Dedication

To parents the world over.

Part One

In Utero

Tomorrow or the next life,
you never know which will come first.
–Haitian Proverb & the 14ᵗʰ Dalai Lama

This is a story as told to me by my mothers.
Some of it I claim as my own.
–JCSZ

CHAPTER I

NOVEMBER 1967

WORD TRAVELS FAST on a ship, as it does in certain countries. Someone had died—a galley cook—a handful of hours out from Rio. Friends of the deceased man gathered on the rear deck to commit his remains to the deep while a group of passengers already lined the railings, keeping safely distant. A tall, statuesque Brazilian stood in close, as well as an American journalist who, out of respect for the occasion, did not take any pictures for the piece she was writing, a profile of the ship's last voyage. Captain said a few words, paused, then cocked his head to port, a signal to lift and tilt the rigid stretcher over the rail. Cocooned in neatly sewn canvas and weighted down with God only knew what, the shrouded body slid gracefully into the waiting arms of its mistress, the sea. Nobody knew at the time that the crossing would be filled with so many endings and beginnings, but all present surely tasted, if only for a second, their own mortality.

Shaking off the heebie jeebies, Claire, whose daily routine up to that point contained barely a ripple of intrigue, carried on with her day. She interviewed crew, organized notes, labeled film canisters, networked. Late afternoon, she took her daily swim in the cavernous salt water pool, hoping to shake any lingering creepies from the morning's burial at sea. Perhaps the watery medium was a poor choice. For as she dove in, instead of forgetting, an inkling of portent flashed in her mind's eye, the image of a gyroscopic tropical storm gathering force a few thousand miles away on the west coast of Mexico. She could not know its name was Márisol—Mári for short. Pronounced MA-ree with a roll of the r. Not Mary. As in Queen. Or Mother.

CHAPTER 2

Mári consisted not of swirling storm clouds packed tightly around an energetic core of calm (though some would argue this was an apt description), but rather a five-foot frame built of mocha curves and a mane of sizzling brown-black hair that spoke a language all its own. Brown eyes comfortable holding a gaze or a stare were always ready to light up, convey strong emotion, although lately they'd found few occasions to do so. Her bosom stirred men, so she played up this sizeable asset by shrink-wrapping it—them—in primary colors with the newly invented wonder fabric, Spandex. Key accessories included white Ray Bans pushed tight to the bridge of her nose or slid back on top of her head, a silver pendant made of Larimar, a pale blue stone found one place in the world, and a man's watch made of brushed steel that roamed freely the territory between her right wrist and the meat of her forearm.

Mári had faced many challenges already in her young life. Growing up agreeably poor and unmotivated in a small beach town west of Santo Domingo, she left home at the age of seventeen bound for Acapulco with a charter group of five other Dominican head-turners. This, under the auspices of an enterprising, future-toupee-wearing parrot-loving Haitian named Max who, lecherous though his game appeared, was somewhat of a gentleman to the girls.

Max had a good thing going. He'd made a ton of money rum-running in Haiti, but under stodgy Papa Doc didn't have a place to invest it. So he floated on over to Aca before it became Aca and purchased two properties. The first, a bi-level guest house situated not far from the best beach in town, *Playa Caleta*. On the outside, the place featured a fresh sign that read *Cosa Del Mar*—Thing of the Sea—a painting error that had yet to be corrected. A generous carport shaded the double-doored entry where high windows let light into a foyer-turned-greeting room. The girls liked to hang out there, before and after hours, drinking cold *cervezas*, dancing amongst themselves, gossiping, raging, missing home. Three rooms on the upper east side housed the girls, while three rooms below were designated as working quarters. Sex wasn't necessarily part of the job, but it wasn't frowned upon, either, and Max made it clear that the rooms along the lower level were available—for a small fee—anytime a guy wanted to be with a girl, or vice versa. For whatever reasons, those ground floor rooms (level with the winding driveway for easy access) were seldom used.

Club Prestige, Max's other property located where the *Costera Aleman* met the *Gran Via Tropical* near *Playa Caleta*, was a nondescript box on the outside, but inside, concrete floors boasted inset lights, ceilings had exposed structural steel painted black, and the sunken dance floor was surrounded by a semi-circle of mod plastic tables and chairs. A mahogany bar—the command center—ran half the length of the joint. All in all, Club Prestige developed a reputation for good raunchy entertainment and boasted a middle class clientele. The girls each paid Max twenty-five dollars a month room and board which included a housemaid *gendarme* who cooked and did some cleaning. They earned five dollars a night plus tips for spending an evening at the Club enticing customers with a dance or something more, and anyone they invited to "the bottom rooms" of the guest house paid the girl directly. Still, most of them were very choosey, of the homespun kind who absent-mindedly crossed themselves when passing a church.

Mári took delight in learning new dance steps and adjusting to working life. She'd been seeing an Italian who was decent enough but who already had a family elsewhere. Overall, her biggest source of embarrassment came from an inability to tell time. Illiteracy was not the cause—she read cheap novels just fine. Numbers were a different matter, and when arranged on a clock face she possessed no reckoning of them. Sure, she could distinguish between a 1 and a 4, a 6, 9 and 20, but the essence of "1:46" or "9:20" escaped her. Something to do, early on, with confusion over the dual role of hands and numerals and the division of an hour into sixty pesky parts. For instance, if the long hand was pointing to the 4, how could that be considered 20? Whereas when the short hand pointed to the 4 it was really 4?

In short, she'd given up on the concept of time, a deficiency that spilled over to calendar reckoning as well. On any given day this meant little. She followed the lead of Sonrisa, her best friend and unofficial top gal who helped her get where she needed to when she needed to. But, as in construction, where the slightest error, if uncorrected, becomes magnified and ultimately corrupts the outcome, Mári's inability to mark the passage of time had a momentous effect on her life. And it was this. The reason why back in March she'd been able to dance so many weeks in a row without the bother of her period or the worry of bulky sanitary pads interfering with the skimpy outfits was because she was good and late. This primary clue went unrecognized, though she was vaguely aware, in a denial sort of way, that something significant had gone missing.

✹

JUNE 1967

Breasts swollen, tender, morning nausea and vomiting most unpleasant; weight-gain in the midriff a puzzle. Sonrisa doesn't say a word, just observes, as do the others. Mári consults with a doctor (not the girls' sanctioned *medico* who gives them oddly frequent gynecological exams, but one referred by the housekeeper), fearing she is about to die from some disease peculiar to Mexico.

"*No, no,*" exclaimed the pudgy-faced MD whose razor thin mustache marked an unsettling perpendicular to the sizeable gap between his teeth. "*You're going to be a mommy!*" He pronounced the news as if it were welcomed.

"*No, I'm not,*" replied Mári evenly. "*You take care, now.*"

"*By my estimation, you are some months along. Maybe three.*" Met with a blank stare, he pouted. "*The procedure is risky, dangerous.*"

Mári exploded from the examination table and clenched the pointy edges of his starched collar. "*You take care, now,*" she breathed, dragonlike.

Since Mári had nothing to compare the experience to, she accepted as normal the splintering pain, the fumbling hands, the pressure, the prick of steely instruments, the tremendous cramping. After withdrawing the final instrument from her inner recesses and removing the vaginal clamp, the doctor announced much less cheerfully than before, "*Ya, tenemos todo, es finito.*" It is done.

She sighed in reply, paid him a fair price, took the prescription and tottered into the sunlight, faint but relieved to feel once again the sticky spread of blood between her legs.

Mári recuperated, returned to work within a week. The nausea disappeared but, accustomed to the swell of her breasts, she couldn't tell if they'd deflated any. And her tummy, well, no appreciable reduction there. Mári accepted her larger self, purchased a girdle and went on with life, though it did mean some annoying wardrobe alterations which, out of pride, she tackled when no one was around. And so, the following scene, some months later, came as a surprise to most, if not all.

The girls woke slowly, some next to and others in the general vicinity of their consorts, a trio of American brothers named William sharing a house in town while they built a new resort. Groggy from too many rum Cokes the night before, they each, in turn, peed, brushed teeth, arranged hair and touched up face. Charlita, the oldest and tallest of the Dominicans, managed to locate the coffee, coffee pot, matches for the stove, and while all that was going, continued her search for sugar, cups, and little spoons. Absorbed, she didn't hear Willy and Bill enter the room. Beer bottles dangling in hand, they drew alongside her and crowbarred their arms through hers. Without spilling a drop, even though she squirmed and protested mightily, they lifted her up and out, depositing her on a stone patio not far from the pool, right up against the house. The third brother, Will, materialized, following closely behind, and when the first two successfully pried Charli's arms up over her head, the latecomer handcuffed each slender wrist to the iron security grate mounted to the jalousie windows.

Will chugged beer, eyeing his progress through the barrel of brown glass. Careful to leave just enough to suit his purpose, he capped the mouth of the bottle with his injured thumb and shook it methodically. Charli could plainly see the blackened nail arcing through the air, the result of the previous night's horseplay. She'd gotten him good while doing the limbo in stilettos—he'd favored the view from the floor and, oh well, she'd not entirely missed skewering his hand. Now, with a calculated grin, Will uncorked his thumb. The frenzied brew erupted on top of Charli's head, flowing down her face in frothy rivulets. Willy and Bill, who'd been shaking their beers like there was no tomorrow, followed suit, poking her here and there, tickling, teasing. Will disappeared inside while the guys dowsed Charli. After a while her objections died down.

Mári, queasy from the rum Cokes and God only knew what else, came out to the patio at the same time Will re-appeared with a five-pound sack of sugar, the same one Charli had unearthed. Older brother Willy restrained Charli's feet so she wouldn't lunge for the gonads, leaving Will free to mash the contents of the sugar sack into her hair. Mári, the shortest person present, shoved him with the effect of a goat buzzing a lion. It did nothing but piss him off. A glance to the other two and Mári was quickly air-lifted to the edge of the pool. From behind, Will had her under the arms. Willy and Bill each grappled with a recoiling leg. Charli stood by in an odd kind of resigned, shackled rage while the two other girls watched, happy to remain unimplicated on the sidelines.

The brothers rocked Mári once, twice—

"No! Estoy embarazada! Qué no!" she yelled.

"Pregnant? In that case," one of them said in English, "too bad this isn't salt water—it's more buuooyant!" The brothers let go on "Three!"

Mári clawed her way to the surface. She rose, sputtering, curtains of heavy hair obscuring her vision. But she saw clearly enough. Had come quite well to terms, in those plunging seconds, with the reality of her present—and future.

CHAPTER 3

Mári spent just about a day mulling over her situation. She sought the input of no one, not even Sonrisa who, for the most part, had been spending her spare time with a female admirer, a fact which, truth be told, made Mári jealous. The overhead fan in their room doing nothing to dispel the sweltering midday heat, she went for a long walk along the *Málécon*, a paved walkway that separated land from sea.

Mári's wardrobe had necessarily gone from minimal to maximal. She wore an Indian print wrap-around skirt beneath a long, flowing blouse. The girdle chafed under the arms and created a suction-like humidity against her skin, making her smell faintly of rubber. She figured this a small price to pay. Her livelihood was at stake—as it was, she'd had enough trouble convincing Max to let her continue her solo act in the

Midnight Show (that's when the girdle first showed up, along with the sari, the veil, and other mysteriously useful props).

Luigi was her biggest problem. Under no circumstances must he find out she was with child—he'd made it clear with cutting remarks and callous snubs that he didn't want any more *bambinos*. Had two back in Italy with a woman happy to receive money wires and an occasional call. A fine arrangement that suited them both.

The Dominican knew she was third spoke in the wheel and did her best not to push it. Nasty as his temper could be, she liked the guy. Theirs, too, was a fine arrangement. She'd spend time with him at his apartment in the heart of Acapulco, near the cliff where divers performed spectacular feats. They'd go out to dinner, dance. He bought her stuffed animals, black market knock-offs from distant factories in Mexico City, but still the real deal. They had fun together, and he'd even asked her to live with him at the apartment, but she didn't want to leave Sonrisa and the other girls who were like her sisters. Being stuck in an empty apartment all day long didn't appeal to her sense of adventure. On the other hand, he didn't like her risqué club dancing but put up with it as long as it didn't carry on into some other man's lair. The jealous type.

These thoughts preoccupied Mári as she lumbered along the *Málécon*. By the wayside, purple pansies and yellow daisies winked and shook their heads as if in on some cosmic joke. Growing weary, she eased her steaming bones onto a bench whose ornate iron back was clearly designed more for show than comfort. Grateful for the respite, she caught no one's eyes, her own secrets company enough for the moment. But not for long as, distinct within the ambient noises of gulls, horns, chatter and surf, an off-beat one-two rhythm gained a momentum that Mári couldn't ignore. Becoming louder, the unfamiliar sound broke through her single-minded daze.

Scratch—drag, scratch—drag.

Could there be sandpaper under someone's shoes? Mári's vague curiosity turned to mounting alarm when the scratch—drag got quicker and closer. She resolutely held her head high and straight, hoping to signal aversion and ward off an approach from behind. In so doing, a ship on the move presented the perfect focal point, its billowing smokestack, onyx hull, and cookie-cutter portholes providing the perfect mock fascination. She could even make out the shape of a huge anchor at the front and a billowing flag at the rear. Was it American? Full of exotic cargo? It seemed so powerful, competent. Her focus prodigious, Mári squinted to see if she could spot any people, but not even fantasizing about who or what might be aboard distracted her from the moment's most dominant sense perceptions—three aggressive jabs to her knee.

"*AYY!*" Mári scolded, scooting to the far side of the bench.

"*Dithculpe theñora, dithculpe, pero nethethito dinero, poco dinero, thi?*" said a gravelly voice with a gravelly lisp, both of which rose unflinchingly from somewhere near the ground.

Mári stared silently for a few moments at a man who spanned less than half the height of the average adult. Piercing blue eyes lit up a tanned, weathered mariner's face. Congealed spittle stuck at the corners of his mouth which he held open, exposing a pink tongue that protruded through the gap where two front teeth had once docked, lending him the appearance of a panting dog anticipating a bone. Traces of orange peeked through a frayed shirt that had, over time, transmuted to brown from a triad of sun, sweat, and dirt. Cloth looking like it did double duty straining coffee grounds draped his lower half, the waist cinched by a nautical rope. Finally, a thick pad of newspapers and cardboard tied to where ankles should've been scraped away at Mári's heart and in one deft move she reached into her bosom, extracting a soft leather coin purse. Secreting it from view like a card sharp guarding her hand, she manifested an accordioned *peso* and gingerly handed it to him. In his eagerness to seize the bill, he smothered her hand and gave several big happy squeezes, as if everyone welcomed such exuberance from a legless beggar.

"*Grathias theñora!*" he croaked, gay levity interrupted by the sight of another mark further down the quay. Without further ado, the half-man bounded off, skating from one stump to the other, waving all the while, whether to the new target or her she couldn't tell. Maybe it was just a way of propelling himself faster.

She blew out the air she'd been holding inside her lungs, took a deep breath, let it out. In…out. In, out. A faint taste of ashes climbed up her throat, lodging at the back, as if something deep down raged and this was its residue. How did that man find the will to live? Where on earth *did* he live? Mári gazed at the horizon, a razor's edge befriending bottomless ocean and topless sky. In a crystal clear moment of knowing nothing was more important, she vowed her baby would not be born in Mexico.

As if in response, a soulful blast of the ship's whistle sailed through the air, tickling the small bones in her ears and electrifying her brain. She now knew something as surely as she knew the sun would rise.

Later that night at the Club, Mári dazzled with a heartfelt dance to the Drifter's *Under the Boardwalk*, complete with doo-wop moves, undulating hips and hula arms. Convincing in her outward presentation, she sold the dance but inwardly could think of nothing but ships. The bigger, the better. Mári knew nothing about them, and it was this very lack of knowledge that engendered hope. Despite hope, there were obvious drawbacks: 1. The cost of tickets unknown, she was sure she couldn't afford one; 2. Visas to countries like the United States were impossible for people like her to get; 3. She didn't know a single soul with boat connections.

So she mimed love gyrations for all she was worth, thinking of other options.

Back in the Dominican the word *coyote* meant nothing—*Hispaniola* had no such animals. But in Mexico the girls learned *coyotes* secreted people over the border, a topic Max's son, a lanky, dark-skinned guy with playboy looks and minimal drive, was only too happy to shed light on while hanging out with the *chicas* in the front room of the guest house—shooting the breeze and downing beers at dad's expense. What Mári learned about crossing the border did not sound fun. Extreme heat, desert conditions, rattlesnakes, testy guys with guns. Stuffed in a hot, cramped, hidden compartment. And if you got caught, *bam*, forget it.

Not at all promising. Under the boardwalk, indeed.

CHAPTER 4

Mári woke early to muggy heat. On her back, she cuddled a stuffed bear and stared at the whirring fan overhead. Though it wobbled in its orbit, she was long past the fear that it would fall onto the big bed. Now, the goofy rotations were mildly comforting, something you could count on as long as there was no blackout. Another awareness struck her—Charli, for some reason, had joined them in bed. Instead of it being just her and Sonrisa, Charli lay to her right, against the wall, and Sonrisa to her left. Sandwiched in the middle, no wonder so much heat so early! Like a cat she arched her body over a snoozing 'Risa, performed a Footsie-type move and landed safely on the edge without disturbing anyone.

Heavy tile floors cooling her feet, Mári plodded to the rattan stand by the door and knelt before a radiant poster of Mother Mary cradling her newborn son.

In the name of the father, the son, and the holy ghost.

Making the sign of the cross, she wondered briefly why this saintly woman had been left out of the invocation—surely there was room for four. Striking a match, she lit a votive in blue glass, bowed her head then quickly looked up. A lightning bolt of identification fused Mári's eyes to the Virgin's face which bore little trace of enthusiasm over her recent accomplishment. In fact, it looked more like Charli's when she'd been handcuffed to the window bars—the face of feminine resignation mixed with profound patience. Genuine heart of sadness, tender and raw. A shiver ran up her spine and wrung her brain like a sponge. Mári always knew she was on to something when that wringing action occurred. It somehow forged her resolve, helping her reach big decisions and stick to them. She thanked Mary for showing her the way. Her child, like the Virgin's, was destined to be born—that much was obvious.

Mári would do her part.

Blowing out the candle, she glanced out the bank of jalousie windows to gauge the weather—sunny and breezy, windy even. At the closet she selected her wardrobe for the day and, as an afterthought, stuffed a man's shirt into her day bag. Once dressed, she anointed her head with a pink and silver leopard print scarf. Italian chiffon, delicate and strong. Her very best favorite, she felt confident and beautiful as Sofia Loren when she wore it. Mári left the guest house through the door at the charcoal kitchen below, stopping for a swig of milk and a quick *buenos dias* to the housekeeper. At the main road a block away she hailed a *combi*, a public minibus, and rode the short distance to the *Málecon*, all the while thinking up a storm.

Forced to look at her future mathematically, numbers now played a greater part in her life than they ever had. This time she'd have to pay heed, the clock was ticking. Something the doctor had said sunk in: *without this procedure you will give birth in early December.* That was only a few months away—even she could figure that out. And if he was off in his calculation, which, given his success rate, was a distinct possibility, the baby might come sooner.

She would have to act fast.

Mári's rap on the back of the driver's seat caused the *combi* to lurch to a stop at the south end of the *Málecon*. After paying, she climbed over passengers on her way to the sliding door, stepped over orange rinds and other gutter trash then strode toward the ocean with purpose. Today, she would leave there with a plan.

Waves chopped at the concrete buttresses, tickling Mári's sandaled feet with spray. A gorgeous day in Acapulco—turquoise heavens, blue-green waters sporting frothy cream-colored heads. The wind was a bit much though, making Mári's scarf behave like a sail. Gusts of wind reached under the fabric, sliding it clear off her head where it came to rest around her neck, noose-like. For the time-being it still did its job, loosely corralling the brown cascade. Funny thing was, she didn't much mind the loss of control. Instead of being irritated, the Dominican laughed, shouted, sang into the wind, hair in flight, feet wet, bladder pressed.

"*Si! Si! Si! Si!*" she yelled, spit mingling with sea mist, fists raised in triumph as if just having scored a goal on the soccer field of life. Scanning her surroundings, Mári's high took a nose dive. There were no ships in the bay. None at the docks except for little scenic putt-putts. Nothing on the horizon. Still, she knew it was only a matter of time before all that would change. Her mood evened. She would admit no more bleak moments.

The man with no legs watched Mári's rooster-like display from behind a bench. Normally he was the one acting crazy, upsetting people's balance. Curious, he shuffled toward her with no specific agenda in mind. Mári stood on the seawall, feet poking through either side of a baluster, anchoring her upper body as it strained toward the Pacific like a figurehead flying above the waves, beauty in the face of turmoil. Not sure what she had in mind, he quickened his pace.

Mári stepped back off the ledge, coming down from her ocean high. *"Hola, señor,"* she addressed the visitor, a half-smile playing on her lips.

"Theñ-o-rita, I thought you might jump," he said with downcast eyes. *"Nothing I could do about that, hey?"*

"Nada, verdad," she replied with a laugh. *"I wasn't going to jump. I can't even swim. Why would you think that?"*

"Don't know, maybe I was juth thinking of mythelf."

Mári greeted that admission with space. *"Como se llama?"* she asked quietly.

"Hector Rioth," he replied, tracing the letters R-I-O-S. *"Yuthted?"*

Introductions out of the way, Mári asked a little shyly, gesturing toward the ground with an open palm, what'd happened to his legs.

"Acthidente, working over there," he pointed at the cargo docks. *"Big boxth, very heavy, many avocadoth inthide. She fell on me, cruth my legth."*

"Are you...ok...now?"

"Jutht a little short, thath all!" he joked. *"The other dock workerth, my friendth, they help, give me money here and there. They feel bad. They don't want thith to happen to them, giving money ith like paying the godth..."*

Mári searched his craggy bronze face, lacey blue eyes reminding her of the docile stones found only, far as anyone could tell, in her hometown of Barahona.

Distracted by the sorry state of his shirt, she remembered to pull the fresh one out from her bag. *"Un regalo para ti."*

Hector thanked her and rolled up the gift, tucking it under his arm. She continued to gaze at him, but wasn't thinking about his accident, his missing front teeth, or his salty woolen hair. She had bigger fish to fry, and edged herself over to a bench for a seat.

"*So, you must know a lot about ships,*" she ventured, crossing her legs prettily. "*I want to leave here. Any ideas?*"

"*You got money?*" he asked in a conspiratorial tone, sidling closer to the bench.

"*No.*"

"*Too bad.*" Hector thought about it. "*A little money?*"

"*I don't know, maybe.*"

"*Every cargo ship got a few cabinth for paying pathengerth. Cost not too much, dependth where you wanna go.*"

"*United States.*"

"*You got paperth for there?*" Successfully avoiding having to repeat *Estados Unidos* with all its "s's", Hector placed two rough, beefy hands at the edge of the bench and lifted himself up with a gymnastic twist, putting himself eye level with Mári.

The subject matter beginning to grate, she played nervously with her scarf, pulling it through one fist then the other, back and forth. "*No papers,*" she admitted.

"*Then how you gonna—*"

A blast of wind cut Hector's question in half and lifted Mári's scarf out of her hands, plastering it, fully unfurled, against two balusters. Off the bench in a flash, Mári crashed after it, but another gust of wind perversely sucked it through before she could snatch it. Indignant, she watched as silver and pink leopard spots agitated freely on the turbulent surf below. Looking around, a quick survey of her surroundings produced an unlikely rescue tool: a deeply varnished gold-tipped cane in the hand of an approaching man dressed in white tropic leisure wear.

"*Con permiso?*" Mári called, gesturing at the stick. "*Solamente por uno momento.*" When the dandy loosened his grip, she took it as a sign of acquiescence and seized it. He let go, perhaps wondering how he could have so willingly relinquished his treasured Malacca with gold ferrule and Bond Street label. Meanwhile, Hector bounced off the bench, hopping up and down with glee and cheerleading for Mári who, striking a most un-ladylike pose, jousted with the truant fabric.

"Math por ahi! Over to the right!" he urged. *"No, aqui—ahi!"*

"Really miss, you must allow me to buy you another one," the stranger suggested in a clipped accent, affronted by the indelicacy of a woman on her knees.

"Mis brazos son cortos demasiados!" Mári yelled.

"Armth short!" Hector barked in broken English.

Mári's feet lifted off the ground with every attempt to hook her beloved scarf which, by now, was waterlogged and close to sinking.

"Allow me to help," said the gallant stranger, preparing to give it a try. But Mári, resenting the intrusion and the implication that she was incompetent, gave her greatest effort yet and with a mighty grunt and thrust connected with the soggy fabric so perfectly that it swooped into the air, flew off the cane and landed on the stranger's head.

"Right then, well done," he testily begrudged, removing the offensive garment.

Mári wiped the walking stick with her shirt, stifling a laugh, for given the man's stature a laugh simply would not do. *"Gracias."* Their eyes met when she handed it back. He looked away, embarrassed.

"Em, I don't speak much Spanish, but YOU'RE WELCOME," he exaggerated the last two words as if speaking to one deaf.

Mári wrung the scarf and gave it several violent flaps, unconcerned with the tall foreigner who stood watching her. In a leisurely manner she wondered how he managed to trim and train the hairs above his lip into such a thin, orderly line, but she was also thinking of something else, some other angle.

"Quiero invitar le al Club Prestige esta noche."

"Mithter, she invite you to Club, on Street Gometh," Hector explained, adding the address of his own accord.

The stranger considered the invitation and eventually rejoined with one of his own. "Would you like… to em…possibly…em…get a drink with me? Now?" he stuttered, somewhat out of his element.

Mári paused her tidying activities and cocked her head. *"Como?"*

"Is that a yes?"

"Si, por qué no," she replied genially. *"But he has to come, too,"* she gestured toward Hector. Otherwise, how would they communicate? She understood some English, but speaking was another matter. And there was more to it than that. Sitting alone with another man at a restaurant would not bode well if it got back to Luigi.

Hector radiated glory, and proceeded to change out shirts. "She thaid yeth, an' me come too!"

The stranger quelled a volcano of revulsion by turning to lead the way.

"I know a place we can *all* go."

CHAPTER 5

The trio landed at a nearby VIPS, a diner chain popular with the business and upper class of Mexico. Without prompting, the host led them to a table in back where Hector wasted no time lifting himself onto a nicely padded bench and bouncing to the far end with the determination of a jack rabbit. After some hesitation, the stranger slid in after him, allowing Mári the decorum of a seat to herself. People stared, their curious minds concocting versions of what the connection between these three humans might be. Mári seemed not to notice—she was used to people gaping and speculating.

If anyone had reason to feel ill-at-ease it was Hector, who refused to whither under the disapproving scrutiny of attendants and patrons alike. On the contrary, he took full advantage of the stranger's generosity and ordered roast beef with potatoes, spaghetti, and a piece of orange cake he wanted as an appetizer. Mári ordered iced tea, the stranger a beer. Not to be outdone, Hector requested a large cherry soda.

The buffer of the waiter removed, all three sat shyly regarding one another. Hector broke the ice, so to speak, by letting loose a moderately muffled fart.

"Wow, I really have to go to the bathroom, mutht be nervuth or thomething." He poked the stranger on the arm, signaling to be let out.

All diners, it seemed, watched the little big man navigate his way to the restroom. It is possible even Fred himself, in a flight of unbidden curiosity, wondered how Hector managed to use a urinal, or even a toilet.

"Er, how *do* you two know each other?" the stranger muttered. "Ah, never mind. My name is Fred, Fred Stacey," he said more cheerfully, extending a hand.

"Márisol Martinez, mucho gusto."

Beverages arrived.

Hector hustled back to the table and resumed his post, causing barely a stir this time. People were getting used to him. *"Did I mith anything?"* he asked after a happy gulp of effervescence. Mári shook her head.

"I'm so glad my cane could be of service," Fred trailed off lamely. Hector picked right up converting it to Spanish, innuendo lost in translation.

Mári smiled. *"I didn't give you much choice!"*

Fred laughed. Hector gave a final, unapologetic slurp. Hefting the glass up high to catch the waiter's eye, clearly he felt he deserved another.

Since Mári showed no real curiosity or need to flirt, Fred kept up the chatter. "I'm here working temporarily, on a short-term assignment for my company. That's why I don't speak so much of the language," he explained, adding slyly, "otherwise, I'd be able to chat with you directly."

Hector conveyed the essence of Fred's admission—and then some—which boiled down to "he's working in town, doesn't speak Spanish, *and* would like to see you again."

"*My English well, it's not pretty,*" Mári admitted. *"Are you American?"*

"English, that is, from England. How 'bout you, from here?"

A long, drawn out *"Nooooooo,"* followed by the proud proclamation, *"La Republica Dominicana."*

"*Qué bueno,*" Fred ventured, drawing a smile from the Dominican. *"Just visiting?"*

"Me make work, make fun," Mári took a stab, clearly lacking the facility to wrap her *boca chica* around guttural Germanic syllables. "At Club Prestige me dance."

Translator duties on the wane, Hector began the real business of moving extraneous glasses and utensils aside in preparation for the incoming bounty. When the waiter arrived and placed several plates of steaming food in front of him, he eyed the server darkly. *"I'll take that orange cake any time now."*

The other two spoke during the short gaps between Hector's gargantuan mouthfuls. Fred began by asking the question no man should ever ask unless absolutely certain the answer was yes. "Going to have a baby?" he inquired innocently, pointing delicately in the direction of her stomach.

"Nooo, me fat," Mári deadpanned in her best English.

After profuse apologies he quickly followed up his blunder by draining the heavy mug of lager and signalling for another.

"What do you do here in Acapulco?" Mári sing-songed, pressing Hector back into duty.

Cheeks still red, Fred explained that he worked for a very old and prestigious ocean passenger line that was preparing for the first—and last—arrival of its flagship to these very shores.

"I think he'th in the bithneth of tranthporting flagth," Hector offered.

"You've heard of Cunard?" the Brit asked, eyebrows arched in quiet confidence.

"No," both Mári and Hector chimed in unison, the latter having heard of *canard*, which meant duck in French.

"Queen Mary? Hugely famous vessel? Thirty-one years of spotless service?"

"The Queen of England, who ith very large and famouth, ith coming!" Hector posited.

"Indeed! Oceanliner, coming here," Fred mimicked a swimming fish with his hand.

Hector squinted, things beginning to dawn. "What mean 'oceanliner'?"

"Ship, a big, beautiful ship—boat—that carries people from one place to another, on the water." Fred, patiently stupefied, wondered what all had been conveyed prior.

"Why not you say?" Hector berated the Brit. *"Ship! He'th been talking about a ship!"*

"Un barco fabuloso para muchos pasajeros?" Mári intoned as if in a visionary trance.

"Yes, yes! Queen Mary, big fabulous ship coming in December!" Fred gushed, vanquished by their sudden enthusiastic comprehension.

Mári, on high alert, had a million questions. *"Por quanto tiempo?"*

"One day."

"Weech day?"

"Tuesday the fifth."

"Where it go *luego?*" Mári asked, pantomiming the word *after.*

"Long Beach, California."

CHAPTER 6

As Mári took leave of her luncheon companions, *Quin Mári, Quin Mári* ran through her head like a talisman. She could think of nothing else. Absent-mindedly tucking Fred's business card into her bosom, she waved to Hector and the Englishman from her *combi.* The air, hot, humid and stuffy, swam with potential. Electric. She'd met the man of her recent dreams.

Fred was being nice as he knew how to be. He'd tried to give her money, ostensibly for the ride, but she refused, pushing his hand away decisively. Neither appreciating nor criticizing his actions, she knew that a more experienced man would have given cash directly to the driver. This one action told Mári a lot about Fred Stacey. She gauged she could count on his help to a certain extent, but his naiveté would stand in the way of a miraculous offer, no matter what she put out. For instance, he'd never be the type to keep a woman, move her in, and pay all expenses in return for guaranteed companionship like Charli's man had. No, this one was likely to have a brief, nervous affair with a mid-level secretary then call it quits for no apparent reason.

Here's what won't happen she thought, staring out the smudged window at locals riding bicycles and ambling along in primary colors. Fred, like most people, was going with the flow. An occasional intervention to gratify soul and ego might occur, but he would not be one to buy her a ticket, help falsify landing documents, or procure a fake American passport. No, that thin line of a mustache said it all—straight and narrow. Fred might want to bed her, but he'd feel guilty afterward, which would run to her advantage, for out of guilt men did funny things for women.

Mári climbed out of the *combi* a few blocks from the guesthouse. She rarely took a ride right up to it because she didn't like to disclose where she lived, itself a signal for her line of work. Certain people knew, including, of course, Luigi, whose faded red Mazda sat parked beneath the spacious carport.

Mierda. The sight of his car interrupted her set-jaw determination which had been buoyed by a catch phrase she repeated over and over: *"debes luchar para lo qué quieres"*—you have to fight for what you want. Mári, for the most part, had her sights set on a Queen she'd never heard of, never seen, couldn't fathom, and most likely would never reach.

"*Hola Márisol!*" Luigi said in a congratulatory tone from inside the car, as if she should be glad to be graced by a visit from him. Michi, who'd been leaning suggestively at his window, sauntered off to lurk inside the front room within earshot in case things got interesting.

"*Donde estaba tan temprano?*" He forced his voice to remain light, then opened the car door and swung his legs out but made no move to leave it.

"*I was at the market,*" Mári lied.

Luigi played with the fuzz on his face, pinched the chin hairs, then raked his fingers through wavy mid-length locks.

"*What did you buy?*" brown eyes challenged.

"*Nothing,*" Mári said crossly, "*as you can see.*" She held her hands apart, palms toward the sky, to prove her point. A sudden urge to shake free and go barefoot made her bend down to unlatch her sandals. When the business card in her cleavage fell out, Luigi swooped down like an osprey snagging a fish.

"*You forget I'm a goalie, and a good one at that,*" he taunted, beefy talons waving the crinkled object in her face. "*Fred Stacey. Quien es?*"

"*Some guy I met at the market.*"

"*Really.*" He didn't believe her, but played along. "*And why do you have his card?*"

"*He rescued my scarf which blew off my head.*" She pulled it out of her bag. "*See?*"

"*Why is it wet?*"

"*I washed it out—the streets are dirty.*"

Luigi snatched the scarf and touched it to his tongue. "*Salt.*"

"*I was sweaty.*"

"*You were at the Málecon, weren't you?*"

"*So what?*"

"*You met this Fred Whoever down at the Málecon—I can't believe it,*" he fumed.

Mári grabbed the scarf back. "*It was hot, I went to cool off by the water, my scarf flew into the waves and this English man lent me his cane to fish it out. He was a very nice, older gentleman, which is more than I can say for you.*"

Luigi refused to look at her.

"*He's just a business man. At least he's coming to see tonight's show!*" Mári turned on barefoot heels and disappeared inside.

"*You're getting fat, you know!*" he called out, then left in a huff.

Michi, who'd heard the entire exchange from the front room, scooted alongside to their *cuarto*.

"*Are you seeing this new guy?*"

Mári gave her a look and didn't bother responding. She plopped down on the bed, tossed and turned exaggeratedly in search of a comfortable position, and managed to avoid any more questioning by pretending to nap. Eventually the nosey one left the room.

What began as a pretense turned into reality and Mári fell into a deep, sweaty daytime sleep, the kind conducive to drooling and dreaming. In a state of suspended animation, she found herself *climbing…*

…effortlessly up the incline to a rocky perch where cliff divers began their hazardous journey. Alone, she paused to examine the bright, cloudless sky before hurling herself headlong into the crashing blue seas. She broke the water perfectly, crown first, hair a screaming brown arrow. Because she couldn't swim, she let nature do the work. The descent went on and on yet Mári felt no fear. Momentum slowed, her body turned horizontal and she rolled face up, catching one last glimpse of puffy gray-white sands dimly visible below.

As if in a cradle, Mári was rocked by the pulse of the current. The steady rhythm caressed her, unswerving in its purpose. So comforted was she by the roll of the ocean that she let herself go. All muscular tension vanished and a gush of water burst out, an urgent surge between her legs followed by a warm, seeping stream. The lump in her abdomen dropped lower and lower, and a baby breast-stroked its way from her body, arms first, glistening. Mári cuddled the fresh being, all eyes locked in embrace. They began a slow ascent. Somewhere, a ship's whistle blew…

Again she found herself climbing, this time…

…into the trunk of a gold-plated Rolls Royce Silver Shadow. The car, which belonged to a restaurant tycoon who lived in a sprawling compound in Las Brisas, was being shipped to Los Angeles so he could drive it to a Hollywood premier. Mári had been hired as a clandestine caretaker to ensure it was handled gently and arrived safely.

Inside the cozy coffer, Mári felt snug, secure. Somehow she had bypassed all security checks and inspections. Men shouted and barked orders, rolling the car into its place in the hold. They chocked the wheels, set a handbrake. Silence. Metal doors slammed shut. Mári knew she was alone in the belly of the ship. The steady hmmmm hmmmm hmmmm of engines lulled her into a deep sense of relaxation. The whistle blew—two quick honks then a third longer wail...

In bed, Mári stirred. Someone was honking their horn outside, a regular practice with tacky visitors trying to get someone's attention.

Her eyes opened, glazing over the lazy oscillations of the ceiling fan. The dreamscape lingered, the warmth and comfort of it all, until she realized the bottom half of her body was soaking wet. Rubbing her fingers on the damp sheets then putting them to her nose, she encountered pee, not sweat.

"Carajo!" So much for a rest.

By the time Mári washed sheets and clothes by hand in the shower and hung them up to dry on the small line in the bathroom, it was time to prepare for a night at the Club. She selected a two-piece outfit made of white cotton. Tropical and anything but form-fitting, she scooped up the garb and plodded downstairs, the slap of her plastic house sandals syncopating with the strains of a Celia Cruz hit coming from below.

Mári laid the clothes down in a corner of the charcoal kitchen and picked up an appliance straight from the dawn of the Industrial Revolution—a clunky black iron with a nicked wooden handle and lid that opened to admit burning embers. She licked a finger and gingerly tapped its bottom—not so hot.

The singing stopped abruptly when a hefty, towering woman with dark skin, pink curlers, and a tight housecoat entered the kitchen brandishing a broom.

"You want something to eat?" asked Madame Gerard in Creole-flavored Spanish. Cook, housekeeper, guard, and resident opportunist, the power she wielded was nearly absolute, her cheeky pluck tolerated and even liked by most of the girls.

"Not hungry," Mári pouted, blowing on the feeble coal inside the ancient iron.

Nevertheless, Mme. Gerard dished up a plate of stewed chicken over rice with thinly sliced cabbage on the side and resumed humming her tune. She didn't like to sing in front of others, would clam up if someone caught her. Whether due to shyness (unlikely) or politeness (also unlikely) no one could say. As a result, everyone wanted to catch her in the act.

"Eat this while the iron heats up," she said, thrusting the plate at Mári.

Wishing to continue her song, Mme. Gerard placed tin lids on the steaming aluminum pots, stepped out to the courtyard near her little attached guard house and belted a throaty rendition of *Guantanamera,* all the while partnering with her broom in a moderately paced salsa.

Mári sucked at the marrow and smiled. She, too, knew how she would dance and exactly what she would ask Señor Fred tonight. Then she thought of a hitch. To be absolutely clear, she would have to find a middle man, someone trustworthy.

"Madame Gerard, need to ask you a favor!"

Plopping her dish of bones down with a clatter she sped to the courtyard and sidled up to the imposing housekeeper. Whispering something in her ear, the taller lady was forced to bend considerably just to hear what the shorter woman had to say.

"Oh no, no, no! I have to sweep!" Mme. Gerard protested, turning her body to shield her dancing partner.

Mári tried to wrestle the broom away. *"I'll do it! The food is made, I can finish grating the cabbage…Please! I'll give you—"*

"What you gonna give me?" Mme. Gerard suspended her struggles.

"Uh, I can't give, but I can lend you my leopard print scarf—"

"Lend? How generous." Mme. Gerard snorted, handing over her beloved broom. *"So what does he look like?"*

"He's got no legs."

"*Dios mio. What else?*"

"*He's short.*"

"*I gathered. Does he have a name?*"

"*Hector. Just ask around. If you sit there long enough on the bench nearest the water he'll probably find you.*"

"*I want that scarf now so I can cover the curlers. They're not ready to come out, not by a long shot,*" Mme. Gerard declared before disappearing into the small, unadorned space she called home. Mári followed close behind. There were many details to cover.

CHAPTER 7

A *combi* pulled up to the main entrance of *Cosa Del Mar* at quarter to nine. The driver slowed to a crawl but did not stop under the sedate carport as he usually did. Instead, the van, per instructions, coasted down to the lower level where the whole side of the guest house was ablaze with light and last minute preparations, taking on the catty charm and tumult of a sorority. The driver knew better than to bother anyone with his arrival. A lone passenger sat in the back silently awaiting his fate.

In *Cuarto Uno* a territorial storm unfolded as soon as Madame Gerard came in to announce, "*He's here.*" Mári took Mme. G. aside and asked if she would let *him* bathe in the kitchen or somewhere downstairs. "*No,*" came the flat reply. As a result, Mári embarked on some fast bargaining with Sonrisa and Michi, her most regular roommates, to prepare them for the visitor.

Inside the other rooms girls tossed one another hairbrushes, hairpins, hair bands, hairspray, mascara, rouge, lipstick, swapped dangling earrings, sequined halter tops, or a cherished pair of stockings. Squabbling also took place, particularly in *Quarto Tres* when Charlita insisted to two other equally insistent girls that a particular black strapless bra belonged to her by virtue of the fact that it had emerged from one of her own cubbies.

In Max's repartitioning of this former residence into a guest house, efforts had been made to accommodate multiple parties to a *cuarto*. As a result, one side of each room consisted of built-in storage cubicles that resembled small pigeon coops. Generally, each tenant took over a vertical panel of five. The bra in question had been unearthed, moments before and in plain view, from Charli's top cubby. Therefore, whether or not she believed the undergarment actually belonged to her—which she did not—on principle, if it came out of one's cubby, it was one's. This was the same rationale they'd all used the entire thirteen months they'd spent living and working together in Acapulco, but the two hold-outs weren't buying it.

(The above scenario was precisely why Max had instituted a mandatory quarterly rotation of bunkmates. Eventually, the girls had come to see the wisdom in this as it provided a sanctioned and somewhat courteous way to rid oneself, at least temporarily, of an irritating roommate.)

With the muggy heat and common desire to wear cool clothing, the strapless bra was a genuine commodity. Not that they didn't all have one. For some reason, on this night there existed a shortage, and Charli's, though everyone knew it probably belonged to Michi who occasionally bunked in *Cuarto #1* with Mári or Sonrisa when one of them stayed out, Charli's looked so much like everyone else's that everyone claimed it as their own. Dominia and Miercoles went so far as to clamp themselves to either side of Charlita, trying to pry the balled up lingerie from her fists. Recalling her recent squeeze with the three Americans, Charli did not take kindly to the gang up and shrieked down the hall in search of backup.

Chevy, the *combi* driver, heard the shrieking and looked at his watch. Nine o'clock. Yes, someone was usually shrieking by now, as the hour to leave approached. He tooted the horn twice. Not to hurry the girls, who still had forty or so minutes to go, but to signal Madame Gerard to bring him a cold bottle of beer, which she did, nightly and surprisingly, without protest.

"Come see me when you're through with that," she said in a hushed tone. *"And you back there, here's a juice—you've got to stay clear-headed,"* she told the passenger before taking leave.

Chevy was a direct man. Mid-thirties, he'd seen scrapes, tough times, the lot. Toughened by circumstances and by nature a bully, a hare-lip kept him humble. He drove a public *combi* by day, earning a small but steady living. By night, he drove the girls to and from the Club. Possibly, he spent his dwell time ruminating on the successful enterprise before him, admiring a vision that had brought exotic young women to fraternize with local elite, appreciating how every facet served the real money-maker—The Bar. Employees did not have to pay for drinks. From soda water to whiskey, it was all on the house. Like a living form of advertising, the more they drank the more the clients drank, and when clients ordered drinks for the girls, Max naturally tacked their beverages onto the guests' tab.

Chevy tilted back a bottle of *Modelo Especial*, a cut up from the regular *Superior*. Truly happy with either as long as he wasn't paying, there weren't many pleasures that equaled sucking down a *cerveza* so cold it made your teeth hurt, on a night so hot your ass sweat never had the slightest chance to dry.

Life was pretty good lately, he thought as he got out of his *combi* across from the bunker where Madame Gerard lived, gossiped, and re-portedly danced with her broom.

According to the sufficient but dim illumination coming from a bare bulb, he could see well enough through the grates of the metal security door that she was not in there. He moved instead to the door that led to the inner recesses of the main house and called.

"Aqui! Aqui," rang a voice that led him to the kitchen. Mme. Gerard huddled over an ironing board, driving that age-old tool of domesticity back and forth along a tortured turquoise half shirt. In one practiced move she flicked sweat from her eyebrow onto the grey tile floor.

"You see that man out there?"

"The one in my backseat?" Chevy queried, more than a hint of suspicion in his voice.

"Would you please take him upstairs to the shower in Cuarto Uno?"

"Es una broma, si—a joke? I'm a driver, not an escort for filthy infirm beggars!"

"If you don't I will never again bring you a bottle of beer that I, if you must know, take the trouble to put in the freezer one hour before you arrive."

"Does this have something to do with Señor Max? Because the arrangement I have with Señor Max—who pays me—is that I am a driver. I have great responsibilities to take the girls safely from Point A to Point B in one piece. I get paid to drive, that's all, not get suckered into an odd variety of errands and tasks."

"You could say it has something to do with Señor Max since it all does one way or another." She paused before continuing. *"It's to entertain an important guest tonight."*

"Is HE the important guest?" the chauffeur pointed outside.

"I really couldn't say," Mme. Gerard retorted, eyebrows arched. *"If you want to take this up with Señor Max, go right ahead."*

Chevy sidled up to the *combi* and stared at Hector, who sat quietly in the back seat, clutching an empty glass. Sliding the door open, the driver clucked his tongue against the inside of his cheek, indicating "follow me" the way a jockey leads a horse or a person calls a dog. Hector maneuvered to the floor of the van, then lowered himself to the pavement, careful not to break the glass.

Chevy moved into the entry-way, Hector followed, hurling himself up the tall step and gaining access to the inside. He caught a glimpse of Madame Gerard in the corner of the kitchen and peeked into the doorway.

"*Exthellent juth, Theñora. May I athk what wath in it?*"

"*You noticed, eh? Jugo de piña con leche, with my own twist, a dash of nutmeg and grated citron.*"

"*Fabulouth! You know, I've alwayth dreamt of having—*"

"*Vamonos!*" Chevy interrupted, leading him to a staircase that rose, from Hector's perspective, all the way to heaven. He gamely scooted up to the first stair, took a deep breath and, without looking up again, negotiated each step, a painfully slow process that involved much swiveling, swinging and grunting.

Chevy considered his options. He could be helpful, it wouldn't kill him. He did, after all, like the beer very much. Lending a hand, Chevy pulled Hector up each riser, pausing after every hoist to give Hector a chance to stabilize. Otherwise, it would've seemed rude to yank him as if he were a misbehaving child.

At the top of the landing, the door to *Cuarto #1* faced ahead and to the left, no more than fifteen paces. It didn't occur to Chevy to let go of Hector's hand, so when he knocked on the door and it opened, the girls were treated to an unusually touching sight.

Michi giggled and ran to the back of the bedroom while Sonrisa mutely stood by, wondering what Mári had gotten herself into this time.

"*Gracias, gracias, muy amable!*" Mári thanked the driver, who lingered as though wanting to stick around to see what might happen next. Then the thought of another frosty *Modelo* held sway and he left, nodding his head in acceptance of her appreciation. He rested easy, knowing a tip would come sooner or later.

"*Hector, I need your help tonight,*" Mári gushed nervously as she beckoned him into the room.

Hector looked up at her in earnest. It'd been a long time since someone had needed him, especially someone so pretty. *"Thi, thi, whatever you want."*

"It's no big deal, really," Mári said with half her attention on the words, half her attention on the towel she draped over the foot-high ledge of the tub/shower enclosure.

"Remember that man who took us to VIPS? He's coming to the club tonight, as you know, to see me," she continued laying out a fine assortment of toiletries—soap, shampoo, shaver, toothpaste. *"And I need to be able to talk to him."* Mári placed a small bottle of *Jean Naté* near the other articles for the finishing touch.

"Claro, claro," he responded automatically, his hopes and fears stuck on the possibility of bathing in a proper bathroom. The last time he'd been in a room solely devoted to cleansing the body had been in the hospital, after the amputation of his smashed legs.

A handful of days after the operation, a beleaguered nurse had taken pity—or offense, he couldn't be sure—on his sweaty, B.O.-ridden frame and wheeled him down the hall, bloody bandaged stumps and all, to the shower, a no-frills affair which, like the hospital, contained the mere basics. Cramped and narrow, it looked more like a converted janitor's closet. Windowless with one bulb dangling from an electrical cord tacked to the ceiling, the nurse lifted him out of his chair, no small feat given his thick, muscular frame, and plunked him down like a child in the middle of the concrete pan.

"Go ahead and remove your gown. I'll get you a clean one," she directed, and without further ado turned the water on full blast, abandoning him in the stall.

A burst of cold water shot from an unassuming galvanized pipe poking out near the top of the wall. He sputtered, finding the shock of it too much.

"Can you reach the handles?" he heard dimly, from some other dimension.

He used his powerful arms to scoot closer to them. The nurse had turned only one, and he hoped the other might offer something warmer. Straining and reaching up high as he could produced a quarter rotation each time. Eventually the flow stopped. With his other hand he stretched mightily and got the other valve open. Out came water all right, but just like before, if not colder. Hector wore himself out getting the new one off and the former back on. Exhausted, resigned, he swiveled on his rear and scooted forward, placing himself squarely beneath the numbing stream.

Grief wracked him as water wicked away stubborn grime. So this was the kind of life he had to look forward to. Enraged, he bent forward and placed all his weight on one ruined leg, then the other. Pain seared from bottom to top, including where feet, ankles and calves had been. He stood briefly, punching his arms high over head. Faint, he slumped back down. The water coursed, cooling hot emotions. He sputtered, rubbed his head, face, armpits, privates. Bandages mushy and seeping pink, he dismantled them, nearly vomiting at the sight of thick black sutures criss-crossing puffy folds of flesh where his knees had been.

"Can you reach the handles?" someone repeated.

Hector looked up at chrome levers neatly ensconced in cream-colored tiles.

"I can," he answered, eyes regaining focus.

Mári closed the door.

He hoped to have a more pleasant experience this time around.

But just to be sure, he turned the water on first and ran his hand through it. This gave him the idea to scrub his fingernails, which by necessity came into frequent contact with dirty ground. Entering toward the back wall so he wouldn't knock over any of the bath items, Hector eased his body under the spray. Hot as it was outside he wasn't used to getting all wet at once and the warm water shocked his senses, making him recoil. Deciding to take his time adjusting to the new sensations, he began with his arms, ducked his head under, then when the shock of that subsided scooted his trunk forward to expose his backside and whatever else was left. This was good. Hector smiled and lathered up, even hummed a little.

Just outside the bathroom door all three girls cocked their ears toward the unseen—but audible—occupant. For a few moments they mimed what their imaginations pictured. Michi was particularly amused with her own rendition of sudsing between the legs and subsequent rinsing. Sonrisa rolled her eyes, but Mári found it a bit funny. Then all at once they detected a weird gurgling followed by vigorous throat clearing, and looked at each other with squeamish surprise.

"He's getting a little too into this…" Mári scrunched up her nose. *"What's he gonna do next?"* she whispered. The others, knowing what she meant, just shrugged.

A pair of pressed khaki pants and white short-sleeved shirt bobbed in the doorway, with Madame Gerard animating them from behind. Mári took the clothes and stretched up on tip toes to give the older woman a peck on the cheek, which drew forth an expression of exquisite grumpiness. With her other hand Mme. G. held out a spool of tan thread, a needle, and pair of scissors. Transfer completed, she raised her eyebrows, dusted off her hands for good measure and left, singing something under her breath about *Jesus Maria.*

"Hector, almost finished in there?" Mári ventured, appearing to ask the very door itself. *"I have your clothes."*

"Momento por favor." Judging from the silence within, they figured he was in the toweling-off stage. Or so they hoped.

A phone rang loudly in the front room. Racing feet silenced it by the fourth shrill bleat.

"Mári, teléfono! Tu novio!" a voice shouted.

"Tell Luigi I'm busy—"

"He says he'll see you tonight."

"Mafioso," Mári murmured under her breath, re-directing her attention to the closed bathroom door. *"Diii-os miii-o,"* she uttered, horrified.

"Qué?" Sonrisa asked, annoyed by the melodramatic tone.

"We have no underwear."

"Well that's your problem, m'iha," Michi kindly pointed out.

"I have an idea!" Mári said excitedly. *"Michi, Chevy really likes you. It's no wonder, you're the most attractive,"* Mári said, laying the butter on thick. *"Sonrisa's going to help me sew up the pants—aren't you, mi amor?"* She took her friend's hand hostage. *"But maybe you could see if Chevy would be—"*

"Oh no. No, no. Definitivamente no!" Michi cut her off.

"—willing to—"

"Are you crazy? No way I'm doing that. Gross."

"—lend us his underwear?"

"Is this really necessary, you two?" Sonrisa calmly put the finishing touches on her look for the evening—mascara, a dusting of blue eye shadow, and a bit of rouge. *"What makes you think your little friend would wear somebody else's dirty shorts?"*

Mári stopped to consider. *"Good point,"* she conceded. *"Maybe he's got a spare pair? I just don't want there to be any surprises."*

"Gross!" Michi spat. *"Like what, you're thinking he'll leave his fly open?"*

Ignoring Michi, Mári knocked on the bathroom door then opened it a crack, averting her head. *"Here, put these on."* She slid the garments through the smallest possible opening. *"Don't worry about the pants, we'll hem them. Just put it all on and come out, ok?"*

"Ok," Hector replied affably. *"Got a comb?"*

Mári tore through her cubbies, coming up blank. Michi declined to search hers, remaining posed on the bed. Sonrisa rummaged around and came up with a pocket-sized generic man's comb.

"Ever notice how those look like fish skeletons?" Michi, ever the dreamer, observed. The others shot her a look.

"He can keep it," 'Risa said flatly.

"What, just because I wouldn't go get somebody's underpants I'm the bad guy?" Michi continued, petulant. *"I do plenty around here."* Then she was up, noodling through her messy cubbies. Exasperated, she pulled her shirt over her head, nude from middle up.

"Has anyone seen my bra? Hell it's hot." A few more moments of unproductive searching and Michi was out the door, topless. *"I hope he's gone when I get back!"*

Hector emerged shiny and moist from his spa treatment. Except for the bunched-up pants, he cleaned up pretty well.

"You look nice," Mári said and smiled.

She and Sonrisa sat on the floor gathering the excess fabric. Mári took up the scissors and was about to begin snipping away when his agitated hands barred them from getting any closer.

"Don't cut."

Mári stopped immediately, worried she'd triggered a phobia. *"Ok, ok, I understand,"* she reassured him.

"Could we jutht roll them up? Better padding."

Before Mári and Sonrisa could express their relief, Hector whipped off the pants and neatly began tucking surplus khaki into a hollow leg, rolling several sections in on themselves then stopping at what he estimated would be the right length.

He did this quickly, with the skill of a man used to working with his hands. Mári and Sonrisa stood by as assistants, keeping their eyes averted except for one or two quick peeks at his lap which was hidden by hanging shirt tails.

Using the floor as his work table, Hector bent over 90 degrees to begin on the second leg, his back to the door. Coinciding with the deepest part of the bend, a figure appeared in the doorway.

"*I found my*—" Michi declared, stopped short by a bird's eye view of Hector's bare ass. For once she didn't know what to say.

CHAPTER 8

This night, unusually hot, the *combi's* interior transported a bevy of listless females. The usual cacophony of chatter and chiding took a backseat to fluttering hands desperately coaxing air molecules to cool painted faces on the brink of melting. Mári paused in her fanning to execute the sign of the cross as they drove in the direction of the submerged statue of the Virgin of Guadalupe, a ritual she never missed.

Each girl, Chevy and Hector, too, dealt with the pulsing swelter in silence. Charlita worried that her tight bun would begin to frizz around the forehead, endangering her odds of being picked as someone's table companion at the Club. Michi wondered how the satiny red of her dress would hold up while doing even just the warm up dance. She feared the area under the arms would, once sweaty, turn an unsightly dark shade. Scared off by her encounter with the rear end of a legless stranger, she regretted not having changed into something more forgiving.

For her part, Mári bounced and swayed as the *combi* clipped along *Costera Aleman* on the ten-minute ride to Club Prestige near *La Quebrada*. Max had positioned his business well. The cliff divers also performed daring feats at night, drawing crowds that, once the spectacle was over, sought other diversions. A growing number of entrepreneurs willingly obliged. Acapulco was becoming known for its wild party scene, and blossoming air travel brought a steady stream of jet-setters to swarm the coastline by day and indulge in sensual pleasures by night.

Fighting the urge to pee, Mári pictured how she would dance a piece of music she'd newly heard on the radio. Her big white skirt would billow and wave suggestively, she hoped, to a tune called *Up, Up and Away*. Someone had told her the song was about a gigantic balloon. The idea appealed! She'd make incredible moves—smooth turns, a few slides in her tie-up-the-calf Roman sandals, flawless. Fred would admire from a nearby table, bottle of champagne cooling on ice, applauding her skill and artistic interpretation.

Looking out the window, she ceased her projection when the *combi's* tires plowed through a puddle and splashed an impeccably dressed woman holding a baby. Mári turned her head in sympathy. There was no mistaking the agony on the woman's face as she took stock of her soiled clothes, unsure of how to proceed or where to stash the baby while she dealt with the mess.

"*Chevy, cuidado!*"

This had no effect on the driver who, after all, was simply doing his job.

She sighed. And sighed again, realizing she'd left out a key part of her guided imagery. The part where she takes off her blouse.

Mári, the bubbly one of the troupe, was not entirely herself. Bloated and starting to cramp, she dragged two leaden feet into Club Prestige, feeling anything but prestigious. A few early birds—regulars—nursed sweaty beers and smoked extra long Benson & Hedges, an affordable sign of affluence. She walked slowly, escorting Hector to a table.

"*Sit here. Order a drink, ok? But just one, I need you to be sharp. When you see Fred, stay put. I'll come get you after the show.*"

On the way to the back, Mári whispered instructions to Mario, the waiter, who nodded and breezed by, taking whatever she'd said in stride. Shuffling along the trail of aquamarine lights embedded in the floor from entrance to bar, she found she could not get in the mood; the cheery blue spots weren't working their usual magic.

"*What's wrong?*" Sonrisa asked, linking arms.

"*Don't feel so good. My stomach hurts, down here.*" Mári rubbed her abdomen while Sonrisa parted the curtain of beads that separated the public space from the dressing room.

"*Lie down,*" she said and ushered her friend toward the cot. "*Second thought, want Chevy to take you back to the hotel?*"

"*No, no. I've got to do the show.*"

Mári rested on her back. *Sunshine Reggae* reverberated through the walls, the rattling sound of unleashed bass telling them a speaker was blown again. Fighting against sub-par sub-woofers made it doubly hard to entertain.

Rubbing her breasts, Mári palpated their heft. "*I hate the thought of these bouncing around while I dance.*"

"*Want to make it a little fun?*"

"*I guess,*" Mári said, rubbing her tummy. "*It's moving,*" she remarked, eyes wide. "*Feels like gas!*" This made them both laugh. She placed Sonrisa's hand on top of the butterfly flutter.

"*Hello in there!*" 'Risa murmured, giving the mound a little peck.

"*Hombres muy malos,*" Mári said disgustedly. Men are bad.

"*Sshhh, now's not the time. We'll figure something out, mi amor.*" Sonrisa squeezed her hand. "*Come on, let's make it so that when you take your shirt off they won't be looking right at you.*"

'Risa fished around in the oversized leather bag she liked to sling diagonally across her body and soon produced a small container of glittery gold paste. "*A disguise,*" she said, raising her eyebrows suggestively and tracing a tight circle in the air above Mári's nipples.

"It helps to do something unusual to them, that way it seems as if people are gawking at the oddity rather than the God-given parts."

Mári smiled and lifted her shirt as a few girls waltzed through the beaded doorway.

"Ay muchachas!" they screamed in unison. From the looks of their loose limbs and tongues they'd already had their fair share of beer.

"Ay muchachas," Mári mimicked sarcastically to hide her embarrassment. The three stooges crowded 'round as Sonrisa continued the delicate application of dazzle paint on the aureolas. *"What's the matter, never seen a pair of tits before?"* she asked crossly, resenting their proximity.

"Not like those!" Loud smooching and sucking noises followed, much to everyone's amusement and Mári's chagrin.

CHAPTER 9

The Midnight Show usually began a good bit beyond *media noche*. Nobody cared, not the regulars, the dancers, waiters, not even Max, who lorded over the place like a happy father with lots of kids. What was twenty, thirty minutes anyway? Nothing and everything could be accomplished in the span of lateness that heralded the night's entertainment. The only ones who seemed to mind—evident in the tensing of torsos, glances at the watch, tapping of feet, and crossing and uncrossing of legs—were the foreigners.

A category Fred fell into.

Of course, he hadn't a clue. Fred was Fred, in his mind intelligent, not unkind, and above all, punctual. He lived his entire life by the clock. There was no way he would admit to any other possible ratio: punctuality was to reliability as earth was to life—the very ground of dependability. Which was why Fred found himself getting more and more steamed as the minutes ticked by and no one, not even the dark, heavyset man whom he took to be the owner (as he operated the cash register, directed people about and kept a parrot on his shoulder), seemed concerned by the yawning delay.

He'd arrived at 11:40, ordered a beer, and watched the girls warm up. Fred supposed that's what they were doing, dancing with no one or each other, admiring and judging their looks in the mirrored wall behind the dance floor. No sign of Mári, but ever-present Hector was waving at him from a back table; Fred made the fatal error of making eye contact. And even though Mári had asked Hector to stay put, he bumped over and offered his hand. They chatted for an awkward moment but the Brit did not invite him to stay.

12:25 a.m. Fred archly surveyed his surroundings. The details of the Club rather impressed. All the tables and chairs sat on a deeply polished wooden riser featuring a series of triangular promontories, or teeth, jutting into the lit dance floor. Overhead, corresponding triangular teeth formed part of a decorative drop ceiling. Perforated metal mesh loosely concealed the space between the drop and existing ceiling, behind which speakers thrummed. Planted vines hung in overhead containers, and tubular railings in upside-down U-shapes were fixed in key places along the riser to prevent patrons from tripping off the sides and also, Fred let himself imagine, to be used as slinky props.

Thirty past midnight. A travesty. Fred stood to make inquiries but was stopped in his tracks by a commotion that rattled the beaded curtain at the back. Scooting and shuffling noises gave the impression a bevy of peahens was about to burst forth. A hush fell over the Club as speakers faded and house lights dimmed. Green, red, and yellow spots ignited from the ceiling one by one and continued to cycle, a sense of expectancy filling the room. Hector felt it, and was so happy he kept knocking his thighs together as if trying to click his heels. Fred felt it, quieted by a sense of unknowing. Max felt it. Though he'd seen the show countless times, he still got choked up whenever the first girl came out to perform. The Dominicans had had faith in him to provide a setting in which they could earn a living, send money home, maybe even snag a husband. It was not surprising he felt a kind of parental upsurge especially since, like his own offspring, they were always trying to get away with something—credit toward next month's rent, skipping a doctor visit, or talking Chevy into taking them this place or that. Sometimes he put his foot down, like the time Mári wanted to borrow money so she could hire a boat and diver to raise the sunken Virgin whose holiness, she reasoned, must be hampered by tons of sea water.

Mostly Max let them do what they needed to do and sort things out for themselves. Like tonight.

Behind the beaded curtain confusion reigned. The girls shifted back and forth, arguing in strenuous whispers about who would start, first in the lineup being the cherished position for it meant getting the ignominy done with and having the rest of the night to flirt or sneak out for a late snack. It was Charli's turn and everyone knew it, but she didn't stand up for herself and got passed over. One girl would declare herself *numero uno* and part the beads as another objected and yanked her back. Mári's voice finally rose beyond the insistent clicking of disturbed heals and beads.

"I've got cramps, ask Sonrisa if you don't believe me. I should go first."

"So do I, but that doesn't mean any of you would let me go first," Miercoles whined.

"Well if you were nice every once in a while maybe we would," Michi replied dryly.

"But I really do, please," Mári begged.

"Ok by me, it's Charli's turn anyhow," said Sonrisa. *"Maybe she should decide."*

"Sure," said Charli, going with the flow.

"Could somebody ask Mejor to play that new song about the balloons?" Mári asked no one in particular.

"It's too late—go with the song that comes up. Your dance will match anyhow," Sonrisa advised.

Mári drew three deep breaths and parted the beads, showing her fully clothed self to a room full of bachelors and couples out for a spot of fun along with their booze. A faux smile curled her lips, the muscles in her face working hard to override an expression of pain. Inside she felt something tugging down. She wasn't sure she should be having this feeling.

Shoving worries aside, she made her way to center stage, head and eyes on the floor, acknowledging no one. Lights bathing her in golden glow, she began swaying as soon as the first peppy accordion chords filled the room. Mári did not recognize the song, but guessed it was one of Mejor's little jokes. Folkloric and innocent enough, it was about a little dove, *Palomita Titibu*. She knew enough English to realize the pun on words concerning the *Titi-bu* part.

Just her luck.

Waving the excess fabric of her skirt in time with the bongos, her nipples hardened as goose bumps coursed from head to toe. The words of the song unleashed some kind of fuzzy emotion. Something about a *rancho* in the mountains and this little dove for his *adorada*. The distinguished voice of the singer jabbed her with the authenticity she'd been missing. She thought of how Charli had been the first to live with a local named Ricardo, a mulatto with balding crown and buffed loafers who worked at a bank, and even though she'd seen her friend languish for months in depression and self-doubt after he told Charlita she must never seek him out at work, Mári had taken the plunge and become the second...

❋

Luigi relocated to Acapulco four months before the troupe arrived. On assignment from *Electrico Italiano*, he was hired out as a consultant overseeing the upgrade of power distribution along the coastal regions—poles, transformers, lines, circuits, relays. He agreed to the assignment for two reasons: one, to get away from a sour personal situation in Rome, and two, to soak in the warm waters of the Mexican Riviera. An electrical engineer by training, Luigi liked physical work better than paperwork and prided himself on having climbed to the tops of poles the world over. Plus it didn't hurt that he loved the pungent tang of creosote. Used to preserve wood, the black tar-like substance forever changed the sweet sappy scent of pine logs into something boggy, and he liked it that way. The smell reminded him of man's imprint on nature. Luigi was very much into leaving imprints.

When Club Prestige opened, Luigi knew his heart was in the right place. These gutsy girls from the Dominican buzzed with ambition. First time he laid eyes on slender, tawny Michi, the fake-blonde poodle-haired mermaid with a penchant for clingy red dresses, he knew she'd be a handful of unreason, jealousy, and demands, all hot and heavy on the outside, cold and unyielding on the inside. Then there was Mári, on the short side, brunette, bosomy, fleshy, not exactly his type, but the first time their eyes met he fancied he saw a flash, a flare, an ignition— the promise of a steady burn, like an ember of coal.

Wasn't that what generated electricity?

After his first Midnight Show, he invited Mári to his table and ordered a bottle of champagne. He spoke Spanish with her and she teased him about his accent. She even exaggerated the way he said his name—lou-EE-gee, with multiple inflections. When she got a little carried away with the fun of saying his name he gently planted a thick index finger on her lips. Mári took the hint and fell in love with him then and there, his finger on her mouth such a tender, firm act, the confident intimacy shocking from a stranger.

Tears pricked her nose and pooled in her eyes, but she wouldn't let them fall. Instead, she swayed, turned, dipped, made gracious motions with outstretched arms, engaged syncopating rhythms, imagined she looked like an Egyptian priestess turning sadness into joy. Anticipating the instrumental bridge, she unbuttoned her blouse from bottom to top. As the singer launched into a newly energized declaration of love, Mári tossed the garment onto a pony wall in front of the DJ booth.

Arms out in front, palms held up in supplication, she turned slowly, shoulders, hips and golden breasts undulating left and right. Coming out of the turn, Mári's eyes found Fred who, surprised, quickly broke her gaze and furtively looked around to see if anyone had noticed. No one had, including Charli's man Ricardo who, she couldn't help but notice, sat stone-faced and rigid, an unidentified female cozied up next to him.

The song ended to polite applause. Mári bowed, corralling her breasts with crossed arms. Grabbing her shirt and dashing for the beads, she nearly collided with Sonrisa who emerged wearing a hula skirt and halter top. The two kissed briefly on the cheeks, a quick peck of encouragement. Once inside the dressing area, Mári delivered her newsflash. *"Ricardo's out there with another woman,"* she breathlessly reported, waiting for a reaction. None came.

"Did you hear what I just said?" Mári caught Charlita's eye-shadow-applying hand in mid-air.

"I guess that means I'll be riding home with you guys tonight," she said calmly, resuming the all-important makeup application.

"Aren't you going to fight for him?" Mári cried, aghast at her friend's docileness.

"Would you?"

"Yes, I would. The spineless snake doesn't even have the courtesy to tell you the right way. I would make a scene," she huffed, jamming a tiara on top of her head. It sat crooked. *"Would you like me to make one for you?"*

"You know something? The last few times I did a reading on Ricardo it kept turning up Ace of Spades." She smiled sadly, shaking her head. *"The Death card."*

"I hate men, hombres muy malos," Mári concluded, lying down on the cot, wiping sweat off her forehead with one hand and rubbing her tummy with the other.

"Wanna drink?" Michi asked, no hint of emotion in her voice.

"No thanks, just a little rest," she whispered, adding an afterthought, *"did I look fat?"*

✺

Things had not gone as hoped. Caught in a riptide of indecision, Mári accepted the invitation to stay at his place. *Indefinitivamente*—indefinitely, the sum total of Luigi's commitment. But as she soon found out, living under his roof meant he had some claim to her whereabouts. For instance, he wanted her to sever ties with Max and the Club—she'd shriveled inside when he'd matter-of-factly suggested this. Clearly the man was unrealistic to think she'd give up her only family and means of support in Acapulco for a spot in his bed with no hint of anything else. Mári refused and they had a big fight. The first of many.

One item they both agreed upon was no bambinos. To this end, he religiously wore rubbers, kept tabs on Mári's cycle, and made sure she used some kind of barrier. One time, out at the beach, they even tried half a lime but, as might be expected, it didn't stay in place. Before Luigi, Mári never worried about contraception because she never climaxed. All the girls knew there was no way to get pregnant if you didn't *venirse*. She didn't with Luigi either, but maybe that would change.

Mári had suspicions about the nature of his bachelorhood—yes, he'd been up front about the woman in Italy. To that end, he asked her never to answer the telephone. In return, she made a condition of her own—that he never interfere with her work. She liked being with him, *claro*, and would not intentionally arouse any customers. And maybe she could dance a little less, but dance she would. He'd nodded his head in agreement, though his face had taken on a reddish afterburn.

Except for the non-child-bearing agreement, both knew in their hearts they would not honor the other's requests. It was impossible for Luigi to refrain from checking up on his *novia*, especially given her line of work. It was equally impossible for Mári to refrain from answering the phone. Sure, she worked out a signal with her friends—call, let it ring twice, hang up, repeat—but there was no way she was *not* going to answer that phone when he wasn't home. Just as there was no way to prevent herself from ri-fling through every drawer, closet, and envelope. For, bold and direct though she was, Mári could not bring herself to ask Luigi if he was actually *married*.

He seemed not to be—at least not in Acapulco. And what of it? They were happy, mostly got along. Dined frequently on seafood at the big, modern *Hotel Caleta*. Some afternoons they rambled through *mercados* and bought silly knick-knacks—he favored masks and alien-looking Toltec heads carved from obsidian, she preferred dainty boxes and painted birds. Mári remembered the time they bought cheap charm bracelets and wore them around their ankles, laughing all the way to the beach. Luigi had loved the way Mári filled in her black bikini, the way her hair fooled the breeze, windswept strands fusing to her face, the way her toffee skin bronzed before his very eyes, the sheen of suntan oil beckoning the sun's golden rays onto her soft torso and breasts…

She'd made sure he could not complain.

And then Mári, who was never quite regular in her cycle, missed seeing her period altogether. It was months before her denial ran out and she finally brought up the subject.

"*There's no way!*" he yelled accusingly.

"*I know, but remember the time…*"

"*One time? One little time? So one time makes a baby?*"

"*Maybe two—*"

"*I thought you said you couldn't have children—what happened to that?*" He shook her, trying to dislodge a satisfactory answer. Instead, it dislodged a flood of tears and the end of living together.

"*I said I didn't think I could. I guess I was wrong.*"

"*You guess. Well I guess you can guess what to do next.*"

She never told him she'd tried but it hadn't worked.

He flew into a rage of doubt, questioning whether it was even his.

"*Oh yes it's yours,*" she raged back. "*Tell me why you are so against this baby?*"

"*Because in Italy I have two already with a woman I no longer love.*"

Every now and then he couldn't stand the separation and would passionately steal her company. But the sight of her growing belly drove him mad and he pushed her away. Mári grew numb to his actions, affections, and lack thereof. Perhaps things could be different between them afterwards. For now, she had bigger fish to fry.

CHAPTER 10

Mári needed all her strength and faculties to speak with Fred, a crucial moment in her gestating plan. She had to be careful not to alarm him with her mounting sense of urgency, to keep cool, casually interested while learning all she could. Tonight would tell whether or not she was on the right track.

The Brit held out a chair for her. He offered a Dunhill, and she unwittingly prolonged the lighting procedure with her own shakiness. After a few missed tries both laughed at the ridiculousness. Finally he clamped a clammy hand around hers and put an end to the business.

"*Gracias,*" she puffed.

"*De nada,*" he answered slowly, as if reading from a script. "*Aprendo un poquito Español.*"

"*Muy bien, pero quiero hablar contigo, y necessitamos ayuda,*" Mári cheerfully explained as Fred shook his head, unable to follow. Looking around, she gave a start. "*Mira!*" she signaled Hector with impatient waves. "*Qué sorpresa! El puedes ayudame!*"

Aware that her ruse to make Hector's presence seem coincidental was thin at best, Mári maintained the forced levity for as long as it took him to shuffle over. She gauged the pinched look on Fred's face and disarmed him by placing her hand on his.

"*Como estas, Fred?*"

"*Muy bien, gracias. Y usted?*" he said a little reluctantly.

"*Bien, tambien.*"

Mári caught the eye of Mario, the fast-moving waiter who never let anyone's bottle or glass go empty before replacing it in record time. This tactic earned Max a small fortune in liquor sales, and usually the patron was too embarrassed, even if he didn't want the drink, to send it back. Regulars on the alert for Quick Draw McGraw could place a hand on top of their glass before he slid another in its place, but even the savvy ones were often too slow. This kind of pressure, needless to say, weeded out the cheapskates.

A nod of the head was all it took for refreshments to be served. She and Hector got club sodas and lime, Fred another beer. "*Keep them coming,*" she told Mario in a low voice.

"*I am so interested in the work you do, Fred,*" Mári said loudly in Spanish. "*Did you know Hector here used to work unloading ships—go ahead, translate!*"

"I forgot what you thaid."

"I'm fascinated by the work you do WITH BIG SHIPS," she coaxed with nods of her head.

"Oh yeth, and me take cargo from shipth, lotta thtuff," Hector added dutifully, reminded briefly of his faraway life. "Me never forget a name, me never thee ship in dese waterth? Quin Mari?"

"Well, she's never been to these shores I can assure you."

"Time firtht?"

Forcing an interruption, Mári reminded Hector he had to tell her what the man was saying…

More drinks arrived. She could tell Fred was tensing up at the thought of having to buy all their booze, so Mári reassured him since he was her guest there'd be no charge. He relaxed noticeably, undoing the topmost buttons on his sport shirt. A glint of gold made Mári lean in for a closer look.

"Puedo ver le?" she asked, pointing to the small medallion. He nodded. This interaction did not require a translator.

Michi took the floor and Hector became utterly distracted. Fred didn't stray for long, with Mári's fingers so close to the flesh of his neck.

"Santo Cristobal," she mulled.

"Patron saint of travelers. *Viaje,*" he added, proud to know a big word in Spanish.

"Si, si, viaje. Up, up and away!" she laughed, mimicking the vocals coming from the blown speakers. Michi, the dog, had copped the song for herself.

Over the course of the evening, Hector became adept at speaking quickly, since he preferred to direct his attention elsewhere. Mári and Fred practiced elocution with exaggerated volume, as if both were hard of hearing. They relied on Hector only after reaching dead ends. Much was said that does not bear repeating, since much was fluff designed to frame and mask the truly important matter.

"I wonder, if a person like me wanted to see the ship, for a little visit say, could it be possible?" Mári coolly inserted soon as she could.

"Well, you'd have to be an authorized guest, escorted on board by an employee, someone like myself, for instance."

"I've always had a fascination with ships. My best friend's father was a sea captain," Mári said, referring to Sonrisa's dad who did have a weathered face, cropped white hair, and blue eyes but who'd actually worked at a cannery in Santo Domingo until an accident took his arm. *"Plus, I grew up on an island..."* she continued, stretching the nautical theme. *"From what you say, no other ship is so grand as Quin Mári?"*

"Rightly so. Did you know—of course, you probably didn't—but I don't mind telling you, if you stood her on end, she'd be almost as tall as the Empire State Building? And this is a ship, mind you, a vessel built to cross the roughest of oceans—"

Hector struggled with unfamiliar concepts and nouns. "Why put ship on his end?"

"Just for comparison," Fred clarified, making a mental note to keep things simple.

"Ok, how's this? During a typical round-trip voyage from Southampton to New York and back—not Liverpool, that was her first port—over 30,000 meals were served." When Hector stumbled at the large numbers, Fred unsheathed a silver Parker pen and jotted them on a napkin, making the translator's job decidedly easier.

"Cooks had at their disposal 60,000 eggs, 50,000 pounds of potatoes, 11,000 pounds of sugar, 14,500 gallons of milk and 3,000 quarts of ice cream! This and much much more for 2,000 passengers and a crew of 1,200." Nearly foaming with enthusiasm, he produced a wallet-sized image of the ship heading out to sea and slapped it on the table, trump card to a winning hand. Clearly marked on the imposing stern was a single exotic word: LIVERPOOL.

"*Qué es liver pool?*" Mári asked. The pained expression on Fred's face told her what everyone already knew: Hector wasn't doing such a hot job.

"A town in *Inglatierra,* my dear. The ship's original home port," he said slower than ever, glaring at the translator.

But Mári wasn't listening, was trying to remember why the *pool* part sounded so familiar. Then it came to her—*pool* meant *piscina.* For a moment, she pictured herself soaring through the air and landing with a splash—

"Da ship he has pool?"

"For your information," Fred addressed Hector, "a ship in the English language is referred to as a 'she'—mainly because they cost us men a lot of money and, at any given moment, might decide to leave you. Remember that," Fred said, softening, a far-away look in his eyes.

"Where were we? Ah yes, Queen Mary has two, a small one for second and third class which is no longer in service, and a big one for first class passengers. These last years, however, class barriers are completely down, no restrictions," Fred explained, pausing every seven words to give Hector a fighting chance.

"*So anyone can use it?*" Mári ventured, not sure where she was going with this.

"Yes, it was the largest pool ever built into a ship during her day. Very elaborate, mother of pearl, uh, shell," he simplified, eyeing Hector's confusion, "on the ceilings, you know, above," Fred pantomimed to help the translator along, to no avail. Mári was told the very big pool had sea shells on its bottom, or top, he wasn't sure.

"*You know, I can almost picture it,*" and she could, despite the many deficiencies. But she needed to know more, way more. The cold beverage in her hand automatically went to her mouth and her throat relaxed to receive a big gulp. "*It would please me to see such splendor,*" she said as she plumbed Fred's eyes while crushing a nick of ice.

"Oh, but you can! I'd be delighted if you came to my office. I could show you pictures..." Fred trailed off. "There's even a secretary who can translate for us."

"*What a pleasure,*" she agreed. One step closer.

Mario swept up and the girls gathered their belongings. Chevy waited in front, *combi* idling, while Max counted up the proceeds and placed all but the coinage in a canvas bag.

The Englishman and Mári had agreed to meet in two days. Again he gave her his card and drew a little map on the back indicating how to find the office. They shook hands. Soon as his slender, erect frame disappeared beyond the front doors, Hector grabbed Mári's arm.

"*I found out a few thingth earlier, before you came out,*" he said in his best spy mode.

"*I thought I asked you—*"

"*I know, but he looked lonely, like he wanted to talk. He ith one colothal thnob,*" Hector snorted, swiping his mouth with the back of a hand.

"*Tell me what you found out,*" Mári said, ignoring his remark.

"*I wath nervouth and hot,*" Hector said by way of launching his excuse.

"*And what do you think I was, a block of ice?*" As if on cue, Mario brought the dynamic duo a couple of beers. She squeezed his hand in thanks. "*And set me up with a few more for the road, would you?*"

"*The firtht question that came out of my mouth wath about thtow-awayth, and let me tell you, ith not a good idea. They thtone them then throw them overboard.*"

Gauging his translating abilities, Mári was not overly alarmed. "*What else?*" she said, suddenly weary.

"The ship comth Dethember fifth, a Tuethday."

"I remember. How many days is that from now?"

"About twenty," Hector estimated. *"And thtowing away ith not a good idea."*

"Heard you the first time. Did you find out how much it costs for a ticket, or did he say?" she asked hopefully.

"Eighty poundth," Hector said doubtfully.

"Eighty pounds of what?"

"I don't know, potatoeth?"

"I can do that—the ship needs supplies, right?"

"Maybe—"

"What if I got a job with one of the suppliers, then stepped right on board with a very good reason to be there?" she said thoughtfully.

"Exthept you don't jutht accompany a thack of potatoeth—they uthe craneth to load everything into the hold."

"Then I'll turn myself into an egg, or a piece of ham!" She laughed at her own silliness, reached for a beer. No matter it wasn't cold anymore.

They dropped Hector off near the Port. Most of the girls sat back and fanned themselves, not seeming to mind the minor detour, except for Michi, who couldn't resist a jab. *"I hope this isn't going to become a habit."*

Everybody knew the best way to deal with Michi was to ignore her. Even Chevy kept quiet for the sake of harmony. He didn't want to stir the nest of lovely hornets.

As Hector hobbled along toward God only knew where, Mári yelled *"gracias"* out the window. Without turning around, he threw his hands up and pumped his fists, the victory symbol. Mári, all choked up, momentarily saw herself in him, tottering on the brink, sink or swim. She didn't know for sure if that was his circumstance, but it surely was hers. She wanted to take a big step but wasn't sure she could do it. During their after-show conversation, she'd asked Hector if he knew anyone who'd row her out to Quin Mári and he'd said he did, but didn't think there was a chance, even with a blessing from the Virgin herself, she'd be able to climb up the ladder—if there was one—and get on board without being detected. It just didn't work that way.

During the rest of the ride, Mári quietly reviewed her options. The specter of *coyotes* and land-based border crossings loomed.

Chevy slowed the *combi* for a pedestrian. Normally he'd do anything to avoid tapping the brakes but a long-legged hotsy trolling the streets for a late-night catch flashed a smile his way. He whistled out the window and she—if in fact it was a she—turned.

"*Muchacha!*" Mári called.

"*Cayate!*" Charli reprimanded, wishing no guilt by association.

"*Yeah, you! Tell me, how far is the United States?*"

"*Do I know loca?*" The legs ambled away, accustomed to offense.

"*Chevy, do you know?*"

"*No, but I should, since I'm a driver and all.*"

He slowed the *combi* again. Two of the girls rolled their eyes, one shook her head, another slouched in her seat. With Chevy on Mári's side, this could go anywhere.

"*I think Nuevo Mexico is the closest,*" Sonrisa ventured a guess.

"*Take me there?*"

"*I'd lose my job—Max would notice his combi and driver were missing,*" he said slowly, as if giving the idea serious thought. "*Seguro qué si!*" A sudden bright idea made him turn hard into *Hotel Papagayo*. Under the canopy, he pulled alongside a line of VW taxis, spotting a familiar face.

"Gorge! How far is los Estados Unidos?"

A gruff voice emanated from inside a lime green Bug. *"Hombre, everybody knows that. Just ask anyone, they'll tell you."*

"Well then?"

Gorge eyed him suspiciously. *"Closest border point McAllen, Tejas, about 1,400 kilometers. You know someone wanna go? You could make money hombre—"*

Chevy quickly answered *no*, but Mári said *si* louder.

Gorge peered into the *combi*.

"How much to take one person?" Mári squawked, leaning on the laps of Sonrisa and Michi and making them squawk, too.

"Depende."

"Maybe you should have this conversation somewhere else," 'Risa nudged.

"Depende on what?" Mári barked.

"You want me to take you?"

"How much?"

"No sabes exactamente," Gorge hedged.

"Have you ever done it?"

"Not exactly a success, no."

"Silly girl, she's been drinking too much!" Sonrisa chastised Mári to throw everyone off. *"But out of curiosity, because now we're curious even though no one is going anywhere,"* she poked Mári again, *"what makes you think you can do it this time?"*

"Señorita muy bonita, I learn from my mistakes. You I'd take almost for free," he said lecherously. *"A thousand dollars más o menos, up front, no guarantees."*

"Ok, nice talking to you." Sonrisa ended the conversation in a singsong voice and jabbed Chevy on the shoulder to get it in gear.

"Well, that takes care of that," Mári breathed quietly.

CHAPTER 11

Two days later, the hour of Mári's intended meeting with Fred approached but by eleven she was still in bed, languishing from a total lack of energy and a large dose of the blues. She could've sworn she was pre-menstrual, such was her state of mind. Times like this, even the best of life felt like crap. *Pura caca*. As it was, she did not have the best life going. Many months pregnant, an unwilling, selfish boyfriend who would be no father, and far, far from home… Ignoring the salty tears pooling in her eyes, her hands lie rigid by her sides. This was the hardest thing she'd ever had to do.

During these two days of dwelling in the dumps, Sonrisa had made a special pumpkin soup full of chicken, potatoes, and vermicelli, with carrots and onion, too. She'd brought it up to her friend and sat bedside to be sure Mári ate it all. So soothing. She couldn't help but think Sonrisa should be the mother, not her—she always knew the right thing to do. But Mári couldn't get that deep because she knew her friend wouldn't agree with her choice. Together they'd make the best of it, Sonrisa had said. They could get Max to kick in or advance some money to prepare for its arrival, even though Max maintained a hard line against babies.

"*They're bad for business*," he loved to say, and had driven home his point by enforcing monthly checkups by an in-house doc who dispensed pelvic exams and the new birth control pill.

Mári spent her time in bed that morning weighing all options, the mental effort making body heat rise to her face and flush her cheeks. Below in the courtyard, Madame Gerard swept in rhythmic strokes that sent Mári into a daze. She became aware of her heart beating, faster than it ought to for one just lying down, remembering, thinking, giving up. Yes, giving up the stupid notion that she might be able to get to the United States where her child could grow up an American and not be forced to remain poor, or forced to marry so as not to remain poor, or forced to work in its mother's line of hospitality. Plus even if she did sneak away, Luigi would go after her pretty quick, wouldn't he?

The daze turned dozey. On the brink of snoozing past her scheduled appointment, the precursor of something big quickened her pulse even more, then burst into the part of Mári's head just above her eyebrows. She frowned to see it more clearly, and there it loomed, large as life: Marta standing by the wharf, pointing to something in the harbor.

A few pieces of the puzzle slipped into place.

Swinging her feet around and propelling her behind off the bed with a push from her hands, Mári lurched to the window and yelled down to Madame Gerard for the time. Displeased at being interrupted, Madame Gerard grumbled back that it was two thirty. More or less.

Carajo. Even Mári realized she couldn't make it to Fred's office by three. She located his card, ran to the phone in the foyer and, relieved when a woman answered in Spanish, asked whether they could reschedule for four. The woman placed her hand over the receiver, muffling a man's reply, then came back with a nasal *claro.* Of course.

Throwing herself into high gear, Mári quickly dressed in a spacious red cotton skirt, white blouse, and black sandals, yanked her hair back and be-bopped out in search of a taxi. Depending on how the meeting went, she would also have to make an international phone call while in town, to her sister, who still lived back home. Marta was the older of the two by a few minutes. *Gemelas.* Twins. Identical.

CHAPTER 12

Two days after departing Rio de Janeiro, Purser received his first complaint about the new passenger in cabin B-408 who played loud music at all hours, as reported by Miss Claire Zeisse in nearby B-410, a photojournalist documenting the final voyage.

During one particularly rousing series of Brazilian sambas, Claire rapped loudly on her neighbor's door, prepared to unleash the killing-me-kindly-all-smiles Los Angeles brand of making things right.

"Yust a minute!" called a sing-song Latin who did not register definitively as male or female. The ambiguous nature of the voice threw Claire for a loop and she was suddenly unsure how to take aim. "Coming!"

A smile played on Claire's mind and mouth—she'd detected a feminine falsetto.

"Whooh la ~ hello? Can I help you?" the stranger offered, looking for all the world, to Claire, like the most exotic tawny-haired honey-colored aquiline woman she'd ever seen.

"Well what have we here?" Claire produced a theatrical flourish in mock surrender to the golden goddess. "I couldn't help but like your music—it is rather loud, in case you didn't know, and I'm right next door." After a moment's hesitation, she held out her hand. "Claire."

"Guga, simply Guga. Like to come in?"

"Why not."

And that was how Claire and Guga met. As well as Purser, who also made Guga's acquaintance during this time, as fielder of complaints. This was also the day Claire received her first authentic salsa dancing lesson, in cabin B-408.

On days three and four out from Rio, all hell broke loose.

CHAPTER 13

Over and over again, Mári's taxi circled the large block of colonial buildings. On the fourth fruitless attempt, she ditched the wheels and scrambled on foot to find *23 ½ Avenida J. Mina.* The problem was the half—none seemed to exist in the maze of crammed entries and tiled stairways, except perhaps in the figment of some ambitious owner's imagination. She could find no posted sign that read CUNARD, a word she couldn't even pronounce well enough to advance her cause with passersby. Finally, she resorted to asking if anyone knew the office for the very big ship, Quin Mári, coming in December. This drew blank stares as well.

Dejected and hot, Mári stood on the sidewalk, bewildered in the heart of the noisy city. Nose stinging from held-back tears, a moment of sheer surrender made her look up: nestled between criss-crossing power and phone lines was a sign with a cargo ship in royal blue—Marine Global. Picking up her feet, she headed into a long corridor, careful to wipe her eyes and snort back the nose drips before poking her head into the first doorway.

Marine Global consisted of a large rectangular room lined with glass-enclosed offices on the long left side, a wooden counter at the front and an open floor behind which hosted half a dozen wooden desks piled high with papers. Workers on telephones spoke rapid-fire Spanish, using words like *manifest, customs declarations, letters of guarantee, duties, bills of lading, verification.* Mári understood nothing. She wasn't even sure they were speaking the same language.

Skipping any pre-amble in case they weren't, she piped up. *"Disculpe, but do any of you know where are the offices for Quin Mári?"*

A tan young man with black hair mowed down to a velvet crew cut and tensile biceps that challenged the hemline of his short sleeves answered her call.

"You're not from here, are you?" he asked, hurling himself over the half-door of the counter the way slick guys hop into convertibles.

Disarmed by his confidence and good looks, Mári fixated on his white teeth, which featured a pair of pointy incisors.

"Say something else and I'll guess where you're from."

She played along. *"Ok, do you know where are the offices for the big ship—"*

"La Republica Dominicana, si?"

"How'd you know?"

"The way you pronounce—or don't—your s's. Julio. Mucho gusto."

"Mári." Knowing better but under his sway, her hand drifted into his outstretched palm. It was warm and strong. He moved to close in but she pulled away.

"The office you are looking for—and I am sorry it is not this one—is right down the hall. I'll show you."

She looked at him, unable to hide her suspicion.

"Really!" he laughed, exposing the wolf teeth.

True to his word, Julio led her to the Cunard office set up to handle the logistics of ship, passengers, and 70-odd reporters flying in by charter to cover the final leg to Long Beach.

The doorway opened into a good-sized room similar to that of Marine Global, with desks on the central floor and a bank of wood-frame glass enclosures that allowed for a measure of auditory, if not visual, privacy.

A Mexican Sophia Loren, early 40s and all legs, emerged from her tidy desk when she saw the two visitors. She was clearly in charge of the other, plainer, female employees who seemed content with their lot.

Julio flashed his smile and brushed Mári's shoulder, as if trying to elicit a twitch of jealousy from the woman.

"Are you expecting a guest?" he asked playfully.

"I'm not," she said pointedly, steering clear of his magnetic orbit, *"but he is,"* she tossed her chin in the direction of a man behind the glass whose bent posture, white-knuckle grip on the phone, and deeply furrowed brow indicated some sort of mess not to be interrupted.

"You're late," the woman announced.

"Yes, well, the directions—"

To ease the escalating cattiness, Julio presented the two women to each other: *"Lena, this is Mári, Mári, Lena."*

He then put his mouth as close as he dared to Mári's ear. *"If you need any other directions—or want a tour of the bay in my boat, let me know—look for the blue roof,"* he whispered quickly, pressing what felt like paper into her hand, then begged off, leaving Mári with the secretary who, after scanning her from head to toe, sashayed to her desk with no further instructions.

"I'll just have a seat," Mári said and dawdled over to a plastic visitor chair while scratching an itch that wasn't really there. When not inspecting her toe or fingernail polish, she stared at Fred. Cheeks flushed, head propped in one hand, muffled tones coming from painstaking contortions of his mouth—she wondered if he was speaking with someone who didn't know much English. She shifted and angled her body hoping he would look her way. He did not. Instead, his gaze just lingered in the mid-air zone that eyes naturally drift towards in boredom or crisis, an area of soft focus where the visual takes a back seat to the workings of the brain, or non-workings of the brain, as the case may be.

With the ship due to arrive in a little over two weeks, Mári tried to imagine the pressure that pelted Fred from every direction, a virtual hurricane of details to wrangle—flowers for the leis, drinks for the open bar, musicians for the band, thatched roof shade structures for the quay, tenders for loading provisions—the list went on and on. Gripping the receiver so hard his sinews bulged, Fred regarded the alien at arm's length before dismissing it with a slam. He then glanced up at the basketball-sized wall clock, noted 4:30 and shook his head, perhaps thinking not even Mári respected the hour, minute or second.

Despite himself, the sight of her lightened his mood. He didn't know whether she'd done it on purpose, but she was wearing the house colors—white, red, and black, an uncanny display which, intentional or not, did his heart good. Lately he'd felt, given the circumstances of this unusual final voyage, they weren't doing any one thing well as concerned RMS Queen Mary. But those colors reminded him of all the feats that had gone right. Bolstered, Fred rushed out of his office.

"*Maravilloso!* You're looking good! Please—*mi oficina*," he invited with a flourish, proudly displaying his linguistic progress. "Have a seat, *tener un asiento*," he motioned the secretary to come translate.

Mári jumped right in, admitting no impediments, not even the bored, put-out air of the third party. "*Muy serio?*" she asked in a concerned tone, pointing to the phone.

"Oh that, yes, well, troubles you know. Nothing terribly serious…just a stowaway." Fred grimaced at the word.

Mári gulped. "*What did you do with him?*"

"Threw him overboard!" Fred answered merrily, while the translator dead-panned his response. "Just kidding, we are much more civilized than that," Fred quickly added, seeing the look on Mári's face. "We gave him the choice of working or being put off the ship at the next port. He chose work."

Mári's eyes searched the room for a less charged subject and found one in the form of a maritime centerpiece decorating a credenza.

"Ah yes, behold RMS Queen Mary!" With the tender hands of a new father, Fred cradled the two-foot-long model.

"*Los mismos colores!*" she pointed at her outfit, nodding in recognition.

The secretary translator rolled her eyes, but did her job nonetheless.

"Bonito," Mári expressed, not quite sure how to compliment a ship. Her eyes were immediately drawn to pinky-nail-sized couples who stood on a deck surrounded by small boats suspended in air.

"Why so many boats? One big one is not enough?"

Fred explained how the 1912 Titanic disaster forced shipping lines to provide lifeboats for everyone on board. "It took some fifteen-hundred people perishing in the frigid waters of the North Atlantic for practices to change. Horrible tragedy."

Fred's eyes misted over as Lena's monotone kept pace.

"And how many people can be on Quin Mári?" Mári asked, preferring not to think about the need for lifeboats.

Delighted she'd asked, Fred seized a large leather folio and opened to the middle, back-tracking two pages to the desired image. His quick assurance led Mári to believe he knew the volume by heart.

"I once made the mistake of asking the same question," the secretary spoke out of turn in quiet Spanish.

"See these little guys?" Fred pointed to one of the miniatures. "Multiply him by 16,683 and you'll get how many people Queen Mary has ever carried at one time—the record, to this day, for the greatest number of humans on a vessel." He flipped a few pages ahead to an aerial shot of decks crammed with soldiers.

"This does not look comfortable," Mári cringed.

"Of course, that was an unusual circumstance. During World War II the ship was converted into a troop transport and she regularly carried over 10,000 souls across the Atlantic. Very dangerous—Hitler wanted her sunk at all costs. The loss of life would have been staggering—there were not enough lifeboats for everyone. But because of her speed, she was able to avert danger. And because of her exemplary performance, by virtue of officers and crew who fired her with life, Winston

Churchill credited Queen Mary and her sister ship Queen Elizabeth with shortening the war by a year."

"*How many people are on it now?*" the Dominican asked, feeling slightly nauseated by the thought of so much humanity in so little space.

"Only a thousand passengers signed up for this last voyage. Normally, with staff, she carries just over 3,000."

"*Dios mio…*" she uttered, then, thinking this might somehow work to her advantage, she upgraded her tone to a more upbeat, "*Dios mio! Que cosa!*"

Fred showed her the rest of the portfolio, a pictorial history of the ship through the decades.

Giant keel being laid at the John Brown Shipyard in Clydebank, Scotland, mute cranes and scaffolding creating a pick-up-sticks of organized chaos.

Gargantuan steel skeleton emerging on the ways, a whale-like colossus propped atop a crib of poles.

Rusted, headless hulk of Job #534, halted one year after work began because of the Great Depression.

Reverse birth into the River Clyde, hull completed after an agonizing delay of over two years.

Shots of the proud new ship on her sea trials, maiden voyage in May 1936, bows ripping a frothy seam while four 35-ton propellers churned a white wake that bled off the edge of the photo.

War-time service, a dismal grey shot of the ship at sea, prow obscured by flying waves and appearing submerged in a turbulent mess of ocean.

The translator, hands full, worked full speed ahead to keep up.

Mári really paid attention when the interior shots began flipping by, her first exposure to the ship's opulence. Except for vast expanses of teak decking, odd rectangular windows along the enclosed Promenade Deck, and hanging emergency boats that served as a constant reminder of where one truly was, Mári was struck by how un-ship-like it all looked on the inside.

Gleaming, upscale shops and a wide main staircase over which hung a plaster relief of the ship's namesake.

Swirly wood veneers and fancy inlays in staterooms.

Main dining room with capacity for 800, high ceilings lofted with reassuring pillars, clerestory lights and glowing torchières, the fore end of the room boasting a stylized map that tracked Queen Mary's and running mate Queen Elizabeth's daily progress, courtesy of two crystal replicas on tracks.

When the content shifted to artwork, Mári nodded her head politely but didn't pay much attention to this intricate bronze door or that large pastoral painting or this array of fine silver centerpieces for the Captain's table. A shot of two stewards vacuuming the Main Lounge did, however, whet her curiosity.

"Here we have my favorite—the second largest piece of art on board—a carved wood panel overlaid with plaster and decorated in gold and silver gilt, aptly named 'Unicorns in Battle'," Fred rhapsodized.

Lena didn't know what to do with the word *unicorns* and so translated them as *horses* which, in truth, is what they looked like if one overlooked the corns.

The Brit didn't stop there. "Legend has it if two unicorns battled and their horns touched, it would create beautiful music."

Mári's eyes focused on an area above the animals, near the peak of a slender mountain. *"What are those?"* she asked, pointing to five square seams.

"Oh, those are hinged panels that can be opened from behind—for the cinema operator to show movies. If I was going to stow away, that's where I'd hide. No one goes up there much anymore since the cinema is elsewhere."

Mári's pulse quickened. *"And this room is on what deck?"*

"Promenade."

"I would surely love to see something so beautiful…"

Tanned skin hiding most of the blush that saturated her façade, Mári forced a laugh and blurted *Show me the pool!* to cover her excitement.

Fred flipped frantically ahead. "Ah, here we are. The First Class swimming pool."

Mári took in every detail, paying close attention to nooks and crannies, noting murky corners and the general lack of light. *"It's very dark—"*

"It's indoors, forward on R Deck, same level as the main dining salon. Both pools were located inside because of chilly conditions on the crossing route."

"What's behind that?" Mári pointed to stairs with a mid-level landing and balcony up top.

"A public corridor. On regular crossings you'd have an attendant dispensing towels at the entrance up there, while at the opposite lower end of the pool, which you can't see in this picture, there's a long row of changing rooms."

Trying to maintain an air of innocence, she asked about the pool's hours.

"On this trip, seven to seven."

"So it's not open at all?"

Lena interjected. *"He means seven in the morning to seven at night."*

"Funny thing about pools on ships, they drain them when the weather is rough so that the water doesn't slosh all to one side, or out completely, leaving the swimmers high and dry."

"And will the weather be rough to California?"

"Not likely, but you never know."

As Mári asked to see more pictures, Fred instructed Lena to contact Señor So and So to fix an appointment as well as make a host of other calls, leaving the two of them to thumb through the book. Looking like a schoolboy about to recite an ill-learned soliloquy, he then uttered a rough but intelligible phrase that Mári quickly identified.

"Quieres ir con mi...al VIPS pronto?"

Not the question she'd hoped for but her chances were still alive, and while she didn't really want to go to VIPS that afternoon, how could she refuse?

Lena returned and took an unobtrusive seat.

"That didn't take very long."

"No one was een."

"There is one thing I'd really like to know," Mári piped, making Fred nervous she would continue on the subject of their personal dining plans. *"How did you know he didn't pay?"*

"The stowaway?" Fred asked, relieved. "Simple, really. He managed to slip by unnoticed without arousing suspicion, spending the first few nights in an empty cabin that happened to be unlocked. Well, because of increasing heat," Fred fingered his neck tie, "people began sleeping outside. He was one among many who camped out in deck chairs. And because there are numerous buffets and teas offered informally throughout the day, he managed to satisfy his appetite, quite nicely, I dare say."

Fred looked longingly into the distance. "What I wouldn't give for some good English tea and cakes—you needn't translate that."

"How did they catch him?"

"Right. Seems, for one, he borrowed money from a passenger."

"That was stupid!"

"Indeed, since that passenger became suspicious and alerted Purser, who in turn alerted Chief Master at Arms."

"Qué es un Señor de Brazos?" Mári asked, confused by the appellation.

Lena was on auto-pilot and hadn't bothered to ask for clarification regarding the uncommon term. She'd literally translated *Arms* as appendages rather than weapons, and *Master* as its closest relative, Mister.

"It's like the police," Fred answered.

"Oh," Mári said quietly.

"They searched a windbreaker jacket he left on a deck chair. What do you think they found?"

"I don't know—a deck of cards?"

"Toothbrush, razor, mouthwash, deodorant—in other words, all the things that should've been in his cabin."

"Maybe he's just a very clean person?"

"Who knows. But he is American, so he can land in Long Beach with no trouble."

Lucky man, Mári thought. *That will be my legacy if it's the last and only thing I do for my child.*

"What if he was not from the United States?"

Fred quickly held up his hand to stop Lena—he was catching on more and more.

"Deportation, unless he had the proper visas."

Barely audible, Mári uttered, *"Si, comprendo."*

"Well, we should head out." Fred stowed the treasury of memorabilia.

Mári replied her assent distractedly. She had to take advantage of the translator, couldn't risk any misunderstanding.

"Fred, I have to ask you an important question."

The Englishman looked concerned, fearing a possible indiscretion. Mári, for her part, felt like a cliff diver about to jump.

"This means a lot to me. I feel very close to your great ship," she said slowly, with great concentration, so as not to slip up. *"After all, I have her name!"*

"So you do."

"I would very much like to visit Quin Mári," Mári swallowed hard, *"in person, when he—she—arrives."*

"All right."

"I know it's a big request and normally I wouldn't ask but—"

Fred placed a comforting hand on hers. "Yes, ok!"

"Me to Quin Mári?" Mári stammered in English.

"Of course, no trouble at all. We're practically having an open house on board that day anyway...what a nightmare... But I know I won't have to worry about you."

"Excuse me?"

"Stowaways, my dear. Stowaways. We will be taking every pre-caution—this is the hottest ticket in town!"

Dizzy with alarm, Mári asked for the ladies' room. If she didn't go now, she'd pee her pants for sure.

CHAPTER 14

The short walk to VIPS challenged the nerves of both Mári and Fred for they no longer enjoyed the buffer of a translator. Once seated inside the busy restaurant, Fred's mood was further set on edge by the spicy nature of the green chiles drenching his *enchiladas Suisas*.

He, of course, had no understanding of the pressure Mári felt. Sitting in his company she felt every inch the traitor. He'd shown her kindness and she would quite possibly show him deceit. Not a fair exchange, she reasoned while watching him dab a napkin to his reddening lips.

"Hielo," Mári suggested, putting her fingers to her mouth.

"Hello?"

"Hielo para tus labios," she repeated, circling her lips with an index finger.

"Yellow? My lips are yellow?"

Mári laughed, conveying she meant nothing serious. Fred flipped through his pocket-sized English/Spanish, Spanish/English dictionary but didn't know how to spell the damned word in question.

Mári flagged a waiter and, soon enough, a glass of ice arrived.

"Right! *Hielo*, ice!"

"Aa-isse," she pronounced awkwardly, giving it two syllables.

Each was painfully aware of how limited their conversation would be without the help of a third party. After all, a dictionary could take a couple only so far.

During dessert Fred produced a folder containing pictures of the great oceanliner. Wondering why he'd waited so long to whip it out, he hoped it would patch the silent gaps which came with distressing frequency.

Mári studied one 8 X 10 black and white glossy, peering at it for a long time. Fred watched, keen on what she found fascinating about the classic picture of RMS Queen Mary entering New York Harbor for the very first time. It was dated June 1, 1936. Skyscrapers crowded the shore and hundreds of small craft flanked the regal ship as she glided up the Hudson to Pier 90. Fire tugs shot water high into the air, celebrating as her knifelike prow cleaved the light chop, funnels puffing moderately. Thousands of well-wishers out to bid her a warm welcome. Newly beloveds making acquaintance for the very first time.

Mári wasn't able to grasp the mechanical intricacies of the creation that was Queen Mary, but none of its humanity was lost on her. She could see love surrounding the ship like it surrounds a person. And the ship was named after a person. And her own name was part of the ship's name. This awareness of something greater than herself—this tangible vessel and all its attendant glory, accomplishment, and sentiment—filled her with awe. Inspired, Mári's eyes brimmed with salty tears.

"Are you all right?"

Embarrassed by errant droplets sliding down her cheeks, she nodded.

"What is it?" Fred asked tenderly.

Pointing at the image of the ship with a red fingernail, Mári barely got the words out. *"Es mi salvador."*

Fred whisked out a hanky and tucked it in her hand. Had he heard right? *It's my savior?*

He didn't have a chance to ponder the significance of her statement because, at this most delicate and awkward moment in their relationship, a thick muscular man with a head full of bouncing Medusa ringlets pushed through the heavy front doors and peered like a werewolf afoot during a full moon.

Mári shrank in her seat, gamely holding the picture of the Mary in front of her face while Fred developed an altogether sinking feeling as he watched the energetic newcomer who, he surmised, was itching for a fight.

The man conferred none too politely with the hostess, pantomiming with burly arms someone about chest high with long hair and a thick mid-section. The hostess pointed uncertainly toward the back. He spotted the target right away and was there in five ambitious strides. Fred rose immediately. In his haste, his tie dragged through the *flan*, becoming saturated with drippy brown sugar.

"Excuse me, but do I know you?" he gamely queried the gladiator. "No, I'm quite sure I don't and I don't wish to, so please leave!"

"Who are-a you? Thees—" pointing at Mári, "—my woman. Djou know dat?" he spat, English not bad except for the heavy accent.

Mári kept quiet, a sour look on her face.

"Yes, I did know Mári had a boyfriend," Fred lied in hopes of taking some of the sting out. "But I did not know him specifically to be you."

"Wise-a cracker English man, eh?" Luigi snarled.

Mári sensed the inflamed Latin was on the brink of transferring his ire to Fred.

"Not here," she said quickly, getting up. Luigi herded her in front of him as they walked out together. Fred followed a short distance behind while their waiter took up the rear, trying to find the right moment to present the bill.

Outside, Luigi roughly spun Mári around and slapped her face. She slapped back hard, letting loose a barrage of venomous Spanish and a flurry of fists into his belly.

"Leave me alone!" Mári wailed, burying her head in his abdomen.

"I can't, you know I can't." Luigi pulled her close.

Fred watched them get into a dented Mazda—the Italian even held the door open. Mári looked composed, then pleased when Luigi reached into the back and presented her with a teddy bear which she briefly cuddled then plopped on her lap. With Luigi busy maneuvering out of the tight parking spot, she turned toward Fred, who stood on the top step, mutely alert. The car yanked away quickly, jerking her head back as she mouthed one word and waved goodbye.

He motioned a small wave back. *"Gracias* to you as well."

CHAPTER 15

SUNDAY, NOVEMBER 19, 1967

The normal engine vibration most noticeable in the aft was tolerably dampened by the time it reached B-Deck Cabin 410, located just forward of midships, but since they'd left warmer waters the ride had become increasingly rough. There was, however, no dipping and heaving at the moment and for this Claire Zeisse was grateful as she finished applying her right eyebrow. At 37, she was the same age as the grand dame she briefly called home (if you counted back to 1930 when construction began).

And what, exactly, had she accomplished? Published a few noteworthy articles? Supported herself in decent fashion? Visited her conservative parents on the east coast every few years when she could spare the airfare?

Cranky, she stared at her peachy complexion in the mirror—so tinted to make queasy people appear rosy at sea. Indeed. *What a curse*, she sighed, eyeing the crooked brow. Now she'd have to get a washcloth, rub out the failed attempt and start all over, a circumstance that smacked of her chosen career. Time, precious time. It was never on her side. Always pieces to write, pictures to take, people to interview, deadlines to meet. Never enough time. Could never quite put her finger on it and make it stay in one place.

Davey Pragoff shuffled along the stuffy working alleyway, a gray service corridor that accompanied most of the ship's length. Careful not to trip, blue eyes and sandy bangs barely cleared the stack of towels rising like snowy mountains above the ground of uniformed arms. He had forgotten his cart—got called away on the thousandth unexpected errand of the morning—and had consequently left it at the opposite end of the ship. A thousand feet of steel and concrete connected prow to stern, and one could expect to walk that length a good twenty times during a typical sixteen-hour day. Not to mention climbing tons of stairs—from R deck where the working alleyway and stores, luggage, and laundry were kept, up to Main, where the uppermost passenger cabins were situated. Like everyone else toiling below, Davey barely found time for a smoke.

Dumping the heap of fresh towels in the eager arms of the pool attendant, Davey turned to trek back to his cart at the aft end when another harried steward bunted him with an elbow. "Purser wants to see you, something about B-410," the lad shouted, continuing down the hall at a jog.

Cabin B-410 was not normally on his roster. This could only mean one thing—someone really difficult was in it. And today of all days, when they were about to round the Horn, a necessary evil for a ship too wide to fit through the Panama Canal. Many passengers and staff regarded this as the highlight of the trip. Excitement ran high, people rose early to pitch camp on chilly decks, requesting extra blankets, hot tea, all extra chores. The double-decker buses on the poop deck were a sell-out attraction, offering "rides" around Cape Horn for $1, and the pool was full of people eager to claim they'd "swum" around the tip of South America. On top of it all there was the anticipation of foul weather. Davey barely had time to take it in. But one thing was certain: he was beyond proud to be serving on the largest passenger liner ever to round the Horn, the first—and last—three stacker to do so.

What Purser knew that Davey didn't was just how peculiar the tenant in B-410 had demonstrated herself to be. Miss Zeisse, a journalist aboard for the final voyage, simply could not stand the stewardess assigned to her, had suffered through for two weeks since leaving England and now demanded not only a replacement but one of an altogether different gender for good measure.

Their encounter occurred via her room telephone (center dial confidently proclaiming, "Call anywhere in the world whilst at Sea") and his desk telephone on Main. Separated by two decks and six cabin lengths, the impersonal nature of the exchange would have to do. On this day of days, he was swamped with queues and requests for Chilean stamps so scores of people could send off postcards at the next port. A sinewy fellow with crow's-feet 'round the outs of his eyes and a fake bronze complexion, he politely inquired as to the nature of the transgression.

Had Miss Love stolen a personal possession? "Heavens no," came the reply.

Had Miss Love neglected her housekeeping duties? "She was very thorough."

The clear polish of his fingernails took a ride through the bangs of a salt and pepper Caesar cut. Summoning reserves of patience, Purser stared beyond the profile of the liner etched in the glass door of the Travel Bureau. How he loved that view, the main artery of the ship, people coming and going at all hours, countless hands caressing nickel-pewter banisters.

"No, no, no. Everything's fine," Claire insisted.

"Then what, may I ask, is the problem?"

"She reminds me of my mother, cold and critical. The way I hang up my robe—or don't; the way she fluffs it and moves it to the hook behind the bathroom door. Okay, so I should know better than to hang a moist robe over a wooden chair. Could you get me a fella?"

"You know, Miss Love, while a bit stern, is one of our most seasoned stewardesses. You really are in good hands. Such an assignment befits your role here, documenting the trip."

"Seasoned with what, horse radish?"

An experienced pro worth every pound of his pay, Purser could see he wasn't going to win this one. He was, by all measures, amused. Ready for a change. Miss Love was a throwback to the days when class barriers reigned. Those days were over, especially with this new breed of American who no longer tried to be British. Furthermore, at the end of this crossing he would be moving to Miami to secure a job on one of the new cruise ships plying the Caribbean. Assuming, of course, the

37-year-old vessel survived the Horn, a region of chastising winds and chaotic seas that, in the days of sail, had claimed many lives.

Three sharp raps sounded on the door—the hand of someone in a rush.

Within Cabin B-410, Claire hastily finished re-applying her right eyebrow. She'd stirred not long ago, courtesy of the seven-ton noontime whistles mounted high up on the forward funnels. White terry swept the floor all four steps to the door—the compact cabin fit better than the robe—in it, she felt at home. The garment, on the other hand, swamped her athletic five-foot-two frame. A leftover from a lover many sizes bigger. First week out. Big Texan, older, widowed. She could tell he'd fallen for her and so put a quick lid on it. If she saw him again she'd return the robe. No souvenirs. Or would there be? Lately she'd been throwing things to chance. Career nicely put, she could afford to work on another project.

Qué sera, sera.

"Hello mum," the new steward greeted cheerily, respectfully averting his eyes at the sight of her *deshabille*. She stepped aside and he glided by with a tray full of morning victuals.

"Will you ever call me Claire?"

"No mum."

"Come on, this is the last voyage. What could it hurt to lighten up a little?"

"I might have the pleasure of serving you on another ship."

Claire seized a boiled egg perched on a porcelain collar and bit its head off while relaxing into the desk chair near the open porthole.

"Davey," she said between chews, "we barely know each other, but I can see you're trustworthy, smart. I have a mission for you."

"Yes mum." A statement, not a question.

Drawing a deep breath and blowing out the nervous energy, the young steward paused briefly outside B-410. He fondled the crisp American fiver in his pocket, running the tip of a finger along its folded edge. As his feet propelled him aft, along the gleaming hallway floor, he let his right hand glide lightly above the yellowed plastic handrails mounted on the corridor walls. He recalled stories of how the ship's builders hadn't fitted Queen Mary with any safety grips, so confident were they she'd give a stable ride. To their horror, they discovered Mary loved to roll, and not just in heavy seas. Everybody joked how she could roll the milk right out of a cup of tea, but it was true. After the maiden voyage they installed the Roanoid handrails Davey's fingers now skimmed. He, too, would need to keep himself steady, particularly as concerned Miss Claire's mission, since much more was at stake than a mere paper cut—a cut, period—his job.

He checked with his section head steward and reported to dining room duty. Lunch service in full swing, Davey had to fill in the gaps for twelve tables—top off water glasses, empty ashtrays, de-crumb tablecloths, fetch more butter or cream, all of which, if done right, would never be detected by the patron.

Davey felt bad enough about this being the Mary's final voyage, but the relatively poor service—an uncharacteristic trait—embarrassed him, so he did his utmost to mitigate the loss of 250 of the crew who hadn't signed on because management had refused to pay a £75 hardship bonus.

Dining room clatter, clanking, bursts of laughter, he absorbed it all as if taking in the pungent sweetness of a fading rose. Most of these passengers were American—and most, he suspected, lived in California, given their tans and flat accents. Miss Claire, he guessed, must also be from California. Along with the first two qualifying traits, she possessed a confident, friendly, assertive air. She'd asked him to locate a passenger who was beginning to cause a stir, a lone female, as the rumor mill would have it, putting her quarters to profitable use. He was to give the woman Claire's business card, with a simple invitation to meet. Claire was, first and foremost, a journalist with a yen for provocative stories, and she had her suspicions as to who it might be... Who could resist?

CHAPTER 16

Davey flexed his sore feet, fighting the temptation to explore the contents of his ears while standing watch and listening to a muffled repertoire of hilarity. He wasn't used to being upright and stationary for long stretches. Had his fill the previous day, and this was his first tour of duty outside the *next* most troublesome cabin. Altogether too much time to think.

Things had gone very badly the day before. He still couldn't get over it.

After accepting Miss Claire's assignment, Davey, during his normal rotation, had stumbled upon a convulsing woman as he entered a certain stateroom, thinking it to be empty when no one responded to his raps on the door. The woman had raided a supply closet and tried to kill herself by drinking the cleaning solution used to freshen the ship's metal railings. This in response to learning her husband was having a ship-board affair.

Davey knew she'd recently returned from sick bay and was resting comfortably enough while her husband, by all accounts, remained sloshed in the Starboard Lounge. A very sad affair. He wasn't at all sure the woman was appreciative of his intervention but management certainly were pleased—he'd averted a huge public relations fiasco. Still, things were bad enough, which is why he was posted outside B-408, the cabin of Señorita G., the leggy Latin who entertained male guests for a fee. Though she'd paid handsomely for her accommodations, events had come to a head in the varnish incident, leading to house arrest and the rotation of five young stewards standing like lamp posts outside her cabin.

Now it was Davey's turn at watch. He'd heard from the others that she liked to invite them in to share a cup of tea or what not, and though sorely tempted, if only to relieve the sickening boredom, Davey knew better. He planned to politely refuse any invitation, but one of his more rash compatriots, a twenty-year-old from South London they called Roger Dodger, accepted more often than not.

Dodger was in there now—off-duty visits were becoming routine. When he emerged with a silly grin on his face, Davey asked about the muted giggles, groans, and odd slapping noises.

"What on earth were you doing in there?"

"Playin' cards—*canasta*. Plus we snorted a nip o' gin." Dodger leaned in to share his breath. "They're gonna throw her off in Valparaiso—can you believe it?"

Davey shook his head sympathetically, though his loyalties remained with the company.

"Gave me really good advice, she did, about how to win ova this girl back home. Well, gotta go. Cheers!"

"Wait a minute!" Davey may have saved a woman's life but, due to all the commotion, had not delivered Miss Claire's message or business card before the Latin had been sequestered. Now, even though he stood right outside their respective doors and was closer than ever, he couldn't risk communicating from his security post. He knew Purser was currently reviewing the evidence, about to bring his case against the alleged offender. Fingering the five dollar bill, he wondered if there was any way he could salvage half of it. Dejected, he pulled it out of his pocket and pressed it into Dodger's palm.

"I want you to give a message to Miss Zeisse. She's not in her cabin," he pointed directly across the way, "so you'll need to track her down. She may be on deck with all the others, taking pictures of the bloody Horn. Hurry—your new friend's future may depend on it."

❋

Travel Bureau was the hub of passenger planning where Purser reigned supreme inside the confines of etched glass and steel, burl wood, and leather. He made decisions about who bunked where, who sat with whom in the dining room, at the Captain's table. In addition, he was responsible for disbursing the crew's pay, down to a pence. With this power came a down side—he fielded all complaints, and on this voyage there were many, not the least of which was the leggy Latin before him. Purser had all the necessary testimony, which was why he was taken aback when, after presenting his case and the regrettable sanction to be imposed, the arrestingly tall Brazilian's vocals exceeded the Travel Bureau's meager insulating properties.

"You cannot throw me off, I am a paying passenger!"

Purser stood his ground. "I'm afraid the Captain has asked me to convey his wishes that you voluntarily disembark at our next stop."

Eyelashes batted. "On what grounds?"

"I just told you what grounds. We've had some complaints."

"That's news to me."

"Yes, I expect it is, since the complaints have come from two respectable women."

"Where is the proof?"

"One witness, who is now gravely ill, says she saw her husband follow a tall, rather flamboyant lady into a stateroom that clearly was not theirs. She said she stood outside the cabin and listened through the vents in the door. What she heard shocked her. Your cabin number, please?"

"You know perfectly well which cabin is mine," the Latin purred suggestively.

"Don't try that with me," Purser admonished, eyes narrowing to a squint. "B-408, correct?"

A nod.

"Precisely. She heard her husband negotiate with the woman who, she said, had an accent she took to be Brazilian. Are you, in fact, from Brazil?"

"I am, yes," the defendant shifted in her polka-dotted sundress. "And for the rest of your information, I am a psychologist. It is customary for me to talk about fees with my clients. He was merely seeking a consultation. After all, it's no secret things aren't going so well between him and his wife…"

Purser took this in stride, clearing his throat pleasantly. "I'm sure you meant well, Madame—"

"My name is Guga," she broke in a low, slightly menacing tone.

"Riiightt. I'm sure you meant well, *Guga*, but it is the policy of this shipping line that no such 'consultations' take place, nor money change hands, on company property."

"Tipping is not allowed?"

"That's entirely different."

The Travel Bureau door flung open.

"What's all this about?" Claire burst in, face red and splotchy from the cold. She peeled off a scarf and gloves and took up a position alongside the tall Latin who, in some ways, reminded her of a bronze Shirley MacLaine.

Purser stood his ground behind a sturdy wooden desk.

"I'm sorry, Miss, this is a private affair. If you would like to—"

"What I'd like to do is end this nonsense once and for all. She's with me." Claire gestured toughly with her thumb as if ordering peanuts from a vendor at a baseball game.

"Beg your pardon?"

"She's with me. We're traveling together. A couple—get it?"

"Even if that's the case, this has nothing—"

"It has everything to do with me," Claire fired back.

"I can handle this myself—thank you," Guga nodded, extending an awkward hand in greeting/goodbye.

"I know you can, but I don't want to see you go. This dull group, why, I'll shrivel up and die if the one spark of life as we know it is thrown off this aging bucket of bolts."

Claire laid on the Hepburn act thick. "In fact, maybe I'll go with you—to hell with this crummy assignment which is, if you recall Mr. Purser, to document the Queen Mary's last voyage. And document it I will, whether I finish the trip or not."

Purser was quiet. The stakes had been raised. Damned Yankees!

"So how 'bout it? She's with me, you leave us to our business, we'll leave you to yours."

"Yes, it's the business part of it that—"

"My business is writing articles—maybe even a book—and keeping *this one* in line from here on in." She nudged Guga in the mid-section. "Ball's in your court."

The events of the past few days raced through Purser's mind, events that most passengers knew nothing about—a burial at sea, the near suicide, and a missing mess boy who forced them to backtrack for several hours while he was presumed overboard.

Purser clicked his teeth twice, then once more for good measure. It was the most assertive thing he could do.

"Very well, Madame, you win. I will inform the Captain of our new arrangement, and that you expect to file a glowing report about the voyage."

Guga and Claire turned to leave.

"Still, there is the matter of the cabin. In order to pacify the complaining passengers, I will give you two hours to clear everything out of your stateroom and into Miss Claire's."

"I suppose," Guga began, "the matter of a refund is out of the question?"

"Given that the alternative is to ship you off at Valparaiso…"

"All right then, it's a deal," Claire chirped, not at all put out by the sudden prospect of a bunk mate.

"By the way," Guga remembered, halfway out the door. "Who was the second woman to complain?"

Purser chuckled. "Funny thing. A stewardess assigned to your cabin remarked to co-workers on the volume of fresh towels and sheets you requested. Normally this would not raise much interest, but given the fact we're usually at sea for five days—not thirty-nine—there is no adequate laundry service aboard. We are somewhat rationing the linens as they are cleaned in bulk during our shore visits."

The odd couple left Purser to his various affairs, noting that the line for stamps snaked up the main staircase toward the library on Promenade Deck.

"Let's get a drink," Guga suggested, steering them forward. "I still can't believe they made me give up my room. How conservative! I should have picked an Italian or French ship."

"What about your little friends, the cabin boys? Maybe one of them can get you access—it'll be empty, I suppose, 'cause, you know, I'm going to need some time alone during the day to organize my writing."

"*No problema.* Let's work out the details over Bloody Marys."

"I'd like that," she said, curious to get to know her new roommate. "Though I think I'll have hot tea. I've got to go back outside."

They took a seat in the relaxed Observation Lounge, the famous bar at the front of the ship. Sitting high up in the superstructure like a tiara, it afforded a sweeping view of the prow and seas ahead. To their right the snow-capped mountains of *Tierra del Fuego*, Land of Fire, presented an arresting sight.

"Let's hope the weather holds—last thing I want to find out is whether this old Queen really can roll the milk out of a cup of tea!" Claire joked, placing a cool hand on Guga's exceedingly warm one in a gesture of camaraderie.

Oddly startled, Claire pulled her hand back and waited in awkward silence for drinks to arrive. Guga merely laughed, crossed her legs daintily, and smoothed her dress. There was something genuine about her, Claire realized. She'd never been attracted to women before, so she wasn't sure what was going on with this one.

Perhaps in the five-thousand miles and twenty remaining days she would find out.

CHAPTER 17

While waiting for her ship to arrive, Mári focused on two things: the unsettling activity occurring inside her body and packing. She did not take the baby's movement as a good sign. It worried her immensely. There was no way she could allow this child to be born in Mexico. No way. Of this she was sure.

Her hands found themselves flying frequently to the taut, low belly which puckered with a life of its own, instinctively rubbing in a slow, circular motion to soothe both beings. These days Mári no longer danced in the show, even though she did go to work most nights whether or not she felt up to it. Nobody said a word about "her condition," least of all Mári herself. Max had taken her aside to ask about her plans, whereupon she'd fictionalized Luigi's involvement, saying they were working things out, that everything would be fine and she'd be back dancing in no time. Max reacted with softly raised eyebrows and a patient smile, but the parrot on his shoulders knew better and trundled its head back and forth screeching "*Mafioso! Mafioso!*"

Packing proved to be as challenging as dealing with the dissolution of life as she knew it. Mári faced all sorts of dilemmas. Should she bring a suitcase? Common sense told her no—where would she hide it? Couldn't walk around the ship clutching a valise. But a change of clothes would be necessary if for no other reason than to avoid suspicion during the four-day journey.

What size should her handbag be? Would it be subject to search, as when the Dominicans entered Mexico and the customs officials rifled through all of their belongings? If so, she'd better not pack clothes and toiletries in it, otherwise she'd be caught red-handed just like that other stowaway.

These moments of logistical confusion were made all the more difficult because she hadn't told a soul of her clandestine plot, not even Sonrisa, who lounged on the far side of the bed, resting after a late night out. Mári looked over at her friend and ached to confide in her, but knew it would not be well received for, among other things, there was one gaping hole in her plan: no papers. What would happen when the ship reached Long Beach? Didn't want to think about it. One step at a time. Just get there. Get somewhere.

Hampered by secrecy and stupefied by her overwhelming need to make a move, Mári welcomed distractions. The sound of a car pulling into the lower driveway provided a timely one. Grunting through a number of unbecoming poses, she knee-walked across the bouncy bed, stopping to straddle Sonrisa's legs.

"*Mira—quien es abajo? Tu novia?*" Mári cajoled, rolling her friend's hip bones back and forth. She loved to tease 'Risa about *that woman* who seemed determined to pursue the elusive queen to the ends of the earth.

Sonrisa pulled herself up and together they peered through the jalousie windows like canaries in a cage. Neither recognized the car and they couldn't see the driver. Sonrisa was relieved when Madame Gerard yelled Mári's name.

Curious, she pulled on a skirt to go with her oversized blouse and padded downstairs, anticipation building. No one had ever visited her besides Luigi.

Mári stood at the kitchen doorway and ducked her head to see who was inside the car. Fred jumped out, a sheepish, nervous smile his calling card.

"I hope no problem me here," he declared in halting pig Spanish.

"How did you know where I live?" she asked, displaying the requisite suspicion.

"Many times been to club but you no there," he paused, sucking up the courage to continue. *"You ok?"*

"Oh, that. Yes, I'm ok. I'm glad you came by," Mári said graciously.

He held out a little box wrapped in silver paper. *"Nothing much, but might help."*

Mári took the gift and held it to her ear, shaking its contents. Something rattled inside. *"Un regalo para mi?"* With childlike wonder she ripped it open. On a cloud of cotton lie a pen knife branded with the profile of their kindred ship. She gingerly worked the blade in and out, fingering the keepsake.

"Es muy bonito—tank you Fred." Hyper-sensitive, she wondered why he thought it might come in handy. Was this a defense weapon? Hardly. Must have something else in mind. Was he on to her?

"See you Tuesday, the ship here at ten."

"Where?"

"Out there." He pointed toward the Bay. *"If I cannot go with you I will make sure you get on. To visit, that is!"*

"And when does the ship leave?" she thankfully remembered to ask.

"Next morning," Fred squeezed her hand, getting back in the car. *"Not much time."*

"No mucho tiempo," he said confidently, getting the hang of this new language. "Cheerio!" The sedan revved out of sight.

Mári had no idea what *cheerio* meant, but it sounded awfully nice.

✺

"Where'd he say he'd meet you?" Sonrisa asked urgently, hopping down from her perch.

"On the docks? Near the Málécon?" she recalled timidly, a pout clouding her features.

"Clear as mud. Remember I told you to always get as much information as possible?"

"But I did!"

"Especially when this means as much as you say it does," Sonrisa finished, the steam dissipating.

Mári's slack jaw rearranged itself into a jutting sort of sturdy front. *"I would rather die than have a baby born in this ugly place."*

"So that's what this is all about. Can't say I'm surprised, it's just like you," Sonrisa said rather tenderly.

"There's a lot of planning to do but I'd rather not get into details—the walls have big ears and big mouths." Mári lowered her voice and said, *"Besides mi amor, there's something I want to do before I leave and I want to do it with you."*

Shuffling over to a low cubby, she gasped while retrieving a dog-eared issue of Life Magazine, 27 January 1967 being her current favorite for two reasons—an article on bathing suits and beauties in Acapulco, and a secret pair of tickets marked *"Admisión Colibri—Uno Adulto."*

Taking a moment to right herself, she threaded her arm through Sonrisa's.

"Vamos a la playa!"

Whisking them to a *combi* where they jostled cozily next to one another, Mári revealed the crumpled, sweaty tickets clenched in her fist, red dye coloring her mocha lifeline. She laughed it off, explaining how the guy who'd helped her find Fred—a cliff diver, remember?— had given them to her. *"We had some kind of connection,"* Mári finished lamely.

"Some kind of connection with what?"

"A glass-bottomed boat," came out a tad snippish, as if Sonrisa should've read her mind. *"Esta bien aqui!"* she called to the driver. Yanking her voluminous skirt out of the van, Mári clarified her intention. *"I want to see the Virgin one last time."*

CHAPTER 18

The Dominicans stood at a small bridge and pier that ventured into dappled turquoise waters at the midway point between *Playas Caletilla* and *Caleta*. Dozens of self-proclaimed glass bottom boats lie tethered to buoys a short distance from the beach. Scores more bobbed pierside.

"How do we know which one is Colibri?"

"He said it has a blue roof."

"Half the boats out there have blue roofs," Sonrisa remarked, unafraid to state what did not yet seem obvious to her friend.

On a hunch, Mári hiked up her skirt and ran to the far end of the little pier, laboring hard to make her way to a boat that stood ready to cast off its lines.

"Aqui! Aqui!" Mári screamed for her friend to follow. *"Es la Colibri, verdad!"*

Breathless, they each took the hand of the skipper, a sinewy fellow who resembled a knotted piece of drift wood except for a pair of tight blue trunks that remarked his lower half. Mári and Sonrisa took their seats among a handful of other passengers, mostly young couples out on a date. For balance, they were required to sit across from each other. The glass bottom stretched between them, showing white sand, clear waters, and an occasional silver fish. Skipper gunned the outboard. The motor sputtered, then lit up, propelling the long, narrow boat over gentle bay waves toward *Isla de la Roqueta.* A few people clapped in delight.

During their time touring the magical reefs, each woman entertained her own thoughts while allowing the fresh breeze to cool the soul. Mári thought briefly about all the things that weren't getting done, but soon gave in to the rocking motion of the sea.

Sonrisa's mind re-traced the events of a recent, memorable night, when a French woman and a local entrepreneur had showed up at Club Prestige. Evidently, the man knew Max through one business capacity or another. Perhaps they were even rivals of a sort. Whatever the story, the Dom Pérignon arrived in a silvery bucket. The woman seemed pleased enough, but her short-sleeved pink knit shirt and highly buffed loafers gave her an uptight look, even though her bi-colored brown and blonde hair put her squarely on the side of wild. Pedro, a short, slightly rotund Mexican whose kind demeanor belied the many agendas coursing through his blood, ran an upscale nightclub in one of the reputable hotels.

Knowing how these guys operated, Sonrisa, catching sight of an orange starfish climbing on top of another, imagined the prelude had gone somewhat like this…

Earlier that night, Pedro had made a courageous attempt to get into the French woman's pants. While on the dance floor at Mambo, he'd insinuated himself rather explicitly against her skin-tight Capris.

Previous to that, his main weapons had been scotch and sensitive conversation. He'd made progress. Kika had warmed to both. Her English became more fluid despite the French cadence. Eventually, she'd grown glassy-eyed and her hands raked her close-cropped hair more often, as if trying to reap some particular harvest. Sonrisa pictured her poofing her lips out with small bursts of air the way French people express ellipses. They would have smoked and laughed and looked forward to catching the Midnight Show at Club Prestige.

Chuckling to herself, Sonrisa knew Pedro thought his chances looked good. After checking in with Max they were seated at a prime table in front of the dance floor. Champagne arrived. That's when she appeared in the open doorway from outside. Framed under the arch, 'Risa casually surveyed the floor. The French woman looked up and caught her eye. Was there something about her self-assured posture, loose fitting cotton jumpsuit, and big leather bag slung diagonally from shoulder to hip that intrigued her? When Sonrisa moved, she went directly to Max for a quick chat, noticing the woman's eyes trained on her the whole time.

Mári tapped her friend, who gazed out over the sea with a look of sadness and wonder. *"Where are you, mi amor? You haven't even looked at the beautiful corals."*

'Risa murmured an apology.

"What's up with you?"

"I was thinking about that woman I met."

Mári couldn't hide the hurt look on her face.

"Don't be silly." Sonrisa reached across and stroked her arm.

"I always wished you were my girlfriend."

"I know, mi amor. I know," Sonrisa said as softly as she could over the rat-a-tat-tat of the outboard.

"This girl—you like her?"

Sonrisa filled her in.

After surveying the scene from the doorway, she'd checked in with Max, then approached their table. Max had suggested she do so. Sonrisa noticed the woman staring at her, a mild look of suspicion, maybe fear, on her pale face. She paid no mind, eased up and asked for a cigarette. Quick to give her a *Gitanes* from her own pack, Sonrisa held it to her lips, indicating she wished a light, which the foreigner managed with shaky hands. Sonrisa cupped a hand around the woman's to steady it.

Meanwhile Pedro, an astute observer of human nature, saw the pieces cascade into place. He eagerly invited the Dominican to sit with them and they made their introductions. She sat next to Kika, somewhat limited in conversation because the visitor did not speak much Spanish. Sonrisa soon excused herself to get ready for the show. Next time she appeared she wore a bouncy grass hula skirt and no top, swaying to the rhythms of Harry Belafonte's *Day-O*.

"That's a bit awkward, no?"

"Whatever. I was in a playful mood and made eye contact with her many times."

"Mafiosa."

"It was harmless."

"She probably didn't think so."

Everyone on the motorboat paused to admire a huge cluster of purple-spined sea urchins and a foot-long barracuda swimming just below the surface.

"No, I suppose not," Sonrisa said thoughtfully.

After the Show, the trio went for drinks at a bungalow within a private compound. They had to spot the car along the wall so Pedro could climb onto its roof and hop over to unlock the entrance door from the other side. Oddly, when they arrived, lights glowed warmly, ceiling fans purred, the clear blue surface of the pool shimmered, beckoning in the mild breeze. In other words, Pedro seemed to have anticipated company that night even though he hadn't planned for an elegant way in.

"*He must've thought he'd really scored!*" Mári interjected.

Modelos flowed freely. They all stripped and jumped into the pool, Pedro looking like a small, dark whale. Sonrisa and Kika gravitated toward one another, treading water in the deep end, splashing each other with water funnels squirted through pumping fists. Pedro got out and disappeared inside. Shortly thereafter, Kika escorted a shivering Sonrisa out of the pool to a nearby table, where the Dominican made her sit on her lap and called her a *tigre*.

"*You didn't.*"

Still cold, they trekked to the bathroom off the bedroom, where Kika wrapped a towel around Sonrisa then stood behind her and clasped her in a reassuring hug. They looked at each others' eyes reflected in the mirror above the sink, and just stood still.

"*When she hugged me, something happened,*" Sonrisa recounted, "*as if she passed energy to me. I can't explain…*" she said and shrugged it off.

"*She came out of the bathroom last—I was already in bed, beneath the sheets. Pedro sat in a rocking chair across the room, near the wall of open windows, wooden louvers folded to the sides. I patted the bed, inviting her in with me. I could tell she was shy and didn't really want to, but I started things anyway,*" Sonrisa said quietly.

"*Did you kiss?*"

"*No.*"

"*Since then?*"

Sonrisa nodded.

"*A little? A lot?*"

'Risa drew a long breath, couldn't help but smile.

Mári wrinkled her nose. "*What was Pedro doing the whole time?*"

"*Watching, I suppose. He climbed into bed at one point and tried to get some but we shooed him away.*"

Mári gave her a look. *"This girl's bad for business."*

They both laughed.

☀

After chugging around the teal waters of *La Roqueta*, the captain headed his craft north of *Piedra de la Hierba Buena*, a short distance off. *"In 1956,"* he began, *"the bronze statue you are about to see was submerged in these waters as a way for fishermen to secure daily blessings from our Sacred Mother. Behold, the Virgin of Guadalupe!"*

Collective oohs and ahs moved through the boat. Several passengers, Mári and Sonrisa included, made the sign of the cross, finishing with the Latin flourish of kissing the fingers that had traced the Trinity. Mári plastered her face rather indelicately against the glass bottom, aghast at the sight of the life-sized Virgin perched on a mound of seaweed and sand, crown on her head, palms pressed in supplication. Saltwater pools flooded Mári's eyes. She remained fixed to the glass, to the point of not letting others have a turn because she was embarrassed by the sudden rush of emotions. Something about the sight of this Queen of Women forever suffocating beneath the waves tormented her.

"She's not real, just a symbol," Sonrisa whispered.

"I know that," Mári croaked, swiping at the rolling tears. On the brink of losing it completely, she was saved by a pair of snorkelers swimming toward the boat. Amazingly, they turned out to be two women with slinky swimwear, tanned skin, and flowing brown hair.

Mári looked up, impatiently drying the remnants of the water works. *"Do you see them?"* she nudged Sonrisa. *"They look like you and me!"*

"Yeah, if we could swim…"

Each woman held something in her arms which prevented her from stroking freely through the water—a long, shiny cylinder. They dove deeper, maneuvering around the statue with their free arms while air bubbles rose to the surface in violent bursts. After inspecting the base, the divers appeared to settle on something, nodding their heads in unison, giving a thumbs up. Remarkably, they seemed not to notice—or care—that their every move was being watched and commented upon like a penalty kick in a soccer match.

The undersea explorers turned to the Virgin, made the sign of the cross and slipped a bouquet of red flowers from each of their plastic cylinders. Many of the women on the boat chimed *rosas!*, as if following the progress of their favorite drama, whereupon two dozen of the long-stemmed kind were tied to the bull horns upon which the Virgin stood, allowing the blooms to pay out in the currents around the statue's feet. Unexpectedly, the two divers hugged, joined upraised palms in victory, took a last look around and swam away.

Sonrisa and Mári stared at each other, wide-eyed. Applause broke out for the gutsy pair.

"Señoras y señores, you've just witnessed a small miracle!" the captain shared.

People chuckled. The boat revved and headed for shore. Mári kept her face pressed to the glass, unwilling to let the image go. She felt comforted knowing the Virgin had been visited—touched by loving hands. Womens' hands. She was cared for after all, not abandoned.

Statue no longer in sight, Mári sat up. She held the golden, feminine image strong in her mind's eye. *"Mother Mary, I love you. Please see fit to protect me and my child on the ship that—"* Mári's heart thumped in her chest—*"bears your name."* Out loud, she spoke the words *Regina Maria* into the wind. *Queen Mary.*

CHAPTER 19

After eating a hearty supper of roast chicken, rice, and grated cabbage with shallots, a meal prepared by Madame Gerard every Monday night, their day off, the girls lingered. Sitting outside on the riser of a defunct concrete planter, they soaked up the comraderie of their (relatively) like-minded countrywomen. Perhaps they sensed a change in the air. Naturally, basking in the delight of full tummies and a tropical breeze, they fell into their usual roles. Michi teased Charli about her woolly hair. Charli knocked Michi's angular body, saying her corners were so sharp no one dared get close. Sonrisa nudged Mári, suggesting "she had a lot to do," but Mári, in her usual way, let the words flow in and out of her ears without necessarily registering their import. Instead, she found a good-sized rock and collected a handful of ripe almonds strewn beneath a scrawny tree. The girls who liked the bitter-sweet pinkish green flesh nibbled away to expose the inner shell, which Mári took and pounded to extract the nut inside.

"A lot of work for such a small reward," Charli commented, the last to receive her almond. All agreed.

Evening fell and the girls split up, going off to roll curlers into their hair, paint nails, play *canasta* on someone's bed. As luck would have it, everyone stayed away from *Cuarto Uno*, duly occupied were they in other parts of the guesthouse.

First, there was the matter of what to do with Mári's personal belongings, most of which she stored in a small train case. Jewelry, photographs, magazine clippings, several cheap watches. She plucked the leopard-print scarf from the top.

"The rest can stay here."

Sonrisa felt like her friend was preparing for death. Mári made small rummaging movements inside the case, scooting stuff aside to get to something squirreled away at the bottom. Touching the object to her lips, she passed it to Sonrisa.

"I want you to have this," Mári said and offered up a gold braided ring.

"I'll wear it until you return—by then your fingers won't be so fat." Her eyes teared up. *"You really want to do this?"*

"Don't know what else to do."

"You know, Mári, it doesn't make a whole lot of sense."

"Who says?"

Sonrisa knew she had a point and respectfully remained silent.

Then there was the matter of what to bring. Looking like a short order cook, Mári seemed to be checking off a mental list as she laid out her birth certificate, toothbrush, toothpaste, hairbrush, comb, mascara, eyeliner, lipstick, eye shadow, nail polish, file, small mirror, soap, washcloth, mints, and chewing gum. Next came the scarf, a polka dot hanky, sunglasses, bra, underwear, black and tan nylons, all laid neatly on the bed next to her oversized handbag, a large zippered sack made of interlocking leather links and two loop handles. Sonrisa just watched, amazed at the display of efficiency. It was possible she never gave her friend the credit she deserved.

Mári stood in the middle of the room, looking around with her mind's eye to picture what she'd forgotten. Oh yes, a clump of cotton balls from the bathroom and her rose-scented lotion.

"One thing's for sure—you're going to be the best-looking, best-smelling stowaway ever. What, uh, are you planning to carry in your handbag?"

"That's the trick—I can't put this stuff loose in here—it'll arouse suspicion if someone sees in it." She added a small tester of Chanel No. 5 to the growing pile.

"So, I've been meaning to ask you, can I borrow your—"

Sonrisa already had the leather pouch out and was emptying the makeup contents, which looked a lot like what Mári would be putting back in.

"I'll take good care of it, I promise."

"And what are you going to do with these?" Sonrisa pointed to the undergarments she guessed wouldn't fit in the pouch.

Mári's arm shot out like a traffic cop's, indicating she had the answer. In the far recesses of her bottom cubby, she seized an item the size of a mini loaf of bread.

"Close your eyes—ok, open!"

"What is that?" Sonrisa asked, confused.

"Plastic pig—isn't she cute?" Mári petted the hard pink skin then flipped it belly up. *"See this? A secret compartment with a combination lock."* She rolled three numbers into place and popped the door open.

"You're going to put your secret stuff in there."

Mári nodded intelligently, fitting first the underwear, then the bra, nylons, toothbrush, on down the line.

"And you think there is nothing suspicious about a grown woman carrying a toy pig in her purse?"

"Not really."

"Just checking."

While Mári tucked belongings here and there, Sonrisa tip-toed down to the kitchen to see what she could scrounge up. And so the last item that made it into the pig, wrapped in a hanky monogrammed with an "S", was a roll of sweet bread that kept all the other non-fabric items from clanking around the swine's innards.

Bag packed, clothes laid out, Mári and Sonrisa knelt in front of their altar and held hands while praying in a soft hum. After a few moments on her knees, Mári, eyes focused on the flickering flame of the small votive, found she couldn't hold it together. Tears streamed down her face.

"I'm so afraid."

"I understand mi amor," Sonrisa squeezed her hand. *"You don't have to go—we'll take care of everything here, baby and all."*

Mári nodded. Knowing she had a choice gave her new resolve.

She reached for the bottle of Night Train Express kept beneath the altar and swigged hard. Sonrisa did likewise. They left a little in the bottom, for the Virgin, and fell asleep curled up together. Sometime during the night their bodies parted, resting alone, no longer close.

CHAPTER 20

DECEMBER 5, 1967

In the heart of Acapulco, on the tower clock overlooking *Plaza Alvarez*, the small hand reached "10" and the long hand settled on "12". Business and activity ran busier than usual on this special Tuesday, with crowds gathering at the dock, textile vendors arranging stacks of woven blankets and shawls on makeshift benches. The women and children who usually sold *doñates* carried in bigger piles than usual of the colorful bark paintings, and florists tended great buckets of blossoms. The smell of fried fish hung in the air, the local specialty being fish tacos, along with odorless *ceviche*, raw seafood marinated in lemon.

As the long hand of the Plaza clock clicked into place over the one, a series of deep-throated, otherworldly *moos* stopped everyone in their tracks. For a few moments, the beehive of activity hung in suspension then, almost all at once, smiles of recognition erupted on the faces of the industrious: the golden goose had landed. Adults asked little children, or the infirm, to tend their wares and soon the Plaza became quiet and empty as everyone who could headed to shore to see the famous ship.

✿

Early morning hours at the guesthouse were tranquil, except on Tuesdays. Because all the girls had Monday off and weren't required to stay up late, most were asleep before midnight. As a result, rather than slumbering until noon they rose early and caught up on chores: curling hair, ironing, washing, clanking pots and pans down in the kitchen in preparation for the big noonday meal, chatting noisily on the phone in the foyer. Though everyone else was awake, when ten o'clock rolled around Mári and Sonrisa remained conked, snoring and drooling rather indelicately as the sun heated up the room.

"*Fuego! Fuego!*"

Not Michi yelling *Fire! Fire!* downstairs, nor the booming admonitions from Madame Gerard to place *something* in the pots before setting them on the hot coals, roused either one. But when ten-o-five struck, both champion slumberers sat bolt upright as a penetrating series of deep rumbles threw them back to the days of Trujillo. For an uncomfortable minute they assumed it was another of the dictator's attempts to keep the Dominican people off balance with threats of invasions from Cuba or, more ridiculous yet, their poor neighbor to the west, Haiti.

"*Dios mio!*" they chimed in unison.

Cobwebs clearing, they rushed out of bed, jostling with one another to be first through the bathroom door. Sonrisa backed off, not wishing to prolong the agony of a pregnant woman's belabored bladder and overworked sphincter. Squeezing her own thighs tightly together, 'Risa heard a great rush of urine hit the *eau de toilette*. Dancing around, squirming, focused on keeping her own floodgates closed until her turn, she became greatly alarmed when a long peal of gas escaped from behind the door, its pitch magnified by the sealed acoustics of the toilet bowl. As if on cue, Sonrisa ran from the room and quickly found an empty loo in the *cuarto* next to theirs.

Relieved and calmed, the girls met back in their room. Without speaking a word, they dressed, fixed their hair, made their morning routine as if nothing out of the ordinary was afoot.

At lunch, Mári masked her melancholy and lack of appetite with mirth she didn't feel. Who knew when they might find themselves together again? Betrayal nagged at her pounding heart when she thought of how stunned Charli and Michi—less so the others—would be when they found out she'd skipped town. Feeling like a spy, or an alien, Mári watched as Charli shoveled forkfuls of rice into her wide mouth and Michi sucked the marrow out of a chicken bone. She herself ate little, moving the food around with frequent jabs. Sonrisa consumed everything on her plate and remained silent, not unlike her usual self.

At the end of the meal, an air of expectancy hung over the table.

"Anyone wanna play canasta?" Charli's idea of a rockin' afternoon.

Michi begged off, claiming an appointment at the hair salon. Sonrisa mumbled something about going shopping and Mári, at a loss, aped 'Risa's excuse.

"Well then, maybe I'll come, too!" Charli invited herself, eager to do anything but spend the day alone.

"Sure," Mári replied, casting a frozen look at Sonrisa.

"Where you thinking of going?" Charli called on her way to the kitchen with an armful of dirty dishes.

"We'll let you know!" Sonrisa assured, whisking Mári upstairs.

"I'm sorry, I couldn't think of what else to say," Mári pouted on the edge of the bed.

Sonrisa paced the room, trying to figure a graceful way out.

"She could come with us," Mári wondered aloud, *"we could let her in on our secret…"*

"You are turning to cornmeal right before my eyes! What if she blabs to Michi, who blabs to the others, who tell their boyfriends, not to mention Max, and it gets back to some, I don't know, shipping authority, or worse yet—"

"Luigi!"

Neither one wanted to hurt Charli's feelings. Since her breakup with what's his name they'd taken care to include her in outings, fun, and games. Though she bore up well, Sonrisa and Mári knew their childhood friend could easily slip into a deep, long-lasting funk.

"But you're right, we may have to tell her."

Mári flopped back onto the bed, feet dangling off the side. *"Maybe we should just stay here today, then all go pick up Marta from the airport,"* she mused, twirling her feet playfully in the air. *"It would be the easiest thing to do."*

"Ok, fine, but I want my bag back now!"

"No way!" Mári fired, sitting up. *"I just wanted one more moment of laziness,"* she sighed, clicking her heels like Dorothy in her ruby slippers. *"You never did let me get away with anything."*

PART TWO

Delivery

*You must do the thing
you think you cannot do.
--Eleanor Roosevelt*

A SEA OF cars, taxis, and buses jostled for position along the *Málécon*. Hordes of *gringos* milled about, some looking anxious and expectant, others looking flushed and gay, the hatless ones shading their brows with the brims of conjoined fingers. A band blared, its particular brand of hip swaying rhythm delighting visitors and locals alike. But the biggest attraction, by far, was the temporary bar erected at the bend of the famous walkway.

"*Where you girls wanna get off?*" the *combi* driver squeezed through the side of his toothpick-chewing mouth.

"*La Plaza.*"

"*Not today, amigas. Either get off here and walk or it's gonna be beyond the Customs House.*"

"*What's going on?*" Charli asked, last one out of the bus. Mári and Sonrisa shot each other looks.

"*Queen Mary is in town. Ever heard of it? Don't feel bad,*" the driver said, scrounging through his coin tin for change. "*I hadn't either. Big famous ship from England. Go take a look—she'll never be back.*" He peeled out, leaving the trio agape at the spectacle.

First sight of the thousand-foot oceanliner took their collective breaths away. Steel black cliffs, massive and sheer, towered above the water in perfect composure, indifferent to the swarm of small craft vying for a closer look.

"*How beautiful!*" Mári squealed, barely able to contain her excitement. "*I bet they have amazing shows on board, what do you think?*"

"*Like nothing we've ever seen,*" intoned Sonrisa, suddenly filled with expectation and wonder.

Charli shook her head in agreement, but wasn't sure why such a big deal over a boat.

Holding hands in choo-choo-like fashion, the girls threaded their way through the crowds. Feeling decreased strain on her hand, Charli, at the tail end of the train, suggested they meet in front of the Post Office if they became separated. This directive didn't have any visible effect on Mári who, like a child, found herself caught up in the carnival atmosphere. Balloons floated from posts, vendors hawked their cool, sweet wares—cut pineapple, mango, orange—hat sellers made killings on cheap straw wide-brims that were immediately put to use.

She led the human chain like a powerful little switch engine on curvy rail, twice letting go of 'Risa's hand to fondle pretty tin crosses and jars of tape worms used as weight-loss remedies. Both times Sonrisa grabbed onto fabric, unwilling to release her friend. She followed dutifully along, pondering their options. When Charli had spoken the words *if we become separated*, Sonrisa realized this might be the solution to their "tell no one" credo. She saw exactly how it would unfold and tucked the details away until further notice.

Pressing and squeezing, Mári maneuvered them toward a clearing on the edge of the *Málécon*. She stood on a low wall and threw her arms up in salutation to her royal oceanic namesake, pirouetting to the rhythms of a lusty rendition of *Volver, Volver, Volver*. The irony was not lost on Sonrisa, for the words the men sang echoed the sentiments in her own heart—*Return, Return, Return.*

"*Gosh, I didn't know you liked boats so much,*" Charli commented, taken aback by the intensity her companions lavished on ship and occasion.

"*Just this one,*" they replied absent-mindedly, sharing a laugh.

"*Just this one,*" Mári repeated, alone.

Turning her gaze away from the oceanliner, she scanned the sea of heads on the nearby horizon. Disembarking passengers were greeted by hostesses and graced with leis under a welcome banner dripping with flowers. Not far from the bar, a four-piece band played while colorful dancers entertained in the little park between the dock and the main street. At the outer rim, Mári spotted a roving *mariachi* band working the edges of the crowd, an important entertainment factor given the volume of people.

Then she found her mark, her man in white, immersed in a side drama. The main band had just stopped playing, going on extended break. Meanwhile, the *mariachis* ended a song and began stowing their meager gear. All music stopped, the crowd heaved a collective sigh. Flowing complimentary drinks, cheerful sunshine, and shoreside comraderie had created an atmosphere of merriment, but the loss of symphonic distraction challenged the tropical fantasy of those who'd been cooped up for weeks on a hot old ship. Visitors found themselves swatting flies rather than dancing *merengue*, wiping brows, and issuing complaints about the @!!%&# sun. Little persnicketies threatened to escalate as impatience with the dispatching process grew—a backlog of passengers waited for tenders to shore.

Ruddy-faced and pinched in an effort to keep his cool, Fred strenuously repeated something to the mustachioed *mariachi* leader.

Perched on the wall like a lighthouse beam sweeping the seas, Mári followed Fred's jabbing finger. It pointed to his leggy assistant who stood at the bar, pinky delicately outstretched with plastic cup of blood-red drink in hand, flirtatious smiles directed toward male passersby. Mári thought she looked happy, as in three sheets to the wind happy, and feared she would be of no help to the Englishman.

"Wait here—I'll be back," she told her friends, easing herself to the ground. Immersed in the throng, she quickly lost her bearings but regained them when she overheard Fred and the *mariachi* leader haggling in loud voices. Like a bat, she echo-sounded in on her man and stood quietly by his side, waiting for some kind of right moment.

Mári assessed the crux of their disagreement. The *mariachi* player had been hired to perform twelve songs. He'd fulfilled his obligation and was preparing to leave in order to make his next engagement, a birthday serenade for the wife of a local industrialist. Fred had offered him more money on the spot to continue, even to play the same twelve songs over again, but the man had not accepted. The band leader explained he could not afford to alienate his rich client. He reasoned, and Mári could see his point, that the *Regina Maria* people would be there for only one day, whereas Señor Merejo and his long arm of influence, a lifetime.

"Da choose, she is not difficult. I sorry for you," the bandleader pronounced gravely in English, and a flick of his hand signaled *vamos* to his bandmates.

"Bloody hell!" Fred swore under his breath, slipping the Omega off his wrist. "Wait! Will this change your mind?"

The band leader stopped.

"Expensive. Keep it, for your troubles, but please, please play more songs!" Fred held the watch in mid-air between them, smiling wanly.

"You keep time," the musician said courteously, pushing the watch away. Then, plucking pesos out of Fred's other hand, he went into a huddle with his men.

When the band members broke and re-commenced wrapping up, Fred wilted like a cut carnation past its prime, desperately searching each face for some sign of mercy. Not one of them met his gaze. Just as he felt he was going to pass out, the band leader took his arm. "I leave you Francisco. 'Bye 'bye!"

In a bubble of uncertainty, everyone looked around, wondering what one lone guitar player could accomplish. The mood turned. Ten minutes without music proved too much—during the past thirty days they'd endured cancelled stops, reduced time in ports, limited laundry service, threats of water rationing, sketchy service, unbearable heat through the tropics—and for this, they'd paid a tidy sum. Acapulco was the final port of call before reaching their destination. Nerves jangled. One man, white as Canada snow but crimson of face, berated a bartender because he was not familiar with a whisky sour. The bartender, a local man trying his best, kept repeating *margarita? margarita?* Another fixture at the bar, Fred's assistant, also took up the cry for a whisky sour.

Mári had seen enough. She conferred with Francisco who nodded his head vigorously, happy for guidance. *"I've never played solo before such a big crowd,"* he confided. Bracing his lanky frame against the back of a scratched six-string, he began in querulous tones and tinny cords to interpret the old standby, *La Cucaracha.*

As visitors began to tap feet, knock knees, and dip shoulders, Mári rushed over to Sonrisa and Charli who stood faithfully where she'd left them. She spoke quickly and urgently. They all looked over at poor Francisco bravely clutching his instrument. Nodding their heads in agreement, Mári embraced her friends tightly then let go as they propelled themselves to stand with the lone *mariachi.*

Hesitant at first, Charli and Sonrisa swayed conservatively to the music. Mári dug into her handbag and, after unwrapping the baked bun inside the plastic pig, handed the monogrammed hanky to 'Risa who, using it as a prop, grew more bold in her undulations. Charli, taking cue, sang the lyrics.

A petite woman with a thick, black page boy and bust accentuated by criss-crossing camera straps jostled for position in front of the *mariachi* and his exotic accompaniment. A smile spread across her face as she clicked away, switching equipment mid-stream, turning this way and that, capturing faces that moments ago had worn frowns. Folks turned cheery, and many waiting to get back on the ship or go on the land excursions gathered 'round, clapping and humming, appreciating the impromptu display of artistry.

"Damn, forgot the Polaroid," the photographer muttered, making a beeline for the tender.

Sonrisa twirled in place, launching the hanky through aerial paces a hummingbird would be proud of, while Charli sang in a rich, deep voice. Francisco, bolstered by his sidekicks, strummed, flicked, and cajoled the worn guitar into rhythmic righteousness.

Fading into the background, Mári watched the white square of fabric fly through the air. Tears came to her eyes. Fred startled her by putting a fatherly arm around her shoulders—she'd lost track of him.

"Go ahead, take the grand tour. So sorry I can't go with you—VIPs and Press about to arrive," he managed to convey in broken Spanish. Urging her toward the tender, he pulled out a wallet. *"Please take these— pound notes—in case you want to buy a souvenir."*

Mári protested. Something funny about taking money from a man. Fred insisted, pressing the bills into her sweaty palm. *"Maybe we could have lunch tomorrow and you can tell me about your visit? The ship leaves at nine, I'll be free by noon."*

"Is possible…call me later," Mári said, swallowing hard.

CHAPTER 22

Though a slight breeze created nothing more than ripples on the bay, Mári felt woozy before the small, bobbing craft even got underway.

"Hold the boat! Wait for me!" yelled the photographer who'd retraced her steps to find a missing lens cap. She meant business, leaping onboard without a helping hand as the vessel separated from its dock.

Mári, sitting nearby, wondered briefly whether that lady, too, had trouble with time. She squinted at the shrinking images of her shore-side companions and rubbed her belly. When Sonrisa and Charli turned indistinguishable from others in the crowd, she launched her full attention on the knife-like prow and massive funnels that looked nothing like any *ella* she knew. Gender issues aside, there sat the entirety of something known as RMS Queen Mary, a sleek fabrication of mind, metal and muster, blending easily and, somehow, reassuredly, with her fluid host. Mári's hand rubbed the offending midriff sites more quickly, having no effect whatsoever on her pounding heart.

As maritime features became more discernible—looming deck vents, suspended life boats, portholes and doorways cut into the hull, anchor chains, guy wires, flags, and soon even individual rivets—Mári's mind engaged in a crude form of calculation to reconcile how one small being in one small boat could possibly transfer herself onto something so big.

The answer came quickly as the tender captain swung his boat broadside and drifted toward a gaping hole in the liner's side. What looked to Mári like a child's slide hung from the lip of the ship's door, free end bobbing in the waves. Crew members reached out for lines the tender hand threw their way, securing their position, if one could call thin ropes and bobbing ramps secure. On top of it all, a rumbly stomach and clammy feet did not, in Mári's mind, bode well for an auspicious start to her desperate adventure. She hung back, allowing dozens to disembark, watching carefully where they put their various appendages for best results. Confident that a successful, uneventful transfer was indeed possible, as well as likely, Mári sucked up her courage and allowed the strong arm of a jaunty young seaman to steady her onto the gangplank. She took one look back to shore, felt an odd sort of detachment, then stepped through the ship's portal, sincerely hoping someone remembered to shut the door.

It took a minute to become accustomed to the soft light thrown by recessed bulbs and opaque fixtures, and not much longer than that to realize the ship was much more than she'd imagined. Here was an immense, intricately splendid floating world fashioned by human hands and conceived by human minds. A sense of pride welled up, taking her by surprise. Nothing grander had ever made its way into Mári's life.

Touched by knowledge of what had come before—the stalled birth, the troopship days ferrying soldiers to war, thirty-one harsh years at sea—Mári lingered in D Deck's foyer, admiring swirly-grained paneling and nickel-chromed elevator doors that opened frequently to let loose their cargo of straw-hatted passengers. People came and went, chatting happily. Crew members, looking warm in burgundy uniforms and pressed from an overload of work, whizzed to and fro up the wide set of stairs and down endless hallways, lugging fruit baskets and sweating champagne buckets.

"Excuse me, ma'am, can I help you to your cabin?" a steward asked, blue eyes peeking around an ornate bouquet of flowers. The unwanted interaction alarmed Mári who, for whatever reason, had not factored in actually engaging with anyone on board, much less in English.

"Tank you, no," she replied, nodding her head vigorously to signal he was completely free to attend to his other duties.

"Aw, it's o'right. Visitin' our ship, are ya then? Any oidea what yud like ta see?" he asked jovially, shifting the flowers to his left side.

Because of his accent, Mári understood two words, which she repeated back, adding one of her own.

"See ship? Pool?"

"Tek ya right there, going up to R Deck maself. Got to drop these off on the way, then pick up a bottle o' whisky for some passengers," the young man chatted amiably, walking slowly at Mári's pace and keeping any suspicion he may have felt deeply hidden. "Gives me a chance to catch a break, ya know?"

Mári realized that her unpreparedness might've blown her cover. Of course she looked like a local—how could she not? Marked forever as a visitor, what would happen if she ran into this *muchacho* again?

What were the chances of running into the same person twice in a place this big? Slim, she hoped.

After excusing himself, the lad left her off beneath a tiara-like, semi-circular soffit—the entrance to the First Class swimming pool. To the right, the in-wall dispensary where passengers collected towels, and directly ahead, silver-colored revolving doors. She reached out to give a push, the thought of *how am I ever going to pull this off* running through her brain—then decided, quite suddenly, to see the sights instead.

First, she found the nearby Main Dining Salon, the largest ever built on a ship. At the far end, a majestic tapestry of trees, bridges, and loitering animals adorned the wall and engulfed a set of ornate brass doors. Generous windows on either side of the room admitted real sunlight, washing out the features of the staff members setting tables. Mári felt herself pale when one of them waved at her. She waved back, recognizing the friendly steward. Apparently, the size of the ship presented no impediment whatsoever to viewing the same people twice.

She turned wanly around, hoping that by doing so she'd be bolstered by something outside herself, something famous. So it was, a huge mural commanded the fore wall and did not disappoint. Rendered in soft, melancholy tones, black continents loosely framed both sides while puffy clouds of dusty orange filled the heavens, infused by a radiant sun in the lower right quadrant and a silvery moon in the upper left. Mári barely noticed the bright, numberless clock positioned over mid-Atlantic as her eye roved along the bottom to appreciate waves of muted greens and purples that floated both the Queen Elizabeth and the Queen Mary toward opposite ends of the world. She could see the tracks—now empty—where crystal replicas once traced the sister ships' progress during regular crossings, one long groove for the summer route and another just below for the winter route—or vice versa. She couldn't be expected to keep that kind of precise nautical information straight.

Wanting to satisfy more of her curiosity before sequestering herself, Mári strode aft along a shiny, endless hallway with doors on either
side. Fighting the urge to test one of the ivory-colored knobs, she continued until she came to a set of stairs. After huffing and puffing her way
up several flights, she encountered a long, narrow room devoid of people,
its lowered ceiling, thick carpeting, and indirect lighting making her feel
safe and cozy at once. Easy chairs with dense cushions clustered around
glowing torchières. Mári had never seen such décor. She lovingly ran a
hand along the back of a blue-green satin low back chair, nudging it to
get a sense of its heft. It didn't budge. She realized all the furnishings
had to be heavy so they wouldn't topple during rough seas. Amazing,
they'd thought of everything!

A variety magazine sat on a burl wood table, its cover, dated
October 1967, snatching her attention with an overhead view of Queen
Mary underway. Mári plopped down in one of the inviting chairs and
flipped through the publication back to front, admiring cigarette ads
and the latest fashions, unaware that she, too, looked in her element.
She thought briefly—and guiltily—of her sister and hoped she arrived
as planned.

At the very front of the magazine, the contributors peered back
in little square pictures. Didn't she recognize one of them, the one with
the jet black page boy, piercing eyes and playful smile? Certain it was the
woman from the tender, Mári turned to her article about RMS Queen
Mary, and while she didn't take much interest in pictures of engine
rooms and old post cards, she was mildly curious about the author who
seemed to be on this very ship.

A dim awareness of the passage of time poked through Mári's
consciousness like a muffled alarm clock, sounding in her head as she
turned the last page. She'd better get a move on. As she adjusted her bag,
a soothing but firm male voice came across the sound system, communicating information Mári understood none of. She paused, suddenly

feeling very tired, unsure whether she had the energy—or the nerve—to follow through. Wouldn't it be easier to simply continue her tour of the ship then resume life on land, with or without that louse Luigi?

"Yes, that's what I'll do. I'll just walk around, no pressure, see the sights, and return to my friends. Bueno."

This thought calmed her and, in the perversely contrary way the human mind works, inspired her to seek the pool.

Feet skipping along the teak planks of the enclosed Promenade Deck, Mári noticed many local types heading in the direction from which she'd first arrived—down. It occurred to her that it must be time for visitors to leave the ship. All visitors. This realization brought a pang to her chest, and baby kicked in response to the upped ante.

But first, a quick side trip! The First Class Lounge reached out and grabbed her with its softly lit golden onyx urns and commanding marble fireplace, above which presided—all the way to the ceiling—a carved panel, done in metallic sheens, depicting jousting unicorns. What intrigued her most were the outlines of five small doors which, she knew, could be opened to accommodate film projectors. She wandered to a side corridor and found a spiral staircase leading up to the projection room. Unwilling to negotiate the narrow, steep treads, Mári saw enough to know it was dark, cramped, and offered no other way in or out. Not her first choice but a possible back-up; this must be the place Fred would hide if he were a stowaway.

Re-tracing her original steps, Mári reached R Deck. To her horror, preparations were underway for afternoon tea, with tables newly set up outside the Main Dining Salon. A persuasive thought about not calling attention to herself sounded rational, but the sweets looked so good she couldn't resist tucking a few into her bag when no one, she hoped, was looking.

Self-preservation finally kicking in, Mári, trying her best to be invisible, sauntered over to the pool entrance where she pretended to be transfixed by the craftsmanship of the revolving door. As she was about to proceed on through, a tall, hollow-cheeked man in a decidedly non-tropical black suit said something to her.

"Perdon?" she turned, pulse rate soaring.

"You have to leave the ship, Madam. Allow me to show you the way," he said, gesturing for her to follow.

Ignoring the hand, Mári bounced up and down, holding her lower belly and transforming her features into an unmistakable portrait of urgency. Pointing toward the pool, she pantomimed, "Batrum?"

"Yes yes, right this way," the man quickly obliged, his red face registering embarrassment over the immediacy of her need.

"Tank you, tank you," she said, trying to get the words right as she wooshed into the *baño* forty paces 'round the corner.

"I'll wait for you here!" the man called through the wall. His words mostly unintelligible, she nonetheless got the drift and decided to stall in the Ladies Lounge as long as she could. Splashing water on her face, sudsing up with musk-scented soap, and patting her face dry with a starchy towel, Mári almost forgot about her predicament.

After the first round of ablutions, she lingered at the door to check for signs of her would-be escort. Thinking she heard the impatient *harrumph* of a throat being cleared, she stationed herself at a mirror, this time arranging errant strands of hair.

Soon out of ways and places to freshen, Mári hung by the door again, all ears. Up the hall a short distance she'd noticed open double doors with men inside, moving folding tables and chairs about.

"Say matey, lend us a hand for a moment?"

Mári heard words drift from that space—then identified the one presumably named *matey*—her guy—mumble something, the expression fading away as he joined his comrades in the storeroom that had once been the Third Class dining room. Metal clanked, followed by a thud, followed by the grating sound of something heavy being dragged.

Mári took the cue, peeked out and, seeing the coast clear, made a dash for the pool.

Hollow-cheeked matey appeared in the storeroom doorway, mopping his brow with a damp hanky and leaning on a round table, in time to see, or so he thought, the tail end of a red skirt whipping around the corner.

"Did you see that?" he asked his companions.

"See what? Come on matey, we've got three more of these to move, can you spare it?"

And so, for the good of putting out the most immediate fire, matey deferred, but couldn't help think that perhaps the final leg of the old Queen's last voyage might prove interesting after all.

CHAPTER 23

Eager to dash home and count all the tip money plumping out her brassiere, Charli almost forgot about Mári. *"Where is she?"* the older Dominican said, poking a distant Sonrisa in the ribs. *"And what's the matter with you? We just made a killing! American dollars, too!"*

They walked together, one with a bounce, the other with a shuffle. Sonrisa kept turning to gaze at the ship in the harbor, reluctant to let it out of sight.

"Hey, what is it with you two and that ship?" Charli demanded suspiciously.

Sonrisa shrugged off the question, preoccupied with her own thoughts. Should she have offered to accompany her friend? At least made the motion? No, that'd be too much to ask. She'd never liked the idea anyhow. Harebrained. Still, she prayed for it all to work out.

"Admiration binds us, that's all," Sonrisa calmly replied, in her own time.

"Sounds like crap to me. Mári's on that ship, isn't she?"

"Well, maybe—she did want to visit. I expect she's back at the hotel by now waiting to tell us about all the magnificent things she saw."

Charli must've been satisfied with her explanation for she began calculating aloud what the sum total of tips might be, eagerly awaiting the moment when she could extract the moist greenbacks and fondle them in private.

CHAPTER 24

Daylight sifted through the atmosphere, gradually becoming weaker and weaker so that all of Acapulco, at least those able to afford electricity and have a structure to put it in, switched on a bulb or two to ward off the coming darkness.

In the Plaza, shop lights and signs sprang to life, their hum adding to the chorus of chirping crickets. On the Queen Mary, strands of lights illuminated the air space above the ship. Strung from crow's nest to rear mast, they dipped in garland fashion and provided a whimsical complement to the blazing practicality of portholes.

On a street of Medieval narrowness north of the soccer field at Independence Park, Luigi walked, hugging the old shops along the slim sidewalk, eyes straining in that hard-to-see dusk time, feet lifting an inch or two higher than normal, given the uneven nature of the pavement. Elated his team *Los Gatos Azules* had won, Luigi switched his soccer gear to his other shoulder, hobo fashion, and whistled a made-up tune. He'd prevented the tying goal. In the final minutes of the game, their opponents had broken through the defensive line in a furious assault.

"You don't want it to come to this!" he yelled to his sweepers seconds before every one of his muscles and nerves committed fully to the oncoming ball, propelling his form through the air, arms outstretched, eyes riveted on the black and white sphere. Luigi's barrel chest interrupted its trajectory, and his hands clutched the ricocheting object in time to prevent further play in the danger zone. Landing like a sack of rice, his head skidded to within half an inch of the goal post. He lay motionless for what seemed like a long and quiet time, basking in the glory of this fine act, grateful to be the one to have made such a meaningful contribution. Insignificant though a game of soccer might be, Luigi could not shake the feeling that something special had happened. As if a door had opened to his soul. He'd made a few spectacular saves throughout his many years of playing, but this one was different.

"Aha!" he yelled to the Gods, penetrating the heavens with a victory fist. To commit, and wind up holding the prize, like he did that afternoon, was something he could learn from, maybe even repeat. In life. Maybe.

Up the road, the sound of a large and bumpy truck made Luigi cock his head to gauge its distance. It rumbled and rattled closer but, satisfied with his bearings, he allowed his thoughts about commitment to progress to Mári. Thus preoccupied, he instinctively moved away from the street. Whether he'd had a premonition or merely a blind sense of self-preservation, Luigi's foresight proved right—it's just that he got the hazard wrong.

He hadn't counted on the unusually high sides of a stake-bed truck snagging a dipping overhead power line, nor had he counted on being struck by the severed line or receiving a charge that knocked him clear off his feet. As he fell through the air in a crooked spasm, his body recoiled from the shock, the magnitude of which he'd never experienced in all his years as an electrician. A numbing, coursing, jabbing sensation penetrated his right shoulder and shot down to his toes.

That was the last thing he remembered. Luigi's knapsack struck the ground in such a way that the neck came undone and his soccer ball squirted out. The scuffed black and white globe, branded with a set of big, bold letters spelling L-U-I-G-I, bounced away, meandered down the street, gaining speed as it rolled through an intersection without being hit, slipped unhindered beyond the seawall of the *Málécon* and plopped into the Bay where the receding tide carried the play thing out to sea, in the vague direction, if one were taking stock, of RMS Queen Mary.

CHAPTER 25

Mári spun the silver doors and entered the dim recesses beyond. Her senses, including ones she didn't know she had, took a few moments to adjust as she picked her way down the staircase to the pool.

Far as she could tell, the place was empty, home to a shadowy mustiness that did nothing to soothe her spirits. The gloomy atmosphere prickled her skin to the point where she felt clammy even though the space itself was warm. Heart fluttering in fear of getting caught, she made a beeline to the changing rooms.

Picking one farthest away of nine on each side, Mári hunkered down in the coffin-sized enclosure, her claustrophobic tendencies appreciative that the three-quarter door left space at bottom and top. After five minutes of squirming on the wooden bench and staring up at a cylindrical fixture with a weak bulb, Mári grew doubtful of her plan's success. Fresh from her enchanting experience in the Long Gallery and keenly aware of the difference in appointments, Mári's discomfort edged her to the brink of pulling the plug. Wistful thoughts of how nice it would be to see her sister and have news from home seduced her, but she pulled back, not quite ready to give in. She tried once more to get comfortable by placing her bag against the wall and lying down, knees up, head resting on the bag. This felt better.

She thought of all she was leaving behind. 'Risa, Charli, both of whom she'd known so long they were good as family. Her job at the Club, the first one she ever took seriously and did pretty well—at least the enthusiastic guests seemed to appreciate her dancing skills, appearance, or whatever. And then there was that rat Luigi, a man burdened by past experiences with fruitful women. Luigi had once explained to Mári, after spreading a map of Italy between them, that because he was from the great city of Rome he was more passionate than men from other parts of the country. These other parts he dismissed with a wave—Venezia, Firenze, Pisa, Napoli, Milan. It was a blessing and a curse, he told her. Mári believed him, though she certainly had no intention of getting pregnant, and told him so. He was so happy to hear the news that he swept her off her feet.

A flush spread over Mári's cheeks as she remembered that day. And then it all came crashing down when he suspected, though Mári never ever confirmed it in words. She couldn't really blame him. They'd tried to take precautions, but something had gone wrong. Sonrisa had taught her how to count from cycle to cycle, to identify when was the most dangerous time to make love, but Mári didn't have a mind for the math, the dates, or the passage of time. Instead, she relied on the old rumor that if you didn't climax, you couldn't conceive. She wasn't sure about any of it.

A heavy cocoon of drowsiness enveloped her and she rolled over onto her side. One minor adjustment and her head fit neatly into the concave dent in her bag, its gamey smell and rough surface reminding her of Luigi as she drifted off. Overhead, the bulb in her compartment flickered, then, with a *ping*, went out.

Already asleep, Mári did not witness its misbehavior.

CHAPTER 26

Naturally, a crowd gathered around the fallen Italian. A few of the gatherers even recognized him. *"Hey, that's the guy who comes to my flower stand—he always gives a few extra centavos!"* And, *"I saw him the other day playing soccer with kids in the Plaza!"*

Everyone was afraid to touch the foreigner who seemed to have no life left in him, everyone except a rancher who knelt down and placed a calloused hand on Luigi's chest. Feeling a faint rise and fall, the man, whose tight jeans, western shirt, and stiff oversized hat lent him an air of midwife to the cows, announced that the stranger was breathing. He yanked off his hat, gesturing with its brim for the others to go and fetch a taxi to take him to the clinic. Meanwhile, a slender man well-dressed in white and on his way to VIPS couldn't help but notice the small group milling about a pair of soles resting toes up on the pavement. This last detail gave his sense of balance a jolt, for Fred was nothing if not even keeled, even without his cane.

"Doctor, doctor, aqui!" the rancher called, seeing white.

"Make way I say, step aside," Fred rattled in florid Queen's English. He bent stiffly over the body, careful not to touch it. The *it* had a familiar face.

Figures, the one time I left my walking stick at the office, he thought grimly, feeling it would have been especially useful on this occasion.

"What happened here—*qué paso?*" he asked no one in particular, wondering what kind of divine justice had struck. Someone pointed to the electrical line lying neatly in the crease where curb met street.

Without warning, Luigi expelled a great gush of noxious, pent-up gas. He groaned and moved his head slightly but did not open his eyes or move any other part of his body.

As Fred looked around at those who'd gathered, trying to pinpoint someone who could really help, a stocky man with tawny hair stepped up, distinguished by tar-splattered work clothes and a coura-geous form of broken English. "Eyy, you *medico?*" the man dragged the last syllable through an upswell of excitement.

"Just because I'm dressed in white? No, me no medico. God help us." He looked from the shallowly breathing Luigi to the man who'd spoken. "Ambulance? Can you get one?"

"No—me put hospital." With that, the laborer clean jerked Luigi up and over his shoulder. By now a procession had formed, with an unconscious Italian bobbing up and down on the good samaritan's brawny frame, followed closely by Fred, then the rancher, and dozens of interested souls who were, in their own silent ways, hoping for the best.

As they hoofed by *Nuestra Señora de la Soledad*, an odd-looking Catholic church with cylindrical bell towers, Fred was reminded of an ancient religious scenario featuring a fallen saint buoyed by the faithful in their collective moment of need. All that was missing (perhaps Luigi's noodle arms swishing back and forth over his carrier's tush gave him the idea) were the swinging canisters of incense and the mumblings of the pious.

"Christ, how far IS this hospital?"

"Ova dare," the lead man replied with energy enough to point out a two-storey plantation-style building at the end of the street.

The procession dribbled one by one through the pale green doors of *Clinica Médico*, where the small waiting room quickly filled up with Luigi's followers and threatened to suffocate the few patients waiting. Fred spoke softly to the receptionist who sat behind a desk positioned next to the closed door of the examination room. He pointed to Luigi, still dangling from the strong man's shoulder.

"This man has been electrocuted and requires immediate attention."

He was met with a blank, though mildly curious, stare. "*El médico es ocupado—momento por favor,*" she announced pleasantly. Clearly, she'd not understood a word. In fact, she glanced at the red polish on her nails to be sure there were no glaring chips before demurely resting her talons on the edge of the desk.

One of the women waiting to see the doctor caught the strong man's eye, nodding her head and wagging a finger back and forth toward the door.

"Is he with a patient?"

"No."

Fred and the man exchanged glances. The Englishman slid to the door and twisted its handle while the laborer plowed through, leading with his free shoulder.

"What's going on here?" the silver-haired doc bellowed, rising from behind his desk.

"Power line—" the worker grunted with effort, lowering Luigi onto the exam table without invitation.

As time wore on only the faithful remained—Fred and Elias the carpenter who, while waiting, shared the briefest of introductions.

Fred tried not to stare at the receptionist because it wasn't proper. But he found her attractive. She had the semi-dark smooth skin of a Caribbean Islander, reminding him of the Jamaican women he'd seen in London; tawny, beautiful, her look made all the more exotic by a canary-colored turban and dangling translucent stone earrings hanging, in the shape of plump hearts, at her jawline. Preoccupied with figuring out why he hadn't noticed the beacon of yellow before, a loud "Jesus Christ, what chyou-a doin' man!" startled everyone in the waiting room. On their feet in a flash, Fred and Elias burst into the physician's eminent domain.

"You two have got a very bad habit," doc spat as he glared at his intruders, the rubber triangle of his reflex tester drumming his palm.

"He jab-bed a PIN in da bottom of my FOOT!" Luigi moaned in disbelief. "Don't leave me alone, please!"

Ignoring the slight, the short, muscular doctor with yellowing skin informed them in polished English that the patient should be admitted to hospital immediately for observation. This was the customary procedure with lightning victims and severely shocked persons.

"To observe-a what, exactly?" Luigi asked in as strong a voice as he could muster.

"Sometimes with high current passing through the body certain organs behave erratically."

"Which-a organs?"

"Mostly the heart."

"Nothing wrong with my-a heart," Luigi grumbled, raising his torso up off the table. A pain deep in his chest thwarted any further movement and he propped himself up on elbows bent behind his back, afraid to move or take a breath. After a few moments, finding that he could breathe well enough, Luigi gingerly sat up and swung his legs to the floor.

"Ok, I'm all-a yours."

Both men felt Luigi was in no grave danger and could probably take care of his own affairs at this point. Problem was, neither wanted to be the first to leave; on some level this caretaking business had taken on a competitive edge. So it was to Luigi's great amazement when Fred and the carpenter offered a shoulder to lean on as they ushered him into the back seat of a Bug taxi and propped him up between them. Not until they'd practically tucked him into bed at the General Hospital did they feel their usefulness had run its course.

Luigi, too exhausted to express gratitude or register their absence, fell into a deep sleep. Around midnight he woke, wide-eyed, and stared at a pair of mating flies on the ceiling.

"Where's my-a Mári?" tumbled out of his cotton mouth, hand drifting to his neck to check on a treasure he never removed—soccer ball charm on gold chain. In place.

"Where's my-a real soccer ball?" came out thickly through a deep sigh.

The last words Luigi spoke that night.

Out like a light.

CHAPTER 27

The sudden splash jarred Mári awake, startling her so badly she very nearly rolled off the narrow bench. In her frantic attempt to clutch onto something stable, namely the narrow bench, she bent a nail back. *"Carajo!"*

In the pool, the rhythmic sound of arms and legs moving through water paused, then resumed. Gripping her finger to contain the pain, Mári paced the compartment, eyes adjusting to the ambient light. What to do next? Gravel-eyed, she wondered what time it was. Surely it wasn't yet morning.

While she waited patiently for some meaningful thoughts to come, Mári stepped up onto the bench to fiddle with the dark fixture. *This is a bad sign*, she thought, unscrewing and re-screwing the bulb into its socket, to no avail. If the maintenance department latched onto this task it would bring all sorts of unwanted attention, so she switched it out with another.

Her next most urgent priority was getting to the bathroom at the far end of the corridor. Mustering her resolve, Mári scampered past the dressing rooms like a hermit crab using quick little side steps to scoot past the open entry. Prepared to raise a hand in greeting, her scuttling efforts went unnoticed by the lone swimmer whose face, it turned out, was plastered to the water every other stroke, in diligent execution of the freestyle. After watching for longer than she should have, Mári ducked into the single loo. She'd never seen a female swim in so mannish a manner. Mesmerized by the powerful movements and rhythmic thumps, she sat on the toilet without remembering to lock the door.

Finishing up her business, Mári grabbed a slurp from the sink. When the door flew open she whirled away but not in time to prevent a figure from plowing into her. Horrified, both women shrieked. The swimmer backed away, leaving a moist, ragged outline of herself on Mári's outfit.

"I didn't see you! I'm so sorry!" the woman cried out in apologetic alarm. "And in your condition," she took more steps back. "Are you ok?"

"Ok," Mári murmured, eager to get back to her stall and ponder the jet black bob, bangs and narrow eyebrows. "Wot time it is?" she thought to ask.

"Almost midnight." On the blank look, she added choppily, "*med-i-a no-che?* I snuck in—sign outside says pool closes at seven. They must've forgotten to lock it—guess we're both in trouble!"

Mári lingered. Couldn't very well go back to her stall, not while the lunatic midnight swimmer made like a duck in her territory. Suddenly, and right in front of her, the woman peeled off her suit and trotted to the shower across from the bathroom. Mári's modesty forced her into the nearest changing stall. Getting naked in front of her sister, her fellow dancers, and seeing them without clothes was not a problem. Confronting a stranger's perky nipples and pubic hair in a public restroom was, however, beyond her level of sophistication. She gave it a while, flapping her skirt to make it seem as though she was doing something opportune. Eventually, the shower stopped and the bathroom door creaked shut. Two hefty *plops* and the tearing of copious amounts of toilet paper were all the cues Mári needed to hustle on out. Back in the farthest stall, she hoped she'd dodged one. There really was no relaxing, and the mute stall was anything but reassuring. An absent-minded hand went to her rumbling tummy. Now here was a chance she was willing to take: scoring a late night snack.

Driven by hunger and emboldened by thoughts of sumptuous spreads she'd seen in Fred's scrapbooks, Mári reckoned her overall confidence would be bolstered first by an adjustment of clothes. Twisting the skirt around a quarter turn, she re-positioned the wrinkles to the side of her hip where they fell mostly unnoticed—a move, she thought, frankly brilliant. Then, from the top of her bag, she removed a black cotton blouse and switched it out with the red one she'd worn since dressing at the guest house that morning. Resting on the bench, she carefully rolled the red blouse, fighting back tears she knew would wreck her makeup. Her life was already irrevocably changed, she didn't need smeared mascara on top of it.

Mári paused to concentrate on a sound—a drawn-out, two-part metal squeak that, she hoped, had come from the restroom door opening and closing. The interloper must've come out, but where had she gone? Impatient for food and knowing the midnight buffet wouldn't last forever, Mári stowed her conspicuous bag in the dark recesses beneath the bench, carefully opened the door to her stall, tiptoed to the end of the hall, and peeked out. Her timing was such that she saw the rear view of her subject exiting through the revolving door at the far upper end of the cavernous space.

Mári rushed forth, caution to the wind, a liberated buzz filling her with—what was it? Joy? Enthusiasm? Mirth? The satisfaction of a game well played? Whatever happened, even if she got caught and thrown back like unwanted catch, she would always relish this experience. How could she not? Here she was, navigating a huge floating palace and doing it alone, fending for herself. For the first time in her life she felt indebted to no one, relying not on the appeal of her body but on the wits of her mind.

At the silver door, on the brink of bursting through to the pastry-filled world beyond, Mári's new-found sense of self was grazed by an inbound visitor.

"Oh my god, I can't believe this! Not again!"

It was the nautical nut.

"I'm really sorry—I move much too quickly," the woman blurted.

"Me ok, tank you." Mári tried to push by, but the woman stopped her, taking her gently by the arm.

"Are you sure you're all right?" she asked, looking deeply into the Dominican's eyes. "I should see you to your cabin."

Mári tried to control the mounting danger she felt. *"No ingleesh, lo siento señora."*

"Señorita, por favor, no señora!" the woman said with a smile, proud of her Spanish. Did Mári detect a hint of flirtation? The bold one prolonged the engagement, extending a hand to shake. Mári hesitated, then limply complied, noting the absence of a wedding band and the presence of neatly clipped nails.

"My name is Claire. Very nice to meet you." Instead of letting go her grip, Claire pulled Mári along as she searched for something on the ground. "Lost an earring—*oreja?*" She finally released Mári's hand to bend down for a closer look. "It's just nowhere to be seen…"

Mári tried to scoot but Claire headed her off with a quick Pepe Le Pew move and an invitation to her cabin for a drink. Requesting, *"Food, first?"* Mári gave in and waddled alongside the pushy American as they negotiated eighteen steps up to B Deck, another eighteen up to A Deck, another eighteen to Main, where Claire paused to allow her winded sidekick a chance to recover. Head hanging, sucking wind, Mári motioned one more flight up to Promenade. *"Uno más para comida, si?"* One more for the food, right?

After rubbing elbows with casually dressed couples and helping themselves to heaping platefuls of scones, sandwich meat, bread, and frothy hot chocolate, they lugged their spoils back down and slightly aft where, breathing less labored, Mári took in the surroundings. Burl wood aswirl with chocolate and caramel colors, as if fashioned in a confectioner's cauldron, paneled the tight corridors, with ivory-colored plastic handrails which, in the 1930s, had been considered novel and très chic. All in all, she was grateful for the mundane Fred facts that filled her head and abraded her anxiety, for a new reality soon dawned in the form of a closed door, Cabin B-410.

"Here we are!" Claire announced, rather too loudly, Mári thought. Did she want the whole ship to know where they were?

"Guga? Brought you some goodies," she said as she barged into the stateroom without waiting for a response.

Mári took in the cramped contours of the cabin—on the far wall, dual portholes painted mint green and so close together they looked like owl eyes (the scrunched curtains between them serving as a beak), two visitor chairs draped with clothing, a vanity overflowing with papers and just deep enough to accommodate a Royal typewriter, and twin beds separated by a low chest. But the woman reading on the near bed fascinated Mári most, a tanned pair of giraffe legs stretched out beyond a sleeveless polka dot dress, large bare feet and neat red toenails careening beyond the fall of the white, gold, and black swirls of the patterned spread. Never mind the long legs, Mári adored the woman's hair—a tumble of golden blond waves framing a kind, relaxed face. Michi would've given anything for a look like that!

"Well hello there," the goddess breathed in an obvious attempt to mimic Marilyn Monroe. It came out sounding more like Truman Capote with an accent. This was well over Mári's head but Claire raised her eyebrows, wondering what might come next. After all, she didn't know this person very well, had only gathered from bits and pieces of conversation that she was trying to raise money for a trip to Trinidad, Colorado, for some kind of new-fangled operation.

"Halo," Mári called timidly from the threshold, unwilling to commit herself to the claustrophobic cabin and wishing she was any-where but on this complicated ship.

"*Entra entra,* come in!" Guga chimed, gracefully closing the vol-ume of Conrad's *The Rescue* and slinking to her feet for introductions. Towering over both women, Mári couldn't help but be intimidated by the blonde's unusual height. Was this exotic specimen a model, actress, in theater, radio? Fortunately her Spanish-speaking tongue reassured Mári who'd feared a long, tedious and thoroughly unproductive session with the bold American who'd brought her here.

"I nearly ran over this poor dear in the Ladies Room by the pool. Then I lost my earring," Claire pantomimed her words so that Mári could follow along in a general sort of way. "So here we are."

From Mári they learned, with Guga translating for Claire, that she'd boarded the ship in Acapulco on her way to see her husband in California. This was why they hadn't seen her before.

"Such an attractive girl, we would've noticed!" Claire admitted then, realizing how it must have sounded, quickly added that after three weeks on a floating hotel a fresh face was delightful.

"*You got on in England?*" Mári asked, in awe.

"That's right. I'm a journalist. I take lots of pictures and talk to lots of people then get to write about it."

"*I got on in Rio,*" the lanky diva purred in Spanish, jutting out a hip and tilting a goldspun head, her tone and manner deep with insinu-ation. "*So where are you?*" Guga asked cagily.

Mentally Mári ran through her limited options. "*I am on…D deck, yes.*"

"Which cabin? Wait, let me guess, I love guessing games. 414?"

"Near there. That's why Claire found me at the pool—I couldn't sleep and decided to explore close to home."

"My cabin is empty—they kicked me out!"

The Dominican merely nodded, not quite sure what to make of this volunteered information.

"I'm still famished. Let's go get more food, come on," Claire said, latching onto Mári's arm and twirling them out the door.

First stop on Claire's agenda took them past the frosted storefront windows of the Travel Bureau, where Mári paused to trace her fingers over the sleekly etched silhouette of the ship. They continued forward where a lounge had been converted for use as a Press Room. Someone appeared to be standing outside the door even though Mári assumed everyone who'd joined the ship earlier that day would be partying elsewhere, given the late hour.

Fifty paces away, Mári's heart leapt into her throat as she recognized *Devee*, the kind steward who'd shown her the way on R Deck an eternity ago. Fortunately *Devee* was attending to his fingernails. Quickly spinning around and mumbling, *"Baño, baño,"* Mári reversed course.

"There's a *baño* in there, food, too," Claire said and pointed toward the Press Room.

"Estómago malo, muy malo," Mári countered, widening the gulf between them. She turned her head enough to make eye contact, pantomimed "sleep" and pointed downward.

"I could bring something to your cabin if you're not feeling well—"

"No ingleech! *Buena noche!*"

It took a moment for Mári's eyes to adjust to the dimness. Once they did, she was relieved to find no chatty figures on the lounge chairs or in the pool. Not overly fond of pools herself, she couldn't imagine anyone voluntarily bathing in this one.

The one nice feature was the vaulted ceiling—it looked like mother of pearl, catching tiny flickers of light and bouncing them through space. Somehow one of these little orbs managed to land on the ground where it lingered long enough to cause a persistent glint. Mári squinted for a better look. Something *was* there. Her narrowed eyes tracked in pursuit; she didn't dare break her line of sight, otherwise the *something* might vanish.

Upon closer inspection, she nodded the confident nod of a detective solving a mystery. No more than the size of an American dime, a sensible gold hoop earring lay next to an ashtray stand in the middle of the port-side walkway. She stared at it, not sure she wanted to pick it up. Made for pierced ears, it had the kind of straight, thin arm that penetrated the lobe and, when pushed down, docked in a tight u-shaped clasp. After a moment's thought, she scooped it up, knowing full-well it must belong to Claire. Funny thing was, the earring was clasped. How could that be?

Mári slid the ornament onto her pinky. It settled comfortably at the first joint, imparting an odd, not unpleasant constriction she'd never felt that far up on a finger.

Relieved to find her stowed bag as she'd left it, Mári curled up on the bench of her cubby and squeezed her eyes shut. Four whole breaths later her eyes popped open as she recalled the dab of light at the pool. How exactly, and why, had it landed on the one item that connected her to that unusual American? Thinking the supernatural must be involved, she set about making the sign of the cross, repeated several times for good measure.

Senses on high alert, Mári stared at her handiwork—the working light fixture. The bulb flickered—then came back steady. Were all the bulbs in this part of the ship suspect, or was something more sinister going on? She tried to calm herself by thinking of her friends in Aca, but her mind's eye wouldn't quit. She knew this 31-year-old ship had seen its share of death. Even the pool area had been jammed with bunks for soldiers, one on top of the other, barely able to sit upright. Then there were all those German prisoners confined near the bow and engulfed in boiling heat. Good God, what if she came face to face with a ghost?

Mári gathered herself and the answer came. If something otherworldly presented itself, she would remain very still. She would tell it she knew this was its home and that she was a visitor, would it please leave her in peace while she was there. And it would vanish, unlikely to bother her again.

She wasn't sure how she knew all this. But her throat constriction eased, fingers unlocked, and she dared to shift her weight, wiggle her ankles and cold feet. She drew a breath, then another, deeper, and another, deeper still. Eyes stinging from fatigue, Mári nestled into a fitful sleep that left plenty of waking moments to wonder just how resolved she truly was.

CHAPTER 28

By eight the sun had made surprising progress in its westerly course, rays of golden light unfettered by clouds. Fish romped near the idle hull, happy to be acquainted with a benefactor that belched up so many tasty scraps. Some passengers, mostly those not privy to parties from the night before, lingered on the open decks, leaned on railings, stared at the shore, sunned themselves on deck chairs. The trip was coming to a close. The air of calm still pervaded, though an alert eye could pick out heightened activity, preparations for departure.

Crew members on the bow started motors and readied winches to haul up a pair of 16-ton anchors. Unseen below, men in boiler rooms, the heart of the ship's motive power, supervised the extreme heating of water to create high-pressure steam that spun hundreds of thousands of hand-set turbine blades, which in turn rotated the propeller shafts. On the bridge, the previous watch was relieved by officers of the next shift, the transfer completed with clinks of steaming mugs and, far as they could tell, the promise of smooth sailing all the way to Long Beach four days hence. Captain reviewed with his navigator the course they would follow, due north, hugging the coast.

Though technically no longer an RMS, or Royal Mail Ship, Queen Mary had held to her end of the bargain, Captain judged as he strolled onto a muggy docking wing and regarded the gentle hills of Acapulco. Admittedly weary from constant complaints about decreased port times and tropical heat, frayed around the edges from leading the Mary into what was, for both of them, uncharted waters, a tad more grey from the rough weather encountered just around Cape Horn, Captain nevertheless felt a tug at his heartstrings as he patted the warm steel of her skin.

His position on the wing this morning was largely symbolic, more out of habit than necessity as there was no quay to pull clear of. In fact, this was Captain's favorite spot on the entire ship—suspended 80-feet above the water, thrust well beyond the reassuring bulk of the superstructure, impervious, in all her years at sea, to defect or failure. Tracing the outline of a hand-driven rivet, one of ten million, Captain nodded his head in affirmation, in honor of this great ship. She'd held up her end of the bargain all right, and as he swiped his eyes with the backs of his hands, he determined to hold up his.

One last time.

Captain shifted his slender trunk away from the sunny beaches and towards the length of his ship. One thousand nineteen and a half feet of hull mated with azure water, and his eyes locked onto the waterline in a habitual scan of the ship's integrity. The unexpected sight of a black and white ball lapping against the hull just this side of midships made him smile from ear to ear. Ever so grateful for the distraction from overwhelming nostalgia, the seasoned mariner threw a good bit of attention on that little sphere.

"Gracey! Marks! You're wanted on the bridge!" he called to two able-bodied hands swabbing the deck below. At first it struck him as ludicrous that his men should be engaged in the age-old chores of the sea, especially on a ship soon to be wed forevermore to land. Then he realized how right they were to carry on. Carry on until the very end, when the Union Jack comes down, Stars and Stripes go up, and Captain, officers, and crew return home, by airplane, without their beloved Queen.

The man's reverie was broken by the arrival of the two deck hands.

"See that ball down there? I'd like you to fetch it and bring it to me." Noting their skepticism, he concluded business with a crisp, "Right, then, off you go. By whatever means, gentlemen."

After they left, Captain rubbed his hands together. "Let's have a little fun, shall we old girl?"

The crewmen calculated the ball to be somewhere between cabins 445 and 430. Gracey thought the first, Marks the latter. They laid a wager—whoever guessed to within three cabins either way would pony up for the first pints back home.

Skipping their way down stairway after stairway, they avoided the elevators which were generally reserved for passengers. To get to D deck near the waterline, the men ducked into the crew's mess where utility stairs led them down a level to an alleyway that hummed and vibrated depending on its proximity to an engine room. After disturbing half a dozen female employees resting in their cabins, the hands finally located the bobbing ball. They fashioned a net of sorts from worn nylons gleaned from their recent, good-natured intrusions, a sort of elongated stork sling to be hung out on a piece of wood. The smaller one, Marks, stuffed himself halfway through a porthole and, after a few swipes, landed the prize. Neither man seemed terribly disappointed that it'd been recovered at Cabin 450, two beyond the limits of the bet.

On the bridge, Captain set aside tea and scone to receive the dripping object. An odd curiosity stirred in his mind, though he wasn't sure why. Turning the ball over in his hands, he made out two names. One, in neat block letters, read "Luigi", and the other, "Josepho Marinella" in a nearly illegible scrawl. Captain recognized the latter as an Italian World Cup hero. The former, he assumed, belonged to the ball's owner.

"Marks, Gracey, find out for me, would you, if any of our passengers is named 'Luigi'. This is, after all, a collector's item..."

The men *aye aye'd* and took their leave.

"...if you're Italian, that is."

In her changing room, Mári slept the sleep of the dead. After tossing and turning through the night, she'd finally found a comfortable enough spot and, exhausted, fell into a deep, dreamless slumber where she remained for some time, oblivious to all the unseen activity and excitement permeating the ship, particularly that occurring right there in the pool, where the water bumped rhythmically from end to end. Of its own accord. Animated by none other than the up, down, and *forward* action of the ship.

Queen Mary was on the move.

Wednesday, nine a.m. Acapulco time. Anchors away, outer screws turning slowly down amongst the fishes, tenders lashed, gangways stowed, hatches secured, breakfast well under way. By virtue of combustible fuel, unstoppable steam, and countless precision hunks of whirring metal, the floating hotel took on the attributes of a ship. To complete the departure routine, an officer on the bridge alerted passengers via loudspeakers that Queen Mary would soon sound her whistles. Placing the heavy black handset in its cradle, another bridge mate pressed a series of buttons on the Tyfon control panel, activating a trio of seven-ton horns mounted high up on the forward funnels. Air molecules compressed at 140 pounds per square inch escaped out the mouths of six-foot long trumpets, forming three surprisingly low, long and, some would say, mournful expressions.

For those on the bridge and upper decks, the sound penetrated to the very soles of their feet. For those inside the ship, the bass A timbre was muffled but still gave pause. And for those on shore, particularly folks lined up along the *Málécon* to witness their golden goose depart, the blasts stirred a deep sense of reverence for the abilities of mankind. Of those, three were more deeply affected than most. Two, unable to sleep due to sticky heat and factors of a more emotional nature, found themselves awake early. Sonrisa and Marta (who'd arrived the previous afternoon to seamlessly pick up where her sister had left off) had slipped out of the guesthouse and headed to the seawall shortly before nine. When they saw the black hull, white superstructure, and trio of red stacks in the bay, though by no means a surprise, it was as if they'd been punched in the stomach, so abruptly did their breaths retreat. Both women clasped their hands to their hearts and looked at one another, faces distorted from strain. Through a haze of brine that welled in their eyes, Sonrisa and Marta regarded the ship, each with her own ideas of where Mári might be. Each feature became a tantalizing detail. Was Mári behind *that* porthole? Had she walked by *that* hatch, stood beneath *that* lifeboat?

"*Es imposible,*" Sonrisa muttered, blowing her nose with impatience.

"*Yo sé,*" Marta agreed, honking into her own hanky.

"*The anchor's been raised,*" 'Risa sniffled.

"*Smoke's coming out of the stacks,*" Marta croaked.

Neither woman dared take her eyes off the ship for fear she might miss some signal—what if Mári had changed her mind and wanted off? Or worse yet, what if there was some last minute not-so-nice removal underway of a captured stowaway?

Gray smoke poured more thickly from the funnels. A sense of anticipation rose from the crowd of well-wishers who lined the *Málécon.* Others, just ambling by, also realized something was about to happen and stopped to watch. When the whistles blew their piercing goodbye, Sonrisa and Marta joined hands and whispered silent prayers as RMS Queen Mary slipped away. They watched until she became a speck on the horizon, her wispy, smoky trail the only proof she'd ever been there.

Feeling as though they'd just sat through a tear-jerker, the two Dominicans gathered themselves and strolled the rest of the way to the Plaza. Somewhat relieved—not totally, but somewhat, now that the deed was done—they remained silent for a time, fervently hoping for the best outcome.

So far as they knew, Mári had made it.

CHAPTER 29

Luigi lay unmoving on the rumpled sheets of his hospital bed, its chipped frame sitting squarely in the middle of a long row that ran the length of a mint green wall. A peaceful ward, its quiet was only occasionally disrupted by the sound of someone calling for a bedpan or slapping flies from exposed limbs. Dimly aware of a seething, electric-like force coursing through his veins, the faint desire to smile teased Luigi's dry lips into an involuntary upturn. Tingles and pinpricks traveled from feet to thighs, swirled around buttocks, skipped across his back, and terminated loosely at the Atlas vertebra. He likened the awakening of his body to a block of ice beginning to thaw. The transformation, he knew, was imperceptible. Only after time did the results show up, and Luigi wondered if the slowness of this inexorable process made it more painful.

He sensed a presence in the next bed. Shocked to see Mári swathed in white sheets, spread legs exposed and bent at the knees, calmly giving birth to a child. In the vision, Luigi stood by her side, holding her hand and cooling her brow with a moistened towel. The crown of the baby's head emerged from its journey through the grand canal and Luigi encouraged Mári to push with all her might but the baby made no progress. Knowing something was wrong, he ran out into the hallway yelling for a doctor, a nurse. Not a soul in sight. A loud crash sounded and Luigi ran toward it, desperate for assistance. As he rounded a bend he collided with a no-legged man hurriedly making his way through stainless steel trays and heaps of fallen surgical instruments. Knowing deep down that he alone was responding to the call for help, Luigi scooped him up and labored back to Mári's bedside. Along the way, an unpleasant thought lodged in his stomach. *What if Mári is gone, vanished, too, like everyone else in this hospital, by the time I get back?* Instantly, he regretted leaving her side. Just as instantly, he realized it'd been necessary. He redoubled his efforts with this thick trunk of a man clasped in his arms. Breath grew short, muscles burned, and the giddy rider slapped his shoulders twice for every step he managed, spurring him on.

Finally, Luigi jerked their bodies into the room. Standing there, panting, the legless man felt him sag. The empty bed crushed his soul.

"You must have the wrong room—try another!" the rider yelled, more whacks followed.

They heard a weak voice some doors down crying, *"Estoy aqui,"* I'm here.

Relieved to the brink of tears, Luigi deposited his load and rushed to Mári's arms. All eyes gathered on her pubis. The shining crown nudged out farther, farther, farther still, stopped, then retreated suddenly, silently and completely.

All that's missing is the sucking sound, Luigi thought, reminded of spaghetti slurped into a voracious mouth.

"Now what?" he whined, growing impatient. *"What am I going to do?"* he spoke the words into Mári's sweaty, lethargic face.

The legless man tugged on Luigi's shorts. *"Include her!"* he pointed gruffly.

Confused by this foreign concept, it took a moment for him to catch on. Gently, he burrowed his face into Mári's neck and whispered, *"What are we going to do?"*

Mári stirred, took a deep breath and pushed. Nothing.

Luigi broke away and spun around the room, clutching the roots of his hair.

"You have to coax the kid out," the legless man croaked.

Though Luigi found him repulsive, he looked deeply into the man's sea blue eyes.

"How?"

"You have to want it."

On the bedside stand, the hands of his wrist watch reached the ninth hour, and three soulful blasts of a whistle woke him up once and for all.

Without waiting for an official discharge or bothering with other formalities, such as paying the bill, Luigi left the hospital in a soccer uniform stiff with dried sweat. Empty ball net slung over his shoulder, he imagined he looked like an unsuccessful fisherman. Chances are he certainly felt like one, and an old one at that, legs wobbly from the sudden exertion of a fast-paced walk to the harbor. Shaken by the eerie, half-remembered daydream, an unclaimed intuition of which he was only minimally aware propelled him along. Why he was driven to go to the wharf he couldn't say. Perhaps it was in search of the forlorn creature that had sounded so wistful to him, a call to something greater than himself.

Luigi ignored, not out of disrespect, but out of single-minded intention, all those who passed by him. He barely noticed the salutes of greeting or the quickly averted eyes when friendliness met an uncooperative demeanor. When a lapping sound reached his ears he knew himself to be close. Gazing out at the water always helped clear his thoughts, gave him strength, room to breathe. He needed that now, but the sight of Queen Mary steaming away stopped him in his tracks. He forgot to exhale for some moments, not because of her majesty but because, well, even he felt a pang of sadness for an old ship on her way to, perhaps, nothing more than a watery grave.

Still, she was a lucky one.

"Arrivederci," he muttered, the lining of his nose stinging. Giving in to the movement of emotion within, Luigi stood on the *Málecon* and driveled like a little boy, salty drops staining the pavement where Mári's feet had recently passed.

Parched and puffy-eyed, Luigi headed for the Plaza with no particular goal in mind except to quench a savage thirst. The semi-rotten aroma of fish infiltrated a corridor of stuffy sinuses and he had to laugh, reminded of the joke about a blind man walking by a seafood market who, mistaking the smell, tips his hat in greeting to the ladies.

"Buon giorno, señoras!" he quipped, his brief display of levity snuffed by the sight of Sonrisa and Mári seated at a shiny new juice stand just beyond the center of the square. Luigi didn't want a confrontation

this morning, in public. They'd parted badly a few weeks ago, hadn't seen each other since, or talked. He felt too vulnerable, might embarrass himself. Plus, she had her toughest ally with her. But he did want to see her, badly. A beefy hand flew to his chest, which he rubbed and rubbed to settle the dispute inside. In truth, his heart ached to be pressed to hers. A lump welled in his throat and he swallowed best he could, approaching the Dominicans with a falsely brave, *"Buenos dias, señoritas!"*

CHAPTER 30

Shortly after the whistles sounded and the details of the morning's departure swung into full execution, the ship's first movements caused the water in the pool to slosh and spill over the surface edges. This sound mimicked the state of Mári's stomach, and so she woke more from the nausea bubbling throughout her abdomen than from the displacement of water. Hands rubbing her belly in a light circle, the gold hoop flew off the tip of her little finger. All she could do was sigh.

Feeling woozy, the thought of coffee hijacked her mind. *Café muy fuerte* and a slice or two of sweet bread would do the trick. She retrieved the earring with a degree of grunting that exceeded the difficulty of the task, then cautiously investigated the pool area. Long, snake-like ripples on the water's surface told her all she needed to know. They were headed away from Acapulco, her friends, her lover, her life. A big, black void gaped before her, ripe with the unknown. Had she made a colossal mistake leaving everyone behind in pursuit of a better life for her offspring?

"My child," she softly addressed her round tummy, *"here we go."*

Like a bubble hell-bent on rising even though it's sure to pop, Mári's need for caffeine drove her up four laborious flights to Promenade

Deck where, clutching a support railing on the spacious landing that overlooked storefronts made of amber wood and gleaming glass, she paused to adjust her poise and emotions now that she was in the presence of others. It was also a handy place to catch her ragged breath—her winded body felt heavy as a whale. Not that it was grossly oversized. On the contrary, she carried deceptively. Few people knew she was as near to delivery as she was until coming within close proximity.

Blue wavelets glided by as Mári scanned the vista beyond the large rectangular windows of the sheltered deck, looking for familiar territory. No such luck—nothing but sea. Inside and just around the corner, however, she struck the mother lode and, dangerous as it was to circulate in public, three tables nestled in an alcove practically beeped a radio signal alerting her to fruits, cheeses, breads, sweets, butter, honey, and coffee.

Feeling flush, she whisked off the trusty leopard print scarf, set it down and, caution to the wind, helped herself to a mound of goodies, smiling apologetically to the attendant who was beginning to pack things up. *If this is the day I'm going to get caught, let it be so!* Pleased with her mature outlook, but apparently unaware of her willingness to sell out the future of her unborn child for a round of tasty victuals, she was doubly pleased with the soothing affect of white cane crystals and thick cream on acrid coffee. About to make off with scarf and bounty, a man thick as a cow and wearing a tan cowboy hat cornered her at the table.

"Mornin' Miss, haven't seen you here before." He winked and smiled, deep wrinkles radiating out past a beak of a nose. "Name's Tex, from San Antone. Pleja."

Mári took a stab, seizing on something that sounded remotely familiar. *"Tejas?"*

"Si! Tay-hass! Abla hispano? Moocho goosto." He thrust a business card her way, extracted in the blink of an eye from a snakeskin folio. "If

ya ever git ta San Antone," he offered, unabashed, "look me up. Ah got quite a spread. Bet chyud like it."

Mári backed away, muttering *gracias, gracias.* Pocketing the card, she scooted across to the starboard side where passengers roamed in loose pairs. Hands full, it was all she could do to maintain her balance and the proper angle of plate and cup as she blindly landed her tush on the calf portion of a deck chair. Perched on the edge, she relished the fresh food, particularly the dripping honeydew balls which soothed a scratchy throat in the wake of an encounter with a dry, crumbly object full of tiny raisins.

As she sat side-saddle on the stretched blue fabric of the deck chair, dabbing bits of this or that into her mouth, Mári pondered why so important a deck paled in comparison to the rest of the splendid ship. They could've done better than drab beige paint and dark brown accents, riveted metal ceilings, plain wooden stairs and dingy light fixtures, *verdad?* After all, this wasn't the *Casa Del Mar* where bare bulbs ruled. This was *Quin Mári*, at least for three more days.

Unsure what to do next, the idea of visiting her B Deck acquaintances sounded potentially appealing but she sensed it might be too early to call on strangers, even if it was to return lost property. Opting instead for a trip up to Boat Deck, the fresh breezes instantly lifted both her mood and her skirt! Mári smiled, inhaling the prickly brine. "*This feels like a ship,*" she proclaimed with the air of a Captain staking her claim. What really made it feel like a ship, though, were the overhead lifeboats made snug in heavy duty arm-like contraptions. This is where the Captain's analogy stopped short for she preferred not to think about what it would mean to board one, not only in the event of an emergency, but as a stowaway. Fred had told her the tale of a young man who, wanting to get from England to New York, used one of these boats as a hideout. How he bridged the distance from deck to suspended hull was a mystery to her. It obviously involved acrobatics beyond her means. And he got caught.

Mári still didn't understand why such a big, sturdy vessel needed twelve small boats on one side and twelve small boats on the other (like the dark side of the moon, she had it on faith that they existed on the unseen profile). Fred had briefly recounted the *Titanic* disaster. However, the year 1912 had meant nothing, so too his description of an iceberg (a bluish frozen fiend bobbing in the sea) or the glancing of said fiend (with its hazardous, invisible, underwater mass) by the doomed ship. Fred might as well have been explaining a complicated medical procedure. Until she heard the words *women and children first*. That struck a chord.

Her hand floated up to stroke a scarf that was no longer there. Stronger than the disappointment of losing a beloved accessory was the fear of leaving proof of her presence behind, so she quickly retraced her steps. Finding no signs of the recently familiar—no tables, no waiter, no *Señor Tejas*, no scarf—she'd count herself lucky if the thing had blown overboard. Otherwise, a link now existed between her and that troublesome fabric with the silver and pink leopard print.

She hoped it would not turn out to be the equivalent of a stowaway's razor.

CHAPTER 31

"Hey, not so hard! You're gonna blast me away!" cried a ruddy-faced crew member, the designated goalie for an impromptu kickaround. Marks and Gracey still hadn't found the soccer ball's rightful owner, having given the effort no more than a half-hearted try.

Drawn by the sounds of hoots and hollers and the desire to get a closer look at the double-decker buses lashed to opposite sides of the poop deck, Mári walked through their little skirmish and up into the port-side bus, easily penetrating a loosely flapping plastic barrier at the rear entry. Since she'd come aboard Queen Mary her courageousness knew no bounds! *Por qué no*, she reasoned, making the extra effort to climb the narrow staircase up to the second level. *Qué vista!* A distant landmass was visible, but the miles of foamy, trailing wake captivated her, so unusual and provocative a sight that it stopped all thoughts except one: *I am alone.*

On the brink of really scaring herself, she focused instead on the novelty at hand, marveling at the bus's overall height and thinking a top-heavy oddity like this would never survive the mountainous terrain of her homeland. Advertisements lined every available wall, a showcase of bright-faced people coyly peeking through curling smoke, or manicured hands cradling pure white soaps. The map of London's transit system did not hold a great deal of fascination for her, but the smell of old leather seats did, reminding her of an ancient barbershop her father visited once a week.

"*Papi, please take me with you!*" she'd cry every time, and every time he did.

The gleaming straight razor buttering a long, shiny strip of hide mesmerized her, not to mention the white foam that disguised her father's mahogany face until it came away in neat white drifts along the razor's path. Her sister joined them once and never again because she'd nearly fainted at the sight of a white-smocked stranger holding a blade against her papi's neck. Deep down, Mári was pleased that she, and only she, had shared this one routine with her dad.

A wild kick shattered her daydreams, sending the ball crashing against a nearby window. Shaking from the rush of adrenaline, she quickly made her way downstairs, a good head of steam building. Luigi and his fanatic devotion to the sport came to mind and she pictured the two of them with a cabin of their own, taking meals together, strolling, dancing, and him sneaking off for a little fancy footwork on the tail end of the most famous ship in the world.

"'Scuse me, ma'am!"

Mári looked up to see the big Texan leaning over a railing one deck above, madly waving his arms.

"Yes you! How-dee!"

Warily, Mári crossed the playing field, taking a long moment to stare down the players.

"Yer scarf! You forgot yer scarf!" he drawled, resorting to a hang-man sort of pantomime when words registered no effect.

Given the repeated knot-tying motions made around his neck, Mári thought he was trying to kill himself. After all, this was about as strange and disorienting a stretch of hours as she'd ever experienced. Then it dawned on her.

"Gracias! Gracias! Donde es?"

"Limpeeando. Kwal es tu cuarto?"

Mári stood stock still. The man wanted to know her cabin number so he could have her scarf returned after it was cleaned. Under proper circumstances, she would give him her name, written down, and ask him to leave it with Purser. This was not a proper circumstance.

"B-410. Hasta luego!" She waved and turned, dismissing any further contact.

Satisfied, the burly Texan headed off, mouthing *bay-quatro-uno-zero, bay-quatro-uno-zero* like a talisman he didn't dare forget. Mári considered heading straight for *bay-quatro-uno-zero* to alert its occupants of an errant scarf on its way, but decided against it. How to explain?

She felt the oddness of the day shift, the way a heavy mist clings to the top of a mountain, then sinks.

"Watch out!" yelled the footballers, voices conveying alarm.

Too late. Mári turned fully into the path of an airborne soccer ball, her upper arm absorbing the impact.

"Pena, si?" she joked about a penalty, then with considerable effort bent to scoop up the leather sphere. Turning it over and over while pondering how best to catapult it overboard, Mári noticed thick handwriting flash by on every revolution. It looked eerily familiar. Flipping to just the right puffy hexagons, she couldn't believe her eyes. The four crew members clustered around, unsure of what this exotic creature might do next.

"Luigi?" she questioned slowly, drawing out the name long enough to look each player in the eye. *"No es posible."*

"Are you Luigi?" someone asked. "Chaps, we finally found our man—enjoy the ball, Missus!" They nudged and winked at one another, leaving Mári holding a soggy hot potato.

CHAPTER 32

As their rumps swiveled on the stools of a new juice trailer, Sonrisa's and Marta's expressions petrified into frozen stares at the sound of Luigi's voice. *"Buon giorno!"* he bellowed again, jolly as an off-season Santa. His forced jocularity caught them off guard, particularly Sonrisa, who knew Luigi seldom went out of his way to be friendly. He even bent down to place a chaste kiss on Marta's flushed cheek, pausing as he did for some kind of emphasis. Perhaps he wondered where her new dress hailed from but had the decency not to ask. She shot a confused glance to Sonrisa, who in turn patted the air space in front of them, signaling *calmate.* Stay calm.

"Dos jugos de piña con leche por favor," Sonrisa called to an invisible attendant.

"Eh heh! Mith amigath! Mith amigath!" cried a gravelly voice from parts unseen.

Sonrisa tilted her head down to catch sight of Hector, clean-shaven and wearing a tidy green smock over the white shirt and tan pants they'd sewn up for him. Behind the counter, he thumped excitedly back and forth along a raised platform that compensated for his diminished height, pointing emphatically at the sky. The captivated female patrons looked up, shielding their eyes from the sun. Luigi just stared, stunned to see the legless man from his dream.

"No, no! Por ahi!" he insisted, crooking his whole body at a dangerous angle, stumps lifting off. Sonrisa caught on when she saw a large green sign announcing *"JUGOS FRESCOS de HECTOR"* on top of the stand.

"Si, si, qué bueno," she remarked in her slow, low voice that came off as sexy without trying.

Relieved, Hector plopped back onto his platform and confirmed that this was, in fact, his juicy fruit stand. *"Portable, too,"* he said, shoving pineapple wedges into a new blender. *"I hire a truck every morning to move it from the shipping yard to here."*

With a steady hand, the juiceman poured the frothy mix into large cups and deftly tucked sprigs of fresh green carrot tops into each drink.

"For you, my friends," Hector intoned and slid the cups out toward the Dominicans. *"Yours is next,"* he curtly informed the Italian while still facing the women.

"Really, this is all possible because of you," he choked, the moisture level in his eye sockets rising, then tumbling over. Getting a hold of himself, he adjusted his smock for no good reason, then his eyes lit on Marta and stayed there long enough to make everyone uncomfortable. He frowned, staring intently, poised to say something then dismissing it with a wave. He was a businessman now, couldn't afford to alienate customers with idle speculation even if he knew he was right.

"Excuse me for interrupting, but Mári, how have you been?" Luigi's voice lifted a note or two like some adolescent boy voicing a puzzled question. Before she could answer, he remembered the dream and asked again, gently, how she'd been.

Over her initial shock, Mári's lookalike fell right in line. *"Pues, muy triste verdad, pero ahora estoy casi feliz."* Well, very sad, truly, but now I'm almost happy.

Sonrisa sat rapt. Hector, for his part, watched the scene unfold like a nervous midwife, wringing his cleaning rag one way then the other. Every time his eyes magnetized on the shorter Dominican's face he caught himself and his hands flew to wiping an already immaculate countertop.

Mári's twin patted her stomach. *"You haven't said anything about this,"* she arched her eyebrows and pointed to a decidedly flat abdomen.

Sonrisa couldn't believe her ears. Hector stopped wringing and wiping. Luigi squirmed, trying hard to keep the whine out of his voice.

"I didn't want to, not in front of everyone," he said between gritted teeth.

"These are my friends, Luigi, get over yourself." She sipped nonchalantly at her juice and wiped the mustache away with an un-ladylike swipe of her hand.

Dying inside, Luigi's eyes grew wide. *"I wondered, I mean, I was going to ask. What did happen?"* he asked in a resigned tone, as if not really wanting to know the details but knowing they expected him to possess the decency of curiosity.

"You mean to our baby?"

"I suppose," he replied, scratching his head in a feeble attempt to deflect the force of the question. Mári seemed a new woman.

"I had it. A beautiful baby boy, with all its parts," Marta added matter of factly, catching Sonrisa's eye with a little wink.

Luigi warmed to the news, shifting his weight to a more receptive stance. *"Well, can I see him?"*

"You cannot."

"Why?"

"Because I don't have him," Marta said, beginning to feel strange. *"I gave him to someone who could care for him better than just me."*

Emphasizing these last words, she stared angrily at Luigi's shocked face.

What could he say? How could he argue with her, beg her to reconsider her drastic actions? Even if he wanted to start a family with her, which up until yesterday he was sure he didn't, once she'd made up her mind, General Trujillo himself couldn't persuade her otherwise. He fought the urge to hide behind silence and, once begun, the words spilled from his mouth.

"I would like to talk to you more about this, about what you have gone and done. It is—an accident."

"You're a little late," Mári's twin reminded him.

"I am late. That is correct. But what you don't know is I almost died the other day." Luigi's hand traveled to his chest. *"All I could think of when I woke up was you. I think you saved my life. I think maybe you're the reason I came back."*

His words were spoken so softly that Sonrisa and Hector had to lean in to listen.

Pobre culito, 'Risa thought, *he's spilling his guts to the wrong woman.*

What was that all about? Marta wondered. *Can't even tell the difference between us.* Granted, to the untrained eye, only a few subtle details distinguished one from the other; for instance, Mári kept her hair longer and her breasts appeared larger, but still, *Dios mio, how could he be so blind?*

Luigi sucked in his breath then blew it out forcefully. Silence was so much easier. *"I would like to call on you, take you out to a fine meal, maybe to the Xaragua where we can be alone to talk."*

Marta quickly ran through her options. She could kiss his ass, dump his ass, or keep his ass suspended over the gorge of her superior knowledge.

"Let me think about what you've said. Call me later."

With that, she and Sonrisa slurped the last of their fruit drinks and left Luigi to commiserate with the legless shopkeeper who, instincts humming, nervously wiped the counter in a peripatetic hen-like motion that lulled Luigi into a semi-hypnotic trance.

"Excuth me Theñor," Hector began, treading lightly.

"I'll have another."

Both men looked in the direction of the shrinking females.

"Theñor, dithculpe, but, I don't know how to thay thith," Hector wheezed in his best Peter Lorre.

"Give me my juice then tell me straight, man. What—don't like the way I smell?" he joked, feeling he could afford to be glib. After all, what could this guy say that would rock his boat?

"I don't think thath your girlfriend." Seeing no violent reaction, Hector continued with the puckered lips of a professor. *"Mári ith rounder, plumper and, well, her hair fallth differently, thoft, around her shoulderth, like cathcading water."*

"Maybe she's having a bad hair day?"

"Don't know," Hector admitted, sliding over the juice which Luigi downed in no time, his Adam's apple bobbing with each glub-glub.

"That's right, you don't know. But I'll tell you this much—I'll find out for sure, soon." He tossed several coins onto the buffed Formica and left Hector to puzzle over kooky foreigners.

CHAPTER 33

Thoughts of a son droned in his head. But he had to play it cool. Luigi pulled into the driveway of *Casa del Mar* a little after the agreed upon time. He tooted his horn then sat waiting, jiggling his knees and tapping his fingers on the steering wheel. He'd wanted to pick her up earlier but Sonrisa and Marta had strategized a later time, agreeing the darker outside the better for prolonging the deception.

'Risa was grateful her friend Mári had more time to unfurl her plan, bless her, whatever that was. Marta, indignant, couldn't believe she was going to accompany this *pendejo* to a public place, much less while posing as her sister. This wouldn't be the first time they'd pinch hit for one another, but it would be the first time the other sister didn't know about it.

Luigi greeted his date with an *hola* followed by a suspicious gaze and a cheeky *your hair looks different.* They rode without speaking after a curt *I curled it.* Music from the car radio—Tito Puente, Celia Cruz— bridged the gulf.

At Xaragua, a buck-toothed *maitre d'* smiling a fake but none- theless striking smile led them to a middle table in an effort to extort money for a more favorable—and less visible—one. The ruse back-fired. Luigi, who never paid for things he could take himself, whisked the menus away and led his date to an intimate spot by a large window overlooking the bay. The host trailed lamely behind, putting up no resis- tance. In the end, he held the chair out graciously for his female patron, clucked his teeth, turned on his heels and walked stiffly away, muttering something about *machos.*

Luigi caught M– stifling a giggle.

"Did you see those choppers?" he asked cautiously, as if his well- being depended on her answer.

At the mention of teeth she burst out laughing, the tension of the last few days pouring out of her mouth in a ridiculous release. Pleased by his success, Luigi placed his hand on hers then wished he hadn't when she yanked it away, glowering.

Something about that glower looked unfamiliar—he'd never seen this particular scowl before. Mári was feisty, but this, this spoke of red hot lava bubbling close to the surface. Absent was any sign of lingering affection or sentimental attachment for all they'd shared and could possibly share again.

"I've decided to become a lesbian," M– declared in an attempt to curtail analysis.

Sputtering on *chianti*, Luigi smiled. It was his turn to laugh.

"That's good! You know, I almost believe you," he said confidently. *"With who then, Sonrisa?"* He meant it to come out breezily, but his voice rose in concern.

"I'm not saying—you might get jealous," she taunted, enjoying the upper hand.

"Me? Jealous? Of another woman? It would take more than a fuzzy coco to make me jealous." Luigi flushed, warming to the topic. *"Another man maybe, I admit."* He paused to swill wine. *"But a woman? What can you build with another woman?"* Dismissing the thought as ludicrous, he asked with a snort if she was ready to order.

"Si, como no," M– said in a coy mimic of Mári.

Luigi's eyes twinkled. The wine, the beautiful woman, the prospect of food, all conspired to bury his doubts and soothe his soul with ripples of reconciliation and love.

Until Marta ordered a rum and Coke.

"Why a rum and Coke?"

M– glanced away and back, straining to keep the "uh oh" note out of her voice. *"Because I like it?"* she answered with a question of her own.

"I thought they made you sick."

"Not since the pregnancy ended…" she replied, coolly sipping the drink. *"Muchacho! Más hielo por favor."*

Luigi looked on pensively, a hint of menace gathering, taking shape.

"Ice? I've never known you to like much ice."

"Yes, well, since the—"

"Don't tell me," he cut her off. *"A lot of changes have taken place since then, and in not so very much time."*

"What are you trying to say?" she asked, glaring through narrowed eyes.

"That sometimes I feel like you're a different person than the woman I love."

"I am different. I've been through a lot these past months, and mostly alone."

"Have you ever kissed another woman?"

"What kind of question is that?" M– responded, certain she didn't like where this was headed.

"You're the one who brought it up. I'm curious. So have you?"

M– could think of nothing witty to say, so she picked one of two answers.

"No."

"Then how do you know you want to be a lesbian?" Luigi smoothly asked.

"Because men are mafiosos…"

"Now you sound like my Mári!" he bellowed, draining the last measure of blood-red wine in his goblet. *"Waiter, bring me a Cuba Libre!"*

"I think I'll join you mi amor," Luigi said when his drink arrived. *"Here's to new beginnings,"* he proclaimed and banged his glass against hers, sending some of the contents flying.

"Such a brute, I apologize," he said, fussing to wipe up. *"By the way, how was your flight?"*

"Excuse me?"

"Come on, I know it's you Marta," he said rather good naturedly.

The imposter holstered the shock without a flinch, managing a convincing laugh. *"You've lost your mind!"*

"I don't think so. Here's why. Mári once told me she'd kissed another woman—"

"And you believed me?"

"Wait a minute—if you're Mári, why didn't you say yes?"

"Maybe I didn't want to admit it again."

"She said, one night when we were sharing little secrets, that she'd kissed a woman and that woman was her sister." Luigi stared intently at the person sitting across the table. *"I could ask you what secret I divulged, but I don't think that'll be necessary."*

Marta blushed. This was true. They'd shared a kiss once, in parting, when Mári left for her journey to Mexico. It had not been an altogether chaste kiss. Something had gotten into them at the airport in Santo Domingo, hugging hysterically, unwilling to let go. One of them, she wasn't sure who at this point, kissed the other's mouth and cupped a hand behind her head to increase the tender impact.

Lost in the memory and the feeling that each sister in that long ago moment had infused the other with courage, fortitude and love, Marta folded.

"I can't believe she told you that!"

CHAPTER 34

Feeling like a bloated castaway, Mári shuffled along hoping the fresh air would infuse her with comfort. Instead, slightly chilled, she wrapped her arms tightly around the soccer ball, resting it on a ballooned abdomen that, with each crampy throb, brought back memories of her long-absent period. Increasing pain cried out for quick relief, and she went back inside the double-decker bus, grateful for its shelter and warmth. Resting sideways on a bench seat, the internal wrenching subsided. She wiggled her feet, realizing she couldn't see them because of the double-extensions of stomach and ball in front of her. For some reason this made her laugh. She stretched back against the window, feet poking into the aisle. Relaxed as if in a religious sanctuary, Mári dozed until, heavy-lidded and drooling, she woke to the sound of clanking glass. The source of the noise turned out to be a svelte blonde in a skimpy bikini spilling a sack of wine bottles onto an upper deck. Mári wondered about these foreigners, thinking them strange and highly unpredictable.

A man snapped picture after picture of the athletic blonde hamming for the camera, holding a bottle in the air like a prized catch then flinging it overboard, body pressed hard against the railing to track the projectile's progress from one element to the other. After a few such repetitions, the man hugged her happily, stowed his gear, and left the woman to wrap up.

Mári decided to take a closer look at this beguiling ritual on her way to the Prom Deck's lure of food. Without giving thought to how strange she must appear, she casually tucked the soccer ball under an arm and headed up. Out of breath at the top, she grasped the dark wooden handrail and bent over, trying to regain her wind. This succeeded in making her nauseous. A searing pain ripped through her abdomen, jack-knifing her as far as she could go with a ball wedged beneath her breasts. The blonde immediately sprinted over.

"Are you ok?" she whispered, holding her robe closed with one hand and extending the other to the stricken passenger.

"*No—ah, si, si, posible,*" Mári replied weakly, clutching Luigi's ball as if it was the one thing keeping her afloat. She didn't dare let go, didn't dare drape her arms around her abdomen and feel how much lower her cargo had dropped.

The woman pulled up a deck chair and beckoned her to sit. Stretched out, she felt relieved enough to point to the bevy of bottles and ask a question. The woman didn't speak Spanish, but she quickly put two and two together.

"Hold on, back in a flash."

Mári watched the woman disappear inside the ship. She had no idea what she'd said, but Mári was in no hurry to move. As she started to relax, a wave of pain stormed the beach of her anatomy, leaving behind a rigid still life. Sphincter awareness had never been more keen, and she felt a certain gratitude that it was able to hold back whatever threatened to come flatulating out since she was not, after all, in the privacy of her own stall. Were these hunger pangs? Or something much worse?

The spry woman returned carrying four items: a turquoise Parker pen, a piece of parchment, a corkscrew, and a bottle snatched from the pile. Sitting cross-legged, she undid the cork, letting loose a "pop" which, though not loud, Mári blamed for precipitating her next bout of internal uproar. The woman, intent on finding a way to draw out the contents of the bottle, didn't notice the ghastly grimace on Mári's face which reflected a new-found fear that she might be turning into a werewolf or some other ill-fated creature.

At this moment, the blonde discovered a serious flaw. Short of breaking the glass, it was virtually impossible to remove the message which had been pre-inserted by the publicity department. The scroll had expanded and not even a scantily clad hourglass figure could coax it out. The bathing beauty, who looked as though she might be named Helga, abandoned her cocktail-mixing moves with the bottle and handed Mári pen and paper. So what if the bottle had two messages in it. Odds were no one would find it anyway.

Emerging from the grip of her body's protestations, Mári clicked the ballpoint out and in while contemplating what to write. The bright color and measured action of the pen reassured her, prompting her to jot down two words that came persistently to mind: *te quiero*. Dating and signing her full name, she kissed the paper.

The nice bikini woman tied a gold ribbon around the declaration then dropped it into the bottle where it nestled inside the first message. Mári wanted to know what that one conveyed but had no way of asking. She hoped somehow the two would go well together.

The model led her to the side railing. Mári held the bottle by its skinny neck and practiced cocking it back and forth over her shoulder until she felt capable of hurling it clear of the ship. On the mental count of *tres*, she released the bottle and watched as it smacked the water and did a little skip, floating further and further away from its provenance.

The two woman quietly threw the rest of the bottles overboard, pausing every now and then to interpret signs of an impending squall. Helga suspiciously eyed the advancing ceiling of gray that devoured fluffy popcorn clouds in its path. Mári eyed the front with a mixture of trepidation and relief. On the one hand, the approaching storm upset her balance. On the other, she welcomed the external turmoil as a sort of wake-up call. What was she doing here? Was she insane? Had lifelong tropical heat scrambled her brain to the point where she'd made this bizarre, almost unthinkable, choice? With a tinge of sadness she looked on as Helga picked up her empty bags, adjusted her robe, and squeezed Mári's forearm warmly on the way to the rest of her life.

Mári watched her go, wistful at the sight of those shapely, strong legs and her unapologetic attitude. She would have no shame, either, when she got her body back.

In the distance, she had no idea how far, a flash of lightning lit up the foggy mess that'd made astounding progress in a few short minutes. She wondered if it was dangerous to remain on deck with such a storm overhead. *Probably so.* Maybe the lightning would seek her out, a kindred spirit full of energy with no proper place to go. Maybe it would strike and in one single moment reduce her—*them*—to a smoking mass of flesh and bone. She shivered at the thought.

"Madre La Virgen, ayudame." Virgin Mother help me.

The glass vessels rose and fell with the rhythm of the Pacific, growing more distant with each passing moment. The interior of her nose stung and a blink released two large teardrops onto the shiny teak rail but they blew away before she could touch them. This moment of lost opportunity caused a flood of tears. Mári's vision blurred and she didn't care. The whole ocean spread before her, its details lost, but none of its immenseness. Sickeningly enchanted, as if being swallowed up by this great body of water would be terrible at first then somehow all right, Mári felt the synchronous spread of moisture between her legs. Shifting positions, her thighs reported back wet underpants. Propriety aside, she reached a hand down and patted her crotch. Relieved not to see blood, she sniffed at the wetness, concluding it must be sweat. She rubbed the "v" of her skirt against a bead of moisture traveling down her leg and leaned toward the ocean, unsure of what to do next.

The storm bore thunder. Nature's throaty expression rumbled through the ship's elements, entraining them like a tuning fork. Mári was surprised, then realized that, although man-made, Queen Mary was every bit a part of the natural world, straining and stretching, absorbing and dealing blows.

Dollops of rain tumbled from the sky, staining the decks with saucer-sized disks. Wet enough, Mári retreated to the overhang for shelter. Unlike on land, she detected no earthy smell as a result of the downpour. Instead, the briny bite of saltwater prevailed, stirring up dormant things lying on, and just beneath, the surface.

CHAPTER 35

"Where is she?" Luigi asked while dunking a rolled tortilla in the last dregs of blood red enchilada sauce.

Marta crinkled her face, casting her offended features out toward the view.

A waiter cleared their plates. *"Algo más?"*

Chomping away, Luigi ordered two *flans*, then asked Marta what she was going to have. *"So where is she?"* The Italian swirled his glass then tipped it back for a deep slug. When Marta said she couldn't tell him, he sucked a piece of ice into his mouth and pulverized it with powerful thrusts of his jaw.

"Is she staying at Charlita's?"

Marta could see the prominent muscles express themselves every time he bit down. It reminded her of a horse's cheek.

"Bueno, then tell me this." His hand, cold from the drink, seized hers, and this time she didn't pull away. *"Did Mári really give my son away?"*

She was starting to feel a little sorry for this lug of a guy. What could it hurt to throw him a bone?

"As far as I know…" the minute the words tumbled out of her mouth she knew she'd stumbled, but she pressed on smoothly, *"…she hasn't had the baby yet."*

"What do you mean 'as far as you know'? You make it sound like you haven't seen her lately. Like she's in some far-off place."

The desserts arrived none too soon. Luigi's spoon dove into the firm custard, eager to deliver sweet milkiness to an agitated mouth.

"I mean since I last saw her—this afternoon. Anything could've happened between then and now." Marta picked at her chocolate mousse.

Luigi hugged the second terrine close to his chest and polished off its contents. Without looking up, he said he'd find out where she was, one way or another.

"I don't doubt you will."

❁

After Luigi dropped Marta off at the hotel, he circled around the block then pulled back into the lower driveway, cutting the engine and coasting the last ten feet. Madame Gerard popped a headful of rollers out of her fortified quarters, scowling at the intruder. Luigi beckoned, unfazed by her bearing. Peeved at the interruption of her end-of-the-day ablutions, she nonetheless shuffled over, heels dragging. When her bulk finally reached the driver's window, she planted her hands firmly on the roof, waiting for him to make it worth her while. He held out a rolled bill and waved it under her nose. One hand swept down like a raptor on its prey, but he quickly withdrew the money.

"Mári aqui?"

"No lo sé." Puckered lips and a roll of the eyes said as much as the words.

"Can you go check?" Luigi countered with raised eyebrows and a look of strained patience. He waved the bill. *"Por favor?"*

Taking a deep breath, Mme. G. boomed up to the rooms, *"Chicas—Mári esta aqui?"* Nothing. She yelled again, doubling the volume while lowering her head so some decibels pierced the occupied car. *"ESTA MARI?"*

"NO!" came two separate replies which, unbeknownst to Luigi, set up a chain reaction of girls asking one another where Mári was, had anyone seen Mári?

Mme. Gerard leaned on the frame of his open window, clearing her throat. He handed her the note, which promptly vanished down the valley of her bosom. Mid-way through her return shuffle, Mme. Gerard heard the squeak of a car door. Guessing at his motives, she flew like a goalie to block his advance through the kitchen. Her hands went to her hips. He huffed and fished in his pants, knowing full well the only money in there was a large note too steep for such a small bribe, but he had no choice. Grudgingly, he withdrew the bill and pasted her upturned palm with it. She moved aside.

"Five minutes," she warned. *"Chicas! Luigi esta subiendo!"*

This, too, set off a chain reaction of girls running for cover. Many, caught in a relative state of undress while preparing for an evening at the Club, threw on bras & blouses, panties & skirts, as none of the doors locked and no one knew when and where Luigi might pop up.

Sonrisa and Marta, who were not able to find a suitable hiding place in time as Michi occupied the bathroom and was producing a particularly smelly bowel movement, heard a quick succession of footsteps leading directly toward their *cuarto*. Of course Luigi would check there first.

Heavy raps sounded on the door. The girls had no choice but to face the music unless, unless…

Of a mind to share the wealth, 'Risa flung open the bathroom door and fanned it back and forth to spread the stink. Marta ducked in, holding her nose. Michi cursed and protested from the throne, but Marta shushed her.

"Entra!" 'Risa chimed sweetly.

Luigi came in all full of himself then stopped, looking like he'd been sprayed by a skunk. Choking back the nausea, he uttered a lame, *"Esta Mári?"*

"Claro qué estoy!" an exasperated voice yelled. The bathroom door slammed shut and those in the room continued to hear a muttering rant asking the Mother of God why nothing was sacred and how could a girl get a little privacy and of course she was here, where else would she be?

Partially satisfied that he'd had a near encounter with the real Mári, though not convinced, Luigi decided, mainly out of embarrassment, to call it a day. It did not help his mental fortitude when, after closing the door, muffled guffaws accompanied him a good way down the stairs.

CHAPTER 36

After changing her sopping undergarments, Mári took what turned out to be an extended nap in her marine cubby. When she woke she was, as usual, ravenous. Deciding as an afterthought to take her bag, she drew a deep breath to bolster near-empty reserves of confidence before emerging from the nickel-chrome portal into a foyer filled with passengers waiting to enter the main dining room. Mári's first instinct, after spotting the antagonistic steward trying his best to placate a handful of fussy blue-haired ladies, was to spin right around and seek the safety of her cubicle. Somehow, inner wisdom prevailed and she kept her limbs moving smoothly and with purpose off to a side hallway, quickening her pace until a stairway took her up to B Deck where she found her shaking hands rapping on the door of cabin 410.

Detecting no signs of life within, Mári, close to despair, formulated a plan B, figuring the red bus would make a good hideout until things died down in her neck of the woods. Turning to walk away, she heard the flush of a toilet, seemingly just beyond the wall. She knocked again. Inches away from making contact, her fist lurched through the air as the door unexpectedly swung open. There stood Guga, eyebrows arched, pantyhose plastering ringlets of gold. Mári's knuckles stopped short of Guga's unmade face, but not by much.

The ridiculousness of the moment caused them both to crack up.

"I am so sorry to bother you," Mári whispered breathlessly, expecting the steward to round the bend any second. *"But here—I'm returning this—it's your friend's, I think."*

Guga put the earring next to the typewriter and graciously pulled up a visitor chair. *"Sister, no bother. Do I look like I'm going anywhere?"*

"Not on your life," Mári admitted, feeling comfortable in the presence of this odd bird.

"*Ehh, cuidado!*" a metronome of a finger wagged. "*I'm very fragile, you know,*" said a voice surprisingly quiet and undramatic.

"*Me, too.*"

"*In that case, I think we should lighten things up with a little rum and Coke,*" Guga cheerfully shifted gears.

"*Just the Coca, my stomach bothers me lately,*" Mári rubbed her belly with a semi-puzzled look on her face.

"*Yes, Coke is good for the upset stomach, no doubt. Here you go, Señora—?*"

"*Loprete.*" She stumbled over unfamiliar syllables, grateful to have remembered Luigi's family name.

"*Married to an Italiano? Qué rica, qué caliente,*" Guga mimicked in show-girl mode, fanning the faux flames of *amor* and clinking high-ball glasses.

After a second round of drinks and general chit chat during which they both carefully steered away from the topic of spouses, careers, and reasons for traveling, Guga laid all the cards on the bed. *Canasta* cards.

"*You do play?*"

"*Claro qué si!*" Mári's pride bristled as if she could not imagine a single human being who did not play the game.

Guga patted the twin bed and Mári found it not at all awkward to accept a seat on a bed in a ship with a stranger who defied classification. For one, her own fun-loving, outgoing temperament customarily led her into situations that also defied the norms. She thought nothing of basking in the kindness and generosity of a casual admirer, and rarely felt any sense of obligation to return the favor, one way or another, because she didn't see it as a favor. If someone wanted to lavish food, drink, perfume, clothes, and jewelry on her in exchange for her dazzling company, so be it. Sonrisa regularly lectured her about this prevailing attitude of innocent opportunism—it could get a girl in big trouble.

Mári, in turn, had a habit of getting on Sonrisa's case for being so *dere-cha*, straight. Still, even Mári had to admit, as she admired Guga's long, narrow, sensually dexterous hands shuffle two decks at once, this was the most unlikely encounter yet.

Nothing but night sky showed through the open portholes. A breeze animated the squiggles, lines, and symbols of the satiny curtains, their geometric pattern foreign to Mári's tropical sensibilities. In fact, the entire décor of the Queen Mary was refreshingly foreign—fabrics and rugs boldly celebrating simple shapes, swirly woods reflecting back a confectioner's blend of light and dark, furniture so dense it was hard to move, not to mention the whole ship-board look of riveted steel, smoking funnels, and perpetual motion. Mári loved it all.

Squealing with delight, she particularly loved the hand she'd been dealt. Guga eyed her grumpily, pulling Indian-style legs in more tightly.

"I'm glad someone is happy."

The first round of *canasta* progressed nicely. Though Mári wanted nothing more than to study Guga's unusually tall body, take in its toned contours, she kept her eyes for the most part on the cards. Why not— they were excellent! Normally her patience caved and she went for easy points, laying down quick three-of-a-kinds and building piecemeal onto sequences already deposited. But here, tonight, aboard a famous luxury liner in a cabin with a mysterious Brazilian, her hand held a preponderance of clubs working their magic in precision line ups. Mári breathed a quick prayer of thanks, elation turning to fret as she wondered how long her good luck would last.

"Did you say something?" Guga asked inquisitively, picking up the entire discard pile.

"Me? No, why?" Mári answered innocently.

"I thought I saw your lips moving," Guga mumbled, sorting cards to and fro.

"I was strategizing." She looked devilishly at her opponent, who laid down a mere two sets of three, leaving behind a boatload of cards in hand.

"Your turn," the Brazilian said politely.

Slowly, with effect, Mári divulged seven clubs running sequentially from two to eight. *"A pure canasta and wait, I'm not done."*

Pointing to her opponent's three queens, she put down one of her own and framed a ten, Jack, and Queen of hearts with a nine and king.

"I'm out!"

"I can see that," Guga moaned, counting up a handful of negative points. *"You are evil. And to think I took you in."*

"Two seventy five for me," Mári gloated. She made a move to collect the cards for the next hand but Guga stopped her.

"Wait a minute—that's not a pure canasta. It's got a two in it. Two's are wild."

"Not in this case—it's not used as a wild card."

"But you counted it as 50 points anyway, didn't you miss it's not used as a wild card? Women!"

The night stretched on pleasantly as the two acted like a couple of juveniles from the Pajama Game. Claire breezed through to switch out a pair of light weight pants and blouse for a bubbly polka dot dress. Guga proclaimed the garment a favorite with gestures of hand over heart, while Mári admired Guga's own bright yellow sundress, a sleeveless number with an Audrey Hepburn cut and plunging neckline trimmed in lace.

Mári couldn't have felt fatter or frumpier.

"Where you going, hot date?"

"Dancing or cinema, not sure yet. *How To Steal A Million* is playing—" Claire said, flying out. "If you wanna join us, I'll be with Tex."

Hours slipped by for all cradled within the aged liner. Eventually, Guga put an end to Mári's winning streak by yawning excessively and issuing an ultimatum: we either leave this stuffy hole and get some air, or I go to sleep and put an end to my misery. *"So which is it?"* Guga asked through another broad yawn, stretching out fully on the bed.

"It's late, I should be going."

"You didn't even have the decency to let your hostess win, not even once!"

"Thank you for your company," Mári said sincerely, flushing out the wrinkles of her skirt.

"Not so quick am I letting you off the hook. I'm going to get my revenge on the dance floor," Guga said and smiled wickedly.

"How do you propose to do that?"

"Hmmmm…"

"I'm hardly dressed for—"

"Go get changed, I'll wait."

"I think I've had too much fun already," Mári lamely explained. *"But thank you."*

"No, no, no mi amor," Guga announced through clicks of pearly white teeth, grabbing hold of Mári's arm and guiding her firmly to the closet door.

"There, take your pick. Claire's just about your size."

The Brazilian rubbed two elegant hands together in anticipation of a good old-fashioned girls' night out. *"Try this."* Out came a roomy two-piece black chiffon with ruffles. *"I'm going to shave,"* Guga announced matter-of-factly, heading to the bathroom.

The blouse dropped down neatly onto Mári's shoulders. A few corners here and there needed adjusting, so she pulled at them, satisfied enough with the results to continue outfitting her bottom half. Mári had the slacks midway up when the bathroom door swung open, Guga's face hidden behind a crop of shaving cream.

"Yes, honey, that will do!" came the same encouraging feminine voice. However, the visual didn't match—a practiced hand mowed the razor back and forth through drifts of foam. Mári, stunned, stood bent, butt in the air, pants suspended knee high. The process of dressing took a back seat to curtailing a barrage of stupid questions. Instead of trying to justify the odd image of a woman shaving her face, Mári turned it around and concluded that Guga must in fact be a very pretty man.

"So I'm supposed to dance with you?" Mári recovered quickly. *"I'm not a lesbian, you know."*

"Neither am I, honey, neither am I," Guga beamed, closing the bathroom door to complete the transformation.

Admiring the figure she cut in the rose-tinted mirror (except for what she called "that bloat"), Mári was not at all certain she welcomed the portent of several soft knocks on the cabin door. Guga peeked out the bathroom door, equally edgy.

"Who could THAT be? Maybe Claire lost her key?"

The Dominican briefly wondered why Guga was edgy about a surprise knock at the door, then she forgot about it and turned the knob.

"Miss Zeisse?" a chirpy steward began, cradling a small object wrapped in tissue paper.

Mári glanced over her shoulder to see if Guga was around, but the door was closed with water running.

"Yes?"

"For you, mum. From the laundry," the little guy grinned, pleased to have accomplished his mission.

Mári fished lamely around for a pocket that might contain some coin for a tip. Finding none, she warmly grasped his scrawny forearm to communicate her gratitude, then tore open the package, pulling the fresh leopard print scarf to her nose.

"Bienvenidos."

It occurred to her she should've packed a clutch. When planning for this trip she'd envisioned holing up in some decrepit dungeon, not rubbing shoulders with paying passengers at buffet tables and on dance floors.

"Do you have a lipstick?" she called when Guga opened the door and peeked out from its steamy interior. *"Better than to go down to my cabin…"* she patted her big bag, knowing full well it contained more than a few.

Guga ushered her into the bathroom and stationed her in front of a medicine cabinet that contained a neatly organized mini-Macy's of powders and paints.

"Who was at the door?"

"Oh, just a package for me," Mári replied unthinkingly, preoccupied with the application of a certain color scheme to her face.

Upon Guga's quizzical look, Mári dismissed the subject. *"It's complicated."*

Giggling like a pair of debutantes, Guga and Mári careened down the endless hallway, so-called because the built-in sheer, or dip, didn't allow them to see the far end. They searched for stairs—any stairs—that might lead up to the Prom Deck lounge. Surprised smiles and surreptitious looks greeted them as they skipped by gringos who tried to characterize their relationship. These reactions only brought the odd couple closer as they assaulted the conservative world of the Mary.

"Why don't we just go to the movies?" Mári suggested, her voice trailing into a wheeze as air diverted from vocal cords to more vital parts.

"How to Steal A Million? Seen it a million times, and that's just on the ship," Guga grumbled. *"My social life has been…curtailed, but not tonight!"*

Mári wasn't sure she liked the Brazilian's tone or the dappling gleam in those clever hazel eyes. She strained to maintain a semblance of belonging and poise as they walked through the double-height doors of the main lounge, a sizeable but intimate space designed to placate the senses of those most fortunate of humans.

Pounding heart and pulsing abdomen took a back seat to the novelty and splendor of the crowded lounge—her eyes went right to the silver and gold unicorns (not horses) frozen in perpetual battle over the fireplace, but that was nothing compared to velvety smooth Johnny Mathis who enchanted from the stage. Mári couldn't begin to explain why she felt at home. It was nothing like she was used to, what with the famous singer, parquet dance floor, honey-colored grand piano, onyx fireplace flanked by glowing, human-sized urns. Grand as it was, it settled her like a favorite piece of clothing—it just fit.

Guga found a vacant seat along the back wall, not far from where dozens of couples swayed to the mellow tones of *Chances Are*.

"Be right back—going in search of chairs—and men."

Mári undid her scarf, draped it over the seatback as a place holder then went to explore the tableau of unicorns. Head filled with misty boreal imaginings, a stab of abdominal pain reminded her all too severely where she was and why she was. Panicked, she made for safe haven four decks below without delay.

Huffing and puffing, Mári pushed on the revolving door to the pool. It didn't budge. With more force she tried again but the portal remained shut. Propelling herself around the foyer, she headed toward the Third Class dining room turned storage area and leaned on the double doors hoping to find another way in, but nothing moved.

Wearily, she retraced her steps. A well-dressed couple announced their approach with loud whispers and glided by. Forewarned, Mári appeared to be busily reading a small posted announcement near the service window. Using an index finger to trace each sentence, she exaggerated her level of concentration, hoping to look not so out of place. What was not an exaggeration was the moment her finger stopped at the following short combination of numbers and letters: 7 am – 7 pm. The pool was closed. Really closed.

In search of relief, Mári plodded to the nearest water cooler. Her feet hurt. Everything ached, burned, felt all twisted up, and the nagging, quivering pain behind her belly button wasn't getting any better. There wasn't any movement—kicking, turning, punching—associated with the pain, which scared her. What if something was terribly wrong? How would she know? What would she do?

Pouring a third cup, Mári considered her options while rubbing her cargo in what she hoped was a soothing motion. Most tempting—though laborious—was the notion of slinking along endless hallways cautiously testing doorknobs to find an unlocked and, more importantly, unoccupied cabin. If by some miracle she found such a door, she imagined slipping in, kicking off her sandals and sprawling on the bed, head sinking into a big, fluffy pillow.

Mári crumpled the paper cup and tossed it into the bin, knowing full well she was headed back upstairs to the lounge. Maybe she could rely on safety in numbers.

Going on midnight, the live entertainment ended and the lounge thinned out, making it rather hard to blend in. Mári nervously took a seat near the unicorns and tried to fall under the spell of a crooning voice emanating from speakers when Guga spotted her and crossed the room with a companion in tow.

"We've been looking for you—you've met Tex?"

"Yes, yes, tank yu far…" her voice trailed off as she fingered her bare neck.

Not wishing to prolong her agony, Tex reached into his coat pocket. "Looking for this?" he said with a mischievous grin. "If ah dint know better, I'd a thought you was tryin' ta lose this article of clothin'. Funny, in't it, how I'm the one keeps findin' it?"

Mári looked at Guga, who understood her bewilderment and translated, finishing with, *"At least that's what I think he said, he has a funny accent."*

"Tell him please, I don't think it's funny he's the one who keeps rescuing my scarf. I think it's destiny."

Guga stared at her blankly. *"You really want me to say that?"*

Glazed eyes and a peaceful expression met his look, so Guga repeated her words while Tex's own ruddy complexion deepened a hue.

"Ma'am, would you be inclahned ta dance with me?" he said as he offered a beefy forearm and gestured with the other toward the parquet.

"Si, como no," Mári accepted, and though not at all in a dancing mood she felt stimulated by the possibilities of the next few minutes which would determine the course of the next few hours and possibly even the next few days.

Finished with an impromptu networking opportunity that took her briefly away from socializing, Claire ducked back into the main lounge and immediately made a beeline toward a not-so-solo Guga who was sidled up to a short, curly-haired fellow.

"Can I speak with you? Please excuse us," she said in a voice sweet as dark chocolate, her hand firmly guiding the Brazilian by the elbow. "What ever happened to keeping a low profile?"

"The trip's almost over! What are they going to do, make me walk the plank?" Guga ran a sultry hand over slender hips, followed by a few timely lip purses.

Claire shrugged, her heavy bangs swooshing like drapes as she shook her head. "I guess you have a point. Hell, I'm sorry."

The song ended and a foursome was born when Tex and Mári joined Guga and Claire.

"Hows 'bout we wrap this up here and you good folks join me at the Verandah Grill," Tex radiated the good will and forthrightness of a preacher.

"I *am* hungry," Guga announced, hands setting off in search of imaginary kinks and wrinkles to smooth.

"Not a bad idea," Claire agreed, gathering her wrap.

Happy to be headed toward Queen Mary's most exclusive lounge, Mári recounted to Guga, who translated to the others, how the décor had caused quite a stir in 1936, the focal point of the controversy being the room's black carpet which, as they entered, they could see was still black and still risqué. Mári's rapture lasted for the better part of an hour as she observed other details of the famed Verandah Grill. Not so famous that her Dominican friends would know about it, but meaningful to a whole group of moneyed people who rode in big boats from one place to another just for the fun of it. What were Fred's words? *Getting there was half the fun?*

At a cozy table for two not meant for four she sat crammed next to Tex. None other was available; this had been reserved months ago he explained, a buffalo arm resting protectively against the back of Mári's chair. No one was surprised by his attentiveness to the odd-girl-out. He made sure her bread plate was always full and her water glass never dry. Wine flowed but she took just the occasional sip as the tart drink made her mouth dryer than a cotton ball.

Mári's limited command of English contributed greatly to her wandering eyes while the three English-speakers gabbed on and on. Oddly enough, an old woman with an entourage of old women kept catching her gaze and smiling knowingly with a little wave of her skeletal hand. She was a few tables away, distance enough for Mári to fend off the unwanted attention. Seeing her puzzled look, Tex put two and two together.

"That's Mrs. Dalloway—she's harmless, a regular with time and money ta spare. She's probably just remarking on your beauty, don't mind her one bit."

Mári's self-consciousness faded and long instants passed observing walls painted with flying horse chariots and semi-nude women holding giant pitchforks and sombreros, radiant light fixtures affixed in places not normally hospitable to such things, curved glass panels flowing between railings of silver metal and etched with crisp designs of bubbling martini glasses and violins, plump circles with stems, music staphs. She spent a lot of time on a pair of silhouetted heads that were joined, facing away from each another—a female with long tresses and a male with shorter hair that, at the top, flew into two forward-pointing upturned prongs of coif that, the longer she stared, most assuredly resembled horns. Devil horns.

This put someplace in her psyche on high alert, but not the part that scarfed a dizzying array of stuffed romaine lettuce, narrow french fries, sizzling chops and parsleyed carrots. Tex did his best to include her in the conversation by peppering his sentences with Spanish words he knew. It worked to a certain extent. At one point he leaned in to mention his *esposa muerto*. This made Mári sad since, in retrospect, the whole time he must have been talking about his dead wife. She hadn't even picked up on the expressions of sympathy that the other two, er, women, had offered.

"Como se llama ella?"

"Polly."

The timber of his voice took on a sturdy tone, he sat up straighter in his chair, an animated hand occasionally brushing the back of Mári's blouse. Tex went on about Polly, and at the end of another rush of words she couldn't understand, he uttered one sentence, slowly, a look of remembrance in his eyes. Surprised by the import of these few words, he asked Guga to translate.

"I spoiled her, and she spoiled me."

Mári's very full stomach flip-flopped and she placed a commiserating hand on his. From across the table, whether by virtue or intoxication, Guga dropped a loving palm on top of hers while Claire took hold of Tex's free hand and topped Guga's with her other, an image worthy of an etching in the glass of the Verandah Grill.

Two of the women at the table found themselves needing to use the restroom. Though she'd consumed her fair share of gin tonics, Claire's discernment remained sharp. When she noticed Mári looking around a little too urgently, she offered up a friendly word.

"Baño?"

Whisking the Dominican off with a flourish, Claire announced to all who would hear, "Follow me." For one brief moment, Mári felt as if she was in one of her nightly numbers, about to ramp up for the visual climax. The thought made her grin—imagine a production like that on a ship like this! She pondered the possibilities while peeing into an immaculate porcelain bowl. Through gaps in the stall's partitions she could see Claire wetting her fingers and smoothing her bangs.

Her mind still on the fake shipboard orgy, Mári, feeling bold, used her foot to engage the flush lever, then turned to fluff her clothing, an action cut short by a terrible, throaty moan emerging from somewhere above. Before it faded entirely, Mári dashed out and right into Claire who, though surprised, burst out laughing.

"It's ok! Really—ok!"

"*Oh no, ruido muy malo.*" Mári declared the noise to be evil and, recalling the tomb-like timber of the groan, turned to go.

"*No problema—mira.*" Claire guided a *muy* reluctant Mári back to the offending stall. A growing curiosity replaced outright fright as she wondered what this crazy American was going to come up with by way of explanation—a huge croaking toad? Resident phantom, lonely but harmless?

Instead, Claire offered proof of a mechanical kind. Lifting her foot exactly as Mári had done, she depressed the flush lever. Caught off guard by the innocent whoosh of water, Mári jumped at the first sound of the drawn-out wail from hell. The only part of her fear that was lessened was the part that gave flight to her feet. Feeling foolish, she had no way to convey how deeply she'd believed a monster had lurked in her midst, no way to explain she'd never heard such a mournful sound and had thus assumed it otherworldly. She knew too few words in English to express how knowledge of 49 recorded deaths on board had finally cracked open her shaky hold on reality.

Claire checked her alcohol-induced cheer, sensing the Dominican had experienced something, well, deep. She reached out a hand, which Mári took. Claire drew her into a hug. Perhaps she wanted to caress the brown waves of Mári's hair as a gesture of comfort, but in the end, didn't do anything like that. They parted at the same moment. Looked into each other's eyes. And offered no phony smiles.

Back at the table, a fresh round of drinks arrived. Claire and Guga dove in, but a change had come over Mári. Tex noticed.

"Feelin' all right, *señorita?*"

"*Oh si, no es nada,*" she replied, but Mári's skin paled. She glanced away, barely able to conceal a wince. "*Con permiso,*" she excused herself to make the familiar waddle back to the ladies' room where she sank into a stall. A tremendous pain racked her abdomen. A sickening shift took place within her belly. Instinctively she knew what was happening but her mind would not allow the possibility. There was no way she could give birth on the ship. No way. She had to get to America. *America.* Like a migrating bird, this was something she had to do, without question. Visions of orange oranges and golden arches swam before her eyes.

Then she passed out.

CHAPTER 37

Luigi barely noticed the whirring hummingbirds sampling the exotic coral tree blooms as he single-mindedly headed for Hector's Juice Bar or, as it was formally known, *La Tienda de Jugo Fresco de Aca Hector* who, as it were, had insisted to backers that his name be prominently featured. Being a well-known personality around town (having no legs as a result of a dramatic dockside accident occasionally had its advantages), he felt his *nombre* would add a sense of familiarity, if not appeal, to the venture. However, the lengthy phrasing, which when translated became "The Shop of the Fresh Juice of Acapulco Hector" sometimes served, truth be told, to dissuade potential clientele, proving the adage that one should always convert one's intended product name into as many nearby languages as possible before deciding.

None of these considerations, which Hector had related in detail the night before, filtered through Luigi's one-track mind as he picked a center stool and scooted up to the bar. Hector, in a corner peeling pineapples, hopped onto his platform and lowered a calloused fist onto the countertop.

"*Lo mithmo?*" he rasped.

Luigi echoed *the same* in a grave, joyless tone.

"*Ey, come on,*" Hector rejoined, his gravelly voice pausing between whirs of the blender. "*It can't be all that bad, young guy like you got a job, a woman, bambino on the way—*"

"*It's the woman and the bambino part got me down.*"

Hector wisely dropped the subject and let it hang in the sticky air.

Fingers sizzling with nervous energy, Luigi drummed out a tune on the shiny blue countertop while he worked up the best way to ask The Question. After trying out a few convoluted versions in his head, he took the plunge and blurted out what'd been burning him up.

"How did you know that wasn't Mári?"

Hector knew the man's pride was on the line and intensified his juice-making preparations, exaggerating, for instance, the effort it took to open a can of milk.

"Yo no thei, thomething about her didn't theem right." The blender, possessed with perfect timing, roared to life. Both men stared at the frothy yellow swirl, unaware that the fruity cream united them, bridged a gap that otherwise would never have been bridged. Hector poured more roughly than ceremoniously, spilled not a drop, and set the tall, red plastic cup in front of Luigi, looking him straight in the eyes.

"Wanna know what I think?"

Luigi wasn't sure he did. But before he could take the first sip, a bold hummingbird buzzed in under the awning and hovered near the cup, facing him as if in a dare. The audacity of the tiny bird made Luigi laugh, and it uttered a quick trill before darting away. Swirling the cool nectar around his mouth, he recalled the vivid dream with Hector as co-star. Ok, he might as well hear it.

"Now I'm not thaying thith to betray my beautiful friend Mári, ith jutht that it doethn't make thenth," he cozied up to the bar, elbows propping him up, *"she not theeing you, thending her thithter in her plathe, ethpecially during a time of need and all…"* he trailed off without broaching an obvious sore point.

"Yesterday, the Mári-imposter said she still had the baby."

"Ahh, do you believe it?"

"I haven't seen Mári so I don't know what to think, except that they are trying to throw me off track."

"Know what?"

"Dime."

"I think your anther lieth in that big thip, the one that left yeth-terday." Hector paused to be sure Luigi wasn't going to slug him. The Italian's frown grew, but his eyes remained receptive. Hector would tell him what he knew about Mári's quest for a way to get to the United States. Not because he liked Luigi, but because he loved Mári.

After consuming the third *jugo* Luigi ordered a fourth. Feeling aimless, in a haze, he realized he'd stopped listening to Hector's blather shortly after the first bit of information. He meant no disrespect. It was just that for every ten helpful words the juice man threw in fifty useless ones.

"Know what elth I think?"

Luigi, sorely tempted to blurt something rude, grunted instead. Hector rubbed his sandpaper hands together.

"I think—yo creo," drawn out with unabashed glory, *"Mári did thith jutht tho you—"* he ground a stubby finger into the countertop, *"would go after her."*

"How can I go after her when I don't even know where she is?"

"Are all Italianth thith blathé? I told you where she ith."

Luigi offered up a defeated groan and hung his head in his hands. *"My wife would kill me if she knew I was having a baby with a Dominican dance girl."*

"And your mama, too, eh?"

Luigi passed on the urge to slug Hector. The fella did, after all, have a certain kind of kooky logic.

"Oh boy, here comth the proof you're looking for." Hector turned his attention to a new arrival. *"What'll it be, theñor?"*

"Watermelon juice, if you please," said the gentleman in white.

Hector leaned in toward the Italian, more than pleased to exercise a conspiratorial tone. *"Did you hear what he thaid? WATER melon. Ith that proof or what?"*

The two patrons nodded to one another with sidelong, superficial tips of the head. There was so much water under the bridge between them that neither man wanted to be the first to break the ice so they just sat there, feigning undue interest in the proceedings of watermelon dismemberment.

Luigi had to pee, but a force greater than urine kept the seat of his pants glued to the barstool. The presence beside him of this Queen Mary fellow made his eyes narrow in suspicion. Mári'd spent time with him. What was the *maricon's* name again?

"Theñor Fred, you juith."

On instinct, Luigi decided to engage. "You-a ship, she left town, no?"

"Yesterday morning," Fred said quietly, nodding in between sips of pink. He continued nodding, as if trying to come to grips with some very sad occasion that everyone should know about. "Headed for Long Beach. Who's ever heard of Long Beach?"

"California?" Luigi asked, old gripes forgotten.

"Near Los Angeles." Deep sigh. "How is your—how is Mári?"

Luigi noticed he brightened at her mention.

"Ees ok. When you see her last time?"

"Seems to me I was going to escort her right before the band stopped playing…ee gads, what a nightmare."

"Last time, Mári?" Luigi's hands finished the question.

"Right! Two days ago—Tuesday afternoon. Did something happen?"

"Tella me. Mári an djyou…interesting in subject similar, no? Da Queen Mary?"

"Indeed! She has a remarkable thirst for knowledge, especially for someone so unaccustomed to such things."

"Please! Easy de Engleesh!"

Fred slowed down, a good excuse for better elocution. "We both love the ship. I remember one of the last conversations we had—about the swimming pool. How she wanted to see that pool! Does she like very much to swim?"

"Mári? Swim-a?" Luigi wasn't sure what to say. "Have you picture, me see?"

"Why don't you follow me back to my office. Things are a mess, what with packing and all, but you can take a look at what I have. Sounds like you've been bit by the Queen Mary bugaboo."

Luigi hadn't a clue what being bit by a bugaboo meant, but he was fairly sure everything Fred said was true. While they finished their drinks he peppered the Brit about the basics, dimly aware of how seemingly useless information might come in handy. "So, how fast-a go da ship?"

CHAPTER 38

Wind whistled through the windows of Luigi's faded red sedan, lifting his jet black ringlets into a bumper crop of hydras that jousted with a mirrored pair of Ray Bans. In his mind danced images of the ship he was now certain held his girlfriend captive. Luigi pressed the old Mazda into service almost, but not quite, beyond its means. The rotary engine whinnied and frothed to provide its mount with a few good horses, achieving an anything but smooth 102 km/hour. Not bad for a rusty old beach car. He knew it put out way more than he put in and so couldn't be cross if a piston stuck or the exhaust backfired every now and then. This set of dynamics struck him as oddly similar to his association with Mári—he'd been skating for some time. Setting his teeth and gripping the thin, hard plastic steering wheel, Luigi resolved to toss a little extra of himself into the mix.

The rattling zephyr tore up the road, flinging pebbles in a staccato of flicks and pings, a plume of gray exhaust left to co-mingle with dust. Luigi wasn't exactly sure where he was going but he knew he was going right. Peering out at the shimmering water, watching pleasure boats set sail, his eyes targeted those headed the opposite way, for points north. He imagined the bouncing crafts cutting through the long-gone wake of the grand liner. And, in this imagining, Luigi knew he had to follow in that wake, somehow, some way, to reclaim his woman.

In this same state of focus, a crystal insight came to him in the form of a name. Roger. Followed by another name. Mills, Millet, Milton? No matter, he had it. Had the shape of a solution. And somewhere along the eighteen kilometers of coastal roadway he would find the solution itself.

All Luigi had to do was ask any one of the regulars whose lives unfolded in the open-air shacks that served *cerveza y ceviche, mariscos y mujeres.* Erected on the beach just far enough from the surf to stay dry, the rustic palm frond *palapas* reeked of fried goodies and Luigi, poking his head out the window for a better sniff, was sorely tempted to stop for a couple of tacos and a few questions about an eccentric American who ran a small float plane operation.

Luigi recalled the start-up days of work between his employer, an Italian power company, and its Mexican equivalent. In order to move technicians throughout the sprawling country, higher ups in Rome— those who governed from afar—courted romantic notions of the *Out of Africa* sort when they heard about an Aca-based pilot known as Rogero (Row-hair-o). This avenue ran into a brick wall as the mucky-mucks pronounced Rogero *completamente maniaco*, a huge relief to Luigi, who hated flying so much he didn't know if he'd ever make it back home as long as airplanes were involved.

Rumors in the bars ran something like this: Rogero had once been a bush pilot running supplies in Alaskan backcountry—bagged game, food stuffs, and building materials peppered with a load of ammo here and a pallet of liquor there. Rogero apparently felt no need to obtain licenses for the transport and sale of ammunition and alcohol, relying solely on the permission of the one entity he held in highest regard—himself. The government saw things differently. Acting on a tip from an aggrieved customer who ran a hunting outfit for tourists, Federal agents met Rogero's plane as it landed on some lake or another.

This was where the story diverged. Some of the more whiskered patrons at *La Pantera Rosa*, a little dive near the naval base at the southern end of Acapulco, insisted what happened next was an ambush that led to Rogero pumping the woods so full of buckshot that agents sought refuge behind the fattest pines until the renegade ran out of ammo (while taxiing) and took to the air, unscathed.

Others believed a tamer tale: on approach for landing, the intrepid pilot spotted a group of men arranged in a conspicuous semi-circle near the docking pier. When a large megaphone caught Roger's eye, he knew the suits were on to him. Most agreed ol' Rogero simply opened the throttle and kept on going. A few locals didn't end the tale there and loved to tell, with absolute faith in their words and their *Modelos*, how Rogero had the *cojones* to dip the wings in a final *up yours* as the little plane buzzed away, never to return.

Whatever the real story, Luigi knew beyond a doubt that if anyone could help him, this Rogero character could.

Hitting the straightaway near Icacos Naval Base with accelerator floored, he gave no thought to pushing the aged machine so hard; something else nagged him to slow down. The base provided a haven for businesses located around it, some of them off the road and hard to see. Bordellos and bars had multiplied given the built-in clientele and protection, of sorts. With the Mazda reduced to a crawl, Luigi craned his neck to the right to see if he could spot signs of float planes or a *gringo* business. Not a single clue jumped out at him, only the faded pink and orange sign of *La Pantera Rosa*, which he kept in mind as a last resort.

Beneath his distant gaze, the needle of the speedometer rose with each progression of the shift stick. The car picked up speed. This Roman relied on passion to fire up his world and sharpen his senses. There was always slow. Slow was for turtles and old men. Now was fast.

He did not prepare well enough for the abrupt bend ahead. Downshifting madly, the Mazda careened into the opposite lane, narrowly missing a motorcycle whose feeble horn bleated a desperate warning. A series of curves forced him to drive moderately until the open road near Observation Point, after which he slowed again in anticipation of the next landmark, a small, remote bay known for tame seas. *Puerto Marqués* had been one of Mári's favorites where she enjoyed the gentle lap of ankle-deep waves and a lack of competition from other female sunbathers. Luigi liked it because there weren't a ton of people to see him out with a local showgirl. After a while, less concerned about what others thought, he began taking her to more visible venues. He prided himself on outgrowing that odd reluctance, but maybe he hadn't grown out of anything at all. Maybe he'd just grown into a bigger jerk.

Luigi's self-immolating train of thought ended abruptly when a heart-stopping view of the docile bay seized him. Calm water. *Calm water!* Triumphant, he whacked the steering wheel so hard the top third broke off. The bottom two-thirds remained attached to the sturdy struts of the half moon horn. Once the surprise wore off, Luigi laughed, even fancied himself a pilot as he gripped the newly modified yoke and banked to the left, then to the right, complete with body English to mimic the tilt of a plane.

This had to be it. His eyes scanned every notable feature. He drove past the section of light brown beach Mári and he had enjoyed, past their favorite *palapa*, one of only two in this lesser developed part of Aca. Doubt began to take hold as the Mazda headed toward the rough waters of *Playa Revolcadero*. Unsure what to do next, something caught Luigi off guard as it darted in front of the windshield and hovered, its copper body ablaze with attitude. A hummingbird. Brakes slammed and the car slid to a sloppy stop. Luigi kept watch against outright attack from this highly maneuverable trickster, taking in its long, slender bill and coal fire eyes. It stared at him and looked downright mad.

Quick as it'd come, the daredevil gave one final buzz, squeaked, then zipped off down a dirt road leading to the water. Something told Luigi to follow, to witness the feisty acrobat soaring high up into the air and dive-bombing back down, eventually to disappear behind the tail of a much larger kindred soul.

Luigi swallowed hard and jammed the car to a stop. Out on the water, close to shore, bobbed the most beautiful little floatplane in the world.

The Mazda pulled off the washboard road and parked outside a canary-yellow structure with a pitched metal roof that appeared to do its job well. The rear of a white Ford pickup stuck out from behind the building and a couple of plump dogs lazed on the shiny landing, sun warming short fur and freckling pink tummies. They glanced up to assess the trick or treat potential. Deciding the odds for either were nil, they clacked their tongues and plopped heavy heads back down on concrete pillows, ending their command performance with adamant sighs.

The canine lethargy which had put Luigi at ease was suddenly disrupted by the appearance of a dart-like beak and intense buzzing that took up right in front of his face—the hummer was back with a vengeance! Luigi dashed inside, more afraid of the two-inch bird than the four-legged watchdogs.

Cooler air greeted him from the whirring ceiling fans. Luigi took stock of the gear for sale—rods, tackle, line, lures, floats—hanging limply on the walls above dusty dock bumpers, cast metal anchors, and red buoys. Swinging around to complete his survey, he encountered the most unexpected item on display—a very hefty white man ensconced behind a counter. He wore a powder blue *guallabera*—or rather, it wore him, its pleated cotton sagging at the breasts but stretched taut over a berm of belly. Luigi had no idea these staples of casual Latin men's wear came in that large a size.

"Ken I help yu?" clipped the man in a strong voice of upbeat English.

Luigi, confounded by the logistics of toting so much flesh around, answered simply, "Looking for da Roger."

"That's me," he drawled and placed pudgy hands squarely on the countertop, palms down, index fingers and thumbs forming an arrow with the tip pointing at the newcomer. Luigi heard a clunk on the Formica then noticed gold links biting into wrist flesh, a black dial divided into white circles with a triangle at the 12 and an outer notched bezel. A Rolex. Luigi instantly felt comforted by the wealth and precision clamped to the man's arm.

"I here because of bird, uh…uh—" Not knowing the name in English, the Italian flicked his finger to and fro then made beeline swooping motions to convey flight. He grinned awkwardly, no doubt feeling foolish.

Roger put him at ease. "Darned little things—pull pranks on me all the time. Finally figured out what kind they are—Rufous. Fly faster and farther than any other hummer it's said. Always with me for some reason, buzzin' in ma face at the worst possible moment. Why, just yesterday—"

"Pronks?" Luigi interrupted. "What is please?"

"Jokes—*bromas*. Anyhow, what kenna do you for?"

Luigi pointed in the direction of the unseen plane.

"Oh, so you're here to see Ethel, not me," he quipped to dead ears, Roger realized, when Luigi lamely bleated, "Etel?"

"The Beaver—airplane. I call her Ethel. It's a lousy story we'll skip fer now."

"Beevair?" Luigi repeated suspiciously.

"In some cases, a small, furry mammal with big front teeth. In this case, the finest bush plane ever built. De Havilland Beaver DHC dash 2 single engine high-wing monoplane," Roger spouted. If he was put out by the language barrier he didn't show it, just kept on going as if Luigi understood every damn word. "She ken take off 'n land just about anywhere, snow, water, top a yer head…"

"De top of my…? Ha ha, *bravissimo!* I get funny!"

Roger stiffly rotated out from behind the counter, enabling Luigi to fully gauge the man's girth. At his widest point he judged the man to be the equivalent of two soccer players standing side by side, as when guarding against a penalty kick. He could not fully hug this man in celebration of, say, a goal, if he tried. Would have better luck hugging a Cypress tree—at least he could compress the needles to his advantage.

They walked to the plane, feet crunching on gravel then clomping on a splintered, weather-beaten dock. The aircraft bobbed serenely like a pelican—a somewhat tattered pelican.

"Is too old?" Luigi asked, feeling certain it was ancient.

"Built in 1948—makes 'er 19 years young. Built ta last."

Luigi wasn't sure how Roger assessed age, but 19 sounded pretty old.

From afar it looked magnificent. But up close, dents the size of golf balls pocked the silver pontoons. Fistules of rust marred a faded, splotchy underbelly and the white upper half bared its metal skin in more places than Luigi could count. To top it off, the propeller was missing and the motor assembly in pieces. It looked every minute of those 19 years. Luigi wondered how many more, if any, could possibly be left.

As if reading his mind, Roger explained. "Salt water's been rough on her. Up north I used to work lakes—fresh water. But she's sea-worthy, air-worthy, too." Roger fiddled with a flap. "Want me ta take ya somewheres?" He peered at the visitor, emerald eyes narrowing.

This is it, Luigi gulped inwardly. "I want go to Queen Mary." There. He'd said it.

"'Scuse me?" Roger's eyebrows went vertical.

The Italian squirmed, moved in closer. "Queen Mary. Bigga boat? Me go."

"Ok ok, no need to get testy, we all have our fantasies about float planes."

"Me true! Uh, serious! Have money—how much?"

"Now hold on. What's yer—"

"Luigi."

"Luigi. We can't just head up the coast—"

"Whya not?"

"Well fer one thing we dunno where she is."

"I do." Luigi's mind reeled with numbers gleaned from his interview with Fred.

"Really. Hmm. Okee-dokee." Roger rubbed his hands together. "When would you want to leave?"

"Now."

"Whoa big fella, this adventure a yours is gonna cost some pretty pesos. Let's go inside, work out the details."

Though a mere few hundred feet of flat ground separated pier from building, Luigi noticed that Roger's two main activities—breathing and walking—were labored. He swung his arms furiously, as if urging unwilling legs forward by example. Despite a pleasant breeze, sweat broke out on his forehead and he paused every so often to mop up with a limp hanky pulled from the waist pocket of his *guallabera*.

"I'll catch up. The ol' knees—wired together. Korea."

Back inside, they resumed their positions at the counter.

"Ok, let's get down to the nitty gritty."

"Neety gre—"

Roger shook his head, leaned forward on bent arms and looked up slowly. He resembled a gigantic praying mantis.

"What time did she leave yesterday?"

"Who she?"

"The ship—all ships are she."

"Nine in de morning."

"Average speed?"

"I tink 21."

"Whaddya mean you tink?"

"Some part of 20 maybe."

"We'll use 20 knots—don't wanna overshoot." He rattled around in a drawer for a pencil and paper. "Ok, first things first. Nine to nine makes 24 hours—it's almost noon now, so we got 27 hours cruising at 20 knots per hour, that makes 540 nautical miles, or about 620 miles." Roger drew dark, thick doodles around the numbers. "Hmmm…"

"What eez it?"

"Got a maximum—and I mean flyin' on fumes kinda maximum—range of 800 miles. That puts us at Cabo, really pushin' it. Even if we left this minute, I'd have to refuel somewheres before making it ta your ship."

Keeping an arm firmly extended as counterweight, Roger fished noisily beneath the counter, sliding objects, making thumping noises. A dusty brown World Atlas emerged, and Roger flipped to a dog-eared page devoted to Mexico. "There."

Luigi struggled to identify the dot, looking hopeful. "Yes?"

"Puerto Vallarta. Just under 600 miles. We can do that." Roger rotated the book and slid it towards his visitor.

"*Andiamo!*"

"It's gonna cost this much—" Roger wrote a number down and underlined it three times. "Up front."

Luigi yanked a wad of pesos from his pocket. "We go now, yes?"

"Wish we could—soonest I can get her ready is 4am."

"Her?"

"The plane—also a she."

"I help."

"Well ok then, this should be fun," he muttered not quite under his breath.

CHAPTER 39

Thrashing her head from side to side didn't wake Mári, but the rousing burp that escaped her lips did. Chasing the sour taste away with clicks of a dry tongue, she came to enough to register a gray sky telescoped by dual portholes. This she could see, and it was real. She could also see that she was in bed, in B-410, and alone. Her hand went to the scene of so much uproar. Belly still taut, intact. A little kick signaled all was well. *Gracias Dios.*

From her supine vantage point, she took in the tidy cabin. One feature stood out as new—a bouquet of white carnations. In pursuit of their sweet scent, Mári put discomfort aside and rolled within arm's reach of the desk/table. Grateful for the company, she pressed her nose in and let her senses drown in the dense, moist petals. A card poked out of the arrangement. The first word startled her: Mary. Could this mean her? A short sentence followed, punctuated by the only other word she recognized: Tex. She plucked a blossom from the bunch and sniffed away, imagining what it would be like to live on this beautiful mother ship, travelling from port to port, crossing the oceans in luxury with food, friends and flowers. Sadly, she remembered their mission—life as they both knew it was about to change forever. Mári closed her eyes and took simple comfort in the flower. She'd always loved the white ones, creamy and delicious like ice cream made with sweetened condensed milk.

As it so happened, the thought of sweetened condensed milk drove her into the washroom where she accomplished a serviceable overhaul, enough to make herself presentable. A bit of sunlight was in order, along with whatever else she might find in the way of nourishment.

Mári climbed the steps to Promenade Deck and found "her" table duly stocked with an assortment of glazed, frosted, and powdered goods which found their way onto a hefty ivory-colored plate and in a manner well exceeding the reasonable border suggested by three thin blue lines near its edge. Feeling surprisingly light on her feet, she hauled her booty up to Sports Deck, the uppermost public reaches of the ship. The only things higher were the navigation bridge, captain's quarters, and funnels. At the top, she strolled from the rear of the ship to the front, pausing at faded hatch marks and boundary lines and wondering how, in the face of cold and wind, anyone would have wanted to hang out there, much less play games. In the shelter of the forward funnel, the one nearest the bridge, she dusted the crumbs off the plate and clutched it to her chest, not knowing where else to put it. A venture to the nearby port-side railing afforded an unobstructed view of the element bearing them aloft—an agitated, gray-blue body with white teeth chopping in random bites. Not at all friendly. Not something she'd want to get to know better.

Glancing back at the reassuring stature of the Mary, Mári relaxed, comforted by the liner's bulk and grace. Her mind's eye shifted to an image Fred had shown her—an aerial view during wartime, upper decks crammed with soldiers on their way to battle. No defense except speed and vigilance, something about the ship being a target with much money promised to the Nazi who could blast her to kingdom come.

Mári turned to regard the towering red-orange stack with its black collar, unable to picture it in jagged pieces on its way to the bottom of the sea. As she craned her neck to inspect the oversized twin whistles mounted near the top of the fore funnel, an announcement crackled through the PA system. Startled at first, the unhurried, matter-of-fact tone did not signal any danger, so the following words, spoken in melodious Queen's English, fell on enchanted and uncomprehending ears:

> "Your attention please. The ship's whistles are
> about to be blown for testing purposes. Will parents
> with small children on the open decks please take
> necessary precautions, as the children are liable
> to be affected by the noise."

After a pause, the speakers again crackled to life and issued another unintelligible notice in the same calm voice, but this time unease crept into her psyche. As a precaution, she positioned herself within sight of the bridge, hoping to glimpse anyone who might indicate an actual cause for concern.

> "May I have your attention please. This is your
> Officer of the Watch speaking. In one minute's
> time the ship's whistles will be sounded. This is
> for testing purposes and the first blast will be a
> time signal for 12 o'clock."

Increasingly anxious, Mári wondered whether they'd struck something—another ship, like the collision that had doomed *Andrea Doria* (such a pretty name) back in, when was it, the 1950s? Or maybe they had to change course to rescue a sinking ship, like *Ile de France* had done for *Doria's* passengers. Wrapping her arms tighter around the plate and her midsection, Mári's mind continued on its disaster path, replaying snippets from Fred's historical overtures. Was there a fire raging on board? Worse yet, what if they'd issued a "wanted" notice for her capture? All of these thoughts—and more—raced through her head, stoking her adrenaline.

Officer of the Watch, facing the rear bulkhead inside the wheelhouse, hooked a heavy black handset onto its cradle next to a bank of switches and phone-like instruments that formed the communication center of the ship. His hand hovered over the horn buttons which, at a mere touch, unleashed a deep bass A that would travel ten miles or more. Certainly one of the most thrilling parts of the job!

As all hands on all clocks throughout the ship slid onto the numeral 12, the first of three blasts ripped the air immediately above Mári. Loud and low, the sustained disturbance caused the muscles in her body to reverse course. Her right hand opened, the plate shattered. Knees buckled and back slumped as quads, hamstrings, and erector spinae relaxed their grip on the bones holding her upright. Mári crumbled to the deck. Internal cavities, gateways and organs pulsed with new purpose.

The Officer who'd sounded the whistles stepped out on the port docking wing to scan ship and seas, looking for anything untoward. As he turned counterclockwise to check aft, pieces of broken crockery glinted from the deck below. He would've gone back inside and rung a steward to clean up had he not also spotted a sandal with toes pointed to the heavens and strapped to a horizontal calf. He didn't wait to see more.

Dashing through the wheelhouse, he ordered a mate to dispatch Doctor to the front base of the fore funnel. "Right away!" he bellowed, taking the exterior stairs two at a time. When he reached Mári she was already sitting up, between labor spasms.

"Ma'am, we've got to get you down to the medical ward," the smooth-faced officer declared, kneeling gallantly on one knee.

She felt oddly calm. The charade, the dream, was over. Her child would come and they'd both be sent back like two undeliverable pieces of mail. She didn't know how it really could've been otherwise, how her offspring might've grown up with the benefits and opportunities of a citizen of the United States, but she knew it *could have* happened. *By some miracle.*

In the still clarity of revision, Mári looked up at a newly arrived silver-haired gentleman dressed in white. Bending to hook his arm through hers, she noticed three slender black bars sewn onto the shoulders of his uniform.

"*Gracias capitán,*" she gushed tearily, overwhelmed that the boss himself had come to her aid.

"*Pardon, but I'm a doctor.*"

"*I am fine,*" she assured in her native tongue, pleased beyond words the Queen Mary's *medico* spoke some Spanish.

"*I must examine you,*" he continued, dismissing Officer with a nod.

"*That is not necessary.*"

"*I would prefer—*"

"*Please, my husband will be wondering—I've been gone too long.*"

"*If that is your wish, but I insist on accompanying you.*"

Mári tried to shrug the doctor off at the door to B-410 but he wouldn't hear of it.

Using his pass key to open up, he escorted her into the diminutive cabin, got her seated on the near bed, and drew water from the bathroom pitcher. She reached for the glass just as something awful lurched inside, threatening to erupt. Willing her hand to stay steady and her face to convey pleasant gratitude, she took a sip. He patted her shoulder. *"I will return in a few hours to see how we are doing."* She thought it odd how he said *nosotros, we,* not knowing that it was a common linguistic habit to speak of *one* as *we* in Queen's English.

As Doctor's slender frame slipped out the door, a thundering series of jolts rolled Mári onto her side. Clutching beneath her belly, trying to squirm the pain away, a wail emerged from the depths of her being. She buried her face in the pillow.

"This is it! I am going to DIE!"

Another wave rocked her—eyes bugging, heart pounding so hard it nearly leapt from her chest. *"Sweet Jesus what did I do to deserve this?"* she panted, hiking up her skirt and flinging her panties. *"Madre mia!"* She struggled to be free of the awful pressure and stabbing pain by pushing, pushing, pushing down there. Sweat seeped from every pore. A variety of unpleasant smells wafted up from between her legs. Checking the progression with her hands, she felt like a blind woman groping for unseen features.

A slimy crown made itself known.

Straining, swearing, sweating, untold effort produced no further gain. Dangling her head upside down off the bed, she glanced back toward the sky beyond the open portholes and pushed with all her might, appealing to the heavens.

Let it come please Jesus let it come ok?

Desperation—or answered prayers—prompted her to action. She hobbled to the bathroom, crying, whimpering, cursing, cramming herself into the nook between the toilet and tub where she fiddled with four bath knobs. Once the right combination of turns produced a warm and salty flow she ditched the skirt and settled in, knees raised and spread, body submerged so that only her nose and eyes poked out like a cranky crocodile.

With the tub water deep as she dared, Mári scrunched forward to turn it off. As she did, the crown and everything else popped out—head, neck, shoulders, arms, hands, torso, hips, wee-wee, legs, feet. Mári stared at the closed eyes, puckered mouth and scant hair matted with blood and mucous. His color turned more blue. Racking her brain for any tidbit about birthing babies, she grabbed the boy's feet and bobbed him up and down with emphasis on the down. Fear gripped her—something was wrong. She wrapped one hand around both ankles, marshaled what was left of her strength and dangled him in the air, thwacking his bottom, upper back and back of head until the upside down periwinkle face contorted and let out a forceful cough which launched a flying clump of mucous. Baby then made use of his newfound breath by wailing at the top of his lungs. Mári laughed a relieved laugh, popped the drain plug out with her foot and watched the stained water swirl away. She thought about cutting the cord, knowing it was something that had to be done. It pulsed with life, looking altogether too energetic to sever. Perhaps it wouldn't hurt to wait a while longer. Separation would come soon enough.

Mári would've been surprised to see, as she dozed in exhaustion in the starfish-colored tub, the corners of her mouth upturn without any effort on her part. The worry frown that'd cleaved a deep vertical groove between her eyebrows smoothed into little more than a hairline fissure. A load had been lifted, delivered. Barely conscious, she yanked a towel from the rack and draped it over both of them, pulling the shower curtain closed for added warmth. The boy and Mári rested. She had done all she knew to do.

The rest would be up to fate.

CHAPTER 40

"When I said soonest I could get 'er ready's 4am, I meant *if we're lucky.*" Roger pinched his nostrils then threw his arms in the air, shrugging.

Luigi stared at the man, comprehending plenty of body language if not all the actual words.

"I stay anda help. We leave four in de morning."

"Whatever you say boss. By my reckoning Queen Mary'll be nearly 1,100 nautical miles out by 2pm tomorrow. We'd have to leave here no later than—wait a minute. We'll be losing daylight early, bein' December and all that," Roger rattled on, moving to the back room. Luigi flipped up the counter and followed, sensing an important logistical moment. His host moved among caved-in boxes and spare parts. A large window at the back looked out onto the water, and Ethel.

"Which means we better try an' shoot straight for Cabo, refuel, get a fix on the ship then go get 'er." Roger nodded his head in accord with his own sound logic and pursed his lips twice.

"Ees good?"

"Hell yeah! We'll have to run lean and mean. No extra weight." Roger cleared his throat. "Fuel tanks filled to the brim. Which reminds me, gotta go to the store. Here—"

Roger grunted from the effort of lugging a two-bladed metal propeller over to a work table. "While I'm out, file this down, nice 'n damn smooth, yes?" He pointed out the pits and divets, then Luigi felt the surfaces for himself.

"Salt chop—murder on the blades. Smoother you get 'em farther she'll fly."

"Soft-a like de ass of *bambino*," Luigi said in all seriousness.

"You got it. Back in a jiff."

✸

Luigi possessed the mindset of a man on a mission. Choosing not to be unsettled by the scattered bits he felt sure belonged on the plane, he filed, sanded, blew dust, caressed and closely inspected the worked areas, wiped hands on shorts, then filed and sanded a great deal more. All of the drama of the past months was reduced to a few simple motions that scoured away imperfections, corruptions. The scraping of one hard material against another restored integrity.

The meaning was not lost on Luigi. Plain and simple—he wanted his woman back. Though they seemed diamond hard when clashing, surely their union could produce something impeccable, no? Time would tell. Complications and other ties aside, he'd give it a good try but first he had to find her. The tantalizing vision of a solution—the bobbing Beaver—propelled him. He hoped, prayed, the old boat carrying her farther away with every passing minute would hold up. He remembered what'd happened to the Italian liner *Michelangelo* the previous year when, during an Atlantic crossing, the ship was pounded by 50-foot waves so forceful that cabins were ruined by the intrusion of seawater. At the time he hadn't given the news a whole lot of thought, but this knowledge presently hounded him like a rum hangover.

Mári is on such a ship, and Mári can't swim. File. Blow. Sand. Blow.

✸

Whistling when he banged through the door, Roger yelled, "Innkeeper, I'm home!" and plopped a stack of cardboard boxes on the customer counter. Except for the initial greeting he seemed oblivious to the presence of a relative stranger making a symphony of grating noises in the back room.

"Let's see—sardines, tuna, crackers, forks—check!" Roger barked, taking inventory of his recent purchases. "*Frijoles*, hmm, maybe not a good idea—" he paused to banish three cans of beans. "Cheese, yup. Knife, loaf a bread—*Pan Bimbo!*" (Any occasion to utter the Bimbo Bread brand was a joyous one.)

Luigi power-lifted his propeller and joined Roger in the main shop where he found the big man inspecting three lengths of *chorizo*. "We'll have to eat this sooner than later, *comprendé?*"

Reacting to the scowl on Luigi's face he quickly added in fluid Spanish, *"Don't worry, everything'll get done needs ta get done. Gotta take care of ourselves."* He gestured widely over the larder. *"Lemme see that prop. Um hmm, uh huh, yup, looks good. You can set it down in the back, we'll mount it to the crankshaft very nearly last,"* he said, preoccupied with re-packing certain of the provisions.

"Gotta ton a gas cans in the truck you can carry down to the plane. Five-gallon jugs, heavy suckers. We'll be fillin' the wing tanks once I've ser-viced the cylinders. She goes through about four a those an hour, thirsty girl! May have to make a few more runs to the Naval Base for fuel. God dahm, forgot how much work it is habla-ing Español," he switched mid-stream to his mother tongue. "Got an arrangement with the Colonel in charge over there, they like ta keep a few planes and a chopper at the ready." Roger closed the flaps on two cartons and slid them closer to the front door. "Here, take these, too…"

"Gas pump stopped working ages ago. Might think about gettin' that goin' now I'm back in bidness," he said almost to himself, drifting back into English so as not to burden his customer with too much information.

Luigi sensed Roger's loneliness and excitement. *"You speak Spanish very well…"*

"My wife was Puerto Rican. Died six years ago, left me with half-a-dozen Chihuahuas."

"What about the ones outside?"

"Them mutts? Just dogs in the sun, makin' 'emselves comfy wherever they are, pile a dirt, slab a concrete, makes no difference, they adjust. Yeah, I'd say we're all just tryin' ta get comfy on our own little slabs. Trouble is we don't do it near as well as they do."

Roger delved into the parts box—lube grease, grimy screws, thick bolts, colored wires, tense coils. *"Mira,"* he said, offering a suction pump as happily as he might have offered a sausage. *"Need ya ta pump water outta the floats. There's eight holes on the top of the skids—do one at a time. Easier said than done with all that bobbin'. Do yur best. More ya get out farther we fly."*

Luigi worked the pump to check its action.

"And speakin' a flyin', clear away those nests—hummingbirds been at it again. 'Preciate chya."

Luigi pumped the air a few more times. *This is sure to make them mad,* he thought unpleasantly, heading out to begin a grand tutorial of the ancient Beaver.

CHAPTER 41

Claire breezed into B-410 to check on Mári, kicking off sandals as she went. They landed next to a pair way too small to be Guga's. *That's strange, wonder where she is…* Momentary strangeness was replaced with the relief of unloading her camera gear onto the little desk, after which she plopped on the bed, musing over Captain's press conference which encouraged patience with the de-boarding process, the collection of luggage according to deck and cabin number, and with finding one's greeting party in the crush of humanity sure to be waiting on the quay. Claire did not look forward to the madhouse two days hence but she realized these were details common to all large passenger ships.

What was uncommon were all the other circumstances; for instance, the gallant silver-haired Captain who'd be out of a job when they tied up in Long Beach, along with the rest of his crew. RMS Queen Mary herself would be permanently retired as a sea-going vessel and, since that'd been her bread and butter for 31 years, also faced a very uncertain future. These harsh facts, along with the lingering—but lessening—heat, took the wind out of her sails. She ran a finger along her neck and winced at the stickiness. A shower was definitely in order. Claire began undressing in front of the portholes, chuckling at Guga's most recent favorite joke.

Q: Why are portholes round?

A: So the water doesn't hit you square in the face!

Traipsing into the bathroom while wrestling her hair into a ponytail, the partially parted shower curtain allowed her to inspect the shower head which she tilted down so the spray wouldn't hit high on the back wall, something she'd learned to do since sharing a bath with a tall Brazilian. A sudden awareness of thirst spun Claire to her left where she poured a drink from the wall-mounted pitcher—she adored these milk bottle-sized containers, so British. Maybe she'd install one in the bathroom of her Hollywood apartment—or kitchen, if she settled in long enough to warrant adding such a permanent fixture.

Quenched, Claire grasped the shower curtain and, sliding it to the right prior to stepping in, noticed a pair of unmoving legs. As if that weren't bad enough, rivulets of blood meandered toward the drain.

Sensing she was not alone, Mári let out a startled screech which woke the baby and set him to wailing. Claire bounced up and down as if she had to pee, ran out of the bathroom and back in again trying to get a grip.

"Are you ok?" she yelled in Spanish, plunking herself down on the toilet.

"*Creo qué si,*" Mári replied weakly, unable to muster the chuckle she'd intended.

"*Y el bebé?*" Claire asked, wiping vigorously.

"*Tambien, pero…*" Tears came as she picked up a bloody, membranous object and held it, a look of horror on her face. "*Es otro bambino no bueno?*"

Claire reassured her it was not a malformed infant but her baby's feeding sack. As the trio shuffled to the bed, two snappy raps at the door gave meager warning of its inward swing. Guga, not expecting the company of three disheveled, mostly naked beings, let out a shrill, "*Ay dios mio,*" before clamping a gaping mouth.

"*Qué pasó mi amorrrr?*"

Mári did look the sight. Messy hair, bloody legs, a ruddy newborn in her arms. Guga's eyes fixed on the prize. "*Pero qué gran ocasión!*" Tawny fingers shot out like divining rods toward the alert and large-headed infant who, as all could see, was able to hold up his noggin from the get go. "*Qué gran ocasión,*" Guga whispered, mesmerized through a film of tears with the repeated clenching and unclenching of baby's fresh digits.

"Help them get comfortable?" Claire nudged the Brazilian, remembering her camera. "This *gran ocasión* calls for pictures."

Switched into photographer mode, first priority were the close-ups. She reeled off shot after shot, snapping fingers, goo-gooing, fixing the boy's swathing towel, arranging Mári's hair, anything to coax them into symbiosis with the lens. Medium shots came next, a few with Guga by their side. No one thought to take a picture of Claire with them. Why would they?

"*Anda le pues! Let's cut the cord so he can be free!* Claire, I'll need hair ribbon and some big bobby pins."

Duly advised, she scraped together an assortment of clamps.

"Good," said the intrepid Brazilian, tying the last knot. "But I still need—" Guga pantomimed a cutting motion. Mári got the gist and pointed across the room. *"Mi bolsa."* Not shy rooting around inside another woman's purse, Guga dug deep, casting aside spare undergarments, mini-muffins and the like. Mári knew her secret would likely be blown at this point. She couldn't have cared less.

"Perfecto."

"Es perfecto, verdad," Mári peeped, fondly reconnecting with the Queen Mary pocket knife Fred had given her.

Rubbing alcohol was liberally applied to metal and skin alike. Claire and Mári preferred not to watch as the withered lifeline was cropped near the infant's belly. There seemed no ill effects and both women were grateful to have such a hands-on transsexual somatic shrink on their side.

"Now, what about a name?" Guga asked coyly, bouncing the tot and twirling the severed umbilical. The baby seemed taken with the cord, lunging and smiling and making cooing sounds. Guga kept the object just out of reach, noting with genuine interest that it was beginning to look like an electrical cord. Mári laughed at all this but Claire didn't appreciate the teasing.

"Not to worry, mi amor. First of all, he is amazingly alert. As such, he can learn from the very first day that not everything in life is easy. That, in fact, most things—"

"All right, we get the point. Let's think about something fun, like a name."

All eyes turned to Mári, even the little one's. She blushed and pulled the covers over her head, sensing the weight of a moment she wasn't ready for. Through a veil of linens she saw the outlines of the others hovering nearby. This odd view gave her a squirt of courage— amazing how with just a minor shift, things could appear so different. Raking through dead end thoughts and constipated whimsies that'd built up for months, she remembered The Name. She'd dared not place a proper *nombre* upon the creature while it inhabited her—Mári kept their relationship impersonal but somehow infused with love. Maybe not infused with love, maybe a mother's instinct. That could be called love, couldn't it?

The Name returned in a rush of confidence. Flinging the sheets back, she declared *"Let my son be called—"*

Two soft raps sounded at the door, interrupting the proclamation. A brandy-smooth voice identified Doctor who'd seen a certain young lady a few hours prior. He wished to check on her spirits and health, both of which had appeared rather down.

"Is the young lady present, and may I come in?"

Mári quickly asked her adult companions to go into the bathroom and take baby with them. *"Shut the door,"* she whispered hoarsely. *"I'll explain later."*

Doctor had taken the liberty to open the door a crack. Mári reapplied sheets to chin and raised her knees so that her reduced bulk would not be evident.

"Hola señora, how are we feeling?"

"Good, tank you."

"You look somewhat better."

"Yes, me good. Mucho good," she insisted through clenched teeth.

"I'm not at all certain about that." Taking advantage of her exposed face, he thoughtfully placed the back of his hand on her cheek then slid it down to her neck to gauge temperature and pulse. "Should you experience any discomfort, please ring my surgery through the ship's operator and I will come at once."

The melodic tones of his voice calmed her and, better yet, the man did not seem suspicious. That was all she could ask for at the moment.

✵

Many of the personnel on board, like the ship herself, were ending their careers at sea, their somewhat advanced years and trim gray experience apt final escorts for the Grand Dame of the Atlantic. Doctor was a case in point. Having served on board a host of liners he would, in two day's time, fly off to England to join his wife for a life of gardening and countless strolls through Holland Park to feed un-wild and overweight birds. Perhaps this new life would suit him. Perhaps it would not. He would find out soon enough.

Personal thoughts such as these broke through his professional veneer more frequently, mildly alarming the physician whose mind for decades had mostly swirled with medical details and symptomatic clues. He was, he could only conclude, going soft in the head.

Doctor eased his posterior into his wooden desk chair by placing all of his weight on sinewy arms and lowering himself smoothly into place. He only performed this juvenile maneuver when completely alone. Settling in, he contemplated the details of his visits with the diminutive Latin lady. In this department he concluded, again, he'd gone soft in the head.

That she was soon to give birth, no doubt. That she was stretching the truth about her room arrangements, little doubt. All he had to do was check with Purser to see where she rightfully belonged, and instincts told him it would not be a pretty picture for Señora Mári. But the good Doctor had no need to pry. It was better for all concerned if he knew nothing. The less he knew, the less he would be mandated to report. The young lady had influential friends. Miss Claire would be publishing articles—maybe even a book—about the Queen's final voyage. Why create a scene now? Perhaps she had pulled the wool over the journalist's eyes, but she had also apparently gained the woman's trust. And he was aware that Miss Claire was fast friends with Mr. Tex, the wealthiest man on board.

Doctor pressed himself up and out of the chair to take slow, pacing turns in front of a porthole. They were 48 hours from their destination—why should he be the whistle blower? A force inside him toed the line against company protocol that required he turn the matter over to higher-ups. *What was it?* He stared out at navy blue waters dressed in crisp white top hats. An entire world thrived beneath the surface even though he couldn't see it. Didn't mean it wasn't there. The magnitude of what lie beneath stunned him into humble realization. It was the same with the little Latin woman. Her courageousness inspired him. Yes. Kindness over protocol would prevail!

An idea came. His stomach flipped and a brief shiver infused his brain, as if squeezed. These physical reactions confirmed the germ of an idea, something to do with betting pools, finished with engines, gaining sympathy, and funds for a mother and child whose futures were anything but set. He would need to see Purser once he had it all worked out. This was most unlike him, getting involved. Still, the juiciness lingered.

First things first.

Doctor stood outside B-410 wondering what to do. Something felt terribly askew, emboldening him to open the door a crack and pop his head in. About to ask whether he could have another moment with the patient as it was his sworn duty to safeguard against medical calamity by conducting a proper examination, he never got a word out. The scene had changed considerably from the time before. The journalist lady sat on the bed next to Mári while a tall Brazilian woman (whom he of course remembered from the scandal) cradled a newborn.

"So you did have the baby!" Doctor blurted, revealing his presence most inelegantly.

"No, no! Ees not my bebé!"

All eyes turned to Mári.

"Ees not my bebé!" she gulped, emotions firing with unstoppable clarity. "Ees for her!"

No one knew what to do, or exactly what she meant.

Mári regained some composure. "Es for her de bebé." She jabbed a finger almost accusingly at Claire, who was too intrigued to deny the statement.

Guga drew the subject property close, hurt not to have been chosen.

"Entiendo. But please." Doctor knelt by the bedside and gently pried a white-knuckled hand away from the sheet. *"It's very important I examine you and, eh hem, whom so ever's baby this is, si?"* He ducked into the loo for a scrub.

Mári's eyes softened. She allowed him to draw down the covers.

"Would you please give us a few moments of privacy?" he asked the others, who duly re-stuffed themselves in the bathroom.

Positioning himself at the foot of the bed, Doctor placed a warm hand on each of Mári's knees and pried her legs apart enough to remove a soiled wash cloth wedged up in there. During the course of the exam which, by necessity, required he place his face somewhat close to the area being inspected, Mári involuntarily clamped his head a few times, requiring him to patiently re-set their respective positions. She finally relaxed enough to let him do his job.

"You have a small tear," he stated, producing a needle and suture from his black bag.

"Ay ay ayy! Por qué este?" The evil looking implements made her slam her legs shut. *"No no, nunca vas…"* she rambled on as the Brazilian peeked out, babe in arms, to see what was happening.

"Please tell her the region is already quite numb and she won't feel much, if any, pain."

"Easy for you to say," Guga whispered before translating the good news.

The battle of keeping legs spread resumed. "Can one of you ladies please lend a hand?"

Guga handed the baby to Claire.

"Keep her knees apart while I swab the region with antiseptic. We'll have to do a bit of a shave, too."

The entire procedure, during which it is unlikely the likeable Doctor got Mári to crack any kind of a smile, took under ten minutes, including a thorough inspection of the withered placenta to be sure no bits remained inside.

This was the first time Claire held the baby in her arms. She tip-toed around the cabin then parked next to a porthole, admiring the oceanic vista while bouncing her frisky bundle in tune to the rhythm of the waves.

The infant seemed delighted by the swirl of colors kaleidoscoping from the polka dots on her blouse, if clutching and gumming to the maximum possible extent were any indication. Claire felt a strength of body and spirit within the child, a force of will emanating from his compact form, coffee brown eyes, crooked smile, elfin hands, thumping feet, and yes, bowling ball head. How was this possible? All of these features conspired to create a connection, one that Claire found hard to ignore. Was it possible this brand-new being had melted her heart, and she his?

"One other interesting bit, just a side note, mind you," Doc said as he wiped his hands with a towel. "While inspecting the placenta, I found evidence of a twin. Can't be sure, just a hunch. Heaven knows what happened. Nature must have eliminated the other early on."

"Must have," Claire echoed, distracted. Had Mári really meant to give the boy up? All present had witnessed her act of disownment. What was going on? Doctor, for his part, persuaded the brand new mother this was her child to care for. With input from Guga, he explained a certain type of sadness and other reasons why she might not feel motherly toward the wriggling mass of flesh and bone. Mári listened quietly.

"Perhaps you two ladies can take some time alone to sort out anything that might, well, need sorting out," Doctor said for Claire's benefit, urging Guga into the hallway with him.

"This is really quite something," Guga breathed in a soft voice.

"Indeed."

"I was thinking of asking Claire to marry me."

Doctor's eyes opened wide, barely concealing amazement.

"Oh, didn't you know?" he feigned innocence. "I'm a man. Still have the parts, but don't like to use them—it—particularly."

"I see. You're a transexsyul," Doc pronounced in a most clinically British manner.

"I consider myself a *gran sexual!* Anyhow, I was going to see if Claire would marry me so I could live in the United States."

"Of course," Doctor agreed, preferring to leave well enough alone.

"There's this operation I've heard of that re-arranges—"

"So I've heard, ground-breaking stuff."

Guga was impressed. "You think it's ok?"

"My dear sir—madame, what you are called to do you are called to do. Medically, it is viable."

"Don't have much money and it's not proper where I come from in Brazee-ou to ask for a lady's hand with few resources, but it could work!"

"I see what you mean." Doctor nodded his head, preoccupied. "Say, would you care to join me in a stroll? I have an idea I'd like to propose to Purser that could be financially rewarding for the new mother."

"We don't exactly see eye to eye," Guga replied, eyebrows askance.

Taking the medical man into confidence, Guga shared the highlights of her renegade presence aboard ship, how it intertwined with Claire and the Dominican. By the time they'd wandered all the way up to Boat Deck, strolling arm in arm in fine fashion, Doc began to wonder how many other law-breakers had made the trip without being caught. It was a tad embarrassing.

With the Purser route and betting proceeds momentarily out of the question, Doctor prospected his thoughts for nuggets that might lead to a simpler approach. While the unlikely couple stood gazing at the roiled ribbon of wake, Master at Arms prowled self-importantly on the poop deck below, making sweeps of the double-decker buses. Wearing a look of forced casualness, his puffed-up frame soon disappeared from view.

"Yes! That's it!" Doctor slapped the railing in triumph. "Here's what we're going to do!"

Part Three

Driving Forces

If you believe in a principle,
never damage it with a poor expression.
You must go the whole way.
—Charles Parsons

THE COMING OF dusk found Roger far enough along to do a pre-flight inspection. Tools littered the dock; all nine cylinders had been serviced, the prop mounted, cowling sections re-assembled, oil changed, battery topped off, charged and tested. Luigi watched in awe from the bobbing platform as the big man contorted his bulbous upper half just far enough into the cockpit to remove the control lock and turn on the master switch. Gauges sprang to life. He motioned Luigi to the far side of the plane to drain the wing fuel sumps. The Italian nervously hopped from one skid to the other where, from his slippery perch, he did his bit. Next, Roger inspected the flaps, looking for anything out of the ordinary. Luigi did the same on his side, not that he would know out of the ordinary if he saw it. At the tail, the elevator moved smoothly up and down in Roger's hands, boosting the Italian's confidence in the weathered craft.

"Look at the safety bolts on that side, would jya?" Roger called, pointing at his peepers with V-shaped fingers then swinging the V around toward the bolt heads.

"Ok, gotta double check the oil before we start 'er, it's on yer side in the cabin near the floor." When Roger hefted himself onto the float nearest the dock the plane tilted and dipped forward, nearly tossing an unsuspecting Luigi into the drink. A wing strut prevented the dunking, and a few choice expletives made him feel slightly better.

"Music to my good ear! Beautiful language yours, even got the gist of summa them words!" Roger pointed to an area near the would-be passenger's left foot. "See that red top? Open it and pull the dipstick."

The long, slender indicator registered low.

"Shit." The engine still needed oil and Roger didn't have any on hand to top it off. "Too good to be true," he mumbled, preparing to execute his acrobatic maneuver off the plane and onto the dock. "Was hopin' we'd get outta Dodge with time ta spare," he grunted, gingerly hoisting himself off the float. Mumbling all the way, Roger gathered an armload of spare parts and waddled back inside.

Thinking he should play follow the leader to lend a hand, Luigi's helping spirit was hi-jacked by the twilight magic show emerging on the western horizon, its sky full of mutating gold, red, and turquoise ribbons. To the east, the occasional man-made silhouette (such as the chapel cross atop *Las Brisas*) punctuated the undulations of darkened hills. But it was the twinkling cadence of watery lights that made his heart bang out a few extra beats.

Acapulco's crescent shore pulsed with energy. He observed the greatest concentration along the beach fronts and his eyes followed the phosphorescent trail all the way north to the far-side of town. Luigi wondered if the waters surrounding Queen Mary looked like this and if they did he hoped Mári saw them. The beauty arrested him. In those moments he made peace with his present and nearest future. He embraced *the rescue* even though he so awfully hated to fly and had no idea what the outcome would be after trying so hard. More than anything, it was the lights—in the water and the ones twinkling in the city—that inspired Luigi to commitment. How could he not be reminded of his hero, Nikola Tesla, who'd harnessed invisible atoms and delivered them to the service of mankind in the form of alternating current, long distance power transmission, and radio communications. If Tesla could accomplish all this, surely he could fly in a speck of an ancient airplane with an oversized human piloting his destiny.

CHAPTER 43

"Jesus Cristo? You want to name him Jesus Christ?" Claire pointed to the innocent in her lap.

"No exactamente," Mári corrected. *"Cruz. Jesus Cruz, no Cristo. Es perfecto, si?"*

Claire's mind drummed up a quintet of reasons why *not* to name the boy after the Christian savior but what could she say other than, *"Bueno, of course, it's your choice."* She lifted the tot toward Mári who pushed him back, shaking her head.

"Mi niño es para ti," Mári said, a faraway look in her eyes.

"My son is for you," Claire repeated. *Ok, she's not giving up on this.* Then another thought. *Does she mean this metaphorically?*

"He needs you more than he needs me." Mári's eyes cleared.

Again, Claire couldn't believe her ears! Part of her resented such boldness, wanted to spurn such outrageousness, hand the child over and storm out of her own cabin. But that's not what happened. They both stared at the infant. Something about the little guy made every unruly notion under the sun feel right, or at least workable.

What was it historian Henry Adams had said? "Chaos often breeds life, when order breeds habit."

Unbidden, his nickname popped into Claire's head. Seaborne, with an "e" in a nod to the Brits. She smiled and kept the secret to herself.

CHAPTER 44

In search of oil, Roger maneuvered himself into the driver's seat of his pickup. Luigi hopped in, expressing his most pressing need: flowers. He'd come to the conclusion that he should arrive with an armful to woo his beloved.

Roger grunted, grinding the tall, thin shift stick into reverse. "Fer all we know she's spent the entire voyage in the brig. Flowers ain't gonna sweeten that my friend."

"What is dis 'brig'?" Luigi asked suspiciously.

"Jail. Prison. Behind bars."

"No. Mári is-a ok. Free," he reassured himself. "I need da—"

The sentence was interrupted by frantic downshifting and a sudden, skidding, sharp left turn into the dimly lit entrance of the *Base Naval de Icacos*.

"First things first, then we'll worry about chyer gol dern flowers."

Roger handed a business card to the guard. *"Quiero ver el Comandante. Soy Rogero. Es sobre un avion."*

The gates opened and so began the task of tracking down the Commander via telephone because it was late and the man was long gone. Once Roger assured the officer he wouldn't face repercussions for disturbing his boss after hours, the big man cashed in on the times his mechanical services had been rendered promptly, and got the ok for the favor of some oil. Luigi and a spare guard made quick work of hand pumping the lubricant out of a 55-gallon drum and into smaller containers.

"Not much time," Roger shook his head. "Not much time at all. Haven't even started the damn engine yet." The rumbling of the washboard road drowned him out.

Luigi said nothing. Maybe he could buy flowers on board the ship, that way they might have a fighting chance of actually getting there without inviting a jinx.

"Jesus H. Criminee," Roger moaned. "Who am I kidding," he seethed while backing the pickup alongside the dock.

Again, the acrobatics fell to Luigi as he balanced on a narrow float while tipping a bulky container into just the right spot without spilling it all over. Roger kept a flashlight trained on the work area.

"Say, how much money you got?" He didn't wait for a reply. "'Cause I'm thinking we could rent another plane. Faster one," he huffed, passing Luigi the last jug. "If that ship a yours really been steamin' at 21 knots, we just might be entirely skee-rewed." Roger looked out at the quarter moon rising, quiet for a moment. "But if the old boat is doin' anything less, we're in luck."

"Luck-a!" Luigi yelled, recognizing a word at last.

Roger patted the Beaver's fuselage and wedged his girth into the cockpit as Luigi held the plane fast to the dock. Switches got flipped, instrument panel lit up, dim displays got tapped, fuel mixture set. Electronics hummed, wing lights flashed. Roger took a deep breath then bellowed, "Clear!" out the mini window in his door. The engine sputtered, the prop cranked a few times, then died. Wispy smoke seeped from the cowling.

"Crapola. Let's try again, Ethel, give it yer best shot. I need all 450 of yer horses, pronto."

Sputter, *crap*, whine, grind, half spin, hesitate, full spin, sputter, smoke, catch, gunning noise, deafening, blades whirring, feather back mixture, ease in choke, idle settling into nice rhythm, still roaring, uncanny vibration.

"Good enough fer government work!" Roger beamed from the cockpit, double checking knobs, levers, and indicators.

"We go now?" Luigi yelled.

The engine shut down. "Not yet—got some adjustments to make, and we better take a quick nap before we load 'er up."

Luigi stretched out on a metal cot in the corner of the back room, arms behind his head, finding it impossible to sleep. Until recently he'd held romantic notions of seaplanes as objects of majesty and grace, thanks to early news reels extolling the virtues of Pan Am Clippers. They were, after all, among the first passenger planes to span the oceans, audacious flying boats that bridged the Atlantic and Pacific as early as the 1930s. The de Havilland Beaver sloshing around in Acapulco Bay on that December night did not in any way resemble the grand vessels of yore. It looked like a little old airplane missing proper landing gear. He could not reconcile the fact that, if fate would have it, he'd soon be thundering along in that very machine.

Contrary to expectations, Luigi dozed. When he awoke, the loud creaking of his cot did not disturb the slumber of Roger, who snored softly in a crackled recliner.

Luigi ducked out for a breath of air as the back room had become stale and warm, smelling vaguely of fart. Scooping water into his mouth from an outside spigot and brushing his teeth with a finger, Luigi caught sight of the Beaver. Trepidation mounted. Not even re-casting Ethel as a mystical dragonfly bearing him to unseen adventure soothed his nerves. He watched the stream of rinse water squirt from his mouth and undid his fly, initiating a stream midships while snuggling decorously against a cinderblock wall.

Luigi was not quite through stowing his personal cargo when the big man came out, laboring with some of the trip's provisions. Tucking himself in quickly, he rushed over to help.

"There's more inside the door, next to the *bathroom*."

The Italian stood on the dark dock, mooring rope in hand, while Roger stuffed himself in, checked a few things, looked out the window and barked, *"Clear!"* Ethel fired right up, straining at her lines and forcing Luigi to muscle her close. He would not let his port of embarkation get away!

Luigi had never been inside the spartan plane with its engine running. A deep reverberation underscored the pop of nine cylinders firing at the lower rpms, drowning out all thoughts. Rattling surfaces and a cocooning tightness unsettled his empty stomach. Exhaust fumes made him light headed. He was fighting forces he knew he might not beat, and to make matters worse, the arrangement of the windshield over the fat, stubby nose made it hard to see directly in front.

When Roger leaned in and yelled over the crushing noise to fasten seatbelts, fumes of old coffee and decaying dental work harmonized with the other unpleasant smells, a condition soon forgotten once the amphibious vessel began to move. Luigi was temporarily comforted by the notion of *boat*, because nothing about the experience thus far resembled that of a dreaded airplane.

Pulling away from the dock, the vessel bumped slowly along light chop. "All good!" Roger bellowed after checking flaps, elevators, rudder, fuel, oil. He pulled and twisted a lever to close the cowl flaps which, when open at slow speeds, circulated air through the engine. Then, somehow in the darkness, he sighted his best angle of attack for takeoff and opened the throttle.

"Blast off!" Roger shouted, unconcerned with the fragile state of mind of his one and only paying passenger. Luigi felt like throwing up and they weren't even airborne. The little plane labored through the water, struggling much too hard, it seemed, to gain speed. The racket, the jostling side to side, up and down, reached a peak then unexpectedly smoothed out when the right mix of velocity and lift was achieved. Old Ethel took to the air.

"Short take off 'n landing—gotta love it!"

Rigid in his seat, Luigi was so nervous he didn't register the comment. Nor could he bring himself to look at the twinkling, shrinking view of Acapulco on his right. Instead, he fixated on a flickering guage light that Roger tapped every now and then.

Despite deafening noise—which eliminated most chit chat—and nerve-tingling vibration, Luigi dared to sit back. Still, he was by no means out of the woods, for the higher the plane climbed the more his stomach wrenched itself into a knot. He hated heights. This had proved a major challenge throughout his career since many electrical jobs required high wire work. He'd learned to cope by never looking down, thereby denying the existence of a gaping void between him and the ground.

"Hows about grabbing me the jerky from in back?"

"Da what?"

"Jerky—long pieces o' dried meat? You shud try it." Roger held his hands about six inches apart and made gnashing movements with his teeth.

Luigi was not in the mood to get out of his seat and go fishing for food, especially in the dark, but he did as he was asked. Settling back in, he tried not to notice that Roger, besides making minute adjustments to the throttle, fuel mixture, nose pitch, and steering yoke, also noisily chowed fistfuls of the brown dung-looking stuff. Glancing over, thinking he might try some to take his mind off of everything, he caught sight of Roger's canines tearing into a leathery piece of old cow and the nausea rose. To calm himself he concentrated on Mári and formulated a picture of where she might be, what she might be doing, and who she might be with at that very moment on board a liner named Mary.

CHAPTER 45

Doc and Guga snooped outside the partially open door of Police and Fire Headquarters, a small office which housed the files, fodder, and occasional folly of Chief Master at Arms and his deputies.

"Still can't believe we haven't found her," one deputy bemoaned.

"Waist high to my knees she is and no sign of her," said another.

"The waif must have inside help," their boss said disgustedly, sucking loudly on a frayed toothpick.

"Hello Chief!" Doctor chimed in his best Cary Grant voice, popping in. "How's the search for the stowaway coming?"

"In between monitoring fire stations and doing the required tests with a short crew, we haven't had the usual resources to devote to a search." Chief remained perched on the edge of his desk while the deputies begged off.

"If I may be so bold, perhaps in some sectors the, er, will is lacking?" Doc hinted.

"Hardly."

"Well, I've found her," Guga peeked in.

"What are *you* doing out?" Chief stood, hiked up his pants, and tugged on the hem of his jacket.

Guga's lips pursed and eyelashes batted in Marilyn Monroe fashion. "First, the reward money."

"Reward? What are you talking about?"

"I happen to know how these things work." Guga winked at Doc.

Chief stared at the two. "Inside job indeed," he grumbled, thrusting a hand into a narrow desk drawer. "Never thought of you on the take, Doc."

"Come on, let's go get your stowaway," the *medico* invited, trying hard to let the slight roll off his back.

Guga led the way while counting out seventy dollars worth of pound notes. "Don't worry, Chief," the Brazilian added flirtatiously, "this can be our little secret."

"Yes, well, my reputation is at stake. I already let *you* go," he fumed.

Wrapping thrice on the cabin door, Guga quickly stepped aside. "All yours!"

Chief swung open the door. As he crossed the threshold to confront Mári a flashbulb went off, stopping him in his tracks. From the bathroom doorway, Claire documented the moment while Tex stood by, bouncing the infant in his tree trunk arms.

"Pictures of the raid! Whaddya think the headlines will read, Claire?"

"'Heartless Shipping Line Arrests Stowaway Mum Seeking Better Life,'" she whispered distractedly, firing off shots as frequently as the flash permitted.

"Doc, you can now add blackmail to your ever-expanding list of qualifications," Chief said almost good-naturedly. "If you accept, Miss Claire, I also place this woman in your custody. Please see to it that she does not leave the cabin—for long."

He spied the infant. "Good looking chap," he said, shaking his head. "I take it *everyone's* debarkation papers are in order?"

"Qwat so," Tex bluffed in a poor imitation of an English accent.

✺

Nobody, it seemed, was overly awed by the fact that an infant had been born in a salt water tub, on a ship, by a woman who could not tell time and who, for whatever good reasons known only to her, had bequeathed her firstborn to a complete stranger.

No one except me.

And, it turns out, Claire.

✺

Later that Thursday afternoon and deep into the evening, Claire kept busy interviewing and photographing all manner of crew—from laundry workers and kitchen help to cabin stewards and electricians. Most, she discovered, would be going on to their respective jobs aboard other ships. Others, such as Lez Devine, a smooth-witted Brit from Bournemouth who, in his spare time, devoured American Jazz, would be taking land jobs. In the engineering department, Lez's duties involved replacing burned out bulbs (thousands of them) and greasing lifts. And while he was not particularly going to miss the messy, claustrophobic elevator-servicing, insane hours, or heat and noise in the engineer's workshop on E Deck (directly above the aft turbo generator room), he was going to miss the comraderie and good spirit of the Mary.

"She's a happy ship," Lez said in an interview with Claire, his tone serious, as if the mind's knowledge of this, her final voyage, had finally caught up with his heart. "A beautiful, beautiful ship." Then he shrugged off his solemn tone, mischievous blue eyes twinkling. "Do you know I'm the only person who's ever ridden a motorbike—a Norton—up the aft gangway, through the working alleyway and back down the fore' gangway?"

Claire declared that she did not know that, amused at how people opened up when offered the chance to share their experiences.

"Some of the crew bet me—they lost a few quid on that one. 'Course, I got quite a talking to by the Captain—Captain Marr. Still, I could see him trying not to smile…"

The ocean-going end figured so near for the proud vessel and its human lifeblood that Claire many times during that busy Thursday found herself wishing she could hole up in an empty cabin, a gaggle of rum punches within arm's reach, and just cry her eyes out. Instead, she slouched back in her chair in the Pig 'N Whistle staff cafeteria, stowed her stack of work notes, and slow-sipped a beer. The emotion of others' goodbyes along with her questionable status as a single mom made her wonder if she could withstand the unending stresses. This ship had withstood the ups and downs of 31 years. Born out of the Great Depression, survivor of World War II, she'd safely conveyed countless souls within her spirited frame. Surely, in her own human frame, Claire could accomplish a modicum of something wondrous. The dignified RMS Queen Mary and those who cared for their floating township would serve as an inspiration for the rest of her days.

This determination energized Claire. She knew she could face each challenge, one at a time, without becoming overwhelmed. Like the ship, she'd ride the troughs and the crests while maintaining poise and presence.

What a loada crap—who am I kidding?

If this was what'd come her way would it fly in the face of destiny to resist simply because it was inconvenient? Was she capable of allowing herself to slip into something less comfortable?

For the past decade and a half, Claire had relished the life of an independent woman free to pursue photojournalism, travel, art, and any romantic ties she chose. She'd lived fully, messily, successfully. The overriding question, nicely framed by this last assignment of a ship at a crossroads, was *now what?* She had no real ties; the east coast relatives rarely bothered with her except for the occasional holiday phone call or greeting card. Living situation consisted of month-to-months in Philly, Savannah, Miami, or wherever the work wind blew. Most recently she'd hung her hat in a studio apartment around the corner from Grauman's Chinese Theater on a side street bookended by the Hollywood Roosevelt Hotel and the Magic Castle.

She had it all—a solid career with her photos and stories carrying enough momentum to finance two passions: painting and Caribbean art. And yet, despite her accomplishments and varied interests she still felt a rush as fresh brush strokes showed up in bold, primary colors on a bare stretch of her life's canvas.

Re-invigorated, Claire rushed back to check on her brood. Inside B-410, Tex's broad back eclipsed the doorway. She put a hand on his shoulder—as far up as she could reach. "How's everyone doing?"

"Sleepin'."

"Where's Guga?"

"He's—she's—there. Baby's on his—her—lap. Mama's conked. How 'r you?" Tex sighed, blue eyes fixed on hers.

"Excited, scared witless!"

"You've given this plenty a thought, right?" He drew out the *right* so it sounded like *raaat.*

"Hell no."

"Lemme hep you out." Tex gently hooked his arm through hers and led her for a stroll. "You can't make chicken soup outta chicken shit."

"You're lucky I didn't take that the wrong way!"

"What I mean is ya don't have ta do this."

"I know. I think I want to."

"Ok then. On the upside, ever' so often they make you weep with joy. Then they grow up and leave the nest, most times, and usually still on speaking terms, though sometimes just barely."

"That's the upside?"

"Downside? Havin' a kid's like wipin' yur ass with a hula hoop— it just never ends."

"Speaking from experience?"

"Yes ma'am. And I got another piece a Lone Star wisdom fer ya."

"What's that?"

"Don't ever let an alligator mouth overload a hummingbird ass. Neither one of 'em—the boy or the—Guga. Think on that a while."

They reached the open Sun Deck where the combined glow of ship lights and quarter moon cast fuzzy shadows of life boats and davits onto worn teak planks. Tex traced one of these phantom shapes with a Hush-Puppy toe.

Claire broke the ice. "I never did ask. What brought you on this grand voyage?"

"Wife and I used to take this very ship over ta Europe once, twice a year most years. She was about yer size. Beautiful. Mother of our two children, boy an' a girl. You remind me of the woman she coulda—maybe even shoulda—been, but she married me instead. Independent, feisty, stood up for her beliefs. Eight months ago doctors found cancer in the pancreas. Not a blessed thing they could do. Two months later she was gone." He turned to face the seamless ocean.

"This is ma first—and last—trip on the ol' QM without her."

Both stared out at the Pacific and watched flickering clusters of Mexico's coastal towns recede in the luminous wake.

"But enough a this sober stuff, let's go shopping!" Tex took Claire's hand and examined it. "Yup, 'bout right. I gotta buy a ring for a lady friend who," he leaned in slyly, "is right 'bout yur size. *Vamonos!*"

"You think the shops are open this late?"

"Ain't but one way ta find out," Tex drawled, and on to Piccadilly Circus they went.

After being a ring model for Tex, Claire ducked into the Observation Bar for some serious refreshment. Her cabin was off-limits, as it now contained many of the people who might drastically alter her life. If she let them. A cool Mohito soothed her heated mood, fresh mint and lime accenting rum in a deliciously brave way. Her mouth swilled the lovely liquids, her legs swiveled off the bar stool and plopped her in front of the curved bank of picture windows.

Dead ahead, the massive arrow-like end of the ship—the prow—held steady in a sea of darkness. Silhouettes of great chains, capstans, and winches possessed the deck in a random order that, even in dim running lights, resembled the bumpers and traps of a pinball machine. Beyond the ship, inky water and velour sky crowded around moon and star light.

"My god," Claire inhaled, nearly swallowing a shard of cracked ice. Choking crisis averted, she was left alone with a raw, genuine heart.

The Tex part confused her. Was he going to propose? Is that what the thinly veiled "ring shopping for a friend" pretext was all about? He'd told her if she ever needed his help, say, to arrange a personal interview with LBJ, anything at all, to call. He'd also invited her to visit his *San Antone* ranch, all expenses paid. Was this a sugar daddy in the making she wondered, embarrassing herself with a morbid slurp to commemorate the demise of Mohito numero uno.

Though she did enjoy his rock solid presence and can-do attitude, Claire knew any kind of serious, romantic relationship between them could never work. True, he could fund her travel and exploration of the arts, but she was able to do that herself. True, with a child to support her lifestyle might become considerably more complicated and *rushed*. This felt dark. She liked her life the way it was. Why was everyone trying to change that? Was she, in fact, trying to change that? Was she just so well off that people naturally wanted to thrust pieces of themselves at her? As a journalist she'd learned to keep a professional distance when working with others. She hated to think of her personal life in terms of an agenda, but that's what it boiled down to. What was good for Claire? Could she even answer that question?

An additional Mohito helped her see that there was probably more room in the frame of her life than she imagined. *Perhaps even limitless capacity* the Caribbean rum whispered.

If only she truly believed.

CHAPTER 46

As the sun took its stand in the sky, a voice droned out the engine's steady commotion: *comin' up on Puerto Vallarta, point of no return!*

Startled, Luigi woke from a doze.

"Hell," Roger said, eyes darting back and forth between the fuel gauge and his Rolex. "If we push on to Cabo that'll be a total of about 750 miles. Ethel's range is 800. Supposed to take into account destination, alternate airport—scratch that one, we got the whole ocean—plus 45 minutes." He peered at his watch. Back to the gauge. "Whadya say, *hombre*? It's yer call. If we stop at PV then again at Cabo to top off the tanks for the round trip to the ship and back we waste a boat load a time an' less chance a gettin' that girl a yours."

"But-a, what if we-a run out?"

"Then we gave it our best shot. I say we goose it to Cabo."

Watch. Gauge. Minute calculations. He shook his head resolutely, triple chins working overtime. "Think we can make it," he feathered back the throttle. "Little luck and a tail wind'll go a long way."

"Okay, goose."

Luigi, who'd been looking forward to using a proper bathroom, now had to figure a graceful way to broach the subject of peeing into a bottle.

The hundred additional minutes yawned eternal, the Italian nearly catatonic, nose pressed to a small gap of fresh air he'd ferreted out eons before. Throughout the trip Roger kept up a constant chain of munching. His latest snack, sardines with mustard and fresh garlic he'd minced with a pocket knife while also flying the aircraft, filled the cabin with a smell not unlike fishy bunker fuel. Then there were the ever-present farts to contend with. Tailwind, indeed. He couldn't exactly ask the man to step outside. Sausage afterburn, fish fumes and the indelible stink of garlic coming from both mouth and ass. Luigi couldn't wait for this to be over.

Sensing his client's dejection, Roger tried to lighten the mood.

"They got the best brown sugar cookies at a little shack next ta the aviation building in Cabo. I'll get us a dozen er so, though last time I did fine a course black hair in one…"

When Roger lined up the Beaver with an imaginary oceanic runway and pushed the yoke forward, Luigi inwardly rejoiced. Normally opposed to extra moves such as a change in elevation or an extended fiddle with a knob, he sat engrossed in all the switch flipping, lever turning, dial readings, and radio channel searchings it took to get the plane safely down and snuggled up to land, where his own urgent mission would be to air out the interior and score some Alka Seltzer.

Roger merrily shook hands with his passenger and told him to hurry on out to secure a line. "We'll fuel up and see if we can get a fix on the Queen. I reckon she's midway up Baja by now, just this side of the point that juts out between here and Tijuana. We'll get 'er, no two ways 'bout it. Damn helluva fine day!" concluded the man with a bush pilot's heart.

With a bounce in his step, the big man waddled out of the terminal swinging a grease-stained paper bag. "Whatcha lookin' so down fer? Made it this far haven't we?" Roger joined Luigi at the moored plane.

The Italian offered a weak smile and rubbed his tummy in reply.

"Why din't you say something? Climb on back there and grab that small case. Fix ya up in no time. Meanwhile, got some interestin' news. A DC-9 took off from the coast a few hours ago, headed fer yer ship."

Luigi let out an extended burp. "What mean, 'headed'?"

"In the direction of…toward."

"But-a why? Like-a us?"

"Not exactly. Get this—the plane dropped a load of flowers onto the decks. Some kinda farewell gesture. Point is, we got a real good idea where she is."

"Who?"

"All the Marys ever born. Your ship!"

"Flowers…" Luigi's voice trailed off.

Roger released the mooring line. They climbed in, squeezing themselves back into the cramped cockpit which reeked of fuel once again.

"Pretty tacky don't chya think?" Roger went through the pre-flight routine, muttering this and that. "After all, was planes put that ship outta business…" Pausing to look at the panel indicators and nodding his head in satisfaction, Roger yelled *CLEAR!* Ethel roared to life. Apparently, she wasn't going to miss this for the world.

CHAPTER 47

The morning fly over did not go quite as hoped. Only a small portion of the gobs of red and white carnations actually landed on Queen Mary's decks—most dribbled pathetically into the sea. To wit, the majority of passengers, confused by the ever-changing time zones, missed the actual event by an hour. Claire photographed the anti-climactic scene from the port docking wing, but instead of being congratulatory, the jet's low-flying actions smacked of spreading flowers on the grave of one not quite dead. She knew it was a nod to the ship's 1936 maiden arrival in New York when World War I ace Eddie Rickenbacker dropped carnations from a DC-2, but it didn't play well this time around.

Eager to leave the cool, overcast elements behind and indulge in a full breakfast, Claire hurried to the warmth of the main dining room without conducting a proper sweep of her work area. While nibbling on bangers and mash she half-heartedly readied her gear for the Captain's final press conference and found a small accessory pack missing. Dashing back to the bridge, she mumbled apologetically to familiar faces that she was there just long enough to retrieve a misplaced item, not to trouble themselves, she'd see herself out to the wing, knew right where to look.

One of the kindly officers listened patiently then found an opportune time to inform her they'd already sent the item to her cabin. As she turned to leave, another officer uttered the first words of an intriguing overture, and so Claire dawdled, mumbling further apologies while remaining in position to hear the following:

"Quick, give this to Captain. There's a small plane on its way to pick up a lady—Cabo controller might have said 'stowaway,' not sure—the comm broke up."

Claire's journalistic instincts bristled. She tailed the messenger down stairs and into a short hallway, past the steward's galley to the Captain's quarters. "I'm hoping to get a quick interview with him, you know, before the press conference," she said gamely. "Very important."

"One moment, ma'am." The fellow rapped twice then went in. Claire put an ear to the door, thinking she heard the plane was due in around 2pm.

When the door opened suddenly she was prepared, innocently gazing at the shiny floor.

"Captain will see you now."

Large for a ship, the cabin held a tidy wood desk off to one side and an ample lounge for small gatherings. Sleeping quarters were not visible. The tall, gallant man in charge greeted her courteously with an unhurried air, offering an easy chair next to a small round table not far from the desk.

Anyone passing by at that moment would've heard an excited female voice relaying, "There's a plane on its way...you probably know about the stowaway...just a hunch, but these two may be related...I think you should hear the whole story..."

At the end of the quick run-down, the dashing Captain had this to say: "I've found throughout my life and career, through the wickedest storms and unexpected twists of fate, that there is something inherently workable in every situation."

"Is that so?" Claire breathed, impressed by the gentleman's steadiness.

"It really is about giving up all attachment to the outcome. You see, once you do that, it takes the pressure off and frees you to work through any given set of circumstances, pleasant or otherwise." The handsome Captain checked his manicure. "Let's see how it unfolds. Endings masquerade as beginnings—and vice versa. Either way, it's really not a problem. And you can quote me on that."

CHAPTER 48

The glorious old Beaver rattled and creaked and strained and bumped her way over the open Pacific and, once again, Luigi's heart resided in his throat. Jittery beyond belief, his mouth oozed saliva that just wouldn't clear up no matter how often he swallowed—what he wouldn't give to spit. The last time he felt this way was right before the most important division match of his life, one that decided whether his team Roma would advance, leaving Lazio, their arch enemies, in the dust. Then, like now, his nerves tingled with something, he had to admit, that felt like electricity. A pounding heart mimicked the rhythms of his tension—relaxing one moment, tightening the next. This time, though, the Beaver's maneuvers were not entirely to blame. As both Mary's loomed closer he realized he had not fully believed they would ever be reunited. Now the good fortune, good mechanics, and good fuel just had to last a little while longer, no more, really, than a palmful of sand in an hourglass.

Luigi took a big gulp of air and swallowed hard. Ethel, unaware of his fragile state, hit an air pocket and dropped her drawers for a few jolting seconds, forcing his awareness down to his gut which went into a free fall of its own. Luigi did not clench, offered surprisingly little resistance, and actually survived the ordeal.

Roger gave him a sidelong glance. Luigi returned it, smiling weakly.

Things were looking up.

"There she is!" Roger yelled, jabbing an arm toward the 11 o'clock. "I'll be damned!" Ethel banked sharply left and down. Luigi nearly barfed. Fear and panic set in, his body filled with adrenaline at the sight of the toy-sized oceanliner steaming north. They were still too high up to see any people but that didn't matter. He knew they were there. Knew *she* was there. He *knew*.

Roger barked excitedly into the radio handset. "Beaver N12376 to RMS Queen Mary, we're comin' atchya!"

"Queen Mary to Beaver, what is your business?"

"Wish ta reunite my man with one a yur women."

"Highly unusual request. Stand by."

Silence…then the airwaves crackled.

"Beaver N12376, 'twill take us 10 minutes to stop. Position yourself accordingly on our starboard side."

Roger rubbed his hands together. "We'll just circle 'round," he noted to the blanched person beside him, even though it was obvious what they were doing.

"Sabes qué…" the pilot began in a gush of Spanish, *"…never told jya this but I prepared a little ruse in case they didn't buy the romantic side a the story. I mean, how often do ships stop for pesky little seaplanes?"*

"No mucho," Luigi managed.

"Exactamente! Which makes me suspicious. Maybe someone on board is corroborating our story. Or—never mind."

Luigi knew the part he left out had to do with Mári being found, detained, and awaiting a non-shipping line-sponsored return trip home.

"So my idea was to fake engine distress. Had it all pictured in ma head. I'd fly Ethel directly over them smokestacks—real low—pull out over her bow…" Roger lapsed into English, never once glancing at Luigi who sat oddly comforted by the pilot's feisty monologues.

"…then off to the side, dippin' my wings as if outta control, bumpin' the plane up 'n down, modulatin' the throttle like crazy, then when I felt we was far enough ahead I'd make a rough landing and wait for assistance like a lame duck."

"But how I get-a in de ship?" Luigi had been paying close attention, working hard to weave the English words he knew into a semi-intelligible web of intrigue.

"Two ways ta handle that." Roger pulled out of circling mode and aimed the Beaver's nose at an area well beyond the ship. "Both involve a medical emergency."

"Sí?"

"First one has you, the passenger, with something like appendicitis. Throwing up, grippin' pain in yer abdomen. That woulda been convincing enough to get chya on. Ships at sea gotta help those in need, 'specially those with medical staff and equipment like that one down there. Then, *amigo*, it'd be upta you to convince the Doc why you were really on board."

Roger banked the plane and craned his neck for a fix on the ship, straightening Ethel out once satisfied with their relative positions. "I realize the language thing mighta been tough so I had another plan in mind."

Luigi quickly chimed in, eager to pin a frailty on the big man. "Heart attack-a for you? Dat explain-a de crazy not so good landing? I right?"

"Yeah, pretty much, but that one'd be hard ta believe since I'm so young and fit."

Both men laughed as Ethel's silver skids dallied with blue Pacific swells.

"Now we wait and try not to get run over."

CHAPTER 49

Tripping over the Captain's foot as she left in controlled haste, Claire dashed back to B-410 where, tossing the door open, she blurted, "We're running out of time!" and sent the whole peaceful setup into an uproar. Tot cried, Mári flew out of the loo imagining the worst, and Guga, well, Guga kept nail filing but at a faster rate, as if suddenly realizing there was much work to do.

"They're coming for her! They're coming for her!" Claire bugled like a modern day Paul Revere.

"Want me to translate?" Guga calmly asked.

"Wait—no—tell her there's a small plane… No, wait. Tell her I'm beside myself because of work…hell, make something up, I don't care."

"*Ella es loca, nada más que esto,*" Guga reassured Mári who, thus reassured, sequestered herself back in the bathroom.

"What is going on?" Guga put the file down, head tilt suggesting a wise old crone.

"I need you to get Doc. I need him as a witness right away."

"Witness to what?"

"To Mári giving up her baby."

"Is that really necessary?" Guga's face crinkled.

"Plane's coming to get her. My guess is it's that man of hers."

"Shouldn't he have the right—"

"Not at all."

"How rrromantic," Guga gushed, rolling the r's. "I wish someone would come after me like dat."

"I'll come after you like *dat* if you don't get it into gear and fetch the Doctor! And if you can't find him, get Tex."

"Least I know where he is. Ciao!"

"Wait—how do you know where he is?"

"Shopping for a ring."

"Another one? Man likes his rings. *Rapido!*"

Claire bumbled about, jumpy when things spiraled beyond her control. Started to change clothes, then decided against it. She became, instead, transfixed by the infant. Swaddled and surrounded by a carefully constructed moat of pillows, the tike tested his arms and legs in jerky, gyrating motions that smacked the bed hard. Arms twirled, fingers and toes clenched and unclenched, legs pumped. Dark eyes wide open, sparse black hair slick with sweat.

Good God, he looks like he really wants to get somewhere...

A smile followed by gurgles transformed his demeanor from one of feverish effort to one of genuine delight.

Passing wind for the first time, are we?

Claire sensed all she really needed to know about his character in those few moments. No doubt such a level of drive, self possession, and adaptability would serve him well.

Guga returned to the cabin with both Doc and Tex as well as a freshly pressed pair of black pants and lavender dress shirt. Smiling from ear to ear, the Brazilian chameleon chucked baby under the chin, greeted the two ladies in waiting, and hung the outfit inside the vacant—for a change—bathroom. Doctor cleared his throat, requesting everyone's attention.

"In the expediency required of us, I hereby ask Señora Mári to state whether she permanently surrenders all parental rights to one J. Cruz and transfers said rights to Miss Claire Zeisse."

Guga translated then ducked into the bathroom.

Turning her back to the others, Mári held the boy with purpose, bouncing him every so often in her arms to make a point, looking deeply into his eyes and murmuring short phrases. At one point she stood at the porthole, took his hand in hers and pointed out toward some unseen target. Was this their covenant, a request for understanding and forgiveness? Or was she merely preparing J. Cruz for the scene to come?

"*Sí,*" she answered quietly, her watery eyes finding the Doctor's.

Guga emerged buttoning the lavender man's shirt, a rarity which, under other circumstances, would've caused a stir.

"Miss Claire, do you accept the responsibility bequeathed to you?"

"I do."

Mári swiped her soft eyes and offered her child into the arms of Claire. They hugged. Squished between two sets of bosoms, J. Cruz squealed with delight, barely noticing the blue stone pendant Mári slipped around his sausage neck.

"Both of you please sign and date here. Mr. Tex and er, Miss-ter Guga, will you also sign and date as witnesses to the exchange."

As the paper altering J. Cruz's life course was passed around, Doctor mentioned one more formality. "I have taken the liberty of drawing up a birth certificate with all details accurately recorded but one—Miss Claire, I have listed you as the birth mother. This, though by no means typical, I saw fit to do in order to avoid questions from the immigration authorities you shall encounter tomorrow at landing. It is binding for life."

Doctor paused while Guga explained to Mári who, after swallowing this final act of erasure, nodded graciously. "*Entiendo. Es normal.*"

"Thank you for your foresight, Doctor." A whale of a lump formed in Claire's throat. This was it—this was real—she was a mother. On paper at least.

Doc paused, sensing something unseen. "Do you feel it?"

Claire looked beyond the porthole. The ship had stopped. "Would you all excuse us?" She took Mári's limp hand and lead her into the hallway where they shuffled along, arms draped around each other, crying an endless corridor's worth of tears. One could not say where the joy began and the sadness ended, both emotions seemed as one, but by the return trip eyes were dry and the women gently swung linked hands to and fro, content as two sisters.

"Mári, I have to tell you something."

"Jyess?"

"Your *novio* is coming to get you."

"*Si, es normal.*"

"Yes, I suppose it is."

CHAPTER 50

Ethel bobbed in the water, the size of a cork compared to the drifting hulk of Queen Mary. Roger and Luigi sat nervously hoping they were out of harm's way when a hatch opened near the waterline and a narrow rope ladder spilled down the ship's side.

"I don't dare get any closer, can't run the risk uh damaging the plane," Roger quacked out of the side of his mouth.

"Look-a! A leetle boat!"

Three crewmen lowered an inflated dingy and one climbed in, rowing toward them.

"Drop anchor!" Roger ordered, and Luigi, by far the more nimble of the pair, did just that.

"That'll hold 'er. I'm coming with ya—wouldn't miss this for the world!"

Junior First Officer, tracking the visitors' progress from the starboard docking wing, updated the bridge. "Two men nearly off the seaplane!"

"Nearly off the seaplane," echoed Chief Quartermaster at the helm, followed by a curt order from Captain.

"Let me know when the stowaway and her entire entourage are assembled in Chief's office."

Ever since he'd been interviewed, Lez couldn't stop thinking about the Mary's last hours as a seagoing vessel. Sure, he'd done his job organizing the engineering workshop for its new American owners, but the ship no longer belonged to him. It was an odd, unsettling feeling, and most everyone he knew, including himself, behaved as though this were just another voyage. Lez supposed they had no choice. They'd all invested so much energy running the ship that the prospect of shutting down engines for good had not been duly considered. He had to laugh, thinking back on these last few days when the maintenance schedule had called for servicing the elevators—just his dumb luck.

Lez was sorting light bulbs according to wattage when he heard shouts and footsteps rushing along E Deck. Before joining the fray, he peeked out the porthole and spied the object of commotion: a small seaplane was nearly upended as a very large man launched himself into an inflatable.

Packing could wait.

✹

Few on the ship knew what was going on. Rumors had been circulating among the passengers about a stowaway, the predominant speculation involving a poor woman running away from a harsh husband to seek opportunity and fair treatment abroad. Feelings generally ran in favor of the young lady, and a certain Mrs. Dalloway made sure the gossip remained flattering having, from afar, taken a deep personal interest in the affair. A regular spitfire by all accounts, widowed Mrs. Dalloway loved to rally others to a cause. Early on, after having had the luck of being within earshot of Chief Master and his men grumbling about an elusive guest, her social prowess had enlisted several like-minded ladies to patrol outside the Captain's, Staff Captain's, and Chief's working quarters. They would stroll leisurely up and down, back and forth, tea cups in hand, watching for signs of intrigue, keeping tabs on who came and went.

Since Mrs. Dalloway was a frequent presence on company ships, the crew knew to be extra careful around her. She'd earned her reputation as a snoop ages ago, back when RMS Caronia was a happy go lucky green cruiser and it was natural to assemble a dendritic network of spies who regularly convened over all manner of drink tall and neat.

Still, no matter how careful staff were, she always managed to dig up just enough to make her a royal pain in the arse.

"The eagle has landed!" came the cry from old ironsides herself who, at 2:10 on the afternoon of Friday, December 8, not coincidentally found herself taking air on the Sun Deck with a posse of sherry-happy companions when the de Havilland Beaver landed nearby. News of the radio message had whipped the spy network into a frenzy, mobilizing the group to block any potential threat from a troublesome husband seeking revenge on an elusive wife or something along those lines.

Tex had other ideas. Having some knowledge of Mári's situation he knew beyond a doubt she would require a dauntless champion but wasn't sure that champion should be him. While alternating between folding clothes and thinking such thoughts, he heard the buzz of a low flying plane waft through the open portholes in his stateroom. Tex wagered this was Mári's guy. A ruddy man of 62, he stopped packing, secreted two small silk pouches—the white one in the right and the crimson one in the left pants pocket—then quickly skipped over to see Doc.

Doc, too, had been tidying up, clearing shelves, dusting, anything to relieve the storehouse of nervous energy while waiting for the big event. Together, he and Tex would have to persuade the powers that be to partake in a momentous send-off. But first they had to round everyone up.

A knock on the door signaled it was time.

CHAPTER 51

Bits and pieces of the story emerged from the winded seaplane pilot as the landing party poked its way through the ship's innards. Every once in a while Lez, bringing up the rear, thought he heard the Italian talking to himself. Sensing the emotional and somewhat unstable nature of the monologue, the Brit asked for clarification.

"My-a wooman, she keel me if no flowers."

"Got you covered old chap." Lez raced ahead and ducked into an area where refrigerated goods were kept. "Go on, I'll catch up!"

❀

Tex and Doc listened outside the Master At Arms bureau, alert for any activity. Hearing none, they pushed the door open and loitered within its tan interior. After running out of things to pretend to read, Tex remarked on the room's lack of decor. Doc agreed, saying this bare bones style, if one forgave the pun, was typical of working spaces which most passengers never saw.

"Least it's got a punkah louvre an' a fan." Tex sucked his teeth and snapped his suspenders, gearing up for action.

A commotion in the hallway made them stand at attention. The door swooped open, with Chief Master remaining in the corridor as ladies entered first—Mári, Claire with newborn, and Guga who, though dressed as a man, still counted as one.

Chief entered and surveyed the scene. "I think we all know why we're here?" he queried in his best West End tenor.

The stuffiness of the room threatened to steal the scene as the conspirators played a game of hot potato, bopping, dipping, and twirling the willing infant between them. Tex laughed heartily, and J. Cruz's glee infected even the Chief who managed a smile before stepping into the hallway to receive the next group—Mrs. Dalloway and her faithful.

"Chief," said the trim widow whose hematite hair imparted a level of authority not easily dismissed. "I wish to visit with *our* stowaway."

Chief twitched visibly.

"I've come with an interpreter. Do stand aside, we've little time to spare."

Chief mumbled and held the door open. The revelers turned to hear what the merry widow had to say, courtesy of a blue-haired woman who issued a halting, prepared speech in Spanish.

On cue, Mrs. Dalloway produced an envelope and handed it with great pride to Mári.

"Now, be sure to stress she can only keep it if she refuses the advances of that man who's pursued her and is, I'm afraid, shortly to join us. Otherwise, it goes to the Seaman's Fund. Go on, tell her!" Mrs. Dalloway needled her interpreter.

Mári self-consciously thumbed through the assortment of pound notes, a currency which might as well have been from Mars. Mrs. Dalloway intervened coolly, her rusty companion still stumbling through the conditions.

"That is worth five hundred American dollars, my dear. Seed money for your life as an independent woman, one who will, as you've no doubt done in the past, work hard to pave her own way."

"Just as you've done, Doris?" the interpreter jabbed, momentarily shirking her duties.

"There now." Mrs. Dalloway clamped her blue-veined hands around Mári's while projecting a sidelong glance of displeasure toward her friend. "Good luck to you."

Mári half-listened to the interpreter's odd words as her attention turned to the sound of heavy feet shuffling closer and closer. A Deputy whisked the door open and entered with the same unchecked velocity, only to be stopped short by the crowd of people inside.

"Uh, Chief, sir, they're here," he mustered, red-faced.

"Well, what are you waiting for? Send them in!" Chief ordered with a flourish, having waited, it seemed, his entire career to pronounce words such as these. "And summon the Captain!"

Luigi entered first, ducking as he crossed the threshold even though, as all could plainly see, the doorway easily accommodated his height. He stood to one side of the door and stared at Mári, expressions of tenderness and pride alternately clouding his face.

Next came the big man who, taken aback by the cramped quarters, backpedaled into the hall, but not before murmuring *do something* to his charge and covering it with a cough.

Luigi knew he had to *do something*. He had no flowers, which was really, really bad. All eyes were on him—except Mári's. Far as he could tell, she hadn't glanced at him once. Except for her, he didn't know a soul among them. Who were all these people? He'd stumbled into a beehive and felt as though any wrong move would precipitate an attack. This called for extreme measures.

He brushed by a scowling, steel-haired lady and nodded to a trio of oddballs—a short pale woman holding a baby who looked familiar, a tall man with a purple shirt and feminine hairdo, and a barrel-chested cowboy with hay-colored Stetson. Once by his intended's side, he held out his hand, palm up. Softened by the tremor she saw, Mári allowed the gesture and lightly placed her hand in his, keeping eyes downcast.

Emboldened by her receptivity, Luigi bent down on one knee. The crowd parted. Roger filled the doorway to get a better view.

The Italian swallowed hard. *"Mári, mi amor, mi unica amor, quiero estar contigo. Puedes vivir conmigo, como mi esposa?"*

Dewy-eyed, the sweet old interpreter relayed the endearing marriage proposal.

"Don't fall for it!" Mrs. Dalloway railed. "This smooth talking rather handsome man will just take you on another ride down a lane of deepest sorrow…"

It rang like a line from a Victorian novel, and a cheap one at that. No matter, it had the intended effect. Everyone perked up, shifted in place. The oddness of the expression lingered, causing tense, shallow breaths, few and far between.

"Hideous man, upsetting you to the point that you ran off all alone, an act of desperation, making it nearly impossible for him to follow. Yet here he is, the plague!" Mrs. Dalloway said with a quick glance at Tex.

"You're better off without him!" she concluded, triumphant, confident in her confidence that no one in the world could possibly believe otherwise.

For the first time, Mári looked at Luigi, who remained dropped on a knee, sweaty hand still gripping hers. She knew this position pained his hip, that he'd come a long way and endured a death-defying trip in a plane. Mostly she knew that he'd just proposed to her in front of all these strangers.

…And she did miss the comfort of his thick body smothering hers…

"Este hombre muy malo de veces!"

"Esta mujer muy mala de veces, y es la mujer para mi!"

"Y tu, Luigi, eres el hombre por mi si puedes, finalmente, enséñame leer un reloj."

The interpreter stepped away from Mrs. Dalloway before repeating the impromptu vows in which they agreed they were both equally bad, equally good, and decidedly meant for each other, as long as Luigi agreed to teach Mári how to tell time once and for all.

Mrs. Dalloway begrudged a crooked smile as Mári surrendered the envelope.

"Keep it—I was simply testing you my dear!"

Luigi, still on a knee, lavished Mári's hand with tender kisses while Tex leaned in and handed him the crimson pouch, parting the flap to privately reveal its contents. The Italian accepted gratefully and removed the delicate gold band set with a small diamond. Placement of it on Mári's finger sealed the deal, and two contrary lovers were joined as one. Captain, sharing a space with Roger in the doorway, spoke up.

"I now pronounce you man and wife! Your marriage shall be binding only for the duration of this voyage; it is not legal. Someone please translate!"

Still on his knee, mostly because he was stuck there, Luigi hushed the room when he asked, in Spanish, *"Where is the child?"*

"What child?" came the chilly reply from his temporary bride.

"That's why you left, isn't it?"

Silence.

"What did you do with my child?" Luigi rose stiffly to his feet.

Silence.

"Is that my child?" He pointed at the dozing infant.

A gasp escaped from the crowd as Tex and Guga gathered protectively around Claire. Roger uttered "Uh oh" from the doorway and hiked up his pants.

"Claro qué no." Of course not.

Luigi stepped closer, inspecting the boy, comparing his features to the woman holding him.

"Dis you-a baby?" he asked Claire.

Prickly silence.

Luigi pried the boy from her arms. He woke, finding himself in rougher hands than he'd known, but didn't cry. Luigi bounced him a few times, nodded in appreciation of his heft, one compatriot to another, examined fingers and toes.

Mári, fearing the worst, flung herself around the boy and pulled, initiating a tug of war. *"No es su hijo! Es unicamente el mio!"* she screamed, clean-jerking him out of Luigi's arms.

"It's not his baby!" the old interpreter breathlessly reported, neglecting to add the bit about the child being hers and hers alone.

Luigi suddenly dropped all resistance. "It's-a ok everybody, okay." He dispelled all the worried looks by tapping the boy playfully on the nose. "What his-a name?"

Happy to have understood a bit of English, Mári blurted *"Jesus Cru—"* but Claire cut her off before she could finish.

"Seaborne. It's a nickname I gave him."

"Ok, Sea-a-borne." Bending over, he pressed his forehead to Seaborne's and whispered magic words.

Claire couldn't help herself—she grabbed the Polaroid and fired off a few shots of the nicer interplay, hastily offering the bulk of them to the odd pair.

"What did you say to the boy?" the steely haired maven felt inclined to ask.

"A secret, between me and-a heem."

A commotion in the hall diverted everyone's attention.

"Flowers! Flowers! Get your flowers!" Lez ducked beneath Roger and lofted a bouquet of red and white carnations into the room. Claire reached up and instinctively caught the airborne flora.

At first, no one knew what to do. Then, the old interpreter clapped, followed by others. A deep blush colored Claire's face.

Tex prodded Guga and slipped him something small.

"While we're on the subject," the Brazilian turned to face Claire, "would you be interested in marrying me? I can help with da baby, help you with fashion and decorating…"

He offered her a ring and curtsied gallantly.

"I know what you're getting at, but yes! Why not!" Claire laughed. "It's the best offer I've had lately!" she said, winking at Tex.

"Right then, hate to break this up," said Captain, tapping his wristwatch, "but we do have to be going."

Roger agreed. "If someone could show me back, I'll get a head start…such an ordeal that rope ladder. Nice meetin' everyone, best a luck!" His voice trailed off down the endless hallway as he was rapidly escorted by Lez and two Deputies.

Mári absently looked beyond the empty doorway, pound notes limp in the hand of the arm that still held her son. She realized what this moment meant—leaving behind the beautiful ship that'd cradled her at her most vulnerable; leaving behind the beautiful strangers who'd shown immense kindness; and leaving behind the little human she'd managed to bring forth. Mári hugged each one of them, kissed her son, wrapped the leopard print scarf around his neck and handed him back to those other newlyweds, her clear eyes penetrating theirs.

New beginnings for everyone.

The remaining wedding party raced to the upper decks to witness history—a stowaway retrieved by her new groom on a seaplane at mid-sea. Claire clutched Seaborne and stood with Guga next to Tex and Doc. The plane made a slow, lurching turn to find the right wind. Once located, the old engine revved for all it was worth and Ethel the Beaver taxied the length of the Queen Mary, from bow to stern, generating hoops, hollers, and tears from assorted well-wishers. Airborne, the flying boat dipped her wings three times in farewell, and as the plane shrank in a sort of reverse metamorphosis, Claire pulled Seaborne tighter to her chest. She had gained a living, breathing keepsake of the occasion. Whether or not she was up to the task was no longer a question to entertain. Motherhood had dropped in on her as suddenly as it had left Mári.

☀ ☀ ☀

PART FOUR

Ra Ra Happens

Bricks and mortar sing us no audible tune;
the heart opens only to the human chant of being.
—Indian Sage

ONE OF THE first major crises in Seaborne's life happened a few days after arriving home. The ground floor studio apartment on North Orange Drive—in the grungy, energetic center of Hollywood just around the corner from the Chinese Theater—barely had room to accommodate the addition of a piece of luggage much less two more humans. Stacks of magazines rose like stalagmites from the short crop of tan carpet. Padded boxes with flung open lids spilled out lenses, filters, reflectors, camera bodies and straps. A long, Spanish-style wooden table dominated the room, a third of its surface claimed by carvings, rattles, fancy bottles, and pin-cushions topped with feathers and neatly tied bows.

Claire hadn't thought much about their living arrangements; after all, what could she do from the ship? Guga's resourcefulness and gratitude saved the day, as he jumped in, grouping things neatly against the wall and beneath the table, leaving just enough leg room so she could work. But that didn't solve the problem of the one bed, a twin, which also served as the couch, so Guga made a snug nest in the corner between the window and the foot of the bed for the infant, while he slept in a slightly musty sleeping bag which Claire picked up from a thrift store.

The uncomplaining Brazilian cooked, made formula, cleaned, laundered, and stayed home with Seaborne while Claire made the rounds interviewing and writing articles to boost what she earned as a freelance photographer.

The zany family became slightly more adjusted with each passing day. But Guga, on the morning of day three and in a spasm of true parenthood, realized nothing solid had passed from Seaborne's rear end. No feces had yet to mar the downy whiteness of the doody cloth. Both adults became alarmed and uptight as new mother cats. They did all but lick his orifices (as a mother cat would have done) to stimulate passage of a long-awaited turd; they rubbed his abdomen, cozied warm water bottles up under him, dangled his feet in sink water.

"Should we take him to a doctor?" Guga asked.

"Maybe we could try an enema," Claire pondered, bouncing the baby up and down in an attempt to move his bowels.

"En-e-ma. Good idea!" Guga plucked Seaborne from Claire and tossed him as high as the cottage cheese ceiling allowed.

Seaborne must not have liked the sound of the word, or perhaps he sensed the impending, deeply personal intrusion. He fussed in Guga's arms, squirming and pushing, to which Guga responded with equal and opposite force by plopping the little tike onto the bed and holding him down gently while Claire ran warm water and got the kit.

Seaborne quieted himself, a look of deep concentration scrunching up his features. Hands flexed and opened in a kind of meditative mudra. Toes curled inward, then splayed outward. This went on for a minute or two. Then Seaborne became very still. He cried out and struggled to roll over onto his tummy. Legend has it he broke into a sweat trying to coordinate the movement of all four limbs in an attempt to crawl *in the direction of the bathroom*. At such a young age!

Given these momentous clues, Guga and Claire anxiously unpinned the diaper, where lay a smooshed, pasty off-white turd the likes of which neither had ever seen.

They were elated, and so, too, the little one, if the truth of the matter be known.

J. Cruz Seaborne Zeisse. From his Italian father and Dominican mother he inherited olive skin, easily tanned to a golden walnut. Hair, jet black with serious kinks in all the wrong places. A real challenge to get it to lie flat. Only after wearing a hard hat or helmet did it even come close.

Exhibited bouts of anger as a child. From cradle to adolescence often became red-faced, features distorted in a painful look of frustration, hands pushing something unseen out of the way, a remembrance, a glimpse of the future. Didn't lash out at others—no, it was something within that got his goat. The tendency to be inner increased over the years. When he finally got his own bedroom, Seaborne covered the window with foil to block out light. When that "look" proved unacceptable, his parents taped a thick black fabric to his side of the window, standard white curtain presenting normally to the outside, as if the heroin users chasing dreams on nearby Hollywood Boulevard gave a damn.

Young Seaborne often spoke of a desire to live in a cave. Anything about Carlsbad Caverns was sure to please, although this flashy expression of the earth's womb troubled him at times, especially the man-made lighting.

"Caves were meant to be dark," he'd spout and shake his head disagreeably while peering at crystalline voids in his red View-Master.

"But if they were dark, no one could see their beauty," Claire usually responded, avoiding any deep psychoanalytic guano.

"I'm dark, does that mean you can't see my beauty?" he would taunt, and Claire, who'd never pictured herself married to a cross-dressing, man-loving man much less raising a child who belonged to neither of them, always came back with something like *you're beautiful inside and out*. And that would usually be the end of it. Eventually Seaborne mistook his mother's seeming lack of depth and interest (after all, he hadn't come from *her* cave) for what was simply a lack of skill. For the most part, everyone in Seaborne's life did the best they could. But try proving that.

Seaborne became noticeably fascinated with transportation around the age of six when he tried to make his Radio Flyer wagon propel itself by fashioning an oval Tupperware pedal and coiled rope to the front wheels. It didn't work, but the attempt impressed the grownups.

He could name practically every car on the road, much to everyone's surprise, and bore an unusual fondness for the AMC Pacer, that wide, inelegant bubble of economic thrift and questionable design. To him, it looked like a spaceship.

Then there was the fascination with shifting. After much hounding, at age seven, Claire relented and let him move her Bug's gear stick on straight-aways when there wasn't much traffic. He already knew the pattern of first through fourth because he'd been watching intently as early as anyone could remember. Still, there was the matter of timing. Starting out, Seaborne was inclined to shift gears before Claire depressed the clutch—mostly she fended off his dominant left hand in time, but when she didn't, the staccato movements of the little car really did resemble those of a bumbling beetle.

Eventually, Claire coached Seaborne to wait until the clutch pedal made it all the way to the floor. Even this seemingly fail-proof method didn't always work, and after being yelled at more times than either liked, the boy invented a reliable trick of simply waiting for the telltale sound of decreased revs as his cue. Sometimes though, the engine RPMs, in his estimation, ran too high for too long, making him yell *shift mom, shift!* She was grateful for these reminders—usually it meant she had other things on her mind, never enough time in the day and all that jazz.

Since the day he could distinguish a cigarette butt from something truly valuable (in the early stages of his evolution everything was subject to a taste test), Seaborne pocketed treasured bits and pieces, mostly rocks. As he grew older, he became more selective, as noted by

Claire who, after the umpteenth stone retrieved from pockets destined for the washer, noticed that many of them had a theme. Some more than others, to be sure, but the notch at the apex, the conjoined twin lobes full at the mid-section and curving down into a point, these features, however chipped and marred, unmistakably conveyed the features of a heart. Funny thing was, they didn't always resemble the perfect greeting card heart. The last one that got away and knocked around in the dryer glistened purple maroon when she pulled it out, roughly scored by dark lines—life lines—and lighter veins that looked like bits of fascia. The bottom tip was sliced off, exposing a smooth, deep red that reminded her of the way a peeled beet oozed. This scarred stone looked unsettlingly close to the real thing.

After making this connection, Claire often caught Seaborne's hungry eyes devouring the most colorful object on the wall of their flat where, centered among a collage of black and whites prints, hung a fabric heart made out of what looked (to a young boy) like shiny silver, pink, and black fish scales surrounded by small wagon wheel spokes. The size of a placemat, this image followed him wherever he went, the most amazing thing he'd seen since *Lost In Space!* Early each day it dazzled from sunlight streaming in the window and somehow flung its shimmering flecks onto the faces on the wall, over Claire's long wooden work table, even as far as the compact kitchen. A true mobile of light.

He didn't care, nor was he aware, that the scales were sequins, the wagon wheels symbolic of the eight directions, and the heart itself central to a *vévé*, or depiction, of the goddess of love, *Erzulie*. A fine specimen of Haitian Vodou flag, albeit a decorative one. Claire longed for one used in processions, the real McCoy. A flag of the people, a symbol of empowerment.

Claire knew how much the flag delighted Seaborne and offered to hang it in his (dark) room when they moved into a larger place in the same courtyard complex at 1769 N. Orange. He must have agreed in principle only, for when she came in with the cherished item Seaborne threw a fit, barring her way with his spindly frame and penetrating whine. When Claire put her hands up in surrender the boy settled down, insisting she arrange the flag and photos the way they'd been in their previous apartment. If she could've gone inside his head, if he could've explained his consternation, they both would've learned that the shimmers of light made the people in the surrounding pictures infinitely happy.

Seaborne knew the characters by heart, asked constantly who they were, loved turning it into a game. Above the sequined flag an 11x14 print featured four adults of widely varying heights in front of the sweeping windows of a place called the *Vewandah Gwill*: a short pretty woman identified as a friend of the family (being too young to be told the real story), then Claire, Guga and a big man named Tex, all looking cheery (inebriated).

Who took the picture? Seaborne was always bright enough to ask.

A nice steward.

What's a steward?

Someone who takes care of you.

Where am I in the picture?

You weren't born yet, honey.

To the right of the flashy heart, an 8x10 of the short pretty woman holding a baby—him! This much he knew. Both stared at the camera as if magnetized by the lens or caught in some kind of force field. Beneath the flag, a picture of the short pretty woman arm-in-arm with a burly, curly-haired man. They looked preoccupied, or possibly constipated. He didn't know what to make of those two. Finally, to the left of the flag, a picture of Claire, Guga, and bundled infant alongside a nifty double-decker bus. He liked this picture best.

☀

For the better part of a year, during his fear of death phase, Seaborne felt he might make peace with the grim reaper if only he got to drive. He couldn't wait, and the one thought that comforted him was hijacking the Bug and taking the *bumbool-bee* for a forbidden spin. A poor, though workable substitute, he settled for kneeling on the passenger seat (in order to see over the dash board) and co-piloting, pretending his Frisbee was the steering wheel. What had prompted the fear of death phase was the demise of a classmate in the second grade, not one he'd been close with, but just the fact that the boy did a *here today, gone tomorrow* bit. The sudden transformation shook Seaborne's youthful outlook. As a result Guga, an attentive and generous parent, spent extra time giving instructive pep talks about the circle of life and survival of the fittest.

One thing Guga did not do was sugar coat the subject.

"In the animal kingdom when someone dies their skin withers and disappears. Just like what happened to the dinosaurs, right?

"I guess," Seaborne replied, none too sure about the angle of approach.

"You know how we go to the museum and see their bones on display? Nothing too scary, right? Well, that's what happens to humans. They live for a certain amount of time—no one knows for sure how long—and then their spirit one day decides to leave the body, and caramba, you have this!"

Guga presented Seaborne with a small crystal skull carved from smoky quartz. "This is not your enemy, understand?"

The boy thoughtfully fingered the bulbous cranium, inspected the temple indentations, gigantic eye sockets and bared set of teeth.

"Looks like my *Scream'n Demons* motorcycle rider with helmet and goggles!"

So much for lessons in mortality.

✺

In 1978, when he was eleven, the little family up and moved clear across the country to Florida. Guga wanted to spend more time in Brazil, Claire to be close to the Islands for her art quests. Seaborne didn't have a choice in the matter. The most important thing in his mind, by now an obsession, was learning how to drive. He timed it perfectly, increasing his hounding until Claire, doing her best to help the newly uprooted boy adjust, let him operate the Bug in a sandy parking lot. Guga came along to snap pictures (no one knew him to drive in Los Angeles) with an Instamatic while Claire sat nervously in the passenger seat next to a perky and flushed Seaborne.

Things did not go well. He was a little too short to reach the pedals and see over the dash concurrently, meaning at any given time he had to favor one or the other of these essential requirements. His initial exuberance was deflated by several jerky stalls in a row, the Bug hopping forward unbidden, then dying. He had no idea something this mon-strous could happen, and Claire had trouble explaining how to avoid this unfortunate result.

"Hold on you two—what's going on?" Guga ceased snapping photos of the happy occasion which saw Seaborne close to tears and Claire at her wit's end.

"The gas and clutch thing aren't in sync," Claire blurted, finding her words.

"Ah, trying to rub tummy and head at the same time?"

Seaborne nodded, hands choking the steering wheel in a death grip.

"Ok, parking brake on, get it into neutral, start the car," Guga directed.

Seaborne did as he was told.

"I'm going into the engine compartment," Guga called from the rear.

"Excuse me?" Claire whipped around in time to see the lanky Brazilian disappear beneath the upraised hatch.

"Going to adjust the timing higher so he doesn't have to worry about the gas pedal yet."

"You who's never even been behind the wheel?"

"Just because I don't choose to doesn't mean I don't know how." The signature putt-putt of the VW engine sped up, as if just having ingested a Cubano coffee. "I don't sleep with women either, but I know how the mechanism works."

After that, the boy caught on just fine.

Seaborne was a natural born jet setter. At a young age he spent summers with Guga in Brazil, vacations with Claire at Tex's ranch. It wasn't that he loved traveling, he just exhibited such impressive self possession that the adults around him didn't mind taking him places.

In 1975, on the occasion of a Carnival trip to the Caribbean, Seaborne took to the air, prepared. He'd brought binoculars. He always loved takeoff—the quick acceleration, the anticipation of the heavy plane lifting off the runway, jet engines whining, nose lifting, climbing up over the California coast. What excited Seaborne more than the trip itself was the hope that they'd cruise over Long Beach and he'd spot his birth ship. As if the mandatory weekly outings to observe, from the far shore, the ship's conversion progress, weren't enough. Well, they weren't. In those early days, one never knew what shape Queen Mary would be in. One Saturday they showed up and, to Seaborne's horror, found her forward funnel sitting on the shore. This sent them on a mission to find out why. They soon learned that most of the engines had to be removed by cranes through the enormous funnel openings, and that the rusted old stacks were crumbling in the process. The ship would be mostly fun-nel-less until new ones could be built.

"Mom look! There she is!" Binoculars plastered against the plane's window, Seaborne yelled loud enough for everyone to hear. He jostled Claire, whose nose had been buried in a magazine due to nervous flying. Reluctantly, she popped her seatbelt to get a better look.

"See? Way down there?" Seaborne pulled her closer without taking his eyes off the prize. Window too small for both heads, she made some encouraging noises and plopped back down, content to take his word.

The flight from California to Miami was smooth, if not lengthy. Amped up for the first few hours from the mighty sighting of *his ship* along with several refills of Coke, Seaborne gradually succumbed to gravity and remained fairly content playing cards with Claire. Go Fish, W-A-R, and match game were good for an hour. Solitaire, a game Seaborne had seen Guga play over and over in their apartment, still eluded his eight-year-old's skills, especially when it came to the face cards, but he tried. When the tray table proved too narrow to accom-modate seven slippery cards across, thanks to a new deck the stewardess had given him, solitaire was shelved for the rest of the flight.

In Miami International Airport they grabbed cheeseburgers, fries, and shakes at a crowded diner popular with regulars. Both Claire and Seaborne, accustomed to such fare, would have taken more time to savor the char-broiled medium-rare deliciousness had they known they would get nothing of the sort where they were headed.

An hour into their second flight the Pan Am Clipper began a slow descent, with Seaborne's eager face glued to the window. The wa-ters reflected a painter's palette of lapis trailing off into turquoise which morphed into a sulfurous green near the creamy shores.

"Mom, what did the ocean do when it met the beach?" He didn't wait for an answer. "It waved!"

High, smooth mountains rolled velvety brown-green inland from the coast. Ribbons of sand stretched for miles, outlining the limbo place where one element kissed another. White specks dotted the aquamarine sea. Then, Seaborne had a lesson in illusion. The lower the plane flew the more detail came to light, and what had resembled continuously vegetated terrain was really a patchwork of scraggly trees and brush, interspersed with tan fields of rock and dirt. As the plane crouched in slow motion along the Bay, keeping pace with its shadow, Seaborne turned his binocs on the beaches and saw not sand but broken coral and shell. Nothing is what it seems! And those white specks turned out to be small wooden boats, hulls clad in shades of faded blue, sail and mast describing the classic "4" shape. At an even lower altitude, Seaborne saw men straddling logs in the waters closest to shore. Claire told him they must be dugout canoes, a primitive vessel dating back to the days when Arawak and Täino natives inhabited the island. A time before Christopher Columbus.

"You mean before 1492?" Seaborne asked, having recently read a book about the explorer.

"Yes, I suppose I do," Claire said, trying not to feel threatened by his growing command of information.

Seaborne was struck by the imaginary contrast between those splinters of floating wood and the riveted ramparts of his birthplace. Craning his neck for a last view of the water, he was a bit more reassured by the sight of a squat motor vessel putt-putting along. How could he have missed it? A large concentration of brown-skinned people lined the upper decks. It seemed a very popular and uncomfortable place to be.

He was still thinking about the ferry when the plane, low enough to make out (*sans* binoculars) dogs in yards and laundry on lines, made a sudden surge forward, then up, startling almost everyone on board. Seaborne hooped and hollered over the gunned engines until a brief glance at Claire's ashen face dampened his enthusiasm.

"It's ok, mom," he rested his hand on top of her white-knuckle grip on the armrest. "They're just making another approach. Conditions weren't quite right."

Seaborne went back to staring down at lush groves of royal palms, thatched mud huts, and slow-moving figures. On the do-over, the plane swung back over the Bay and the packed ferry again fell into view. From this angle he thought he detected a list to starboard. That was the side affording a view of the capital, where most passengers gathered to see if they could pick out notable landmarks—the white domes of the National Palace, the twin spires of the pastel-colored Cathedral.

"Look at dat country," the man in the seat behind was heard to say. His thick accent baffled Seaborne; the way he pronounced "country" sounded like the verb "count" doing an odd dance with the noun "tree".

"*Gadé pays la*," the fellow in the next seat behind repeated in Creole. Claire, intrigued by the rapid dash of syllables forming mysterious words, also noted the odd air of detachment with which they regarded their presumably native country. Perhaps they'd been away a long while. Perhaps they'd been exiled during Papa Doc's regime and were returning to try their luck under Baby Doc. Perhaps something very bad had happened to them, or loved ones, in the past, and the stance of distance kept fear and uncertainty, and possibly even wonder, at bay.

Claire's mental ramblings ended when an abrupt jolt signaled touch down and a stewardess announced, "Ladies and gentlemen, welcome to Port-au-Prince."

CHAPTER 53

Seaborne couldn't wait to get off the plane. He realized then and there how superior ships were, in comfort at least. Queen Mary's spacious decks came to mind, along with dim stairwells, hundreds of doors and off-limits alleyways. Great places all to seek and hide, dash and dawdle. But, and here was a horrible thought, because the vessel had cabins, you could also be rounded up and put to bed for an untimely nap, which didn't happen in airplanes, a distinct advantage over ships. Seaborne decided that airplanes were, after all, ok. And they had rivets, too.

Passengers finally began to move in both directions down the aisles. Seaborne nudged Claire to follow the group heading out the rear, an exit strategy which amused the boy a great deal.

"I wish Guga could see this—the plane is pooping live people!"

Thrilled by the prospect of dropping out of an aircraft's bunghole, Seaborne stole long looks back at the procession of elimination as he and Claire pecked their way down portable metal stairs and onto the tarmac. Once the potty humor lost its overwhelming appeal, he took notice of the surroundings. Slabs of angular concrete formed *Aéroport International François Duvalier*, its balcony of colorful, waving well-wishers fronting most of the second storey. An octagonal control tower with olivine windows made the structure look like an oil tanker. Various bins linked together like little trains and work-horse trucks idled on the ground while men in blue uniforms leaned against the reposing vehicles. A few skinny dogs with ears folded back like moth wings darted away from the whirring jet engines, their whip tails tucked between hind legs. A trio of musicians strummed loose guitars and rasped a song that repeated words unfamiliar.

"Mom, what does *tea zwazo* mean?"

"Not sure, honey. We can ask Eugene when we see him."

"How will we know which one is Eugene?"

"I suspect he'll find us."

Seaborne stopped short of the building's massive overhang, short of the shade. Bathed in the glare of tropic sun, Scooby Doo backpack dangling on an arm, he looked around, squinting, head tilted up, hand to forehead, nose flaring in a series of quick in-breaths. Claire snapped a quick pic in which everyone who later saw it was hard pressed to tell whether he resembled a golden angel or a golden retriever.

"The air is different here, mom."

"Yes it is," she nodded. "That it is."

More than just a warm breeze. He'd felt warm breezes before, in Los Angeles, when the Santa Ana's came up from the desert and caused people to become edgy as fire danger rose, reminding them of their own mortality or some such thing. Seaborne, of discerning senses, could appreciate the difference. Soothing, gentle, comforting, like the caress of a whisper on a cheek, it made him smile, and so did the jovial, slender man in white who greeted them (and everyone else) with a degree of flourish unrivaled by Liberace himself. He was a fixture at the airport, an icon for as long as anyone could remember, and he took the opportunity, upon learning Claire was a journalist, to invite her on the Department of Tourism float.

The chaos inside the terminal did not make Seaborne smile. Immigration was no big deal. A robust woman inspector looked at him blandly and brought down the gavel of her stamp onto their joint passport, waving them on to baggage claim where the real fun began. Seaborne frowned as a few porters fought over bag commissions, with multiple guys dragging a single suitcase over to customs, each straining against the other in oblique directions. A dismayed Claire snapped photos, which caused a minor uproar—the subjects stopped and turned toward her, not quite with their hands out but with chins jerking up on every salient syllable.

"*Madame, fo'ou bai nou cob pou photo.*"

"You geev us moné for photo," one among them translated. Sweaty, energetic, all were quite suddenly of a single mind.

Claire fumbled in her purse but Seaborne got to his pocket first.

"Can you share this?" he asked quietly, handing the most aggressive man a couple of dimes.

"Dat's ok leetle man."

Seaborne scanned the cavalry of suitcases lining up against the long wall, five deep. The airport had no carousels. Instead, handlers shoved bags from outside through a square opening while those on the inside slotted them in neat rows. Claire was loath to surrender her baggage stubs to the airport workers, identified by tailored gray pants and tops with red insignia, so she and Seaborne scrutinized every new arrival through the hole.

This waiting game gave her a chance to witness how the locals did it—no one had any trouble at all parting with their stubs. They merely said a few words in Creole and off went the uniformed gents. Incredibly, after minimal but intense scanning and a handful—or less—of actual number checks, each porter somehow found the right bag. Claire saw this happen again and again. These men obviously possessed some kind of magnetic ability that landed them in good stead.

With Seaborne working up a sweat climbing between rows and having no success, Claire decided to do the "when in Rome" thing—fan herself vigorously and hail a porter. One just finishing a commission came over, bowed a close-cropped salt and pepper head not much taller than hers, and gently took the two damp stubs. An older, slender man with concave cheeks draped from high bones, he smiled and nodded when she described two brown Samsonite suitcases, one large, one small.

Within minutes the man located both bags. Seaborne couldn't believe it. Fishing two quarters from his shorts, he offered them to the porter who pocketed them quickly.

First the gentleman porter saw them to customs, an open area beyond bag claim that consisted of ten or so long stainless-steel benches manned by inspectors wearing tidy uniforms and deadpan expressions. Finishing up with a traveling saleswoman whose bulging luggage full of sandals and wigs took some doing to close, the next available inspector waved Claire and Seaborne over.

Practiced fingers sprung the chrome latches. "You are tourists?" he asked pleasantly.

"I'm here on a photo assignment, Carnival. This is my son."

The inspector nodded politely while fileting each layer of clothing. Finding nothing untoward, he searched the corners, pulling out bags of film.

"For camera?" he asked, popping open a canister and sniffing a roll of Ilford 125.

"Yes, that's right."

After tucking all contents neatly back he began his exploration of the small Samsonite. Shorts, t-shirts, socks, striped engineer hat. A coloring book with a train on its cover made the inspector smile and whisper *choo choo*. Serious again, he withdrew a clear plastic bag containing two unlikely bedfellows: Tampax and tuna. Claire flushed with embarrassment as the Haitian registered no emotion. She wondered if he'd enjoyed the irony of that one.

Next, the gentleman porter escorted them outside, where a throng of people pressed in to greet newcomers. In a sea of faces, a smile and a frantic wave somehow stood out.

"Madame Claire? It's Eugene! Over here!"

The porter accompanied them to the Peugeot wagon parked close by, completing his duties for another 25 cents, all Seaborne had left. Whether he was happy with that no one could say, but the man was gracious enough not to complain to an eight-year-old.

"How did you know it was me?" Claire asked as she climbed into the front seat, a little winded.

"Der was no doubt at all," said Eugene in a rich French/African accent, the happy rhythms of *merengue* on the radio providing the perfect welcome. He checked his watch and glanced up at the sky, smiling self-consciously.

"What does *tea zwazo* mean?" Seaborne blurted from the back.

"Its mean leetle burd."

Satisfied, Seaborne settled in, allowing the Peugeot 404 to wow him. Never seen one before and he liked the cushy seats even though his thighs suctioned with sweat against their brown leather. Besides the front, there were two rows of back seats plus a small cargo area at the very rear. The car smelled like an old saddle and looked like a VW square back, with a fluted, elongated stretch, round headlights and wide grill.

By far the most fascinating feature was the gear shift which resided on the right-hand side of the steering column. *The steering column?!* Eugene gently guided the drumstick lever through its paces, which Seaborne noticed behaved, despite its odd positioning, just like a four-on-the-floor, with first up high and toward the driver, second directly below, third a half-move up, push away and up again toward the dash. Fourth remained to be seen; so, too, reverse. Each time the lever moved it made a squishy Tin Man squeak. How groovy was that?

Seaborne only half listened to the adults chatting up front. He had a hard time understanding Eugene who, for one, said things like "ee 'ad a bro-ken toot, dat's eet," describing minimal dental damage to a peanut vendor he'd accidentally clipped.

After a time, the textures, sounds and smells of the Peugeot gained familiarity and Seaborne focused on the views beyond its windows. Eugene's molasses voice produced a running commentary that faded in and out. They traveled up a paved road called *Delmas* (the "s" being silent), passing concrete buildings with flat roofs and wrought iron grills. Every few blocks the mouth of a cross street opened up to reveal rocky terrain bordered by structures in various stages of existence, including a few with missing walls and upper floors, rebar reaching for the sky, dark patches of mold staining cinder block that might never wear its finish coat.

On the left, Seaborne looked up in time to see a modern sign depicting a cartoon waffle cone with a blob of chocolate on top. "What's the word for ice cream?" he interrupted, digging his elbows into the tops of the front seat.

"*Crème a la glace*," Eugene replied. "You want some?"

He turned the car around and Claire treated them all to real waffle cones with delicious chocolate blobs on top. Upon leaving, a trio of caramel-colored women, joking in lively Spanish, crowded the storefront entrance, causing one of them to bump into Claire. A funny feeling came over the American as she begged pardon and caught a whiff of rose. She'd noticed that lingering scent on Mári. The coincidence tantalized her. She didn't dare stare until back in the car.

"Eugene, uh, were they by any chance Dominican?"

"Yes."

"How do you know?"

"Everybody knows."

"What are they doing here?"

"Dancers at a club in *Pétionville*. For da rich."

After a few moments, Claire got up the nerve to ask where the club was.

"Eet ees not a place for you and da leetle one."

"I have something else in mind, don't worry. But the club—"

"Visage."

CHAPTER 54

Back on the road, Seaborne watched locals meandering along on foot, bicycle, the occasional bony horse or donkey. One such long-eared creature was loaded with sooty sacks of jutting, charred wood. The animal labored uphill, led by an equally slow woman who balanced a bulging basket on her head, arm upraised to steady the weight. Their spare movements worked in sync. Seaborne had never seen anything like it. Both loads looked like they hurt. He wasn't sure who he felt more sorry for, the animal or the lady.

After giving it some thought, the donkey earned the lion's share of his sympathy; the patient, resigned look on its gray-brown face made the case that it didn't have much choice in the matter.

Eugene left the *Delmas* thoroughfare and drove through the residential neighborhood of *Place Boyer*, located in the wealthy enclave of *Pétionville*. Proud stone houses, multi-storied with balconies, mature trees and mossy green shade adorned the narrow, curvy road. A peculiar organic smell permeated the air. Seaborne rode with his head out the window, alert as a hound to sensations from beyond.

"Many important peepool in dis part—embassies, ambassador residences, beeg shots, and famus restaurant *La Lanterne*." The quiet pride in his voice spoke volumes. He took a moment to deftly cock his wrist, checking the time on a stainless steel Omega.

"What's that smell?" Seaborne blurted, yanking his head in.

"Very rich dirt mébee?" Eugene chuckled, checking his watch again.

"The smell of money," Claire chimed.

"Smells like fried green peppers to me—yuck."

"Curious place, this," Claire mused. Seaborne had heard that tone of voice before, usually when Claire talked about things that really turned her on, like paintings. She'd get a dreamy look, too, like she did when she ate ice cream or spaghetti. He wondered what had so enchanted her this time.

The afternoon downpour began precisely at four. Evidently this was a matter of some importance to Eugene, who gave his watch a final calculated stare and tapped the dial three times. His physiognomy brightened despite their unenviable position at the base of a steep incline on the final approach to *Hotel Ibo Lélé*. The more it rained, the more the wheels spun and the rear end of the Peugeot fish-tailed, making forward progress impossible. Eugene seemed unconcerned, glowing in his seat with some private preoccupation.

"Eugene, um, do you have to be somewhere else?" Claire pointed at her own watch.

"Oh no madame! You see, instead of playing de *Borlette* numbers—my wife she no let me do dat—I play de weather. A few friends we do dat. Today I win! I get a chick-en! My wife she have no idea why I bring home chick-en she no ask for!"

"If you had lost, what would you owe?"

"Same, a chick-en," he said off-handedly, as if everyone's currency was tied to poultry. "Ok, wait please," a sing-song voice ordered as he slid out of the car and rooted around the roadside. He quickly found several big rocks, popped them into the cargo space and soon they progressed slowly, but surely, up the hill.

The slick road had a drop-off on the other side, but to their right, a loose stand of tropical trees anchored the inclining land. Seaborne noted with curiosity that many of the grayish brown trunks sported long, finger-width trails of raised material that looked like coffee grounds.

"What's that brown stuff on the trees?"

"Oh, dat. Termites. Ees where dey live."

Seaborne, on to the next best thing, climbed into the way-back. "Look at me, I'm ballast!"

The boy had not given much thought to the reason they were in Haiti—*Carnival*—but whenever someone mentioned the word, which was often, he thought of two things: merry-go-rounds and funnel cake. Claire had tried her best to convince him neither were likely to be found on the island.

"Then what is Carnival?"

"Well, it's a time of celebration."

"Celebrating what?"

"Life, I suppose."

"Why do we need to celebrate life?"

"Well, to put it simply, we never know when we're going to die."

And so Seaborne's preoccupation with death was reinforced, a phase that never really ended. As a youngster it made him anxious to go to sleep for fear he wouldn't wake up. Some kind of background noise was needed—fans worked nicely—to trick him into believing everything was all right, secure, for once he closed his eyes he often saw an endless darkness scattered with occasional pinpricks of light. On and on went the darkness. He tried to fathom infinity but his brain just could not compute. It spun out, losing traction like the Peugeot's tires on a rain-slicked road.

Ever since she told him death was lurking 'round every corner things had never been quite the same, and when his mother started quoting an author whose name sounded like Carlos Castanet, Castaneda or some such Spanish word, he started to pay attention. One of the sayings, easy to remember, went something like this: "All paths lead nowhere, so choose a path with heart."

That's when he began collecting all manner of stones for the heart.

CHAPTER 55

Eugene handled the bags, freeing Claire to admire the bright mural painted on the wall of the long, covered entryway of *Hotel Ibo Lélé*.

Seaborne darted in and out of columns on the open-air side, run-sliding when he could on the burnished tile.

"So, you are here to see Carnival?" the crisp front desk clerk said as he cheerfully slid paperwork across a varnished mahogany top. "That is very brave of you, madame!"

Claire pulled Seaborne to her side, which he submitted to for a few seconds before breaking away to explore. She fought the urge to tell him not to wander far. What could possibly get to him here? This was a top-rate hotel with a good reputation.

"Mom! Maaahm! Oww! Over here!"

Claire dashed around the corner to find Seaborne next to a giant cactus and cradling his left arm.

"I—tripped—and—fell," he sobbed, "trying—to—scratch—my—name!"

Claire shot a quick glance at the dueling cactus where she saw for herself the many crudely etched block letters on its thick trunk and upraised limbs. To be fair, Seaborne was only one in a long line of visitors inspired to leave their mark.

She gingerly extended the injured arm.

"Ouch! It hurts! Look!" He pointed to a patchwork of green-yellow spears growing from his elbow and forearm.

"We can take care of this," she tried to sound confident. "Let's get my magnifiers and tweezers."

"Allow me, madame. These things do happen from time to time," said a muumuu wearing, thickly-accented, impeccably spoken woman who appeared out of nowhere. "I have one hundred percent sook-cess removing kacktuce queelss from little boys' arms," said the woman whose aqua blue eyes with matching eye shadow, long silver hair, and bronze tan constituted her fourth, fifth, and sixth most striking features.

Seaborne was immediately disarmed by two things, and allowed himself to be ushered down a small flight of stairs to the sprawling open-air restaurant—and pool—below. The way she pronounced "kack-tuce queelss," and the little blond dog that materialized from the same nowhere.

With a fruit punch the color of sunset before him, a wooden bowl of scorched peanuts, and a pooch to pet with his good arm, Seaborne suffered the quill removing process undramatically. Bits and pieces of the adults' conversation drifted into his head and out. He learned, for instance, that the exotic woman was the owner of the hotel. He couldn't remember what the name *Ibo Lélé* meant—something about snakes and gods. Way too deep, so for the most part Seaborne focused on the mongrel. This dog of no discernible breed sat placidly while the boy fondled small ears doubled over in a neat fold, the tip of one jagged from an old wound. Traces of healed scars criss-crossed its muzzle, and Seaborne noticed it walked with a limp, tail down not quite between his legs, but almost.

"I see you and Mortified have an understanding already. He doesn't let just anyone touch him," the lady said. "He's very, how shall I say, shy."

"What did you call him?" Seaborne asked, wincing from an abrupt quill yank.

"Mortified."

"What does that mean?"

"Embarrassed, a leetle ashamed." She paused, ocean-blue eyes peering over granny glasses to connect with his.

Seaborne took a moment with those words. They described how he felt when he'd gotten up from his fall.

"He doesn't seem that way now," Seaborne said quietly.

"Not so much now, you are right, but when we met he was a mangy, cadaverous street dog. Do you know what those words mean?"

"I think—*ouch!*"

"That was the last one. Well done. You are very brave."

"How did you meet each other?" the boy asked, slurping the remains of his punch.

"He wandered into the hotel one day a year or so ago, just the way you came in, along the covered path into the lobby. Fortunately for him I happened to be behind the front desk rather than one of my employees. Some people, you see, are not fond of dogs the way you and I are."

"Why not?"

"That's a longer story, for another time. I'm sure you'd rather go swimming."

"Not really," Seaborne declined. Mortified yawned, stretched, and curled up a few feet away.

Thoroughly used to such a captive audience, the owner continued. "I heard scratching and grunting, the sound of little nails tippy-tapping on the floor. I thought one of my Chihuahuas had gotten out."

"Do you still have the Chihuahuas?"

"Three of them."

"Mom, she has three Chihuahuas! Can I have another fruit punch?"

"I heard dear, and yes," Claire said pleasantly, motioning to the waiter.

"There he was, right on the other side of the front desk, patches of fur missing, scabs all over. A real mess. Somehow, though, he was not afraid of me, nor I of him. I scooped him up, nursed him back to health and now, as you can see, he is a fat lazy old fellow!"

"I think his name should be Lucky," Claire offered, not quite as deeply charmed by Mr. Mortified as the other two.

"Luck has very little to do with it," the hotel matron smiled kindly, a knowing look on her face.

"Why do you still call him Mortified? Isn't he over that part of his life?"

"That's a very thoughtful question, young man. What is your name?" she asked.

"Seaborne," he replied proudly. "With an 'e' at the end. It's the British way."

"Very mighty. Is there a reason you're called that?"

"Because I was born at sea on a big, big ship," he beamed.

"And you are how old?"

"Eight," he chirped, displaying all but two of his fingers.

"You mean to tell me that eight years ago you were born—on the sea—and here we sit, much time has passed, and you're still called Seaborne?"

"I think I get it," he said, grinning.

"It's not such a bad thing to remember your past. Do not ever be afraid of who you are, where you came from, or what you are called to do."

"Did you want to tell her your real name?" Claire hinted.

"It's Jesus Cruz Zeisse. Seaborne is just my nickname."

"Well, a name is just a name, anyhow. What does it really signify?"

"Who I am?" he answered after a long pause. Both women laughed.

"You are a human being. It's up to you to discover what that means."

The sound of muffled, rhythmic horns bleating off-kilter with metallic scraping and percussion beats slowly permeated the air.

"Saved by the Ra Ra!" The hotel maven clapped her hands in joy. Mortified leapt up and slunk out of sight. "This time of year, during the run-up to Easter, Ra Ra happens. They'll be passing in front if you want to experience it."

Claire drained her glass, grabbed her camera gear and, ever so glad to be doing something active, took Seaborne by the hand. They retraced their steps, stopping first to scratch "SZ" and "CZ" into the green flesh of the offending cactus.

"Ra Ra happens—I love it!" Claire yelled, standing in the middle of the street, reeling off shots, the Ra Ra band not more than a bus length away and gaining, expressive song of voices and instruments infusing the moist air, getting louder.

A few advance guards wore red sashes around their waists, cracked whips and pointed at the *blanc*, a local word for foreigner, mimicking her actions, dancing a curious pirouette around her while maintaining a playful but respectful distance. Seaborne, loaded down with camera bags, watched nervously. He knew his mother sometimes got crazy in the heat of a shoot and tended to forget her own safety.

"Look out!" he called, warning her of an oncoming car honking its horn in sympathetic time with the revelers.

"Honey, bring me a fifty mil lens—hurry!"

Two flag bearers arrived first, slightly ahead of the pack. Waving shimmering banners heavy with multi-hued sequins, they danced a figure eight around the foreigners, laughing and engaging them with *how are yooos* and *see ya laders!*

"My God those flags are beautiful!" Claire yelled, torn between staring them down with her naked eyes and capturing them on film. "Magic flags, magic!"

The body of the Ra Ra band swarmed past them. A woman in an orange trench coat and Lombardi hat conducted the musical troops with erratic toots of her whistle, the shrill trills syncopating with the beat of sweaty drummers in a crazy, unpredictable way. Clapping hands, stomping legs, thick truncated reeds blasting a nasal "moo moo" when panted into, graters rubbed with crooked sticks and sheet metal fashioned into crude metal horns with oversized trumpets, red shirts everywhere, bottles clinking, women with heads covered in scarves, all bouncing up and down, side by side, zany happy, carefree for a spell, some dazed and rapturous, others less possessed, gyrating hips swaying and shuffling to the unified force. Seaborne clung to his mother's side as the big, loud, colorful, and stinky sea washed over them, jostling, bumping, bathing them in hope, fear, and wonder.

The mass turned as one. Like a school of fish suddenly changing direction, they encircled the foreigners, pressed in while the bleating, frenzied music intensified. One man's grizzly face stood out—bulging eyes bloodshot and unblinking bore down on the boy. Something passed between them that made Seaborne's knees go weak, a moment when no one could predict what the man might do.

It broke, the wave passed, sweeping Claire along.

"Mom!" Seaborne yelled, dashing out of the mayhem to a place just beyond the pack.

"I'll be right back!" she yelled, Nikon furiously clicking.

Breathless, Claire soon returned to Seaborne, who sat on the hotel entry stairs, arms tightly wrapped around pulled-up knees, trying to shake the lingering jitters. "Did you see the flag with the sailboat?" he managed.

"Yeah, and the one with the big heart?"

"It's way bigger than the one we have at home."

"Gonna have to track those down," Claire said under her breath. Seaborne heard nonetheless.

Ra Ra happens.

CHAPTER 56

Eugene picked them up from the *Hotel Ibo Lélé* on Sunday at 4 o'clock, his new favorite time of day. Destination: midtown Port-au-Prince. Claire had decided that rather than drive around trying to follow the Carnival action through town, she'd shoot from a stationary vantage point—the spectator stands near the triple-domed National Palace. They no sooner squeezed themselves into the bristling bleachers, with Eugene as escort, than the first floats trundled by, music blaring from stressed speakers and surrounded on all sides by thousands bouncing up and down in time to the *merengue*. Realizing she needed to be in the crowd for full effect, Claire coached Seaborne to hold onto her blouse and not let go for any reason. Eugene said he'd keep an eye out.

At street level, elbows knocked chests, bumped shoulders, groins ground into the first available piece of flesh ahead, knees clobbered thighs, feet tripped feet. No problem! Haitians made merry in practical and ribald ways, overlooking, it seemed, any collateral damage. Claire had to laugh at one cardboard effigy bobbing on a stick above the crowd, a crude rendering with articulated arms and pelvis that repeatedly jabbed the air with a stiffly upturned phallus.

Floats continued to drift by. One GMC flat bed truck accommodated an energetic ten-piece band on its expansive deck, snappy tunes frenzying the crowd into double-time hip moves. A bottle of rum passed into and out of Claire's hands, and Seaborne was offered a pacifier full of the stuff.

A moving palm tree appeared on the horizon. Thinking it might be the one she'd been waiting for, she reminded Seaborne to stay glued to her.

"Like white on rice, you hear?" she drilled into his ringing ears.

They pushed their way closer. Eugene followed.

The palm tree heralded the Department of Tourism float, a fact confirmed by the jolly figure of Monsieur Jolicoeur, a rail of a man perennially dressed in white suit, walking stick, and generally known for his effusive airport greetings. With the bearing of a dancer and a dove he presided over the crowd, waving and smiling graciously. Claire made her move and climbed aboard, confident the tug on her shirt and the little hand in hers was Seaborne's. Nodding politely at introductions, she turned her head fully expecting to see the familiar tangle of wavy brown hair, but in its place stood a neat little Afro.

"Halo lady!" the imposter beamed.

"Where's my son?" she cried without caring whether or not he understood.

"Down der," the spindly Haitian boy said, pointing good naturedly.

Sure enough *der* he was, alone in a sea of strangers with fornication on their minds, Eugene nowhere in sight. Seaborne stood stricken, mouth open in a silent wail, tears streaming down his face, gulping air best he could through snot and saliva.

Seeing the frantic look on her face and the separation growing as seconds ticked by, the local boy asked, "You wan me get eem?"

"Yes!"

The boy leapt off the float, his landing softened by a man wearing, off all things, a Nixon mask. Claire watched his every move as he threaded through a miscellany of body parts to reach her confused and paralyzed son. The Haitian boy grabbed Seaborne and spun him in the direction of the swaying palm tree where he saw his mother flailing her arms, letting fly the SOS with Mr. Jolicoeur's pristine white jacket. He dodged toward the float where a relieved-looking Eugene edged out Nixon and swung him airborne into the welcoming arms of his mother. The Haitian boy disappeared in the crowd, unaware of how much gratitude he'd earned that day.

CHAPTER 57

April 1986, Port-au-Prince (11 years later)

Ti Mouche felt light on the balls of his feet as he walked, a jaunty, bow-legged jig—enjoying the spring in his step and the breeze on his face. He smiled at the warmth of the sun. The blue sky welcomed him, and Mouche raised his arms to greet the air. It was kite season, his favorite time of year. He didn't have a kite, but he had a knapsack, and its bounce thumped reassuredly against his back, filled as it was with his worldly possessions: an actual toothbrush (he considered himself very lucky on this front); a hotel sewing kit; a Chicago Bulls cap he'd have to grow into; pencil, pen, and small notebook (in case he resumed school); a tin of something called Altoids, and though the curiously strong mints were gone it did house several of his baby teeth, a British coin of lovely gold color and hefty weight (purely ornamental but it made him feel rich), an American Indian head buffalo nickel from 1936 only to be spent in a dire emergency; and (not in the tin) a large brass keychain which he kept even though he had no keys and didn't anticipate getting any. Tourists gave him the damnedest things.

As he walked, Ti Mouche knotted his hands behind his back to ease the thump against his spine and contemplated the hard paving beneath his worn Converse hi-tops.

This concrete is the mountain over there, he thought, looking distant to the enormous swell of uplifted rock and earth that formed Haiti's central range. He could make out a small white patch and knew that's where they dug out the gravel. Though young, he had plenty of experience with this level of transformation, of catastrophic change.

The backpack felt good (it had belonged to a wealthy boy named Eddie Bauer, according to the fancy sewn-in tags). Good like in the days when Mouche went to school at *L'armée du Salut*, Salvation Army, behind the foreign lady's business where his parents worked and they all lived. Those were really, really good times. The knapsack was a reminder of those days, being an accessory to the navy blue and white checkered uniform with black shoes. He'd felt so proud as a student but had to quit during the 2nd grade when *papa* died of *SIDA*. The dentures Madame had bought for his father wound up being too big for his mouth after a while. This his father seemed to regret the most, loving those dentures like he did (Ti

Mouche carried them in his backpack until he finally had to sell them for money).

After his mother passed he became married to the streets. A younger brother had already died from pink blood and fever, leaving him with a sister who went to live with an aunt. He never saw them.

As for his old life, only the backpack remained. He knew his alphabet, could write his real name, knew how to make change and pay with the right coins and bills, which was all he really needed to know, besides somehow learning to drive a *camionette*, his dream.

CHAPTER 58

APRIL 1986, MIAMI

The day started off unlike most. Not only had he gotten up earlier than usual—pulled off his job as brakeman for the local shortline to do track work—but a weird interplay of fresh past and stale present had settled into his pre-dawn mental fog.

Seaborne grabbed his satchel and plopped a scratched-up "easy rider" helmet on his head without bothering to thread the strap. He'd made a deal with his mom to always wear it; her permission still counted 51% of the time since the apartment was in her name, even though she spent most of her days traveling the Caribbean in search of Art and, he suspected, Romance, in addition to unusual stuff to photograph and write about. She was finding it, too, according to their last static-filled phone conversation in which she'd breathlessly mentioned discovering a town called *Jeremie* with blue-eyed black natives, descendents of God-only-knew-which-imperialists, and reached from Port-au-Prince by a 140-mile round trip ferry ride.

"Good luck with that," Seaborne chuckled, picturing chickens and goats crowding the decks as they seemed to do in all modes of transportation on that crowded island.

"Honey, almost forgot. I got a post office box here so we can write each other, might save on these expensive international calls. It's number 2-3-3-0, Port-au-Prince, Haiti, West Indies."

"Got it," he said too quickly to be convincing.

"Write it down mister!"

"I've memorized it! 2-3-3-0—there."

"Write to me, k?"

He heard an echo on the line, always a disconcerting sign.

"I will. When are you coming home?"

The line crackled.

"What's that?" came her distant voice.

"When are you coming home?"

"You mean, there?"

"Uh, yeah."

"No plans to return yet. I'm about to sublet a great little apartment here, things are heating up with demonstrations and rallies since Duvalier left, lots to cover. Maybe you could come down." She hesitated, as if trying to decide whether to continue along this road. "There are some people here who'd very much like to meet you…"

Seaborne didn't bite.

"I'd rather visit a badger in hell!" he joked, then the connection was lost. He waited a few minutes, but she hadn't called back. Their conversation, already a week old, had stuck with him. He looked around the apartment, waiting for Something to Happen. Nothing did, but it was then and only then he realized the big sequin flag with the heart was gone. The one with the boat still hung in place in the living/dining room, but its companion—Claire's favorite—was missing. In fact, no trace was left, no holes in the wall, chipped paint, or scuff marks. As if it'd never existed. When had he stopped noticing?

CHAPTER 59

One day it just happened. Ti Mouche had been keeping an eye on the thinning fabric and knew right where to look to gauge the wear: under the buttocks, where the baggy pant unfulfilled by flesh had developed a curious line on the brink of parting. Also, if full stock be taken, the hems on the cuffs dangled in tassels of liberated thread, but this didn't matter half as much as the fine striations that'd developed above each knee directly opposite the cargo pockets.

An eleven-year-old with no physical complaints, most of his teeth (some still coming in), eyesight good, limbs intact, Ti Mouche watched the dissolution of threads with a curiosity borne from the vantage point of overall good health. Surely a sign of things to come, this cumulative wear. Had he had scabs to pick, sore gums, or rampant headaches like most people he knew, he might not have paid such close attention to the process of decline. Hourly he observed the wear until, without warning, the soft, thin strands ruptured. They had done so independent of his will, after stooping down to pick up a six-sided chrome nut. The holes Ti Mouche named *pétés tonnerres*, thunder farts, for their tattered, clumped strands looked as if an emission of gas had ripped through the weakened fabric. Shards and flaps blew in the breeze, exposing a hand's width of inner thigh not quite to the knee.

Some kind of response was required.

He'd heard there was a new shipment of *rad kennedy*, second hand clothes from the States, that would be ready for sale the next morning.

This was important because, in addition to ratty pants, Ti Mouche's only other shirt had lost both sleeves, a breast pocket, and most of its buttons, forcing him to tie the tails around his waist like some exotic dancer. He seldom wore it, preferring his red hooded Chicago Bulls sweatshirt. Roomy and not too hot, he kept the two ends of the neck cord tied in a knot way down at his chest with a carabiner clipped on the loop. That sweat shirt and carabiner made him the envy of many a street kid. It also garnered him some respect, young as he was, because he looked good, tough, capable. Or maybe it was just the menacing bull face. At any rate, the ensemble gave him confidence.

The process of buying new threads was not a benign one. First, it involved deciding which *marchande,* or merchant, to engage. Understandably, some of them had better reputations than others for consistency and fair dealing. He preferred Madame St. Juste's little territory at the corner of Rigaud Market in *Pétionville,* the richest town in Haiti. Buzzing between Port-au-Prince and *Pétionville* whenever he could scrape up the twenty-cent fare to make the seven-mile trip, Ti Mouche liked to earn money in the latter and sleep in the former where necessities (a dollop of rice and beans, a chunk of deep fried pork) were cheaper. Sometimes it was the other way around. Maybe it was all just an excuse to ride with his favorite *camionette* drivers and observe tricks of the trade.

In the hill town named after one of Haiti's first presidents, wealth lined the streets and it extended to the merchandise, even the second-hand goods. You came to *Pétionville* looking decent and clean. If you didn't, the rich snobs would doubly ignore you. Forget washing their car windows for a *gourde* if tattered pants and a snotty nose were your calling card. His philosophy ran contrary to most who liked to look downtrodden, hoping to elicit a few coins out of sympathy.

Which is why Ti Mouche, on this April day, lit up when he saw the next best thing to cargo pants. Peeking out from a jumble of clothes piled high on a plastic tablecloth on the ground, he spotted a pair of slightly faded blue jeans. Levis.

Ti Mouche pounced. *"Combien?"*

Mme. St. Juste, however, had bigger fish to fry with two house-maids in the market for brand new kerchiefs. As they combed through the stiff folds of never-before-worn polka dots, paisley, and other patterns for which there was no name, Mme. St. Juste knew if she kept a close eye and prevented any sleight of hand she would stand to make a two *gourde* profit, forty cents, on each scarf. She also knew these two young servant women worked around the corner at the Mourra house where a kind-hearted American lady ran the household and gave them food, lodging, and decent wages. They could afford to pay top dollar, especially for the convenience of proximity. Thoughts of profits—however modest, still, they were profits—ran through her head as she waved Ti Mouche off with a dismissive *pantalon yo pa pou ou.*

"Why aren't these pants for me?" he demanded, giving them the sniff test for good measure.

"You can't afford them!"

She was right, of course. He couldn't afford them. Didn't even have twenty pennies for the ride back downtown. He strolled a few feet away, hovering, shaking his head, clicking his teeth. This would not do.

Ti Mouche approached the housemaids. *"Est-ce-que madam gen travail pou moin? M kap palé oun ti anglé."*

"No, we don't need any more help even if you do speak a little English," came the reply in Creole.

Hands and forearms jammed into the expansive front pockets of his sweatshirt, he fingered the heavy nut. This would get him back downtown if he flagged the right *camionette* driver who needed one.

He took mental inventory of his other belongings and realized he did have one or two items that might be of interest to the seasoned vendor. He waited until the housemaids paid their money and sauntered off, knowing full well Mme. St. Juste would be flush with happiness over a successful sale. Slinging his backpack forward, he retrieved a hefty brass keychain with the word EVITA, whatever that was, in big letters, and a date of 25 September 1979, his fourth birthday, more or less.

"Look at this. Very beautiful, also heavy, you can use it to defend yourself. If you have a key you can put it here," pointing to the ring. *"I can show you how,"* he offered politely.

Mme. St. Juste allowed herself to be wooed. This skinny little kid had some charm, neatly trimmed short hair, the whites of his eyes and flash of his teeth prominent against a handsome face.

"Hmm. I do have a key. This would help me not lose it."

"I want those pants AND this shirt," he picked up both, fancying the latter because of its cartoon frog and cheerful green color. Some writing in English had the amphibian saying something, but he didn't know what.

"Non mon chere, just the pants. This is a very good deal," she admonished, the effects of his charm wearing off.

"How about this for the shirt?" He gallantly placed a yellow plastic lei around her neck, then stood back to observe the effect. *"Very pretty."* He regretted having to give that up, too, recalling how a nice lady from a cruise ship had gently slipped it over his head after showing her the sights.

A little more innocent haggling and he got the goods. This was the way life went for Ti Mouche. Things came, things went. Even Duvalier was gone. Somehow, it was all the same. But he felt that by summer his circumstances would change. He knew this sure as he knew if a frog pissed in your eye, you'd be blind.

CHAPTER 60

On the deserted two-lane road, cool air painted Seaborne's face and coiled around his body, rocking him awake. The headlight cut an adequate beam, exposing all manner of flying bugs and scurrying animals, among them, frogs. He made a special effort to avoid these, for when squished, they made for slippery roadways. How many times had he walked ahead of a locomotive, shoo-ing away sun-bathing croakers perched on the rails? Even as a newbie he'd done it plenty. Engineers lauded his efforts for it eliminated wheel slip coming out of the yard bowl, but truth be told, Seaborne could relate to their need for both water and land and the ease with which they passed from one to the other. Trouble was, no one had prepared them for cars, motorcycles, or trains.

Shifting into fifth gear he settled back and allowed his mind to merge with the steady hum of the engine beneath him, glad it was Friday. Since taking the job at the railroad, his first real one, thanks to a friend of his mother's, he'd noticed himself falling into the same pattern as everyone else—TGIF, work all week to make it to those two days off. Sometimes less. If the yard was busy and there was tons of switching to do, a sixth day was required in order to service the local freight clients along the I-95 corridor.

His thoughts naturally drifted to his real love—boats—even though the Honda nosed west, away from the ocean. Vague made-up images of Claire's ferry adventures crossed his mind, then the memory of the listing boat he'd seen years ago from the air wormed its way into his head. Seaborne doused the unsettling thoughts with visions of his birth ship. One of the many things that fascinated him about RMS Queen Mary was the fact, he realized on that early morning of all early mornings, that she'd had a last voyage, one planned and designated as such.

Last voyage.

There was a last time she left her home port of Southampton.

Last time.

Passengers would never again feel her reassuring bulk beneath them or see her riveted flanks pant under pressure from rough seas. New Yorkers would no longer witness that graceful prow slice the Hudson, funnels puffing lightly as she passed (barely) beneath the Verrazano Narrows Bridge. Barnacles, crustaceans, and clams clinging to the submerged Holland Tunnel would no longer instinctively recoil from the mass of steel passing just a few inches above their, well, heads. Never again pull into Pier 90 after hours of do-si-doing with wind, tides, and tugs. And though almost twenty years had passed since she last steamed—his whole lifetime, in fact—he imagined molecules from the Mary still drifting along Atlantic currents. He pictured himself at the beach, immersed in the dazzling remnants. The ship completed 1001 crossings—surely something had rubbed off.

No. RMS Queen Mary hadn't died; she floated in state. Neither breach in hull, raging fire nor the breaker's ball had done her in. Most others not so lucky.

Last sunset. *Last* sunrise. *Last* breath.

Last...breath...

Seaborne looked up in time to see a fireball flare in the aurora sky, a low ball of flame shooting south, the red orange glow of its streaming tail intensifying then *poof*, extinguished. He wanted to follow, search nearby fields for steaming celestial metal that might've made it to the ground, something physical he could take away to mark the day. For a second or two this seemed imperative, the most important thing he could do for himself. Then that, too, faded.

He'd been thinking of his father the past few weeks, wondering who he was, what he looked like, whether he, too, could ever get his fill of meatball subs. Would they ever meet? Surely the fireball was a sign.

"Hi dad!" he smiled, downshifting as he neared the job site. Couldn't bring himself to be nice to his blood mother, not yet. If ever.

There was one more thing about the Queen Mary, that ship of ships, and it was huge, even though it wasn't the thing he usually remembered her for. She'd brought all of his parents together in one fell swoop and delivered him, literally, into their hands. For this miracle, he would forever be grateful.

The work went well, but all day long, in slow-motion spells, Seaborne caught himself picturing what he looked like from afar, as a mother might see him. Never a fun thing for a son. This was a new unfolding of his mind triggered, in part, by proximity to an odd co-worker that day. He often saw his own physical traits in others even when they weren't outwardly alike; a kind of melding took place that made him feel almost woozy with oneness. More an impression, a tone, rather than hard fact, it went something like this.

Carhartt coveralls, their original tan presently camouflaged by patches of oil-slick black. Easy tall, lean, blond brown waves caressed the back of a sunburnt neck that should've been named Earl but was merely Jim. Scuffed white hardhat hid the rest of the 'do, never once removed (that day) to wipe, scratch, or just plain let scalp breathe. Delicate mustache complimented full, rosy upper lip, blond hairs equally mixed with dark. The thing, really, that made Seaborne stare, and where any illusion of similarity diverged, were the bottom teeth. Corn cob sockets. A depressed ridge of porous roach-brown, seething stumps. One could not help but stare in wonder how a working man making good money could let such decay occur.

He of soft-spoken Southern roll, Jim stood tending a small fire most of the day—burning dunnage and stripping copper wire, the latter for beer money. Thick round spectacles magnified his eyes, imparting an old-fashioned studious look until the teeth revealed themselves and *Deliverance* sprang to mind. Seaborne did not wear glasses and all of his sturdy, god-given dental fixtures lorded above clean blue overalls and white t-shirt, and though his hair was darker he fancied some resemblance.

Gentle demeanor, graceful posture, unhurried. Cigarette delicately balanced between his lips, Jim stirred the fire in slow strokes, the spade a lanky, befitting appendage. The man looked good with a shovel. This simple revelation startled Seaborne, and he wondered if he himself looked good with a shovel. It wasn't exactly the kind of question you could ask, he thought, leaning against the long wooden handle, shooting the shit. Still, though beefier and shorter, he felt pretty sure he cut a decent figure.

Seaborne mimicked the older man's pace, so much so that by the end of the day he was completely relaxed. They churned the smoldering remains, prodding the valuable copper wire, willing the plastic coating to melt. The rest of the track crew did the heavy work, but these two just reduced trash to ash, and Jim hastened the process with the bulbous toe of his work boots, old Red Wings, leather singed and darkly smooth with a hint of burgundy, flashes of raw metal at the promontory, heels worn down by a third. Seaborne wondered what the man looked like in off hours, what he wore, how he smelled, if he preferred Pabst over Schlitz, London Broil over liverwurst.

A rip-curl of sadness broke and without warning he felt empty, stomach sour and contrite, for the quiet comraderie they shared that day was something he imagined a father and son might do.

If only this guy's mother could see him now.

If only anybody could see *him* now.

CHAPTER 61

In the afternoon shade, Ti Mouche sat leaning against a street lamp outside the gates of the American Embassy—his favorite place to hang out downtown, watch the *blancs* come and go, maybe practice some English. It didn't hurt that Wilson, the old Haitian cook in the cafeteria, occasionally snuck him food—french fries were the best. Knees bent, back against the sturdy conglomerate pole, work site held practically under nose, needle strokes painstakingly mended a small hole in his new Levis. He'd been there more than an hour. Mouche tied off and severed the last stitch when a white Suburban drove up. Long as a boat, he knew these diplomatic vehicles rarely contained more than two people at any given time. Such a waste, they'd make good taxis! He fantasized about driving one, collecting fares, selecting artwork and sayings for its body, vehicular tattoos that set each one apart.

This one contained six, three Haitians and three *blancs*. All wore dead-pan expressions behind tinted glasses. One of the men in the backseat kept looking nervously behind at something in the cargo area. The driver honked for the guard to hurry up. Ti Mouche sniffed something afoot and dashed over to the Suburban as it moved impatiently against a partially open gate. In order to see into the well he sprang up and down, and at the top of each spring he saw a body, prompting a Haitian man to roll down his window and threaten him with empty words to make him go away. But he got his glimpses. The body of a white woman with coal black hair that clung in messy jags to her neck and forehead, as if wet. Glimpses, as the Suburban screeched into the inner sanctum of the Embassy, of a lifeless body and the blank, open stare of death.

Funny thing was, he knew her—she drove a yellow Volkswagen that looked like a Jeep, license plate *Privé 28739*. He remembered how, after trips to the Post Office, she'd spend time outside, her wide-brimmed hat flopping in the breeze, browsing and chatting with dozens of painters and canvases set up across the street. In addition to being kind, she'd given him a gift once, one he still carried.

God bless you nice lady.

This was all very curious, but Ti Mouche had bigger fish to fry. In search of a private nook between buildings to try on his new pants, he couldn't wait to see how the previous wearer's form fit his.

CHAPTER 62

The flashing message light reminded Seaborne of the fireball earlier that day. He smiled wanly—the only people who ever called him were Claire and Guga. It could wait. He stripped on the way to the shower, a trail of ripe work clothes snaking beyond the living room. The sun's last rays illuminated the lone sequined flag—*Agwe*, god of the seas—the mate to the heart flag, virtual duplicates of the ones the Ra Ra revelers had swooshed around them many years before. Its beauty went unremarked in the rush to cleanse and begin the weekend.

CHAPTER 63

Next morning, Seaborne woke groggily to the synthesized *bing bings* of *Ring My Bell* straining the speakers of his alarm clock—he'd forgotten to disable it. Grumpy, he took stock of three things likely to prevent him from going back to sleep: (1) hunger—conch fritters and calamari from the Oceanside Bar had not stuck to his ribs; (2) urine—had to pee bad from the extra volume of *liquid* consumed the night before; and (3) crap—once he drank water to quench his dry mouth he'd probably have to take a dump, the dirty kind that required a lot of wiping, courtesy of his most recent odd meal.

Throwing back the covers, he resigned himself dully.

It just never ends, he slurred, flushed the toilet, and commenced gathering stinky clothes on his way to the living room. Seaborne felt old compared to others his age who surfed all day and partied all night. He'd taken the railroad job on a lark—to earn money to finish college (should he be moved to do so) or just support himself in relative comfort while developing a trainman's career. It was a lot easier to feel somewhat good about oneself when earning cash to spend and stash.

The message light blinked a pattern that signaled two calls. He maneuvered one index finger beyond the heap of clothes in his arms and pressed the button. *Click. Whir.* The tape rewound, stopped. *Beeeep.*

"Hey mister, how's it going weeth you," Guga's voice announced, more whiney and accented than usual, sounding tired. "Sorry I missed you but wanted you to know I'm on my way to Brazeeou, James is coming with me. *Papi* had a stroke…long estory," he sighed and paused to slurp something. "Anyhow, love to you both. Where is she, anyhow? Tell her it's the same number if she needs to reach me. *Ciao bambino.*" Lips smacked and kisses flew.

"Love you, too," Seaborne called through a mouthful of toothpaste. He could hear well from the bathroom which was tucked behind the open kitchen off a short hallway.

Beeeep.

Deciding whether to shave. Fingering sparse stubble, sideburns, nose hair—was anything growing?

"Ah, hello? We're trying to reach a family member—"

The man speaking sounded American, stiff, official, with an exaggerated evenness of tone, as if reading from a script. Seaborne took notice and padded back into the main room to be near the answering machine.

"—of a woman named Claire Zeisse who, uh, registered here at the Embassy in Port-au-Prince. She listed this phone number as belonging to her son, Seaborne. If this is you please contact us immediately at 011-509-2-4431. The name is Briggs."

All preoccupations, vitality, and veneer flushed to his feet in a freefall that left the space around his head and body crystal clear. Here was a moment of truth. Something had happened to his mother—exactly what, they weren't saying. Guga was far away and Seaborne didn't have his Brazil information. It looked as though it was up to him to deal with what had arisen.

At first he felt glum, sorry for himself. Didn't know whether his mother was in a prison for sympathizing with boat people or in a hospital languishing from some dreadful tropical disease. Deep down, he suspected she was neither. Off-balance, his feelings ran the gamut. He resented the thought of missing work, being pulled from his life, his routine, because of someone else's drama.

Then, as if to instruct in another way of looking at things, key images flashed.

Heart-shaped stones—heart.

Claire clutching a bundled infant on the Sun Deck of Queen Mary.

The *Ibo Lélé* owner allowing Mortified to stay, nursing him back to health.

Guga baking cookies just to see a little boy smile.

Sure, any way you cut it, it all revolved around him, but why not regard the situation as a mission, an assignment, a continuation of his life rather than an interruption, or worse, an inconvenience. Once he decided this, his energy surged and he snapped to.

Claire's life might well depend upon it.

CHAPTER 64

Seaborne called three different numbers to track Briggs down on a Saturday. The Embassy was technically closed. A nice Haitian woman gave him Briggs's home number, whereupon a nice Haitian housekeeper told Seaborne that Monsieur was at the beach. He almost left it at that and hung up, which would've been par for the pre-emergency son with no real fire under his ass. Then it occurred to him to ask which one.

"Ibo Beach."

Seaborne dug through the drawers of a built-in credenza that stored all manner of reference material—menus, yellow pages, owner's manuals, the Haitian *Annuaire*, or phone book. He couldn't find the number, so he rang up a Teleco operator and asked to be connected to Ibo Beach, whereupon Briggs's breakfast was shortly thereafter interrupted.

"I'm sorry to have to tell you this," the American said as Seaborne's nose tingled from the onset of tears, "but we have reason to believe that Claire Zeisse perished in a ferry accident two days ago. We are holding the, uh, body at the Embassy until a family member can make positive identification. I'm so sorry, I know how difficult—"

"I'll be there tomorrow."

"Will you be traveling alone?"

"Yes."

"I'll pick you up at the airport. If you don't mind my asking—how old are you?"

"Nineteen."

"Very young. I'm so sorry."

"Could you tell me…what the…body…looks like?"

"It's in good shape, if that's what you're worried about."

"What color hair?"

"Jet black."

CHAPTER 65

A Yellow Cab dropped him off outside American Airlines at Miami International. Seaborne moved as if in a daze, his mind curiously blank, devoid of all but the most mundane thoughts. He kept replaying his brief conversation with the embassy guy. What'd led them to believe the body was Claire's? It wasn't like she carried a wallet on her—how did they know? He hoped against hope a mistake had been made.

Seaborne stood in line at the check-in area, his only bag a Nike backpack. Around him, small groups of Haitians scooted bulging boxes and suitcases through the cordoned maze, squabbling in sharp Creole. A few tried to cut the line but they were loudly chastised by fellow well-mannered Haitians and slunk to the back to wait their turns.

"Why so busy?" Seaborne managed to ask a priestly-looking fellow behind him.

"Duvalier is gone—people are going home."

Normally this kind of scene would intrigue Seaborne. During his year of college at University of Miami he decided to major in anthropology, a discipline that complemented his tendency to analyze human interactions from afar. Objectively. What a crock. Today he felt like the majority of mankind—just doing what had to be done to get by. Since the phone call he hadn't eaten, slept, showered, or changed out of his old black Carhartts and Megadeth t-shirt. Nothing mattered except getting to Haiti.

The line inched forward. His furrowed brow, folded arms, and clenched jaw proclaimed anger at the world. He didn't want to help, rescue, or make anyone feel better. When a top-heavy rouged woman, bent over in a most unlady-like fashion to deal with a disintegrating box, also lost control of her wobbly two-ton piece of luggage and it landed on Seaborne's foot, he offered no complaint, assistance, or forgiveness. None seemed necessary in light of his own circumstances.

"*Excusez-moi, monsieur, excusez-moi,*" she fretted while clean jerking the offending bag. No sooner would she turn her back than she'd turn around again and plead *excuse, please excuse.*

"No problem. Really." He tried to smile but nothing came.

Claire's published articles about Haiti drifted vaguely through his mind…African slaves (and free people of color) gained independence from the French in 1804—standing joke was that was their first big mistake. With no support from the white world, were they doomed from the outset, a fate more dreaded than any black magic curse? To provide for their families, Haitians, especially the millions living in the capital, needed cash. A slumlord's concrete slab cost $150 a year to rent, then there was the matter of finding cardboard and pallets to build a hut. A two-quart *marmite*, or can, of rice, cost $1.50. Beans, $0.60. Goat or chicken meat, $2 the half pound. Clothing was required, except for the very young who could go naked. Not even schools were free—$20 per year per child. On top of that, fabric for uniforms had to be purchased and sewn, notebooks, pencils, texts and book covers obtained.

Health services, when available, were charged a la carte. At the General Hospital an injection of penicillin cost $2.50. To set a broken limb ran $30, plus the cost of x-rays. And at the very end of the line, when someone's clock finally ran out in the poorest country in the Western Hemisphere, a proper burial could set a family back $600, much of it borrowed from black market lenders who charged unthinkable interest rates.

All of this on an average yearly income of $360. If that.

Talk about wanting to crawl into a hole and never come out. Somehow the hard, objective facts that'd just been words on paper were becoming felt, shape-shifting from black ink to black bodies with eyes, tongues, and hearts.

Up at the check-in counter, the apologetic (and mortified) rouged lady strained to lift her gargantuan piece of luggage onto the stainless steel scale. Afraid she'd fart—or worse—from the effort, Seaborne watched with mild interest from his place in line.

"Too heavy, madame," the ticket agent said dryly, turning her arms into scales and making a weighing motion. *"Peso demasiado,"* she tried once more, in the wrong language. "Overweight fee is $50. And you need a new box for that one."

"Fitty? No have fitty, *oh mon dieu...*" the Haitian leaned heavily on the counter.

"You need two boxes, yes? One to replace the one that's falling apart, and one to remove the excess from the luggage. I can sell you boxes."

"How much da box?"

"Five dollars each."

"Not poss-ee-bul. Fie dolla? No have fie dolla...no ten dolla. *Seigneur,*" the woman wiped her brow, began panting lightly, shaking her head and clucking her teeth in despair.

Seaborne mentally reached into his wallet to plumb the depths of its generosity when he heard a deep voice from behind.

"Allow me, Madame. *Pour les boites.*" A gentleman gave her $10. She nearly fainted from relief and, fanning herself, warmly expressed her gratitude.

The ticket agent wasn't finished. "There will be a surcharge of $25 for the extra box. You're allowed *two* check-throughs."

"Mes amies, qu'est-ce-que c'est? Dix dollars ici, vingt-cinq la, ce sons des voleurs!"

This made people in line chuckle—she'd called the airline bandits, the various charges akin to highway robbery. Her benefactor, stocky, early 60s and sporting knock-out cologne, hefty gold necklace, ring, and Gucci sandals, paid the surcharge and helped the woman shuffle her belongings to the side for re-packing.

Mystified by the two large, flat pieces of cardboard, she complained she thought she was buying *boxes*. Only when her helper began folding the flaps into cubical form did she relax, her dwindling drama eclipsed by similar scenes.

CHAPTER 66

Seaborne stared out the window during most of the flight. He wanted no chit chat, no eye contact. Just Cokes. And pretzels. Puffy clouds looked solid, stationary, like something you could land a plane on. Life had seemed solid, too.

"Ella cumple! She gets things done!" Guga loved to remark about the diminutive journalist who remained very busy making a living to support her family and art habit. When Seaborne became old enough to joke, they both started calling her "Ella Cumple," savoring a ridiculous English pronunciation that rhymed with "Della Rumple" instead of the silky Spanish *eya koomplay.*

If it hadn't been for her, who knew where he'd be. Perhaps a sniveling, sickly, rickety, crooked young man wandering the streets of Acapulco or Santo Domingo who, if lucky, had a job in a hotel or slaughter-house or jeans-assembly factory. To be disadvantaged and disenfranchised in a third world country would not be a fun way to

begin life, much less live out the whole enchilada. This fate he'd narrowly escaped. Mári's scheme had merit after all. Softening, he suddenly felt small and insignificant, overwhelmed by the unknown. His
stomach floated unanchored in his chest cavity, decidedly not where
it belonged. A stewardess making the rounds passed out landing cards
to complete.

Grateful for the distraction, he dug out a pen and right off the
bat experienced confusion over the first question: Family Name and
Surname? After figuring the correct order and content (and leaving out
the name he used most), he proceeded to Citizenship. *American.* Easy
for him to say. Claire—*Ella*—had toiled for years smoothing the complicated circumstances of his nativity. Home Address? No problem. Date
and Place of Birth? Ella had, in fact, persuaded sympathetic city officials
to certify the seaside town of Long Beach as his birth place. After all, she
argued, didn't they own the Queen Mary and hadn't her son been born
on property they owned? Date, 12/7/1967. Nothing to declare. Reason
for trip, business or pleasure? Offended, he wrote "No Choice."

Then the stumpers. Address while in Haiti? Length of stay? *How
the hell do I know?* Seaborne muttered, apparently loud enough for others
to hear, for the kind gentleman dripping in gold twisted around from his
aisle seat directly ahead and, with great effort to maintain the contor-
tion, addressed him thus.

"You don't have a place to stay? Or, if you do and just don't know
the address, which is understandable, a foreign country, funny street
names," the man spoke in a voice rich with tropical notions of coconut
and rum, "you can use mine. I have a hotel on *Delmas*—D-E-L-M-A-S,
the "s" is silent—"

"So I've heard," Seaborne said tersely, remembering Eugene's tutorial years back.

"*Delmas* 31, Hotel Concorde. Write it down." He jabbed a plump
forefinger in the air by way of command.

"I hadn't thought about where I was going to stay..." From his vantage point Seaborne detected a seam between where the man's real hair ended and fake began. Should he trust a gold-loving, toupee-wearing stranger?

"Go ahead, it's legit," the man said, reading Seaborne's thoughts. "If you get in a bind, remember, *Delmas* 31. Ask for Max."

With that, the big man snapped back to his scotch on the rocks as if nothing out of the ordinary had transpired.

On the final approach to Port-au-Prince, the seeds of hope tickled Seaborne with the possibility that this was all one giant mistake and Claire was ok. How could it be otherwise?

The plane glided over sparkling bay waters. *No way those calm waters took her life—she could swim!* He let himself believe she was lying in a hospital bed nursing injuries sustained in the mishap. Maybe his answering machine back home flicked newly red from a message she'd left, her voice weak but reassuring. An air pocket jarred him from his reverie. Passengers gasped then laughed nervously. Seaborne's own heart sank with the plane and did not come back up.

CHAPTER 67

Briggs was lanky with rugged, pockmarked features and close-set blue eyes. A tawny mustache carpeted the real estate below his flared nose, its unkempt bristles curling slightly beyond where they should. He resembled the Marlboro man and looked like he'd be fun to know under different circumstances.

Pocketing the sign that read *American Embassy*, Briggs reached out to shake hands and take the newcomer's papers for ease of processing.

"Any bags?"

Seaborne shook his head. He'd learned his lesson from that first trip. Whether a band played Seaborne could not say, inured to *Yellow Bird* and *ti zwazo* as he was.

"Have you been to Haiti before?" Briggs asked in a gentle twang, unlocking the front passenger door of a mile-long Suburban. Seaborne nodded, choking back the tears.

"Are we going there now?" he asked, body tense, heart pounding. Briggs nodded, let out a big sigh.

The twenty-minute drive to the Embassy stretched endlessly with Seaborne recognizing few of the sights. Toward the end of the eternal ride, a prominent rectangular building, situated perpendicular to the waterfront, caught his eye. Vendors, artists, and beggars milled about with no particular urgency.

"What's that?"

"Main Post Office."

Claire's insistent instructions to record the mailbox number flooded his head. He still remembered it even though he'd only sent one letter.

Around the corner, just before Briggs dialed the steering wheel left a final time, Seaborne glimpsed the vandalized Columbus monument perched near the shore, its canopy and bronze likeness of the explorer once a notable amenity but, since Duvalier's departure, nothing more than a covered ruin.

The vehicle stopped at the black iron gate. Briggs radioed something in a clandestine voice and the gate squeaked open. A Haitian boy tapped on Seaborne's window and, being on the short side, hopped up and down to convey a quick message.

"Wanna see sight? Me guide you!" the boy yodeled on the final downward leg. Seaborne, in the blackest of moods, identified with the kid's shirt which had a perplexed cartoon frog saying *"I'm So Happy I Could Shit."*

"Enterprising little guy—hangs out here. Never asks for money, which is unusual," Briggs shared.

A pair of ramrod Marines flanked the entry stairs to the multi-storey Embassy, a veritable skyscraper by Haiti's standards. Heads inclined slightly, no one said a word. Inside, a deep central hallway stretched immaculate and sterile, terrazzo floors displaying the patina of age. Because it was Sunday, no one was around. It struck Seaborne as all very tomb-like.

At the back of the first floor they took emergency exit stairs down a flight then entered a room full of cartons advertising American brands of buns, mustard, ketchup, sugar, coffee, plastic utensils, napkins, cups.

"Supplies for the cafeteria," Briggs felt obliged to explain. In front of a double-wide metal door he paused, then hefted it open, inviting Seaborne into the cold storage room. Boxes labeled "Hamburger Patties, 100% Beef, USA" which normally would've been kept in the freezer, were stacked on a shelf next to the "All Beef Wieners". To the rear and left, a small door provided access to a much smaller—and colder—space. Briggs stepped in. "This is the moment of truth, I'm afraid."

Why are you *afraid?* Seaborne wanted to say but kept his mouth shut.

Ducking, he joined Briggs inside the freezing, cramped space, bare except for some empty shelves, a table pushed up against the far wall, and a human form beneath a white sheet that still held its fold marks.

"Ready?"

Seaborne nodded even though he wasn't.

First he saw neat black bangs lately infiltrated by rogue strands of silver. He'd expected unkemptness; someone must've brushed her hair. What he didn't expect was the raised bump on her temple, its slit jagged and pale red. Her face lacked expression, eyelashes immobile, garnishing lids drawn over the normal bulge of eyes. Her body had been recovered soon after the incident. Fish had not gotten to her, nor the tides, sun, rocks, or crabs. She was intact, but no longer animated.

He'd seen enough. His mother was dead.

Seaborne's own behavior surprised him. He'd pictured a dramatic scene whereby he'd run bawling his head off, pounding the black gate with all his might to be let out, then dashing along the harbor road, inhaling the rotten egg smell of the bay and deserving no better.

Instead, he felt oddly detached. In shock, most likely. It isn't every day one gets to see one's parent, oldest friend—savior—laid out frozen stiff in a meat locker.

The final details, as far as the Embassy was concerned, were all wrapped up in the mundanity of filing cabinets, typewriters, water dispensers, and Lysol. Yet as he sat in Briggs's office, surrounded by these every day normal things, he couldn't get his mind off of the picture below.

"There is the matter of a death certificate, which will be issued in the coming week." Out loud, Briggs reviewed the information that would be on it.

✺

Name of Deceased: Claire Elizabeth Zeisse
Age: 55
Gender: Female
Race: Caucasian

Birthplace: New York, NY
DOB: May 27, 1930
Marital Status: Married
Children: 1
Spouse's Name: Gustavo Mondavi
Spouse's Occupation: (left blank)
Father's Name: R.D. Zeisse
Father's Birthplace: Milwaukee, WI
Mother's Name: Dorothy Alice Meyers
Mother's Birthplace: Minneapolis, MN
Date of Death: Thursday, April 17, 1986
Primary Cause of Death: Blow to head, drowning
Place of Death: Bay of Port-au-Prince, sinking of ferry boat Pluto
Former Residence: Miami, FL

The information came from the registration card Claire had filled out upon arriving in Haiti. Good thing—Seaborne couldn't have answered nine-tenths of the questions. He lingered over her birth date, a magnificent coincidence. Queen Mary's maiden voyage began the day she was born! Claire was six when the grand ship nosed into its Manhattan pier for the very first time, and though she claims to have been there with her parents, when interrogated, she never remembered particulars.

"There is the matter of the body..." Briggs parked his bottom lip on the mustache and rested it there. "A few things we don't know yet, such as place of burial, date, undertaker's name and address..." He cleared his throat. "I can make arrangements, of course, with a local funeral parlor to carry out your family's wishes..." Off Seaborne's silence he continued. "Or we can arrange to have…the body…flown back to the States."

Seaborne cracked his knuckles. First, the middle joints on his right hand popped in near-unison, then the left, then he pressed the fingers of both hands together and bent them backwards. He left his hands in steeple formation and twiddled his thumbs, otherwise quiet.

"This last option is rather more complicated, but certainly doable," Briggs hastened to add. "You have a little time to think about it, consult with—"

"I'll be making all the decisions," the nineteen-year-old interrupted, preoccupied. "But there is one problem…"

He'd heard Claire express something very emphatically once when the three of them were playing UNO and Seaborne'd asked them to tell (for Guga had been present as well) the burial at sea story for the umpteenth time. On Queen Mary's last voyage a cook had died and, long story short, she'd witnessed the method of his corporeal disposal. The body, entrapped in a tightly sewn shroud, slid from a board tipped by four sailors and floated like a fleecy cocoon on the dark early morning Pacific. The bag took on water, billowing and sinking as the weight increased, becoming dimmer and dimmer beneath the waves as it dropped into oblivion.

"Makes my blood run cold to this day," she'd said, clasping her arms around her chest despite the Florida heat. "Not for me, thank you. I don't want to be dumped in the ocean, buried, burned, rouged, embalmed, or in any way counterfeited."

"Uno!" Guga slapped down his cards and asked, "Then what is your wish?"

"Don't know. I'll leave it up to you fellas."

Seaborne shook his head at the memory of her response. "Mr. Briggs, what do you think I told her?"

"What?"

"I got your back, mom."

"I see your predicament," Briggs said, slightly deflated.

"Could you release her to me?" Seaborne asked after an extended silence.

"Yes, but we still need an undertaker to complete the death certificate."

"Let me work on it." His voice sounded more confident than he felt.

CHAPTER 68

Seaborne glanced at the business card Briggs handed him in parting, on it a reminder to return Tuesday at 10 am for, well, everything. The blank side had his mom's local address, the one she'd provided to the Embassy back when she'd filled out her registration. Having declined the offer of a ride, he took the stairs two at a time and slipped out the pedestrian gate to the streets beyond. Relieved to be outside, he squinted from the glare, eyes narrowed to slits even with the help of cupped hands. This tunnel vision perfectly suited his mood, focused inwardly as he was on his own misery, loneliness and the weight of the tasks ahead.

Oblivious to everything around him, Seaborne wandered aimlessly, immune to the horns and popsicle vendors, zooming enduro-style motorcycles and irksome insects. Nothing made an impact. Not the people staring and pointing as if he were a zombie, not the taxi driver who pestered him for a few blocks then gave up when he failed to engage, not the flies that delighted in landing on his nose and lips. Nothing existed for Seaborne beyond a sad, numb paralysis, as if he moved in a fluid realm with nothing to grab onto. As if he were drowning.

He walked to the edge of the Bay. A brownish surf sloshed up against a cracked and unconvincing breakwater of foot-high concrete. Orange rinds, charred wood, coconuts—some whole and waterlogged, some busted open—a couple of dead fish and aerosol cans floated on its surface. Seaborne had not asked Briggs where she'd been found, why the boat had sunk, or how many other people had died. He preferred not to think about such details. What did it matter? What's done was done.

Her boat should have, he imagined, docked somewhere along the long pier that ran out to sea, about forty cars away (railroad habit made him calculate distance in terms of fifty-foot box cars). A lone cargo ship floated by, a strand of colored bulbs swooping from wheelhouse to stack. He wondered how her body had come ashore. Had it washed up? Given the gently lapping waves, that seemed unlikely. Had someone hauled it in by hand then left it unclaimed, the person not wanting to be implicated in a complicated affair? This would've taken some courage. These folks, according to what he'd learned from his mother, never knew when the wrong side of the law would visit, cleave them in two. A wave of thanks for the unsung hero cracked Seaborne's heart. He began to cry, the drifting sun his solitary companion.

CHAPTER 69

From a distance, Ti Mouche roughly put two and two together. Though he'd had only a smidgen of schooling, he knew the alphabet and numbers, could read at a snail's pace—signs were easiest—and could figure change from a hundred *gourde* note. Well, theoretically. He practiced all the time in his head since he'd not yet had occasion to possess one of those prized purple notes, the equivalent of twenty US dollars. His bright mind a quick study, he saw connections and disconnections everywhere, knew when concordance existed and when it did not. Mostly it did not. He made the best of it.

The scene with the *blanc* across the way indicated a breakdown, a dissolution of threads, just like his pants. Around these parts, attunement to surroundings was key, and all that he didn't know, the book stuff, the grammar, the fancy French, to his knowledge, hadn't hurt him. Yet.

Back to the foreigner with the cool pants of a kind he'd never seen. They had some kind of loop on the side—a *machete* could hang from that! Coming to the Embassy on a Sunday…in the same Suburban the dead woman had arrived in—he knew because he always paid close attention to license plates, tracing the numbers and letters in the air, sounding out words like *Privé* (private), *Location* (rental), *CD* for *Corps Diplomatique*, *Taxi* (indicating rides for fares) or *Gouvernement* (indicating a free ride).

That guy with the wild hair stood facing out to sea, the pack on his back racking up and down, hands messing with his face, snorting snot from one nostril then the other.

Question was, when should he make his move?

CHAPTER 70

Seaborne angrily swiped the tears from his cheeks. The sun, nearly all tucked in below the horizon, shot golden rays into a mauve sky.

She would've liked the sunset.

The water sloshed, a not uncomforting sound despite the look and smell. A pit bobbed in the troughs of gentle swells. Avocado.

Her favorite.

Thoughts from a few days ago filtered back—last voyage, last breath. He couldn't bring himself to imagine what her last breaths were like. Just couldn't.

Was it really only a few days ago life had been normal, contained, predictable?

He kicked a coconut husk. It stuck to the toe of his Teva, wedged tight. Couldn't shake it off. This charade caused an unexpected string of expletives to escape from mid-chest. Finally, a great heave of the leg and perfect ankle pronation sent the coarse brown hemisphere flying into the water. He concluded there was never a convenient time to get a husk stuck on your sandal, and never a convenient time to die.

Seaborne left the shore in deep twilight, drawn to the only place that looked open—a small dingy building with a brightly lit sign on the far side of the Post Office plaza. *Roxy Bar* it proclaimed in neon, blinking the night away in the shape of a windmill, no less.

Soon as he entered the pink doorway he became aware of someone watching from behind. Spinning quickly, on guard, he didn't see anyone threatening, just a young boy who appeared to be tracing Seaborne's footsteps in a time-delayed game of footsies.

A red glow permeated the interior of Roxy Bar, making him think he'd stepped into a giant heart. Life had, in fact, turned anatomical. Things he enjoyed and, to a degree, still possessed, had become painfully obvious by comparison. A beating heart. Red hot blood on the move. He could walk, run, explore.

She could not.

Or could she?

Seaborne could not rectify the extremes of his awareness. The contrasts were intensifying and he wondered if they'd ever go away. Funny thing was, he'd never given thought to any of this when she was alive. Had never given anything a whole lot of thought. Pretty much taken her—and everything else—for granted.

Selfish little bastard. Self-centered prick.

Seemed a cruel twist of fate to be feeling so intensely now that she was gone. Why hadn't anyone prepared him for this? Was a lack of religious upbringing coming home to roost? How far could mottoes like "fight for what you want" really take a person? What if you didn't believe in anything? Why did it have to be her?

Seaborne backed himself onto a tall red bar stool, torso hunched over the scratched mahogany counter. He ordered a rum and Coke and, when it came, protectively cradled the fizzing dark depths that held promise of oblivion.

The bar's most notable occupants were a burly bartender who sported a half-broken front tooth and an older woman who pressed her blue dress suggestively against a shadowy back wall. An overworked sound system infused the room with a fast-paced tune which failed to move him in any way.

Seaborne did not know how long he sat nursing rum and Cokes. Out of the corners of his eyes he saw patrons come and go, the kind he'd seen hanging out in sleazy joints clustered along Miami Beach. Rough men, made brash by a little cash, teaming up with tough women out on business. Here, as in Miami, he couldn't tell if the women were Puerto-Rican, Cuban, or Dominican. He had a low opinion of them all, having known none personally, except his birth mother for a few days, and everyone knew how that'd turned out. Swirling the remnants of a glass, ice cubes long gone, it occurred to him that he'd been dumped by a Dominican woman once. Had a great track record all right; zero for two in the mother department, one gone, the other unaccounted for.

At some unknown hour Seaborne settled his bill and stumbled out of the Roxy. Reeking of cigarette smoke, he brushed off his clothes

and billowed his shirt in an attempt to freshen up. Claire would not ap-
prove. She always gave him a hard time about the way he smelled, and
ashtrays were among the top offenders, right up there with ripe, sour feet.

Doesn't matter anymore.

Venturing a few tottering steps, he barely recognized the dim
square, illuminated in the most minimal way by a lone street lamp and
blue and white *Dominicana de Aviacion* sign next to the Post Office.
The daytime features of colorful people, colorful language, and colorful paintings were replaced by nighttime sentinels—sturdy, thumb-sized
roaches whose alert stances and impressive ground clearance made them
intellectually and physically suited for the terrain; skinny mongrels who
sniffed, poked, and snorted for unimaginable goodies in piles of rub-
ble; rats who, like commandos, darted from one dilapidated cover (a
smashed wooden pallet) to the next (a caved in metal drum). This all
struck him as perfect.

The spinning ache in his head turned nasty, precursor to a single
retch that unleashed a geyser spew without warning, splattering his sandaled feet. A second wave quickly followed but this time he was ready
and managed to keep himself out of the way.

"Mista!" he felt a tug at his shirt. "Come wit me, Mista!"

Seaborne let himself be guided by the oddly confident Haitian
boy who seemed very much at home on these streets. Embarrassed, he
glanced groggily back at the puddles of gunk he'd generated. The dogs
circled, checking it out, and he could've sworn he saw the roaches rush in
for their share of the bounty. The dogs lost interest in the foul brew and
with practiced paws pounced on the roaches. Perfect midnight snack.

The boy led Seaborne to the Columbus memorial, the best place
he could think of in a pinch. It did have three low walls and a roof and
luckily no one else was using it.

There was a good reason for this, Seaborne discovered as he
slumped down, facing the dim waters. From the acrid smell of it, this

was a handy urinal for creatures large and small, probably since it'd been built. In his state, Seaborne couldn't do anything about anything, so he let the mindless carousel in his head play out. Sleep came easily and he was somehow disciplined enough to remain upright.

CHAPTER 71

Particles of light mottled the dark sky shortly before five, according to his watch which, when he woke, he was surprised to find still on his wrist. Patting his pants pocket, the familiar wallet bulge also greeted him. The boy, however, was gone.

Backlit mountains took on greater prominence as the sun rose from the Dominican Republic side of the island. Before it got any lighter, Seaborne took a piss in the Caribbean and a dump on its shores. Rooting around in his backpack while still in squat mode, he found nothing appropriate to wipe with. Desperate and becoming more and more vulnerable to curious flies and eyes, he grabbed a bandana and swaddled away, burying the soiled item with focused swipes at the dirt like an embarrassed cat.

The weight of circumstance, the frustration, burst—he cried a thickly-snotted downpour, thinking of his dead mother, how full of life she'd been and how many stupid, mean things he'd said to her throughout the years months days and hours. It wasn't fair. Worse yet, at the Grinch-like center of his juvenile heart, the other part that didn't seem fair was that he had to involve himself in this decidedly un-fun affair, the dissolution of her life, which had culminated, thus far, in the undignified disposition of a beloved bandana.

Vendors arrived, bundles in arms and baskets on heads, to set up their wares on the wide landing of the Post Office. Seaborne wondered where these people lived. Caught between his own discomfort and true curiosity, he hung back inside the Columbus potty and watched. Industrious painters arrived in multi-colored pickups and unloaded stacks of stretched canvas. A woman pushed a rough-hewn hand truck into position, removing a few boxes and a folding table which she reverently set up, extending its metal legs and sliding the buckles down to secure them in place. The newness of the table surprised him. Common in the States, it must've cost a lot here as it had to be imported.

"She get tay-bool in *dechoukaj*, when Jean-Claude lef few monts ay-go." The boy appeared at his side from nowhere, offering two hot meat-filled *patés*. "Big place, Janicon, sell tay-bool, chaises, deks, on Boulevard Jean-Jacques Dessalines. Dat lay-dee live in de fwont, get tay-bool when people, how you say, stealing."

"I see—she's a thief."

"No, she pay! Feel so bad, she go to bizness boss and buy eet good price, dam-edge goods, you say?"

Seaborne regarded his sidekick in a new light.

"Damaged goods," he concurred, shoving the last of the warm, flakey dough into his mouth.

❀

Early Monday morning. Back in Florida, Seaborne would've already devoured an egg and black bean breakfast at *El Cubano*. He'd be filled to the brim with sweet coffee, a to-go cup balanced on the tail end of a cut of train cars, big pieces of rolling steel he would unlace, roll, place, and tie down. He always got a sense of satisfaction seeing a string of cars or lone car where he'd left it—and staying put. Instead he found himself in the pit of the Western Hemisphere, so-called by the world at large, and his toiletrie display hadn't helped.

But he found it wasn't so bad. The people he saw appeared cheerful—more cheerful than he ever was. He wasn't sure how this could be. Whereas a relatively small thing like a lack of toilet paper had set him off, he wondered how they went about life so easily, taking things in stride. Biases fell by the wayside. Just because they were poor had he imagined they were somehow less human, helpful, generous, or wise? And what about this odd little boy? Ti Mouche, was that his real name?

Christ, that could've been me if I hadn't been adopted!

A possibility that, while exaggerated, did not escape Seaborne who, on top of it all, was beginning to feel the deficiencies of youth rise up. Used to thinking himself so grand and so together, he realized he was mostly a blank slate, this experience blasting tracks deep into the fiber of his being.

"What chyou wan do today?" Ti Mouche asked, slinging his backpack over a scrawny shoulder, ready to move out.

Seaborne stared at the dirty, tan tote with brown leather bottom. Eddie Bauer. He had one just like it. Hadn't used it for years. No idea what'd happened to it.

Couldn't be.

Seized by a sneaky suspicion, he do-si-doed to get a look at the front of the bag, but Ti Mouche side-stepped to stay face-to-face with his competition. This Three Stooges routine repeated itself until Seaborne, by far the larger and taller of the two, held the boy in place while he pivoted to his back where, beneath the etched leather brand name, he made out a faded *JCSZ*. Claire had penned those initials without his approval, a throwback to more infantile days when he frequently lost or misplaced his belongings.

"Nice bag. Where'd you get it?" Seaborne tried to sound upbeat.

"You mama geev eet me."

The American sighed. "You know my mother?" he asked, becoming less and less surprised at events on the island.

"Leetle beet. Me know lotta pee-pool," Ti Mouche said with a touch of pride.

Seaborne scratched his chin and laughed despite himself. "Perfect. My old shit is parading around Haiti with a new life."

Ti Mouche laughed too, mostly because he'd picked out one of his all-time favorite words. "Sheet!" he repeated gleefully. "Sheet sheet!"

Seaborne secretly liked the idea of his stuff being re-used. At least he'd contributed *something* to the world *out there*. What he didn't like was the pokey feel of stiff hairs growing on his face and neck or the rumbling of bowels becoming ever more insistent.

"Speaking of shit, where do we do that?" he asked aggressively, trying to sound tough.

Ti Mouche eyed the pinched look on the *blanc's* face and, judging him to be in serious need, led him to a nook between two walls next to the Post Office. The half-pint pointed. Seaborne's eyes zeroed in on a few moist piles of recent deposits and felt the bile rise. Flies festooned.

"Is there anything to wipe with?" he asked, thinking back on his previous beachfront evacuation. Ti Mouche didn't seem to understand the question, so the *blanc* pantomimed wiping his ass. A dawn of recognition spread over the boy's face and he dug into old Eddie B. and tore off a section of *Le Nouvelliste* newspaper.

"I guess this'll be enough," Seaborne said doubtfully, staring at the chalk eraser size of paper.

Mouche turned his back and stepped away to guard his guest's privacy.

Of all things, the foreigner experienced a loud burst of gas followed by a splat of ill-formed turds. Said turds, he noted with horror, speckled his sandals. Adjusting the breadth of his squat, he ripped the newspaper in two and dabbed strategically. He resisted cleaning his feet in front of his host for fear of looking totally inept.

Ti Mouche led them back to the water's edge and dipped his hands in for a rinse. Seaborne quickly followed suit. After a moment's hesitation, the Haitian boy fished in his backpack and withdrew a sliver of soap wrapped in the ubiquitous daily. He offered it to the visitor.

"Thanks a lot," Seaborne croaked, worn down. He found a clear-ish patch of seawater and washed his face. When he looked up, Ti Mouche was holding a Schick razor at arm's length.

And so, that Monday morning in Port-au-Prince, Seaborne completed what toilet he could by the shores of the Caribbean Sea.

CHAPTER 72

The ride up to *Pétionville* took place in a Peugeot wagon like Eugene's from eight years before. This one had not aged gracefully. For one, excessive use had turned the seats into landmines of coiled springs and sagging leather. Seaborne knew this because his left butt cheek was planted squarely on top of one, with no room to shift, squished as he was between several kindly commuters and Ti Mouche.

These practical *camionettes*, or *little trucks*, Seaborne estimated, probably made ten trips a day up the mountain and an equal number of trips down on paved, but not entirely smooth, roads. At squeeze capacity, the laudable chariots could carry two lucky passengers in relative comfort up front, five slender ones jammed in the middle bench seat and four skinny souls in the way back, thereby adding one to two people per seating arrangement more than the French designers had ever intended.

Welcome to Haiti!

The cost of a *gourde* per person to travel the 30-odd minutes from bottom to top or anywhere along the steep, winding seven-mile stretch therefore resulted in maximum earnings of $2.20 per leg. With the price of a gallon of gas about that, it was understandable, then, why many drivers extinguished their engines on the downhill, relying solely on the car's brakes to deliver them to Port-au-Prince.

Seaborne continued with the math projections, relieved to keep his mind busy. Twenty trips at $2.20 max garnered $44.40, a king's ransom of a daily wage until expenses were subtracted: fuel, oil, parts (especially brake shoes), insurance, car payments. Still, he guessed it was a living since so many men did it.

"*Ok, ça va!*" a voice peeped from the back. When the driver failed to respond, a resonant, "*ça va ici!*" boomed, startling everyone and prompting a spate of laughter. Folks to the right of Seaborne slid out and held the seatback forward so a petite woman wearing an immaculate white dress could extricate herself. She handed two large, dull silver coins to the driver and bid adieu. He eased the car into gear while pulling something from beneath his seat: a dented blue tin that, at the height of its career, had housed a pound's worth of Dutch Butter Cookies. The driver tossed in the fare which clanked a modest addition to the morning's population of coin and crumpled bills.

While looking over the driver's shoulder, Seaborne admired the steering wheel, its circumference wrapped in alternating red and blue plastic strips that created a checkerboard pattern. The shaft of the gear shift was similarly endowed. He'd seen embellishments like these during the Carnival visit and had been so impressed that he'd added similar touches to the handlebars of his Schwinn after returning home. Most importantly, he even scored a (musical) drumstick, wrapped it up and wedged it between the double rails connecting the bike's steering column and seat stem. Riding along Hollywood Boulevard, mostly between La Brea and Highland, 3,000 miles away from the source of inspiration, he pretended to be a *camionette* driver, deliberately pulling over to admit or discharge passengers, miming the collection of money and doling out of change, shifting gears and imagining the squishy squeak of Eugene's Peugeot 404 wagon.

The good old days, Seaborne whispered, slipping back into a morose mood.

"Lemme see address." Ti Mouche leaned to within earshot.

Seaborne handed him the paper, surprised the boy could read.

"We get off soon, I tink."

"Do you know where this is?"

"We see," the boy said brightly, the moment of uncertainty passed.

"*…Num-er-eau huit…Rue…Au…Aubran et…..Ga…Gabart,*" Ti Mouche read the address on the slip of paper, sounding out as he went. "*La Sou…Sou-ve-…La Souvenance,*" he concluded, finished mixing the potion of syllables.

Just past the Red Carpet in *Pétionville* they got off across from a multi-storey hotel favored by missionaries and headed, on foot, down a street lined with stone walls and wrought iron gates, behind which loomed heavily-built homes bathed in bougainvillea. The colorful climber draped walls and balconies without regard for order, its main imperative to flood the optic nerves of hummingbirds and humans with brilliant magenta, pink and, Seaborne noted with pride, Cunard red!

"Up dare, see dat choorch? Saint Therese. Good futbol play bee-hine choorch," Ti Mouche pointed knowingly.

By *futbol* Seaborne understood him to mean soccer, a national passion. Kids played everywhere, setting up on sleepy side streets, using cans for goals and fashioning balls out of socks, stockings, even newspaper when supplies of worn out leggings ran short.

"Here eet is," Ti Mouche announced triumphantly in front of a massive, two-storey, L-shaped spread.

Wrap-around terraces characterized the top floor. Banks of jalousie windows clad in brown bars broke the monotony of white on both levels and, most unusual, along the roof's flank, foot-high buttresses popped up every fifteen feet like castle ramparts defending against siege.

Behind the perimeter wall Seaborne heard the hum of a pump. Jumping to see over, he spotted a crystal blue swimming pool and immediately wondered why Claire hadn't mentioned this inviting feature. Its reassuring hum faded as the pair walked toward the front gate where a decorative wooden sign proclaimed *La Souvenance* and a Renault 11-TSE (looking suspiciously like the *Encore* sold in the States) rested in the shade of the carport, lending proof to the likelihood of fully French inhabitants.

An arrow directed them along a stone path leading back toward the pool and an entrance that was closed. Seaborne knocked several times, eliciting a quick response from a white woman who opened a glass sliding door upstairs and stood on the terrace, peering down at them.

"Hello," Seaborne offered uncomfortably, suddenly aware of unbrushed teeth and a ragged appearance. "Uh, do you speak English?"

"But of course," she replied in an air both kind and meant to put him in his place. "Why are you here?" The lilt of her accent softened the words.

"I'm looking for my mother—" He couldn't help it, the tears came even though he fought hard to keep them down. "She listed this as her address."

"I'll be right down."

The French woman wore her platinum hair in a tight cylinder at the nape of her neck. Not quite a bun, more like a twisted wave with a rideable inner curl. During introductions Seaborne learned his guide's real name was Olivier Saint Aimé. Of course he'd known "Ti Mouche" was a nickname—who in their right mind would name a child Little Fly? The fact that he'd used his birth nomenclature—the one thing no one could take away—moved Seaborne, inducing a twinge of protectiveness that made him lean closer to his street-wise companion. The woman handled herself adroitly, adopting an inclusive air of hospitality so as not to offend the classless but sensitive American.

She called for a servant to bring two Pepsis then invited them to a table replete with cloth napkins poking out of goblets, endless silver utensils and nesting plates set upon a creamy table cloth. The bubbling drinks arrived and Seaborne caught a relieved look from Ti Mouche— at least he knew what to do with that.

The woman waited until they'd sipped their sodas, then spoke.

"And your muzza is…"

"Claire Zeisse."

"I sought so. You resemble her." The woman's gaze pierced him and he blushed.

"She deed stay here for a leetle while, it is true. When we were just starting zuh restaurant. So many rooms, big place. My husband is off-ten a-way. But I am sorry, she is no longer here." On his look, she continued sympathetically. "Sum-sing has happened?"

"She died in a ferry accident near Port-au-Prince," Seaborne answered glumly. "I'm here to retrieve her and her things. This is the address she listed on her registration with the Embassy."

The French woman took his hand for an uncomfortable while.

"Did Claire by any chance say where she was going from here?" Seaborne asked, eager to move on.

"Come to sink of it, she did men-shun a place at de top of *Delmas*, sum small apartment owned by—now who was eet—"

"Yes?"

"Ah, I cannot sink. I am sorry."

Seaborne stood first, followed by Ti Mouche.

"Ah! Where ees my head?" the woman burst unexpectedly, one manicured hand flying to his arm, the other to her temple. "I have sumsing I soospect belongs to your muzza—now you."

She disappeared up a flight of terrazzo stairs and returned shortly, placing a small penknife on the table.

Seaborne picked up the thumb-sized object and stopped breathing when small bits of turquoise (sky), onyx (hull), milky quartz (superstructure), and jasper (funnels) faithfully rendered RMS Queen Mary in miniature. Here was his most enduring mother figure!

"Good," she soothed. "We found eet in her bedroom. But, had it been *Normandie*, I can assure you I would not have parted weess eet," she said, adopting the tone of a stern teacher.

Seaborne smiled, grateful for the levity that quashed the prickly sprinkler system in his head.

CHAPTER 73

The odd pair wandered in the direction of *Delmas*, Seaborne alone with mundane thoughts about how that particular road had been his first introduction to Haiti years back, and how it connected *Pétionville* to downtown's gritty *Boulevard Jean-Jacques Dessalines*, an east/west thoroughfare of crumbling buildings criss-crossed by an overhead maze of power and phone lines.

Memory further carried his mind to a notable landmark located in those parts, the Iron Market. An open air, riveted, minareted structure dating from the 1890s, it sheltered vendors of all kinds beneath its soaring heights, and what didn't fit inside spilled out onto the bustling Boulevard, making travel a game of dodge ball against encroaching mattresses, pigeon coops, hand-carved dinettes, portable radios, tires, and cords of slender tree trunks used as supports in construction. In other words, everything under the sun.

Ti Mouche walked silently beside Seaborne, who continued his inward reminisces, different sights jogging different recollections. There *was* that *other thing* that'd happened on the Carnival trip when he was eight…

Claire had, at the time, newly taken to water colors; her goal, to paint among the people. Eugene suggested a visit to the Iron Market the day after the big Carnival celebration downtown. Seaborne remembered harboring a distinct preference for splashing around in the *Ibo Lélé* pool but his opinion didn't count for much, and as the self-designated protector, he couldn't in good conscience let her go unescorted.

Eugene dropped the pair off in front of the bulging market, opting to stay nearby with the car. As they snaked their way into the building, the locals ceased transacting, nailing, buffing, peeling, squeezing, and measuring, to out and out stare. Seaborne remembered Haitians as being very good starers. After this initial shock, the more enterprising of the lot tried to get the *blancs* to buy from them.

Pleasantly ignoring the masses, Claire took a few reference shots with her Polaroid then set up an easel and began dabbing an impressionistic scene of brightly clad dark bodies and goods clustered around a vertical tunnel of light emanating from the crotch of the roof. Seaborne himself had seen no shaft of light—this was her imagination at work. Or, he thought back, was it?

Curious Haitians gathered 'round slowly, one after the other stepping away from their huddled sales positions to see what this woman was up to. They pointed and commented and tried to pick out threads of realism within the stylized scene. Some murmured quietly, others squabbled over interpretation. When she was done the vendors slowly dispersed. One woman, wearing a red-checkered dress and matching head scarf that reminded Seaborne how much he missed meatball subs, offered an appreciative, "*Merci, madame,*" prompting more cheerful chirps of appreciation to rise from different parts of the market. Not loud or fervent, spoken as if they'd been reminded of something. Seaborne saw tears inching down Claire's face as they packed up and left them to their lives. He didn't get it then, but was beginning to get it now.

❂

Seaborne wouldn't allow Ti Mouche to carry his backpack even though the boy badgered him. How could he even consider letting a four-foot tall spindly adolescent labor under a bag almost half his size? Plus backpacks were absolutely meant to be carried by their rightful owners, especially if the owner was a guy. This was unwritten code.

"I've got it," Seaborne insisted. "It's ok, I'll pay you as my guide—you don't have to carry my bag."

Still, at the end of every block the pestering began anew. Finally, Seaborne asked why it was so important.

"Eef I no carry bag me look lazy, me look bodder you not hepp you. We no oppose bodder tourist."

"I see," Seaborne replied, not really seeing at all. He suspected it had something to do with trust. "Ok, we'll take turns."

Ti Mouche hugged the Nike in front of his slender torso, grinning as the Eddie Bauer rose and fell on his back.

"Say, what's the fastest way back down to the Post Office?" Seaborne asked, coming to his senses. Next thing he knew he was sandwiched between the boy (who was perched on the rear metal rack) and a Baptist missionary, the three of them careening down *Pétionville* Road on an orange and black Honda Trail 110, one of the homeliest motorcycles ever built. And the ride didn't cost a penny.

CHAPTER 74

Back at the *Bureau des Postes*, which was beginning to feel like home, Seaborne stood in line for assistance. A roving vendor tried to tempt him with notepads featuring modest line drawings of palm trees, huts and flying birds. Others tried to sell him stamps, old Haitian coins, and of course, post cards. A one-legged toothless man begged for money, foregoing any attempt at commercial exchange. Each time someone approached, Seaborne uttered *no, merci*, shook his head and looked away. If they became the least bit persistent, the one thing he could've really used from Ti Mouche—intervention—did not occur, and he was, to his mounting annoyance, forced to repeat *no merci* louder and louder while striving to avoid eye contact. Even he knew that once you made eye contact it was all over.

When he reached the head of the line, Seaborne took one look at the woman behind the counter and his heart sank. Her deadpan mouth and unconcerned brow communicated the most blasé look he'd ever seen. Her eyes matched the intensity of a grazing cow. The one bright spot on her face was the blue eye shadow to which he looked for inspiration.

"Bonjour," he stammered.

The bird on the wire stared, dimly parroting his greeting.

"Do you speak English?" Hope and fear scrunched his face.

She nodded and tapped her long fingernails on the scratched countertop. Seaborne wasn't sure this indicated a yes or a no.

"P.O. Box 2-3-3-0? It's for my mama, *deux-trois-trois-zero*, oui?"

"Vingt-trois trente, qu'est ce que vous voulez avec cette boite?"

Ti Mouche stepped in, head barely clearing the counter. He rattled off a dozen words Seaborne didn't understand. The clerk looked down at him without moving anything but her eyelids. He delivered another dozen or so words in a steady voice, knuckles wrapping the hard surface for punctuation. Whatever he said worked, for though her expression never changed she disappeared for a few minutes and returned with a slip of paper. On it, an address and the name *Claire Zeisse*. Seaborne was relieved to see it was different from the outdated coordinates the Embassy had supplied. Still in the hunt.

"Thank you very much, madame. Can I also have a key?" he asked confidently, pantomiming turning a key in a lock.

She explained to Ti Mouche, who translated best he could, that in order for her to give him a key, since its owner's approval would not be forthcoming, next of kin would need to fill out a registration form, put a deposit down, and supply her with a copy of the death certificate.

"Can I see inside first? Please?"

Ti Mouche rattled off a flurry of words that prompted her to rise off her stool and flick a beckoning finger in the air.

The boys kept pace with the clickety-clack of the clerk's high heels, following the sound to the back wall. A door on the bottom row popped open—2330. Seaborne knelt down to take a look. Watchful eyes peered back at him—she was going to let nothing slide on her watch. He smiled appreciatively and removed two envelopes. One was a letter he'd dashed off the day she told him about the post office box. Choking back tears by clearing his throat roughly, he re-established eye contact with the hot coals at the rear of the box. They'd turned predatory, a deep scowl setting in.

"No can take wit chyu," the clerk threatened, reaching her hand clear through, a scary prospect for anyone with a crotch-height box.

The second envelope was addressed to Claire in a loopy, self-conscious script. The postmark, a partial half-moon stamp, showed it was mailed recently from a place abbreviated as *Rep. Dom.* The return coordinates, *Primer Piso D-5-B, Urbanizacion Las Tortugas, Santo Domingo.* Sender's name not included. He felt the outline of something thin and hard inside, the size of a quarter.

He thought about absconding with the mail, pictured himself sitting on the dirty shores crying his eyes out over vapid greetings his mother had not lived to enjoy, then tearing into the other letter, eager to discover what it might reveal. Looking back into the denuded box, eyes glared and a throat cleared demandingly. If he carried out his dramatic theft there could be repercussions for Ti Mouche as well as this woman who had, after all, extended herself.

Seaborne slid both envelopes back in the box.

CHAPTER 75

It was the kind of place his mother loved. Tucked away on a dead-end street away from the hustle and bustle of *Delmas* sat a flat-roofed concrete dwelling dipped in canary yellow. A rustic carport of dark lumber extended from its midsection, flower baskets suspended from the rafters and dripping with trumpet-shaped blossoms clinging to hunter green vines. Just beyond both ends of the wooden structure two identical carved doors marked separate entries, and to the left and right of those, large windows with flower boxes bookended the symmetry.

A duplex. The Post Office address did not specify which unit.

Seaborne took a long look at a yellow Volkswagen "Thing" sunbathing, top down, next to the unit on the left. A hibiscus decal the size of a grapefruit softened the military lines of its front passenger door. Was this hers? If so, why hadn't she driven it on her last outing? Maybe she'd gotten a ride, not wanting to leave the car downtown while away on her boat trip. Was it bought or borrowed? Either way, this was news. He hadn't realized the extent of her digging in. Maybe she hadn't either.

Grief masqueraded as anger. Claire should've been enjoying the fruits of her labor, not chilling in a meat locker. Now he was part of the insanity. Fuming, he searched for a house key, flipping rocks, sending water bugs scurrying, poking flower pots. The Thing got frisked, revealing nothing but an unusually wide glove compartment door that would not stay closed no matter how hard he slammed it.

"*Muchacho ey! Qué paso?*" came a woman's voice with emphasis on the *what's up* part.

Seaborne raised a mad head and did a double take at the short, bosomy brunette standing outside the far door. Far as he could tell, a woman perpetually frozen in time aboard a ship nineteen years back had just been transported to the highly charged present.

"*Por qué estas aqui? Qué estás haciendo?*" she approached the ransacked vehicle while continuing her protective grilling.

"*Uh Claire, mi mama*—" Seaborne struggled to explain, but the feisty Latin interrupted in an outburst of recognition.

"*Dios mio. No es tu, verdad? Jesus Cruz? Sobrino mio?*"

Seaborne didn't know what a *sobrino* was but he sure enough recognized his name before an onslaught of hugs, tugs, laughter, and phrases invoking *Dios* led them to her apartment. Feeling faint, he eased into a floral love seat, never imagining it would be like this.

She brought him a glass of *citronade*, limeade. He downed it in three gulps, grateful for the sweet relief. Crunching ice, he couldn't help but be reminded of a favorite Dr. Seuss book, *Are You My Mother?*

As if reading his mind, she brought him a snapshot taken the day he was born. He'd seen it many times, studied every grain of detail. Doc had taken it of the foursome—Mother, Infant, Claire, and Guga who, with intertwined arms and jaunty hips, did their best to collectively look cheerful but whose tense smiles and bunny-rabbit eyes told the truth.

She pointed at each character.

"*Mári,*" she began. Seaborne thought it an odd way to refer to herself.

"Claire," she lingered lovingly, *"Guga,"* she cooed, evidently recalling a fond memory, *"y tu."* The woman smiled, chucking the celluloid newborn under the chin with a painted red nail.

Seaborne sat there, his mind mushy with what felt like a dense Atlantic fog. How on earth had things gotten so complicated?

He knew his birth mother had a twin sister. So identical were they, he'd heard tell, that one could fill in for the other. In his heart of hearts Seaborne knew which one of the twins this was. There would be no mother/son reunion after all. Shock turned to relief turned to disappointment as broken Spanish and bits of English established the sad purpose of his appearance. Other details emerged: Mári had also lived in the apartment but had moved to Santo Domingo when Duvalier left a few months back. She had a place in Urbanizacion Las Tortugas, near her best friend, Sonrisa (who, according to Marta, was the most gracious and beautiful of them all), and was still mostly with Luigi—his *papi*—who worked for an Italian company helping supply electricity to both Haiti and the Dominican Republic.

"Do I look like them?"

"Exact split down the middle. You have your mother's eyes and your father's mouth. And hair." Seaborne seemed to take this into deep consideration.

"How did you meet Claire?"

"Puro accidente." A masterful combination of facial contortions, mime, and a mixture of languages conveyed how she'd been shopping for vegetables one day, just down the street, when that odd yellow car passed by, stopped, and a woman jumped out and yelling *"Mári? Mári?"*

"She wouldn't believe I wasn't my sister. Maybe she thought Mári didn't want to see her—or you—again. Which was never true. She marked every one of your birthdays, celebrated them with pastelitos and the correct number of candles. My sister always had high hopes for you, that's why she did

what she did," Marta concluded, brushing imaginary crumbs from the plumage of tablecloth roosters.

"There is enough time for all of this—you have other matters to deal with," she said, squeezing Seaborne's hand. A thought took her by surprise. *"You're not left-handed by any chance?"*

"Yes."

"So is your mother. They say left-handed people are conceived as a gemela." Seaborne had done pretty well up to that point but did not know the last word.

"Mári y yo, gemelas, si?"

This was beyond Seaborne's linguistic capabilities.

"No importa." Marta fished inside a kitchen drawer. Shifting items around, she finally produced a key. *"Listo?"* she asked, pressing her palm to his while making the exchange. Without thinking about it, he knew she was sending him energy and good will to face what he had to face. He showed his appreciation by lightly kissing her on the cheek. Marta hugged herself tightly, defense against a heart cracked wide open.

CHAPTER 76

Two things struck Seaborne as he let himself in. One, the pit in his stomach and two, a shaft of light that, through a gap in the curtains, illuminated the mate to the sequined Vodou flag back in Miami.

He approached the flag. A watery, shimmering spectacle of silvers, reds, pinks, and greens filled the heart. Time stood still as he traced its shape and recalled Guga's explanation of why the typical "art heart" did not bear that close a resemblance to the actual muscle beating inside human chests. Something to do with the various layers of energy surrounding the physical body, an aura he called it. Certain people could see them and the different colors at which they vibrated. Claire, Seaborne, and Guga had squinted themselves silly trying, but came up dry. Nonetheless, legend had it the aura was wider at the top, tapering off toward the feet like the shape of an egg. When two people who loved each other stood side by side, their auras merged, the wider domes at the crowns remaining distinct while the narrower base energies came together in a point.

Seaborne pondered whether he and Claire or he and Guga had ever created such a design with their auras. He wasn't sure about love. What was the difference between love and need? Love and habit? Love and fear? The hole left by blind-sided loss, was this proof of love? He traced the whirligigs, doo-dads, hatch marks and spokes. All he could think of were crossroads and stars, heavenly realms. Clamping his eyes shut to cut the tears, he sent a fervent prayer that his mother was above, basking in the glory of her grace and generosity.

The sun beams multiplied, intensifying their influence on the radiant sequins. Peace and a sense of letting go settled in. Tears came and he didn't try to stop them. It seemed as though his emotions were a rag, washed and wrung over and over again, and now he was squeezing them, clean and dry, once and for all. Seaborne wasn't sure where the sensations were coming from. They didn't feel like his own, so he ascribed them to the spirit of Claire. He was grateful for these moments, this final link to his dearly departed.

Wandering from station to station, Seaborne fingered the remnants of Claire's life as if sampling from a buffet. First the dining table, where he jingled a set of Volkswagen keys while reading a To Do list scribbled on a palm tree notepad.

Call Seaborne
Check oil
Check mail
Lunch with Pierre at El Rancho

Pierre? Who the hell was Pierre? He felt the air go out of him, sudden deflation, realizing there was so much he didn't know. It never occurred to him she might be dating—all he'd seen was her close, but platonic, relationship with Guga. The childish ignorance of it all made him feel rotten and selfish.

A few green bananas sat coiled in a bowl. Green bananas— banking on future ripeness. He guessed all humans conducted their lives as if nothing would cut them short. He guessed they had no choice.

Seaborne made a trip to the bathroom, and while taking his time on a much appreciated toilet, catalogued Claire's belongings: Excedrin, Q-Tips, Aim toothpaste, Vicks, Vaseline, Scott toilet paper, travel bag full of eye liners and lipsticks, a dainty bottle of *L'Air du Temps*, tweezers, magnifying mirror. In the trashcan, discarded tissues formed a pyramid. One at the top featured a pair of blotted red lips, presumably hers. Its lacey imprint reminded him of a Kiss poster, a likeness that made him altogether queasy.

In the bedroom, a double mattress sat atop a simple wooden frame and headboard, its yellow varnish imparting the telltale "locally made" stamp. Jungle swirls animated the still sheets, single pillow neatly centered, the case featuring a perched parrot. Seaborne didn't know how anyone could get any rest lying on such a noisy pattern.

On the nightstand, a battery-operated lamp (insurance against blackouts), a few reference books and what looked like a manuscript. Upon further inspection the untitled, inch-thick stack of paper turned out to be Claire's typed account of Queen Mary's last voyage. Cross-outs, miniscule comments squeezed along the margins, and editing symbols he didn't recognize made it difficult to read. This would be for another time and another place, but it *would* be.

He rummaged through the drawer, encountering a flashlight, felt pens, loose change, tape, a green pack of Wrigley's gum, paperclips, X-ACTO knife, purple ribbon, and a folio containing her passport and hundreds of dollars in cash. A black Moleskine notebook lie buried in the miscellany. He almost didn't touch it, fearing an invasion of privacy, but the slim journal held a certain appeal, and when he opened it he found lined pages full of colorfully penned prose and lacey doodles illustrating a woman at home with herself. One entry caught his eye—a sketch of a tumbling waterfall surrounded by boulders and trees, still pools, drawn in spare black lines. Alongside, these words:

> June 14, 1985, Saut D'eau in Ville Bonheur, Haiti
> In this poor village called the good hour,
> I found the grace to live and die in peace.
> Crystal cold water cuts through ignorance and bliss
> Erasing all memory of who I was
> and all thoughts
> of who I am to be.

❋

Sometime after dark, knocking woke Seaborne. He'd flopped on the bed and fallen asleep after spending the afternoon getting to know his mother. The knocking continued. Seaborne got up, his head feeling like a dried sea sponge. Marta stood outside bearing a tray of two somethings wrapped in thin paper napkins and two tall glasses imprinted with green and red flowers native to nowhere. Because everything was in pairs he asked her in. She shook her head and pointed.

"*Para ti.*" Without further ado, the spitting image of Mári turned and left.

A doubt needled him as he took a seat at the round dining table, snapping on the globe light above it. *What if this woman is my mother?*

The two wrapped somethings were ham and cheese sandwiches on French bread. Slathered with good butter, yellow mustard, and spicy bits of cabbage and peas, Seaborne devoured the meal, smacking his lips and chewing like a cow while gulping syrupy *citronade* and allowing crumbs to gather on his face and snatching the bits falling from his mouth with the speed of a black widow seizing prey.

Mulling over the lingering condiments staining his fingers he rallied, regarding his task in a new light. It was a privilege to take care of one's dead, and as her nearest kin it was up to him to dissolve her life sure as if he'd dropped a cube of sugar into the dark, steaming recesses of hot coffee which, incidentally, Marta arrived with in short order. Claire, in all her wisdom, had never expressed how her mortal remains should be put to rest, except to say how she didn't want them put to rest. Let someone else figure it out when the time came. The time had come.

Eager for a distraction he sipped the strong brew and leafed through a brown accordion folder filled with clippings and handwritten notes. A section at the back held photographic proof sheets with many of the thumbnail images circled in red grease pencil. Seaborne located a jeweler's loop next to her Polaroid camera, sunglasses, and hat *(to think she'd recently touched these)* and peered at images of wooden boats in various stages of construction, propped up on support cradles not far from a shore and flanked by the vessels' builders and future captains, village gents from the looks of their tattered shorts and bare feet.

He glanced at some of the papers—interviews mostly, with the craftsmen who built boats for local commerce. Seaborne could guess where Claire was going with this. Anyone living in South Florida knew about Haitian boat people, and no doubt some of these vessels would be venturing farther than anyone cared to admit.

Another paper had the word *Danger* highlighted at the top in Claire's handwriting. Notes and quotes testified to the hazards of marine transport in Haiti, used primarily to shuffle goods between the coastal towns of *Gonaives, La Gonave, St. Marc, Les Cayes* and *Jacmel*. Every year, Seaborne learned, ferry disasters claimed hundreds of lives, sometimes numbering close to a thousand. Most of these souls didn't possess passport, birth certificate, or even an official address. Most were unknown to the world beyond their villages. They didn't matter, had no voice, no economic means to effect change. According to Claire's research, the reasons for the accidents—cracked hulls, unstable design, overcrowding, lack of flotation devices—pointed to a single theme: greed and disregard for human life.

His own mother had been a victim. And she most assuredly had a passport. Would anything change? Could he do anything about it? Anger and a crushing sense of helplessness flooded his nervous system as he read on. According to one of Claire's sources (a retired Colonel in the Haitian Army who wished to remain anonymous), the Haitian Navy was practically non-existent; it possessed in its arsenal a few rusted old mine sweepers, a handful of rowboats fitted with dubiously maintained outboard motors, and a Vietnam-era chopper that couldn't fly. Perhaps an exaggeration, Claire had penned *CHECK* next to this section. Still, there was no denying the Haitian Navy relied almost entirely on the U.S. Coast Guard to protect its shores and rescue its citizens from the perils of the seas, usually learning of local catastrophes too late to prevent casualties.

Almost reverently, Seaborne returned the papers and proof sheets to the folder and nestled the loop back under Claire's sun hat, mindful of the fact that she would appreciate such consideration for her belongings. He'd rarely been so thoughtful.

What looked to be a rolled up poster leaning against the wall near the table caught his eye. Slipping off the rubber band, he exposed a reproduction of a painting with a haunting subject matter. Weighing down the four corners with whatever he could find, he spread the poster on the beige tile floor, beneath the heart Vodou flag, to get a better look. Somber greens, blues, and the offspring of both—teals—dominated the print, and a hazy copper sun cast a warm glow on the cool scene. In a composition reminiscent of *George Washington Crossing the Delaware*, but closer in and more impressionistic, skeletal humans manned the disintegrating ribs of a wide-beamed wooden boat unable to withstand the assaults of a frothy sea. Flesh gave way to bone, wood to water. The tortured faces and writhing limbs foretold a dismal fate. The painting, by Valcin II, stunned him, made him think about things he rathered not think about, but he stuck with the discomfort out of deference for all boat people, particularly those who never made it to the shores of their new selves.

CHAPTER 77

Greedy for fresh air, Seaborne walked the streets. *Camionettes* still ran at this eleventh hour. Men in slacks and t-shirts with collars loitered at little boutiques for a smoke and a chat. An occasional bike rider pedaled steadily along, unhurried but determined to get somewhere. The produce vendors were gone, though Seaborne noticed a few human forms huddled next to their bundles, resting beneath thin sheets. Roosters crowed, the kind that did so all the time, not just at day break. Seaborne liked the night—white skin blended with shadows. No one bothered him.

A short distance away, parked cars clustered around a building set back from the street. The structure, concrete and angular, its single storey built upon some kind of basement below, looked like a house that'd been converted into a club—a popular club, from the looks of the well-dressed couples moseying up the front stairs, smiles dangling infinitely before being swallowed up by the dark mouth of the entrance, lured by fast salsa. An electric sign, dim behind yellowed plastic, identified the destination as *Club Visage*. Smaller letters flickered *Midnight Show*.

From his experience in Miami he expected to pay a cover charge, but this was not the case and he went directly to a small table close to the dance floor. Couples played footsies, sipped a variety of libations, and the unaccompanied men sat in the far reaches of the room. A few women with light-ish features, straight-ish hair, and self-absorbed expressions twirled robotically on the floor, sticking to the darker corners, the hems of their clingy dresses straining against hips and thighs. Everyone seemed to be biding their time.

A male waiter took his order and quickly returned with a frosty Prestige beer. Seaborne drank from the squat brown bottle even though a glass had been provided. After leveling his tilted head from the first deep draught, he noticed other people had beer but no one drank directly from the bottle. He poured the remainder into a glass and downed it, foam and all, then immediately regretted the hasty act of conformity.

Next time, he'd do it his way, no apologies.

Distracted by the terse interplay between etiquette and sincerity, a large figure eclipsed his table, startling Seaborne with a resonant, "May I join you?"

It was the man from the airplane, the one who'd offered him a place to stay.

"I am sorry for your great loss. My condolences," he said through a chocolate brandy voice so deeply authentic it could've belonged to Moses.

"Thank you," Seaborne stammered. "But how do you know?"

"Marta told me. If there is anything I can do to help, please," the man signaled for another round.

"I know your mothers—both of them—from way back. Met Claire in the 70s, she had you along, so that means I've known you since you were this high—" he raised his hand level with the table top. "Well, since before that, if you want to get technical."

Seaborne stared at the big, friendly face, pieces of the puzzle flying into place.

"Wait a minute—you're Max? *The* Max from Acapulco?"

"You see," he chuckled, nodding, "I am somewhat of a godfather to you." Max lightened the tone with a nudge to Seaborne's shoulder, followed by an expansive wave of his own arm out over the premises.

"Take your pick," he offered, bushy eyebrows doing most of the talking.

At first Seaborne didn't know what he meant. Then, noticing a silky girl in a tight, shimmery dress by herself on the dance floor, he got the picture.

"I pick…Sonrisa!"

Max eventually stopped laughing and, dabbing at his watery eyes with a crisp hanky, managed a few words on the subject.

"Sonrisa the queen! They all still look up to her, you know. Nobody else like her. Lovely person," he said with a far off look.

"Is she here?" Seaborne asked hopefully. It never hurt to ask.

"No, no, she lives in the Dominican, married to an Italian—why all these Italians I'll never understand. She has two children I hear."

"And Mári?" he croaked. "Does she have more children?"

"Couldn't say, my friend. Maybe you should find out."

I stayed with Claire in a room filled with shafts of light on the 14ᵗʰ floor of a high-rise in Manhattan that overlooked the Hudson's old ocean liner docks. She lay in the middle of an empty room on a long table fitted with a clean smooth white sheet. I ran a basin of warm water infused with basil and mint leaves and sponged her body while rays of sun streaming through lonely windows did their best to warm her. I stood by her side and held her hand, eyes trained on the dark wooden floor, tear drops staining my

dirty bare feet. While preparing her body I'd had a purpose. With nothing more to do, I struck a match and held the flaming head to the thin cotton beneath her. It caught. I let go of my mother's hand and stepped aside as flames consumed her body...

CHAPTER 78

The heat woke Seaborne, bathing him in sweat even though the sun was only just beginning to swell in the east. He remembered the dream and, preferring not to dwell on certain details, hopped into the shower to cool off and organize his thoughts, reminding himself when he got out to look for Guga's number in earnest.

After flicking a towel over large expanses of skin without paying attention to the more out of the way places, Seaborne dug a pair of Gurkha shorts and t-shirt out of his backpack, grateful for the change of clothes. At the bottom of the pack, which also doubled as his train bag, he found the small crystal skull Guga had given him ages ago. Initially it was there as a reminder to take care around large, moving pieces of steel that could maim and kill. Re-discovered, into the Gurkhas it went, next to his wallet.

Stillness struck him. The uselessness of her sunglasses struck him. He picked them up, turned them this way and that, scraping a fingernail over the rough surfaces where her teeth had scored the plastic. He got to thinking about last times again.

The last time she locked the door to this apartment...

The last time she waved to Marta, or yanked the handbrake up on the Thing.

Last time she called her son...talked with Guga...smoked a cigarette...made love...ate a meal...smelled a flower.

What was the last image she registered before blacking out? The shadow of her own body floating above white sand? The sun streaming through a sea unable to float her once her lungs filled with water? A piece of debris flying toward her head?

The possibilities made his stomach queasy, the way it got when he'd pondered eternity as a kid, a dizzying, circular tail chase with no end in sight. Churning, churning, no pat answers to satisfy the brain. At some point—he'd learned this on the roller coasters at Busch Gardens— you had to let go and stop resisting the plunges.

Seaborne found an empty Pan Am tote bag and began the Easter Egg hunt: Stretchy black jazz pants. Black and white striped shirt—wait, put sandals in first, soles down (Claire would've had a fit if he hadn't thought of that). White button down blouse. Wide-brimmed hat with adjustable cinch cord to keep it in place, very floppy, very red.

Yes, he had the Queen Mary's color scheme in mind!

He supposed underwear was also in order. And the final touch, the famous pink and silver leopard print scarf. Recognizing this as the relic that'd launched the whole escapade, he stuffed it into the front pocket.

Next into the Pan Am bag went beach towels, hairbrush, mascara, and bobby pins. No would-be contestant for *Let's Make A Deal* would have anything on him. Seaborne tested tubes of lipstick on the backs of his hands before going with a tame orange metallic glow.

Finally, Claire always liked a good book. Among those lying around he picked up *Their Eyes Were Watching God*, which she'd mentioned she was re-reading ever since learning that Zora Neale Hurston had written the novel, published in 1937, while on a trip to Haiti. Curious, he scanned the bookmarked page. Nothing remarkable there. Something made him check the first page, knowing that opening lines were sometimes the best.

Ships at a distance have every man's wish on board.

The book made the cut.

Passport, cash, art knife, tape, and camping lantern also made the cut into his backpack. He tossed in her Polaroid camera without knowing exactly why.

Seaborne took one last look around then, by way of signing off, placed Claire's sunglasses at the top. There was a last time she'd worn the shades, but it hadn't happened yet.

CHAPTER 79

On his way to the Embassy, Seaborne stopped at a modern Shell station to fill up. He'd learned from railroading to make a thorough predeparture check which, in this case, included tires and fluids. Engine oil *was* low, he nodded appreciatively, thinking back to Claire's To Do list.

He pulled alongside the black Embassy gate at 10:10. Ti Mouche left his post near the light pole and hopped in without waiting for Seaborne to finish his parking maneuver.

"How you doin? Evryting ok?" he asked enthusiastically.

"Pretty ok, I guess. How 'bout you?"

"Hunky dory, me wait here," the boy announced, once again taking the American aback with his bright nature and odd command of corny idioms.

Briggs was not in his office but would soon be, a woman who resembled Karen Valentine from *Room 222* assured him. Seaborne took a seat in the corridor across from a large portrait of President Reagan who looked as though he might, at any given second, raise a hand in greeting, or sympathy, depending on how much he knew.

Briggs burst out of a stairwell door and whizzed by his visitor. "Follow me to my office," he said edgily, trying to keep his tone polite.

The door squeaked closed.

"Sorry to keep you waiting," he extended a hot hand. "I've been working on your, uh, case. Death certificate is ready." Briggs slipped him a manila folder. "You've got a dozen originals in there, should be plenty. You'll need them for bank accounts, title changes and the like."

Briggs's breathing evened out. "Now for the tricky part. She was moved to a local funeral home late yesterday without my knowledge. Apparently an inspector took exception to the storage of mortal remains inside the food locker. I just found out," he said, adjusting his tie.

"Has anything been done…to her?"

"Can't say for sure, sorry."

CHAPTER 80

Ti Mouche guided Seaborne out of the tight parking space with a series of precise hand signals, as if he'd been a conductor, or traffic cop, all his life. He hopped in once the fenders were clear.

"Ever heard of *Pat's Villa?*"

"Dat way—" Ti Mouche pointed inland, away from the waterfront.

"Ok, but first a slight detour."

Seaborne careened around the corner to the Post Office and located the clerk whose unmoving features registered no sign of acquaintance whatsoever.

"Here's the certificate madame—2330 please."

Taking two stairs at a time, he paused at the bottom landing to stow the envelope postmarked *Rep. Dom.* in a deep pocket of his cargo shorts. He would open this later, after the work was done. Completely done.

Generally speaking, Ti Mouche knew where the funeral home in question was located, and asked for directions only when they seemed off track. His method of doing so at first surprised and embarrassed Seaborne, for the boy would thrust his lanky torso out beyond Thing's frame and, if he could reach, tap a pedestrian's arm, yelling *koté Pats Villa?* Sometimes the tap was more of a whack, causing the startled passerby to blurt, under duress, *jus lot boa* with a pointing finger to fortify the vague *just over there*. Others offered street names and landmarks, but when these proved to be dead ends, the calm instruction of a professorial older man finally got the job done.

Thing purred into a parking spot within a courtyard shaded by mature trees and paved with uneven cobblestones. Decorative wrought-iron bars topped a stone wall surrounding the property, its identity confirmed by cursive letters on an entryway arch. *Pat's Villa*. Purple bougainvillea, white lilies, and red anthuriums were the only three plant forms Seaborne could name. Beyond that, well-tended, exotic greenery spilled from pots, planters and just about every nook and cranny within sight. A faint smell of decay and moss scented the air.

Seaborne approached the double-height Victorian gingerbread, its soothing, cool air meeting him at the porch. Claire would've admired the lush garden, ornately turned banisters, multi-colored wood details along the eves of the pitched roof, the light green, burgundy and white trim…

This will be fine, right? She's in good hands here, given how well everything else is taken care of?

"Except for one major problem." Had he really said this out loud?

He lingered on the porch, delaying the hard sell of the undertaker. A bird cage swayed in the breeze, its suspension chain attached to a protruding roof beam. Two parakeets chirped softly, perhaps enjoying the rocking of their cradle. Out of this stillness in motion, a solution percolated. He sensed it and remained quiet, attuned to the surroundings. A vibrant tree caught his eye, reaching midway to the peak of the roof, waxy deep green leaves arranged in a perfect umbrella. From it, big-fisted avocados dangled, slick and plump. Claire loved them. Her mouth watered—or so she said—just thinking about their buttery flesh. Her descriptions of avocado ecstasy had, in fact, bordered on the obscene and Seaborne preferred not to think further on the matter. Nonetheless, the tree gave him ideas, and foremost among them was this:

Hadn't Claire wanted to be a tree, to bond with its molecular structure and become one? If she hadn't actually expressed this (in truth he couldn't remember her ever having done so), surely she must have thought it. She loved trees almost as much as she loved avocados. Decided. He would see to it that she became a tree. Sooner than later.

"Can I help you?" said a cheerful older woman parting the dim interiors with her East Coast accent and ankle-length muumuu.

"Uhh yes, hello. I'm told my mother is here. Claire Zeisse?" he said self-consciously, as if calling on a living person.

"I'm Pat. Let's have a chat."

Seaborne followed, fixated on Pat's unmoving, yet unconstrained, long yellow-silver hair. He sat across from her, next to a rattan table covered with potted plants. A small fountain gurgled pleasantly on one end of the lush table and struck him as very *Addams Family*. All that was missing was the Venus Fly Trap and the box with the cheeky dismembered hand.

Positioned mid-way between the double front door and the rest of the room, he felt like a guest checking into a rehab villa. Warm yellow light seeped from hip-high torchières, sending cobwebs of illumination into the "check in" space as well as other nooks with wicker settees, cane back chairs and boxes of Kleenex angled just so. Seaborne didn't much care for the effect, kept expecting Lurch to appear, stating *you rang* in his lugubrious, death-warmed-over baritone.

"What did you have in mind for the remains?" Pat asked softly, getting down to business.

"Nothing, actually. There's been a mix-up. I was supposed to pick my mother up from the Embassy."

"I see." She shifted, crossing her legs and nestling her hands in the folds of Indian-print fabric. "First of all, I need to point out, and I hope you understand I'm trying to help…" Her voice trailed off and she fingered a few chin whiskers, at which point long yellowed fingernails came to prominence. "You must begin to make a distinction between 'your mother' the living person, and the 'remains,' what is left of her mortal body."

"Are you trying to tell me that's not my mother?" Seaborne asked defensively, leaning forward in his chair.

"Yes."

"Well, she still is to me. What've you done to her?" he asked, beginning to think something horrid had happened to 'the remains'.

"Just a little packing, standard, nothing too invasive," she replied, softening.

Seaborne's blank face stared back at her.

"To prevent leakage. You see, when a person dies—"

"I get the picture, thank you. I'll be taking her with me now, please. What do I owe you for your services?"

"Not a thing," she beamed, and for the first time he realized she had rich blue eyes that actually twinkled. "But first, I have an idea. How about we dress her? A lady can't go out looking like that."

Seaborne retrieved the Pan Am tote and Pat walked them to the back of the house. The preparation room, filled with light and plants climbing up tall, narrow windows, resembled a gardener's workshop, although some of the tools hanging on peg boards looked more sinister than rose snippers.

"You sure you want to be part of this?" she asked, her hand on the handle of a stainless steel door.

"Uh huh," Seaborne muttered.

"If at any point you feel sick just head for that sink over there. Faint? Head between your knees, ok?"

✹

After all was said (*rigor mortis has passed, she'll be supple from here on in but will start to leak, bloat, discolor, and smell real soon*) and done (packing changed, body dressed, Seaborne did not watch), the crowning touch was the scarf.

"You don't think it's over the top?" he fretted over the effect of a gay chiffon leopard print accessory looped around the neck of a corpse.

"Not at all," the undertaker soothed, strategically inserting safety pins to make it stay. "You sure you don't want me to glue it? A few dabs here and there would do wonders—"

Seaborne shook his head. "It was one of her favorites. Belonged to my birth mother."

"It's sweet of you to have brought these things for her," Pat caught herself. She chuckled, giving in to the moment. "I was going to say, 'I'm sure she's smiling down on you right now,' one of my Pat lines, but it doesn't sound very authentic, does it?"

"Not really…but do you suppose…?"

"Hard to say. All you can know is what's in your heart," she said around the pins in her mouth.

✹

A yard maintenance man with a machete tucked into his belt (who knew what other duties he performed) wheeled an old-fashioned gurney to the Thing. On it, a colorful, supine Claire. In order to avoid the unfortunate outcome of rattling the body right off the contraption, Pat supervised, advising when to lift the rig over serious bumps.

Ti Mouche's eyes widened when he saw the cargo. While Seaborne had been conducting his affairs, Ti Mouche had been chatting with a peanut vendor positioned just outside the gate. It hadn't occurred to him they'd soon be driving through the streets of Haiti with a brightly dressed corpse on display. These *blancs* were so much fun!

Shoving the front passenger seat forward, Seaborne climbed in to position the body from inside. With her head on the seat and legs bent at the knees to fit, Claire looked nothing more and nothing less than a foreigner laid low by a hangover or Haitian Happiness (diarrhea). Seaborne carefully placed the wide-brimmed hat and sunglasses on her unprotesting figure.

Pat nodded approvingly. "Where are you taking her?" she whispered.

"Don't know, haven't much thought about it."

"Here's some friendly advice. First, you might want to put the top up. And you're going to need to do something within the next two to three hours. Decomposition at this temperature will accelerate. Does that Thing have a/c?"

Seaborne shook his head.

"Sometimes when a person dies in cold water their proteins convert to fat and this can help with preservation, but that's not the case here."

"She loved trees," Seaborne blurted, eyeing the big green avocados.

"I see…" Pat paused knowingly. "This is neither here nor there, but there's a pine forest near the border. Wouldn't imagine anyone goes there much. You could probably find a secluded nook…but don't tell anyone I said so, it'd be real bad for business."

Seaborne brightened. "Pine forest. Evergreens. Heaps of fallen needles…"

He saw the possibilities instantly and gave her a heart-felt squeeze. "Thank you for your help."

"Any time. You're a fine young man. Your moms did a real good job."

CHAPTER 81

The yellow Thing with its cadaverous cargo and odd couple of pilots struck out eastward bound, winding through the streets of Port-au-Prince to HASCO, the Haitian-American Sugar Company, at which point they turned onto National Highway No.1, but not before Ti Mouche, ever the guide, proudly informed Seaborne that this was where the sugar cane train used to run.

"Where are the tracks?"

"People take it. No more."

"I see."

At the *Croix des Bouquets* fork in the road they stopped at the Texaco to fill up and double check the oil. In the shade of the small building, off to one side, a *griot* vendor sat crouched next to a crackling cauldron, dropping in chunks of cubed pork, rolling them through the depths and up the sides with a handmade spoon. Seaborne caught Ti Mouche looking in her direction.

"Let's get some of that," Seaborne announced as if it'd been his idea. He slipped the vendor ten *gourdes* for two napkins full of steaming meat.

Ti Mouche, between mouthfuls of piping hot food, availed himself of the opportunity to fine tune directions to the forest. The *griot* vendor, it turned out, was from a village near there and told him which landmarks to look for: *just past three huts a big boulder on the right marks a dirt road. Take that to the left, up and over orange rocks and red dirt past the ruins of a foundation then down the hill.*

Seaborne, for his part, was more interested in the oversized basket behind the vendor, brought to his attention by feeble fluttering.

"How much?" he asked, pointing at the sturdy handicraft. Rather than wait for a reply, he peeled off a fiver—no more *gourdes*—and offered it to the woman who, while maintaining seamless chatter with Ti Mouche, reached behind and emptied its contents—a scarf, plastic sandals, coil of fabric used to cushion her head, clump of sisal rope, and a live, bound chicken waiting dejectedly, it seemed, for death and dismemberment, whichever came first.

"*From there,*" the vendor concluded in her native tongue, "*you can see the big pine trees in a sort of valley and find your way.*" Ti Mouche nodded vigorously, licking his fingers.

The chicken distressed Seaborne. It wasn't so much the notion of poop lining the crevasses of the weaves (an unhappy circumstance, to be sure), but something deeper. Seaborne couldn't put a finger on it.

"*Combien?*" he pointed at the bird which, believe it or not, craned its head and looked him in the eyes, blinking. Its expression was hard to read.

The vendor, ever commerce-minded, responded but Seaborne didn't hear because Ti Mouche threw in a low bid at the same time.

"*Vingt-cinq gourdes,*" the boy repeated in a done-deal voice, nudging Seaborne. Timing was everything.

"Ten is the smallest I got…"

The American got his change in rope, *griot,* and pressed bananas, which the vendor hastened to prepare seeing how hungry—and monied—her customers were.

CHAPTER 82

The chicken, the corpse, the basket, and the two young men arrived at *Foret des Pins* at dusk. Surprisingly cool, a layer of misty fog shrouded the low-lying land. They encountered no one as the Thing puttered along inner paths and circled around clusters of trees cushioned with pine needles. Seaborne appeared to be looking for something, as a dog does when sniffing for the right spot to drop a load. Every now and then he got out to inspect a particular tree, checking the height of its lowest strong branch by raising his arms and jumping up. He performed this ritual several times and on the final sortie, abreast of the perfect pine, stopped the car in a lurch. The chicken—unbound in its basket pen, slid forward and bumped against the back of the rear seat, clucking a great fuss. Fortunately, Claire stayed put.

"Now you cry out?" Seaborne lifted the flustered foul out of the cargo space and dropped it gently to the ground. The bird took off on a dead run, squawking into the approaching night. Ti Mouche shook his head disappointedly. There went dinner.

Seaborne quickly threaded three sections of rope through opposite sides of the basket and tied six big knots on the inside, several inches beneath the rim. The result looked like criss-crossing handles.

"Let's fill it up to here—" he indicated a third— "with pine needles. We've gotta hurry."

While Ti Mouche was busy lining the basket, Seaborne climbed into Thing's passenger seat. Turning fully toward the back, he looked at Claire for a long, undisturbed while. She really didn't bear any resemblance to the animated woman he'd spent the last nineteen years with.

"I know you're not my mom anymore but I love you anyway," he breathed, tears falling fast. Transferring the crystal skull from his pocket to her waistband, he closed his eyes, buried his face in his hands and lost it.

When a prick of irritation emerged, caused by a gargantuan case of nasal stuffiness, he realized the emotional deluge was over and plodded around to the driver's side, solemnly pushing the seat forward. Taking a deep breath, he reached under her armpits, telling himself *don't think about it, don't think about it.* She slid easily, seeming even more petite in death. It was weird how dead she was. No spark of life. Like a slab of meat, truth be told.

Seaborne tugged some more, just far enough so her legs wouldn't fall to the floorboards, then reached in under her knees and scooped her out. Ti Mouche remained by the basket, finished with his task, sensing the American wanted to do this part alone.

While sitting by her side moments ago he hadn't smelled anything untoward (well, maybe something a little gamey that he chalked up to the chicken), but moving her unleashed the hidden forces of putrification and he got a whiff of something unspeakable that clung to his nose hairs like nobody's business. Holding her a slight distance from his body, Seaborne maneuvered awkwardly in an attempt to plug one nostril and blow, then the other, boxer style.

Taking a gulp of air, he hurried over to the basket. Ti Mouche held the rope handles aside while Seaborne nestled the corpse into position. She fit pretty well as long as her knees were bent. Something dark oozed from her nose. Ti Mouche looked away while Seaborne blotted the inky substance with a napkin leftover from their feeding frenzy. Realizing it was high time for her body to get on with its business of breaking down, he carried the basket to the tree that would cradle his mother's decomposing remains.

Ti Mouche saw what needed to be done and quickly procured a long stick with forked branches. Seaborne lifted the basket to his head while positioning himself at the end of a strong bough. Ti Mouche fed the rope handles onto the tree limb then snugged them over bumps and snags toward the craquelured trunk of the hospitable pine. Neck bob-bing back and forth under the strain, Seaborne took his cue and eased out from under the load, making sure the basket held before withdraw-ing all support. It groaned. It swayed. It held. The son of the woman in the basket stepped back to survey his handiwork. Whether it would survive a brisk wind or last for even an hour, Seaborne knew not.

He'd done his best. Truly.

Tired from the day's exploits, Seaborne invited Mouche to keep warm in the Thing while he cozied up to the pine, lantern by his side and letter in hand. For a long time he refused to open it, feeling that once he did, his life would change.

Seaborne drifted in and out of sleep. Startled awake various times during the night by rustling noises, he trained the lantern on Claire, check-ing to be sure she was cradled in her bough. Head slumped forward, knees bent in classic "dozing Mexican wearing a sombrero" pose, he no longer recognized her. In fact, there was nothing familiar about her or her situation.

Finally, the time had come.

Diving in with all his courage, he ripped into the envelope, find-ing a small, blue, heart-shaped stone attached to this short missive:

> *A gift for our boy, who now I expect is almost a man.*
> *If you think it right, please give this to him. It is Larimar, from*
> *my hometown. I'm sure he thinks my heart is stone, but tell him*
> *this stone is my heart.*
> > *With devotion, Mári*

Seaborne circumambulated the tree, for how long he could not say. Every now and then a dark substance dripped from the bottom of the basket onto the ground, making the pine needles shine. Seaborne watched the slick puddle grow, and as daylight dawned, he did not know what to do next. Logic told him he should return to Miami, resume his job, and put it all behind him. But there was another voice, a faint one, telling him otherwise. He could barely hear it. Didn't want to hear it, for it made no sense.

As the sky transformed from dark to light, Seaborne quickly reacted to something coming at him from the east, a flying creature very small and very fast. Cocking his head the way a fighter does to skirt a punch, it zoomed past, repeated the would-be assault then returned to hover right in front of his face. A hummingbird, rufous and rebellious, it's large eyes blazing *follow me!*

Message duly conveyed, the bird buzzed off toward the east. Toward the birthplace of his first mother.

Clicking into high gear, Seaborne woke Ti Mouche and took a quick picture of the youth, telling him not to worry, and would he like to go on an adventure?

CHAPTER 83

Later that morning Thing, Seaborne, and Ti Mouche, corpse-less and chicken-less, slipped across the border. Seaborne had expected much more trouble, even concocted a story about how the little guy was his brother, named after their mother and he, by the way, was named after Jesus. He'd hoped this would throw the guards off, and it did. They stamped his passport and, for twenty bucks, put their suspicions aside as to why a Haitian boy pictured in a U.S. passport had the name and birth date of a fifty-five-year old American named Claire.

❋

The air felt different on the Dominican side. Stickier. Frogs hopped about trying to cross the road. Ti Mouche breezily informed him of a huge nearby lake that had crocodiles. Seaborne wondered if life could get any stranger.

Zoning in on the shimmering road ahead, he mentally replayed his phone call to Guga, the one he'd made from her Haitian apartment a world ago.

"You know, she loved you very much," Guga said, honking like a hysterical goose into a hanky.

"Sometimes I wonder…"

"One time I remember coming home to that first teeny Hollywood apartment and there she was, holding you in her arms like a dance partner. The two of you twirled and dipped around the living room, face to face, giggling like crazy. It was something to see. Do not ever doubt that she loved you." More honking. "People show it in different ways. A feeling of oneness with another is a form of love—the purest."

The eye-works started up and Seaborne tried hard not to blink for fear his blurry vision might run them off the road.

Thing's movement produced a pleasant breeze. They stopped to pee and put the top down. A waxing moon still visible in the sky balanced the bright sun. Both remained silent before and after infrequent exchanges.

"You teach me?" Ti Mouche finally ventured.

"Teach you what?"

"How drive?"

Seaborne had to laugh, remembering his own obsession with getting behind the wheel.

"I don't know, you're kinda young."

"Me know shift."

"That's a good start."

Mouche seemed satisfied.

"Know what this is?" Seaborne pulled something from his pocket.

Ti Mouche handled the slender heart of light blue stone. His face lit up. "Where you get dis?"

"Long story, my mother sent it to my mother…it was in the envelope…"

"*Piedra azul!* Eef we get more we make good money to selling."

"Where can we find it?"

"Not far, Barahona, Republic Dominican! Only place in world get dis stone. And they got train. Den," Mouche said, catching his breath, "Americans making movie Santo Domingo. Filming, you say? *Le Serpent et L'Arc-en-Ciel…*" his voice trailed off, dreaming.

"Le what?"

"Da serpent and arc in sky."

"Arc in sky—you mean rainbow?"

"Mébee."

"How do *you* know all this?"

"Everybody know!"

"Crap, we just hit another frog."

Seaborne weaved in and out of the migrating amphibians, keeping an ever alert eye out for wayward hummingbirds as well.

"You frayed to die?" Ti Mouche eventually asked.

"I suppose, it's just I can't picture myself—like that."

"In Haiti, we say tomorrow or nex life, never know which come first. You see?"

"I do see. It's a good start. A very good start."

GRATITUDES

This is a dream come true! Thanks to all who helped make this book a reality, seen and unseen. Mom, always my biggest fan. Leslie, who long ago made me believe it was possible. Teachers along the way who encouraged and inspired. Nan and Sandy, whose friendship is golden. Maria, for your early input. Frank, for your camaraderie. Andrew, for your talent as an artist. Todd Barselow for your keen eye.

Finally, this odyssey springs from a deep regard for RMS Queen Mary and magical Haiti, Dominican Republic, and Mexico, and all beings everywhere.

ABOUT THE AUTHOR

Janice Convery can spell the word *Oceanliner* with her full name and is convinced she has the ghost of a mariner inside. Born in New Jersey, raised in Haiti, she graduated from Syracuse University with a degree in Magazine Journalism and English Literature which she put to good use working on a monthly business paper and turning the movie "Boys On the Side" into a novel for Warner Brothers. She calls Los Angeles and Albuquerque home.

CPSIA information can be obtained at www.ICGtesting.com
Printed in the USA
LVOW07s2157011014

406883LV00005B/295/P

9 781499 760880